Defiant Enchantress

DOROTHY HOWELL

ZEBRA BOOKS
KENSINGTON PUBLISHING CORP.

ZEBRA BOOKS

are published by

Kensington Publishing Corp.
475 Park Avenue South
New York, NY 10016

First Printing: January, 1988

Printed in the United States of America

PASSION'S FLAME

"I thought you would be in the library with the men," Rachel said, stepping away from him.

"Usually I would be," he said, following her. "But tonight I can't keep my mind on the discussion."

Gray reached out to touch Rachel, but she whirled away, moving quickly to put the wicker chairs between them.

"Good Lord, woman, why are you always trying to run away from me? I feel like a hound pursuing a rabbit each time I am in your company." He came to her side, his eyes boring into hers. "Do you find me so unappealing? If you do, tell me now and I will leave you," Gray said as his large warm hands slowly traveled up her arms and shoulders, sending waves of pleasure through her trembling body.

Gently, Gray pulled her into his powerful arms, and his lips sought hers and caressed them. Under his expert guidance, Rachel's lips moved with his until their mouths melted together in a deep, satisfying kiss. His sheer strength overpowered her, and the rest of the world was lost to her. She was his now, totally and completely, as she had been on that special night so long ago. And as then, she was helpless against him, desiring to share herself with him now and forever ...

Chapter 1

The muddy waters churned rapidly beneath the paddle wheel's relentless turning, propelling the boat through the inky night. Few lights dotted the shoreline, adding to the solitude of the cool evening. The lone, black-garbed passenger who stood on the deck blended into the shadows making her nearly invisible. She breathed in the crisp air. It smelled good. It smelled . . . free. Yes, free. She lifted the black lace veil off her face and allowed herself a small smile. He would never look for her here. Not this far north.

"Mrs. Fontaine?"

She jumped. Good Lord, would she ever get used to that name? "I wish . . . I wish you would just call me 'Rachel,' " she said, and hastily lowered her veil.

The boat's captain joined her at the railing. "If you'd like," he replied.

"It's—it's only that the name sounds . . . strange, somehow." The words came out in a rush.

Captain Daniels nodded sympathetically. "You weren't married very long, I take it."

"No, not very long. But . . ." Oh, why had she started this conversation? She had avoided it so well up until now.

"But you've been alone a long while." He finished the sentence for her.

"Yes, exactly. Many months now."

"It will get easier," he predicted. He knew all too well the anguish of losing a loved one and shared that pain with the young widow. She had stayed in her cabin for most of the trip up the Mississippi, taken her meals early to avoid the crowds, and talked little to the other passengers. He had intruded upon her solitude knowing it wasn't wise to leave anyone totally alone with their grief. "Are you meeting family in St. Louis?"

She cleared her throat nervously. "I wanted to start over fresh and since I have no relatives of my own, I decided to begin anew in St. Louis near his family." She had rehearsed the story since boarding the paddleboat in Memphis.

Captain Daniels rubbed his chin thoughtfully. "Fontaine . . . let me think. Do I know any Fontaines in St. Louis?" Rachel held her breath. She hadn't anticipated *this!* "No, no I don't think so." She heaved a silent sigh of relief. "We will be docking tomorrow evening as scheduled. Don't stay out too late. This night air is chilling," he advised in fatherly fashion.

"I'll be going in soon," she said. "Good night."

He touched the brim of his uniform cap and disappeared down the deck.

She grasped the railing to steady herself while her runaway heart slowed to its normal pace. He believed her.

He was the only person she had told the story to and he had believed her. Rachel pulled her shawl closer with trembling hands. Would it always be this difficult?

The crowd on the deck pressed closer to the railing as the whitewashed houses that bordered St. Louis came into view. An excited hum went through the gathering. This was a stopping place for some, another port along their journey for others. Whatever the reason, they had all braved the chill of the early November wind to mark another milestone in their westward trek.

Rachel stood with the other passengers as the powerful boat drew nearer the docks. For once, she was glad her veil covered her face. It would be very difficult to otherwise disguise the excitement she felt. Moments later she moved with the surge of disembarking passengers only to be halted by a strong hand on her shoulder. Her heart stopped. Slowly she turned and, to her relief, saw that it was Captain Daniels.

"I hope you find a home in St. Louis," he said.

The captain was a tall man and she had to tilt her head back to see his weather-lined face. He stood ramrod straight with square, sturdy shoulders and would look very formidable were it not for the gentleness of his green eyes. He had been kind to her while the other passengers had gone out of their way to avoid her. She hadn't felt close to any man since her youth when her papa had taken her everywhere with him. Business meetings in town, visits to the neighbors, horse-buying trips, riding about Richfield as he discussed the working of the plantation with the overseer, Rachel had been at his side. She loved listening to him almost as much as he loved ex-

7

plaining things to her. Rachel was the closest he would ever come to having a son. Delta, the servant who ran the big house as if it was her own, had put a stop to that when Rachel began to blossom into a young woman. It was high time she started acting like a young lady, Delta had relayed, her mother had said so. And as Rachel well knew, whatever her mother wanted, her mother got.

She pulled her thoughts back to the present. "Thank you. Will you be heading back downriver now?"

He shook his head. "No, I have some business here, then possibly I will head west," Captain Daniels replied.

"And give up the river?" she asked in surprise.

Captain Daniels chuckled. "There is more in life than one purpose, and many types of rivers to conquer." He squeezed her hand gently. "Be careful on the docks. It will be dark soon and it's not a fitting place for a young woman alone," he cautioned.

"Good-bye," she called as she blended into the crowd, clutching her small valise.

The throngs of people that congregated on the docks had been a welcome mass of confusion when she had changed boats in Natchez and Memphis. Those stops had delayed her journey but had made her trail much harder to follow, she hoped. In the swirl of activity who could say that a young woman in widow's weeds was seen getting off one boat and report with certainty that the same widow had boarded another? Yes, it had delayed her escape but she felt it was worth the risk.

Yet the masses who had given her sanctuary in the past few days now seemed stifling to Rachel as she made her way to the ticket office. The constant roar of voices, shouts, neighing horses, and crying babies was unbearable this evening. She had to get away, even if it was only

8

for a few minutes. Carefully counting her coins, she made her purchase, and seeing that enough time remained before departure, she gladly left the docks behind.

She wandered about the streets taking in the sights of a town she had no plans of seeing after today until her stomach reminded her that she had not eaten since noon. She located a clean, respectable-looking tavern and went inside. The few patrons there took little notice as she sat at a corner table facing the wall. She dined leisurely then left. Once outside she was surprised to see that the streets had grown dark, and she became frightened as she recalled the captain's words of caution. Tightening her grip on her valise, she hurried toward the docks.

The streets were quiet in the cool night air adding to Rachel's uneasy feeling. She wished now for the crowds at the dock. A shiver ran up her spine when she heard footsteps behind her, heavy steps that shuffled along the cobblestone. She quickened her pace. The other's hastened to match hers. Her heart began to pound in her chest as fear twisted her stomach into knots.

Suddenly, a giant of a man jumped from behind a building, blocking her path. She gasped and turned to run the opposite way only to confront another man. Caught between the two she froze, too frightened to move.

Each man grabbed one of her arms roughly. From the light showing through the windows of the nearby building she recognized the men as two she had seen in the tavern. By the smell of their foul breaths, she knew they had consumed a large quantity of ale.

"Look at what we got here," the big man said with a laugh.

Rachel pulled against the men. "Let me go!" she cried. Their grip on her arms tightened painfully.

"Wonder what she looks like," the shorter man said, and reached for her veil.

Rachel swung her small foot with all the force she could muster and kicked him squarely in the shin. He howled in pain and released her arm as he clutched his injured leg. Rachel rotated her body and bashed the other man's head with her valise. Stunned, he released her as he went down on one knee.

Panic stricken, she raced away. But she had gone only a short distance when a strong arm closed around her waist and lifted her off the ground. Her valise, the only semblance of a weapon she had, fell out of reach. Her body trembled with terror as he held her suspended in air, and an ear-piercing scream tore from her throat.

The small man hobbled over. "Let her go, Zeke. She makes too much noise."

"If you don't want no part of her, then she's all mine, Artie!" he declared.

"I am not anyone's!" Courage she didn't know she had overcame her fright, and she pounded his chest with her fists.

"Let her go," the other man repeated.

"I suggest you do as your friend advises" came a stern voice from the shadows. A tall, broad-shouldered man stepped into the light and faced the men squarely. Rachel ceased her struggle as everyone's attention turned toward the stranger.

"Get your own woman!" the big man shouted sourly.

Artie took a swing at the stranger but he blocked the punch with catlike reflexes. He drew back his own fist and struck Artie's face with full force sending a spout of

10

blood coursing down his cheek. The little man decided he wanted no more of this fight and ran away as quickly as his injuries would allow.

Zeke gave an animal growl, pushed Rachel aside, and lunged at the stranger. Rachel struck the ground hard, driving the wind from her lungs. She tried to stand but her legs failed her and she fell once more, panting for air. When she looked up she saw the stranger deliver a series of hard, quick punches to Zeke's face and stomach, dropping the man to his knees. A final blow sent him sprawling into the street, unconscious.

The stranger rushed to where Rachel lay in the street and knelt beside her. Gently, he lifted her into his arms. "Are you all right?"

His mellow voice sent a warmth through her body while the touch of his strong arms around her gave Rachel a chill she had never experienced before. "Yes ... yes, I'm fine." Her voice sounded weak.

"I don't think you are," the man said. "Let me get a better look at you." He reached for the veil that covered her face.

"No!" she cried and pulled herself to a sitting position and out of his grasp.

"I won't hurt you."

But that wasn't the cause of her concern. Rachel knew he meant her no harm. He wore well-cut clothing and she could see he was a gentleman. "I know," she said softly, and wanted to be in his arms again.

Rachel tried to stand but the stranger rose first and put his hands around her narrow waist, easily lifting her to her feet. An unexpected shudder went through her. "Thank you," she murmured.

Reluctantly he released her. "I don't think those two

will bother you again, but it's not safe to be on the streets alone. I would be honored to escort you. Where are you going?''

She stood mesmerized by his probing blue eyes. It took a moment before she could find her tongue. "I'm going to the—"

The paddleboat! Rachel grabbed her valise. "I've got to go.''

"I'll go with you.''

"No.'' She backed away as he reached for her.

"It's not safe,'' he insisted. But it was more than her well-being he was interested in. He wanted to see her face and hold her in his arms again.

Rachel broke into a full run. She heard him calling but didn't stop. She made it to the paddleboat only moments before the gangplank was hauled away. Standing on the deck, she watched St. Louis disappearing behind her and her thoughts returned over and over to the dark-haired man who had helped her. And each time, her heart fluttered beneath her breast and a strange mixture of warmth and excitement raced through her. She had never experienced such feelings before and didn't understand why she felt them now.

St. Joseph, Missouri, stood on rolling wooded land and extended more than three miles along the Missouri River. What had started as a fur-trading post had grown into a town as pioneer families heading west began their long journey in wagon trains that formed along the river's banks. It had marked the beginning of many promising new lives, hopefully including that of the widow Rachel Fountaine.

She nervously tightened the grip on her valise as she looked up at the sign marked Cora's Tavern & Inn. It was a sturdy-looking two-story building about a quarter mile from the docks and easy enough to find after she had gotten directions from someone there. But now she hesitated. How would her cousin feel when suddenly presented with a stranger asking for employment? It had seemed much easier when Rachel had rehearsed her request on the paddleboat. Now she wasn't so sure.

She gathered her courage. She had come too far to turn back now, and besides, there was no place to turn back to. She walked determinedly up the wooden steps and pushed open the heavy door.

The large common room was warmed by a roaring fire in the hearth that extended the width of the room. Rough-hewn columns supported the second floor. About half the tables were occupied with all manner of people. Burly fur trappers, families with small children, wealthy businessmen all dined alongside each other. The wall opposite the fireplace held a narrow staircase. A small counter stood next to it where weary travelers could obtain lodging for the night. The delicious aroma of food drifted from the door at the end of the counter. Everything in the room looked freshly scrubbed. Rachel relaxed a bit, seeing that her cousin's establishment was quite reputable.

The kitchen door swung open and a stout woman with neatly coiled gray hair burst into the room carrying a tray of food. Rachel approached her. "Excuse me, I'm looking for Cora."

"You've found her," the woman said briskly and continued on her way. She served the plates of food to a young family and headed back into the kitchen.

"Excuse me," Rachel said, hurrying along beside the woman trying to keep up with her rapid pace. "I'm Rachel. Your cousin. From Charleston."

Cora stopped and eyed Rachel for only a fraction of a moment, then disappeared into the kitchen. Determinedly, Rachel followed on her heels.

In the large room a trim, middle-aged woman stood at the cook stove frying meat and stirring pots of boiling vegetables. Another younger woman was elbow deep in a bucket of sudsy water, washing plates at a frantic pace. Dishes were stacked neatly on the sideboard, pots and pans were suspended over the stove, bins of raw vegetables lined the walls. It was warmer here than in the common room, despite the back door standing open to the late afternoon breeze.

"I'm not looking for a handout. I'm seeking gainful employment," Rachel called as her cousin loaded her tray with a plate of hot biscuits.

"A job? You're mighty frail looking to me," Cora said skeptically.

Rachel pulled herself up to her greatest height. "You haven't got a job here I can't do," she said confidently.

"Cora! You want to look at my vegetables or not?" a man called from the back porch.

"Be right there, Hank!" Cora answered.

The woman at the cook stove pulled a hot bubbling pie from the oven and placed it on the sideboard. "Pie's ready, Cora," she called.

"Cora!" The man called impatiently.

"Need more soap from the storeroom, Cora," the dishwasher requested.

Rachel lifted the veil off her face and dropped her valise. "I'll serve these, then slice the pie. You see to the soap and vegetables." She took the tray before her cousin could respond.

"Biscuits to the young couple in the corner," Cora called.

Rachel nodded and disappeared through the door. She returned a moment later, located a knife, and began to slice the pie. "Is it always this busy?"

"Just since we lost a girl last week," the cook said as she expertly tended the four pots on the stove. "She and her husband got enough money together to head west."

"Does that happen often?" Rachel asked.

"More and more now," the cook said. She wiped her hand on her apron then offered it to Rachel. "I'm Liz. Over there is Jean." Jean waved a soapy hand.

Rachel shook her hand happily. "I'm Rachel Fontaine," she said with a smile. It rolled off her tongue easily this time.

"Sorry about your husband," she said.

"Who?"

"Your husband," Liz repeated, and glanced over the widow's weeds Rachel wore.

"Oh, yes ... well, thank you."

"Been long?"

Rachel wasn't prepared to deliver any in-depth information about her late husband. "No, just a few weeks ago," she said.

The afternoon passed quickly as Rachel worked frantically to keep up with the chores that needed her attention. She helped do the cooking, fetched supplies, dried dishes, and swept the floor. The other women took a liking to her immediately. Rachel was glad to see some friendly faces so soon. By evening when the supper service was over, she was exhausted.

"You did a good day's work," Cora praised. The others had left for the day and she and Rachel were alone in the kitchen.

Rachel dried the last plate and stacked it on the sideboard with the others. "Thank you."

"You say you are Frederick's daughter?" Cora asked, studying the delicate features of Rachel's oval face, her narrow straight nose and wide fawnlike eyes. Her skin was creamy and white. "I haven't seen him for years and met his wife only once, but from what I recall you don't favor either of them."

Rachel smiled nervously. "Everyone always said that. Actually, I don't look much like either of my parents. I'm sort of a blend of the two," she said, and wiped her damp hands on her apron. She hurried to the valise she had left in the corner and pulled out the family Bible. She turned quickly to the pages where the births, deaths, and marriages were recorded and showed them to Cora. She held her breath while the woman reviewed the information.

Cora closed the Bible and handed it back to Rachel. "Seems to be no doubt, Cousin," she said with a wink. Rachel heaved a sigh of relief and tucked the Bible safely into her valise once more. "There was no mention of Mr. Fontaine," Cora observed.

"Who?"

"Mr. Fontaine, your husband."

"Oh, him. Well, you see, actually we were married for only a short time before he, ah, died."

Cora put her arm around Rachel's small shoulder and gave her a squeeze. "Come sit down and tell me all about everything. I've got a lot of catching up to do." She

16

poured them each a cup of steaming coffee and they sat down at the table.

Rachel was bone-tired and she didn't want to face this tonight when her mind wasn't sharp, but it seemed her cousin would give her no choice.

"Let me think, you must be about seventeen now." Rachel nodded. "I never heard of Frederick having other children. Do I have any more cousins running around I haven't met yet?"

"No, there is only me. I think it always hurt Mama that she couldn't have any more children, but she was too proud to admit it. Mama had a lot of pride."

"Like I said, I haven't seen Frederick Samuels in years. How is he?"

Rachel swallowed hard. "Actually, Cora, my father ... passed away."

"Oh, no. Honey, I'm so sorry. When did it happen?"

"About two years ago." *Two horrible years.*

"Frederick was one of the healthiest men I ever knew. What happened?"

Your mother should be telling you this, but since her ... breakdown ... well, I'll just say it, Rachel. Your father died in a tavern at the waterfront in a shootout over a ... a woman of ... questionable reputation."

"It was a shooting accident," Rachel said simply.

"Such a shame," Cora said mournfully. "You know that papa of yours was poor, just like the rest of us trying to farm in Pennsylvania. But he was smart and he had vision. He took that little bit of money his uncle Silas left him and made something of himself. Even got your ma to marry him, and her from that fine, respectable, wealthy Virginia family. Yes, he done himself real proud."

"Your father made some rather risky investments in

17

the past few months and when they began to fail he invested more and more capital until he had mortgaged all his assests."

"Yes, Papa worked very hard."

"What did you and Althea do after he was gone? That plantation must have been a handful to run."

Rachel took a sip of coffee. "Mama and I decided we wanted to start over fresh somewhere else."

"The bank is foreclosing on Richfield. You and your mother will have to find someplace else to live."

"But I heard that all Althea's family died in the big fire years and years ago," Cora said.

Rachel returned the cup to its saucer, afraid her trembling hands would upset it and betray her turbulent emotions. They were all such terrible memories. All her wonderful childhood years filled with the love of her parents, their fine home, beautiful gowns, magnificent parties, surrounded by their many friends, had been smashed to bits in a few hours, the afternoon Althea had collapsed and Mr. Wingate, the family attorney, had finally told Rachel the whole ugly truth. It still hurt to think about it all. *And it was all your fault, Papa.*

"Mama had a cousin in Louisiana," Rachel explained. "She had a big home, similar to Richfield, and she was elderly and wanted to have her family around her."

"You're darned lucky I'm taking you in! I've hardly got enough money to keep body and soul alive. And that doctor is robbing me blind, giving me medicine that does not help me one little bit. I've had to sell off most everything I own just to keep this leaky roof over my head. Times are hard around here so don't think you are going to have a life of luxury here like you had in Charleston."

"We hadn't lived with Cousin Annora for long until Mama died."

"You poor little thing!" Cora explained, and her heart went out to her young cousin.

"She became terribly ill."

Your mother isn't that sick, Rachel, but I can't help her. Annora told me of your . . . circumstances, and it seems Althea has simply lost the will to live.

"Don't say another word," Cora told her. She shook her head gravely. "Such tragedy you've been through. And then losing Mr. Fontaine."

"Mr. Fontaine?"

"Your husband."

Rachel shifted nervously in the chair. "Oh, yes, him. Cora, I'm awfully tired. Do you suppose we could finish our talk another time?"

"Listen to me rattling on when you have just arrived here today and worked so hard to boot." She leveled her eyes at Rachel. "You're a strong girl. It couldn't have been easy losing both your folks, burying your husband, and coming all this way alone. I want you to know you've got a home here for as long as you want it."

Rachel smiled. It was the first genuine smile she had felt in months. "Thanks, Cousin. I think I'm going to like it here."

"Come on, let's get you a place to sleep. All the rooms upstairs are for travelers. I sleep in a room off the kitchen where I do my books. All I can offer you is a tiny room in the attic. It's not much, but you're welcome to it."

"It sounds fine." She picked up her valise and that dreadful black hat she had tossed aside earlier and followed Cora through the common room and up the stairs. They made a right turn at the head of the stairs and

19

went down the hall past the rooms that housed their over-night guests. Cora opened a small door at the end of the hall and lit the lantern that hung there. Holding it high in front of her, she climbed a narrow staircase that led to the attic. The room was indeed small, with a low ceiling. There was a window covered with a thin curtain that overlooked the street. A few packing boxes and an old trunk stood in one corner. Along the wall was a bed and a washstand; an oval mirror hung near the door. It smelled musty and everything was covered with a thin layer of dust, but it was a warming sight to Rachel.

"There are some bed linens and a quilt in that trunk. Do whatever you want with the other things in there and in those boxes. Most of it should have been thrown out years ago," Cora said.

Rachel smiled gratefully. "It's perfect."

"Let's get some sleep," Cora said, and turned to leave. She paused at the head of the stairs and faced her young cousin solemnly. "Folks that pass through St. Jo are all filled with hopes and big dreams. They have got big plans for a better life out West. I like to send them on their way feeling good about things."

"What are you trying to say, Cora?"

"They don't like no omen of what lies ahead for them on the trail. Lots of folks don't make it through to Oregon. Indians, sickness, cholera, it all takes its toll. And we don't hold with all the traditions you southerners have." Cora paused and took a deep breath. "When you get to know me better you will find out I'm not one to dance around a problem, so I'll just say it. The widow's weeds have got to go. You will have to grieve for your husband privately because in Cora's Tavern & Inn travelers see only the best life can offer."

20

Rachel wanted to run to her cousin and hug her in thanks for releasing her from the bondage of the horrible black dress. But she managed to contain her happiness. "I understand and I will abide by your wishes," she said with a somber face. The two women exchanged a smile before Cora left Rachel alone.

The first thing Rachel did was shed the widow's weeds and toss them aside. She never wanted to see that terrible dress and hat again. That gave her the last boost of energy she needed to prepare her bed and collapse into it. It felt as good to her tired body as the feather mattress and silken linen she had slept on as a child. But tired as she was, Rachel tossed about fitfully as her mind was more unwilling to turn loose of reality than her aching limbs were. Finally she dozed off.

Hot wet lips covered her mouth with bruising, plundering kisses. The foul taste of ale assaulted her senses. A heavy weight bore down upon her, crushing her until she could barely draw a breath. She struggled against him but his massive body pinned her beneath him easily. His hands groped at her bodice until the fabric gave way. Panic overcame her as he tore at her soft flesh brutally. She fought harder but could not stop his pillaging hands and mouth. With no way to escape her attacker, Rachel opened her mouth to his, then bit down on his lip, hard, until she tasted his blood. He howled with pain and sat up. In one quick motion she—

Rachel sat up in bed gasping for air. Her heart pounded like the hooves of a runaway horse, her forehead was damp with perspiration. She pushed her tangled blond hair off her face and looked around the dimly lit room. Where was she? She threw back the covers, hurried to the window, and looked down at the deserted street below. Slowly she gathered her wits. Yes, now she remembered. She sat down on the ancient trunk and gazed out the window. Suddenly she wished the dark-haired stranger who rescued her in St. Louis would appear now and save her from that horrible nightmare. She drew her feet up next to her and rested her chin on her knees. But it wasn't just a dream. The whole ugly scene had really happened and there had been no one to rescue her then. It had been only sheer luck that allowed her to escape the brutality—and marriage bed—of Fergus Cavanaugh.

Chapter 2

It wasn't supposed to have turned out like this, Rachel thought as she dressed the next morning in one of the simple cotton dresses donated by the fine Christian ladies of St. Francesville, Louisiana, who had taken pity on her. She had been born to wealthy plantation owners in Charleston, South Carolina, and had had the finest of everything and should still be living the grand life. But her father's foolish business schemes had put an end to that and forced her and her mother out of the home they had loved so much. That had been her first lesson in life; she hadn't known then how many more lessons were to follow.

It wasn't dawn yet and Cora's Tavern & Inn was still sleeping as Rachel located cleaning supplies in the kitchen and set about the task of making her small room livable. When she and her mother had first arrived at Briarcliff, the home of their cousin Annora Carmichael, Rachel had never scrubbed or washed anything in her life. They had expected to find a home much like Richfield and had planned to resume a life-style similar to what they had enjoyed in Charleston. They had no way of knowing that Briarcliff had suffered from years of neglect because Cousin Annora's second husband had run off with her money, leaving the sick old woman near poverty. It was a rude awakening for Rachel but she had adjusted, unlike her mother who lapsed into a deep depression and never recovered. Rachel had worked tirelessly—if not awkwardly at first—in the once beautiful mansion cleaning, tending the fires, learning to cook from the only servant there. She had filled the long days caring for her mother and cranky cousin, reading to them from Melvin Carmichael's extensive library.

Rachel wrung the mop angrily. If only she had left Briarcliff after Althea's death she wouldn't be in this mess right now. She had wanted to go to New Orleans and find a job of some sort. She was intelligent, excellent with figures, and eager to learn a trade. But Annora would not hear of it. She accused Rachel of abandoning her. So finally out of guilt and some misplaced sense of loyalty Rachel had agreed to stay. Deep down she knew it was a mistake, but she didn't know how big a mistake until months later when Annora died.

She jabbed the mop into the bucket as she recalled her final days at Briarcliff. Annora had grown increasingly difficult, though Rachel hadn't thought that was possible. Her failing health had become more evident, making it more and more of a trial for Rachel to face her each day. But somehow she had managed to sit by her cousin and read to her and care for her. Althea had passed away the winter before and, strangely enough, tending to her cousin had helped fill the void left in Rachel's life. She had been with the old woman in the final hours when they both had known the end was near.

"I have done some bad things," Annora said weakly.

Rachel leaned closer; the words were barely audible. "Don't try to talk. Save your strength," she encouraged, and clutched the woman's frail hands.

Annora shook her head. "I was wrong. I shouldn't have . . ." She drifted for a moment then forced her eyes open again. "Forgive me, child . . ."

Rachel could only guess that her cousin regretted the way she had treated her. It hardly seemed important now.

"It's all right, Annora," she said calmly.

"I . . . I meant it for your own good," Annora whispered.

Rachel clung to the wrinkled hands until she felt them relax in her grip and saw Annora's chest rise and fall with the even rhythm of sleep. Quietly she moved to the window and looked out. Where was that doctor? What was taking so long? Damn that Fancy, she thought angrily of the old servant, why must she always travel so slowly? She had sent the servant to fetch Dr. Sommers at first light leaving Rachel feeling frightened and alone in the empty house. She wanted to run from the room and let someone—any-one—tend to her dying cousin. She didn't know what to do. Or what to say. She shouldn't have to face this. Some-one else should be doing this. She should be at Richfield, safe and secure, with her mother and father to care for her and—

Rachel turned away from the window, willing herself to surpress the panic that threatened to overtake her. Gently she massaged her temples with the tips of her fingers. She must get a grip on herself. Looking back was of no help. She was here and her cousin needed her. Rachel looked once again at Annora sleeping quietly; the old woman's white hair and complexion faded into the stark bed linens making her appear translucent. She drew in a deep breath and resumed her position at the bedside.

Finally Dr. Sommers arrived and confirmed what Rachel already knew. There was nothing he could do for her. They both sat with Annora. In her final moments Annora had cried out for her husband Melvin, the man who had taken her wealth and abandoned her. She supposedly hated him, and not a day had gone by that she didn't tell Rachel just that. Yet with her dying breath she called out his name and declared her love for him.

It had been almost a week after her cousin's death when Mr. Rutherford, Annora's attorney, and Fergus Cavanaugh came to call. The house had been so quiet without Annora that Rachel was glad to have visitors, even if one of them was Fergus. She had dressed in a pale-blue gown and swept her hair up in a loose knot at the nape. She appeared older than her seventeen years, with the exception of her deep brown eyes that still held their innocent look.

Rachel poured refreshment from the mismatched tea service and settled herself on the threadbare sofa opposite the gentlemen. "I was expecting to hear from you, Mr. Rutherford," Rachel commented, knowing that he could not wait too long to carry out his duties. But it did puzzle her that Fergus Cavanaugh would be present to go over Annora's business affairs.

Mr. Rutherford sat his teacup aside. "There are certain things that require our attention. Certain business transactions, property settlements, as well as the execution of your cousin Annora's final will," he began, settling his spectacles in place. He unfolded several papers and stud-

26

ied them for a moment. "Most of this will be too much for you to understand," the gray-haired man began.

"I am not totally unacquainted with such business matters," Rachel said.

"Certainly, child," Mr. Rutherford said.

Fergus had not spoken since his arrival. That, and his constant attention to her every movement, made Rachel nervous. She smoothed the skirt of her gown, glad she had selected a dress with a high neckline.

Mr. Rutherford cleared his throat and began to speak. "I am certain you realize that Annora Carmichael had little wealth at the time of her death," he said, and glanced quickly about the shabby room.

His critical stare pricked Rachel's pride. "Yes, I am aware of that," she had to admit.

"The fact is that she was heavily in debt."

"In debt? To whom?" Rachel asked. It was true that she knew nothing of her cousin's finances, but there had always been money in the house for food and supplies and to pay Dr. Sommers.

"The banks would do nothing to help her, given the circumstances. But there was one man who took pity on your cousin's plight and arranged for the funds necessary to keep Briarcliff going," Mr. Rutherford said.

A feeling of foreboding came over Rachel and she knew she would not like what the attorney was going to say.

"That man was Fergus Cavanaugh."

A smile spread slowly across Fergus's heavy lips.

Rachel was able to hide the revulsion she felt. She certainly did not want to be beholden to Fergus Cavanaugh for anything! "That was very kind of you, sir, to help my cousin in her time of need," she said, managing a small smile.

"It was your time of need as well, if I may point out," Fergus said, patting his perspiring lips with a handkerchief.

The truth of his words stung Rachel but she could do nothing except to agree. "Yes, mine and my mother's."

"None of this is very pleasant, but I have to tell you just the same," Mr. Rutherford continued, now anxious to conclude the business at hand.

"Please continue," Rachel bade, gathering her composure.

Mr. Rutherford put the papers down and spoke directly to Rachel. "The final accounting of Annora's affairs is this: she had few assets and a great many debts. The taxes are behind on Briarcliff and there is not enough money to pay them. The cash that is available is owed to Mr. Cavanaugh, and that is not nearly enough to pay the enormous sum due him."

Fear began to spread through Rachel. "You mean there is nothing? Not even the house?"

He nodded solemnly. "The state will take possession of Briarcliff for the taxes. All other money will go to Mr. Cavanaugh." It was a dismal outlook, but he had no choice but to state the facts as they were.

The color drained from Rachel's face and she set her teacup aside with a trembling hand. She knew Annora had very little, but she thought there would be some small amount for her. Or at least the house so she might have a roof over her head. What would become of her now? Where would she go?

As if reading her thoughts Mr. Rutherford patted her hand consolingly. "Don't worry, all is not lost. Your cousin has made provisions for you."

Her face brightened. "What? Please tell me," she urged. There was hope after all.

"Annora's arrangements are twofold, actually. She has seen to your future and to the repayment of her debt."

Rachel was confused by his words. "What do you mean?" she asked, desperately holding her emotions in check.

"Annora arranged for your marriage," Mr. Rutherford explained.

"Marriage!"

"And in accepting your hand the gentleman has agreed to forgive all debts owed to him by Annora."

Rachel's mind whirled. This could not be happening. It couldn't be true! "Marriage to whom?" she managed to ask.

Mr. Rutherford turned to the man who sat next to him. "Mr. Cavanaugh has been gracious enough to accept you as his wife."

She had sold her! Her own cousin! Sold her as a bride to repay her debt to—of all people—that pompous, overweight, lecherous Fergus Cavanaugh! A bride! The man was nearly old enough to be her father! Rachel wheeled the mop angrily jabbing it into corners, banging against the furniture as she recalled. And she had agreed to it! Oh, but not at first. He had hounded her—relentlessly—reminding her over and over that Briarcliff would be sold for past due taxes so that very soon she wouldn't even have a place to live, and that Annora had left her nothing because the cash she had all went to him to help repay her massive debt. She had no skills, no trade, no references, no hope of finding decent employment, and certainly no other marriage proposals since she had lived in near isolation for years at Briarcliff. But dear Cousin Annora had provided for her and arranged her marriage to Fergus. That way Annora could die with a clear conscience, Rachel would have a home, and Fergus would have received due value in return for his extensive loans to Annora. It was the perfect solution to everyone's problem. Everyone but Rachel. She had been livid, indignant, outraged when she learned the terms of Annora's will. Oh, certainly Fergus was wealthy. He had a beautiful sugar cane plantation, and was a well-respected gentleman even though he had lived in St. Francesville for only a short time, but Rachel was sickened by the very sight of him. He had narrow, cruel eyes that made her shiver every time he looked at her.

But in the end, logic had prevailed and Rachel had agreed to the marriage. She had gone to supper at his home to discuss the wedding plans dressed in the garish red gown he had sent to her. After several liberal libations, Fergus had confessed that he planned to buy Briarcliff for the taxes due, a minimal amount compared to the property's value, and sell it for a great profit. Then he opened his cashbox and showed Rachel the money that had been her cousin's. He thought himself quite clever, and said as much, because now he had everything of Annora's, including Rachel. He had leered at her, then suddenly attacked her, tearing her gown, pawing at her ruthlessly. She fought him off and it was only sheer luck that a servant had burst in on them, screaming that the horse barn was on fire. But before Fergus dashed from the house, his lip bleeding from where she had bitten him, he had reminded her that soon she would be in his marriage bed and then he would take what he wanted, as often as he wanted, and there would be no one to stop him.

Rachel had been sick with fear and revulsion, and she

knew she could never live like this. So while Fergus and the servants were occupied with the fire, Rachel took the money from the cashbox—Annora's money that should have been hers when Fergus's debt would be paid in full from the profit resulting from the sale of Briarcliff—and sneaked out of the house unnoticed. By the time she reached home she had formulated a plan to escape Fergus forever. She donned the widow's weeds and wedding band that had been her mother's, gave herself a deceased husband and a new last name, stuffed a few belongings into her valise, and booked passage on the first paddleboat going north. She wasn't even sure where St. Joseph, Missouri was, or if the cousin her father had occasionally spoken of actually existed, but she was going to locate them both, one way or the other, and leave Fergus Cavanaugh high and dry.

Rachel halted her work, her arms aching, her emotions spent. Memories of her recent past were all unsettling and hurtful and it lifted her spirits more than a little to realize that they were just that—the past. Her parents and cousin could never hurt her again. Fergus would never think to look for her in this small frontier town. For once in her life she could go where she wanted and do as she pleased. It would take some getting used to but it was an adjustment she would gladly make.

Cora's Tavern & Inn easily became home to Rachel, and after several days she fell into a routine. She helped in the kitchen some, but mostly confined herself to cleaning the upstairs rooms. Business had slowed so that Liz and Jean were able to handle the food preparation and service, and in an emergency they called on Rachel for assistance.

Her first full week at Cora's was marked by a torrential

31

downpour. The rain had begun as a light shower around breakfast, and by midafternoon it was coming down in bucketfuls. The air was cool and damp and Rachel was anxious to complete her chores upstairs and return to the warmth of the kitchen. She pulled her shawl closer around her shoulders and hoisted the bucket of dirty water. She walked carefully down the stairs and circled wide around a tall gentleman who stood at the counter.

"Mrs. Fontaine?"

The familiar voice drew her attention at once but it took her a moment to recognize the man who had called her name. The lanterns lit against the darkness of the cloudy afternoon sent a shadow across his face. She stepped closer, then her lips parted in an easy smile. "Why, Captain Daniels, what a surprise," she greeted. "I didn't recognize you out of uniform."

"I wasn't certain it was you, either. I thought you were in St. Louis."

"Well, yes, I was there, but only for a short time," she said slowly.

"Whatever made you come to St. Jo?" he asked.

"Seeking employment."

He glanced down at the bucket she carried. "I see you have found it."

"I was fortunate to find something so quickly," she told him smoothly. She cringed inwardly. *The lies keep getting easier. Will I go to hell for this?* "And what brings you this far west?"

"Business. You are sitting square in the middle of a booming town."

"What kind of investments are you considering?" Such matters, though very unladylike, had always intrigued her.

32

"Several different things. I am meeting with some local businessmen later today."

"I'll tell Cora you're here. It's good seeing you again," she said, and disappeared into the kitchen.

Something about that young girl was wrong, the captain mused. She didn't belong with a scrub bucket in her hand. She displayed poise and an easy grace that spoke of refinement and good breeding. He wondered what had driven a grieving widow to a place she obviously did not belong.

Rachel advised Cora that a customer was waiting, but didn't mention that she knew him. The less connections to her past were made, the safer she would be. She was surprised that she would run into anyone in St. Joseph whom she knew, but had no fear of Captain Daniels. She actually enjoyed seeing him again.

After warming herself by the cookstove she refilled her bucket and headed upstairs. When she crossed the common room she saw Captain Daniels sitting at a table by the window with his back to her. Though she would have liked to chat with him longer she knew she had to finish her chores, and she climbed the staircase to do just that.

Before ordering a meal from Cora, Captain Daniels had two tankards of ale to drive the chill from his bones. He was deep in thought, gazing out at the steady rain when a voice intruded upon his concentration. He turned to see a younger man hanging his dripping cloak and hat by the fireplace. He knew that man—he could recognize that dark head anywhere. "Gray Montgomery!" Daniels boomed, coming to his feet.

The man looked up and immediately a smile spread across his youthful face. "Ezra! You old river rat!" He crossed the room quickly on long, muscular legs and eagerly grasped the captain's outstretched hand.

"You are the very last person I expected to find out here," Captain Daniels said earnestly.

"I might say the same of you. My pa used to say that you didn't know how to walk on dry land."

"Times change. People change," he replied. "Sit down, sit down." He called to Cora for another tankard.

Gray settled into the chair opposite his friend and watched as Cora came through the kitchen door carrying his ale and the captain's meal. He turned down Cora's offer of food, preferring to first warm his innards with drink.

"I'm out here on business," Captain Daniels said in reply to Gray's question. "And you?"

"Business." He took a liberal draft from the tankard.

"So far from home?"

Gray nodded and leveled his slate-blue eyes at his friend. "I felt a change of scenery was in order."

"All the lovely belles you left behind must be crying their eyes out over the loss of the Low Country's most sought-after bachelor," the captain teased, then added, "But you are still too young to concern yourself with marriage."

"A man of thirty-two years is nearly overdue for a trip to the altar. Or so my aunt tells me." He studied the bottom of his tankard for a moment before speaking again. "Actually, I am engaged to be married," he said slowly.

Daniels's mouth fell open. "I never thought it would happen," he confessed. He offered his hand across the table. "Congratulations are in order. Who is the lucky lady?"

Gray shook his hand, then downed the last of his ale. "Claudia Danforth. Her father is in shipping."

"When is the big day?"

"As soon as I return from this trip," he replied and called for another ale. "I purchased a plantation for her as a wedding gift."

"A plantation?"

"Claudia thought it would be good for me—rather, us—to settle down."

"You selected a plantation?" the captain asked in disbelief.

"Actually, Claudia selected it," Gray admitted.

The captain studied his friend carefully. "Do I detect a note of reluctance over your impending marriage?"

"Oh no, certainly not," Gray responded quickly. "Claudia is very beautiful. She comes from a proper family, is very well thought of, conducts herself accordingly."

"And you love the lady?" Captain Daniels asked softly.

Cora appeared by the table and Gray eagerly took the tankard she offered. He downed half its contents before he spoke. "My God, man, I've traveled all over and abroad, and I've known many women. Claudia is a fine and fitting lady and she will make the perfect wife." His words carried less confidence than he had intended.

Silence fell between the men. Captain Daniels ate his meal slowly while Gray drained the last of his ale.

"Your father and I go back a long, long way," the captain said thoughtfully. "I miss him."

Gray nodded. "As do I."

"At least he died a happy man. He lived his life to the fullest. God, I've never known a man who loved a woman as he loved your mother. It was best they went together. I don't think either of them could have gone on without the other," he mused. Captain Daniels raised his tankard in a toast. "Here is wishing you the same."

Gray smiled half-heartedly and touched his tankard to the captain's.

"I hate to break this off so soon but I have to meet with some men shortly. Do you have the time?" Captain Daniels asked. Gray pulled a gold pocket watch from his waistcoat and read off the hour. "I see you still have your pa's watch."

Gray flipped the watch over and read the inscription: "To My Darling, With All My Love." It had been a wedding gift from his mother to his father. He snapped it shut and slid it into his pocket. "My pa gave it to me just before he died," he said softly. "But you know that. You were there."

Captain Daniels rose. "I'll return later. Will you be here?"

"I, too, have some business to—" Gray stopped in midsentence as his attention was drawn to Rachel descending the stairs. She looked familiar, but then again, not. He squinted his eyes in the dimly lit room and studied her as she crossed the room and disappeared through the kitchen door. Something tugged at his memory. What was it?

Captain Daniels turned and followed Gray's gaze across the nearly empty room. He saw nothing. "What's wrong?"

Gray shook his head. "Nothing, nothing. It's just that—" He stopped and turned his attention to his friend. "I have a business meeting, then I'll be leaving."

"It was good seeing you, Gray. And congratulations on the wedding. I hope you will be very happy."

Gray settled back in his chair and turned his attention to the rain outside. It was coming down even harder now and he dreaded the thought of going out in it again. But he had a few minutes before he had to leave, so he called for another ale.

After Cora had served him two more, she asked, "Will you be having some supper?"

Gray blinked his eyes to bring the woman into focus. "Yes, yes, ma'am, I believe I will."

Just then Rachel passed once more through the common room. Gray watched intently as her slender figure climbed the stairs and disappeared.

"Ma'am," Gray said to Cora, "who was that girl?" He pointed a wavering hand at the stairs.

Cora turned but saw no one. The dining room was empty save for Gray and a family seated near the door. "Who?"

"A young girl with blond hair."

"Never you mind about that one. She's a widow in mourning," Cora told him curtly. "I'll get your meal."

Gray sipped his ale. A widow? He didn't know any widows—certainly none as comely as that one. Why did he feel pulled toward her? He drew his brows together to concentrate, but his head was feeling quite heavy and he propped it up on the palm of his hand with his elbow firmly planted on the table.

Claudia. He was supposed to be thinking of Claudia. She was to be his wife. A spasm swept through his stomach. *What does she look like? I can't remember her face!* Maybe more ale would help clear his head, he decided, and emptied the tankard in two swallows.

Claudia. Yes, now he recalled the roundness of her full curves, her raven black hair. She would make a fine wife. So what if she was somewhat outspoken? And opinionated. And always wanted her own way. And pouted if she didn't get it. And flew into a rage if pouting didn't work. He

37

liked women with spirit and independence. They intrigued him and presented a challenge. He liked those qualities in Claudia. Didn't he? Gray bit his bottom lip. *Good Lord in heaven, what have I done?*

Cora placed a plate of food before Gray. She could see that he was a bit unsteady from the ale he had consumed and didn't want a drunk on her hands to spoil what seemed to be a very quiet evening. "Eat up. Kitchen is closing for the night. Cook's gone home."

"Another ale, if you please. Better make it two," Gray said, and reached for the plate. It took two tries but the roving meal finally halted long enough for him to lay a hand on it. He chewed slowly and stared out the window at the darkness and the steady rain.

It was much later when Ezra Daniels returned to the inn, cold and wet and anxious for a warm bed to sleep in. His meeting had been successful, but even that thought didn't play as favorably on his mind as dry clothing. He hung his wraps near the fireplace and turned to go up to his room when he saw Gray still seated at the table by the window. "Gray, I thought you would be gone," he said as he stopped at the table. "I'm glad you waited."

Gray rolled his head slowly to look at the captain. His eyes blinked several times trying to focus, then gave up. He tried to lift his tankard but it was so heavy it fell back to the table with a thud. "Ezra, my old ... friend ..." His words were slurred by the thickness of his tongue.

"Good God, man, you're drunk." the captain exclaimed, seeing the empty tankards and untouched plate of food.

"Do ... you ... think so?"

Gray had never been one to overindulge in spirits and it puzzled the captain that his young friend would do so on this occasion. Whatever the cause, it was clear that he was in no condition to tend to himself, so Captain Daniels found Cora in the kitchen and inquired about a room for the night.

"I figured he would be needing one," Cora agreed. "Quietest drunk I ever saw. Much have something mighty important preying on his mind." Daniels nodded in agreement. "I'll get a room ready if you can get him up the stairs," she said, taking the coins the captain offered.

Rachel sat before the mirror in her room gently brushing her thick hair. She had bathed in the tub in Cora's room and washed her hair in rainwater she had collected. She had warmed herself by the stove, allowing her hair time to dry, and now, comfortably dressed in the night rail and wrapper that had belonged to her mother, she felt content and warm.

There was a light tap on her door and a second later Cora appeared on the steps. "I know it's late, dear, but we have got a late guest in need of a room. Could you prepare Room Two for me?" she requested.

Rachel smiled. "I shall do it right away," she promised. She wasn't nearly as tired as Cora looked, she thought, as her cousin walked heavily down the stairs. Rachel followed after her, her bare feet silent on the cold, wood plank floor. As Cora disappeared into the common room, Rachel lit the lantern in Room Two and folded back the heavy quilt on the bed. She was anxious to conclude the chore and snuggle into the warm linens of her own bed. Taking the pitcher from the washstand, she left the room. There was an awful clattering noise on the steps and she waited when she saw Captain Daniels assisting another man to the top, a man who quite obviously had partaken of too much ale. How like the captain, she thought, always coming to the aid of people he didn't know, as he had done for her on her journey up the Mississippi.

"You seem to have a penchant for helping strangers," Rachel commented as the pair made their way into the hall.

"I also have an affection for orphaned children and lost puppies," he said with an easy smile.

"Put him in Room Two. I'm going to get fresh water."

Gray's head rolled lifelessly onto the captain's shoulder and it was all the captain could do to control the man who very nearly matched him in size. They stepped closer into the light, and suddenly Rachel recognized him. Her breath caught in her throat. It was the man who had rescued her in St. Louis.

For a moment she stood perfectly still, unable to move. She felt a rush of emotion that she had never experienced before; it sent her heart racing wildly. Their brief encounter in St. Louis had left its mark on her, and the stranger had since been in her mind a great deal. She watched his every movement as the captain guided him down the hall and into the room.

Finally she pulled herself away and hurried down to the kitchen. Cora's lantern was already out for the night, so she filled the pitcher as quietly as possible. Her mind was filled with the image of the stranger upstairs as she recalled how gallantly he had come to her aid and easily taken on her two attackers. Then with such softness and tenderness he had gathered her into his arms and held her securely. She had never felt such powerful yet gentle arms. His concern for her—a stranger—had touched her.

Yet, more than that, he had touched her heart. And he left her with a yearning she didn't understand.

Captain Daniels turned down the linen of his own bed and stripped off his damp shirt and trousers. He was tired and cold and wanted nothing more than a good night's sleep. He heard footsteps in the hall and swore a mild oath under his breath, thinking Gray had awakened so quickly since he had left him in bed across the hall. He opened the door of his bedchamber and peeped out. To his relief, Captain Daniels saw that it was Rachel returning with the pitcher of fresh water. He watched as the girl went inside Gray's room, and satisfied that all was quiet and his friend was well taken care of, he closed his door and climbed into bed. Immediately he fell into an exhausted sleep.

Rachel's limbs trembled nervously as she quietly entered the darkened room where Gray slept. The lantern was out, but light from the second floor of the mercantile across the street shone through the windows enabling her to place the pitcher in its proper location. She hesitated for a moment and stared toward the bed. She couldn't see him but her pulse quickened. She had never been in a man's bedchamber before, and this being the handsome stranger's sent a double flutter through her stomach.

"Come over here." A mellow, masculine voice broke the silence, giving her a start. She didn't respond. "I have to ask you something."

Rachel saw the outline of his wide shoulders against the windows and she realized he wasn't in bed after all. His words didn't sound very slurred, and he was up and about, so perhaps he was not as drunk as she had thought. Slowly she crossed the room. After all, he was a guest, evidently in need of some assistance, and she knew he would not

41

harm her; he had proved that in St. Louis. And he was handsome, more handsome than any other man she had ever seen. She felt drawn to him, almost powerless to stop herself.

Stepping into the light, Rachel tilted her oval face, and her dark eyes searched the face of the man who stood before her. Her heart raced uncontrollably as she was held in place by some unseen force. She couldn't move. No words formed in her mind. Every curve and angle of his face was etched carefully in her mind as she took in his clean masculine scent.

Though his mind was clouded with too much ale, Gray tried desperately to recognize the young woman. Surely he knew her. But from where? She had the darkest eyes he had ever seen, so dark that they reflected the light around her and made them appear luminous. She was beautiful. Slender and shapely, with gentle curves and thick blond tresses that fell softly about her shoulders. Why couldn't he remember who she was? Why did she pull at his memory?

With an unsteady hand Gray touched her chin and tilted her face toward the light from the window. Raindrops splattered against the glass as she lifted her eyes to meet his, and he saw such innocence and openness there that his arms ached to hold her and protect her. Slowly his hands traced the line of her jaw, cupped her ivory-colored cheeks, then traveled down the slender column of her neck. Through the brocade fabric of her wrapper he felt the fine bones of her shoulders. His hands lingered there caressing her delicate frame through the thin cloth. The rain pelted harder against the window as his senses were overwhelmed by the fury of the storm and the vulnerability of the woman he held. A warmth spread through him, like none he had ever experienced. It was more than just the growing urgency in his loins and a rekindling of the fires of passion. The warmth was from the glow that surrounded the young woman. It penetrated his body, winding its way around his heart and consuming his soul. Reality was lost to Gray as he gave into temptation.

The touch of his hand sent Rachel's heart to pounding furiously. She was frightened and at the same time intrigued, wanting to pull away yet anxious to continue. No man had ever touched her, ever looked upon her with the fiery gentleness his eyes displayed. The depth of their blueness drew her to him, captured her, held her a willing prisoner. His mere presence compelled her to stay and she had no desire to flee. At that moment Rachel realized that there was no place on earth she would rather be. She belonged here.

His warm hands moved upward to knead her nape causing strange pleasurable ripples to course through her. His fingers wound their way through her thick tresses. Cautiously, Rachel raised her hands and touched the bare flesh of his arms. They were strong and muscular, and the feel urged her fingers on to explore his wide shoulders and finally his dark-haired chest. She was fascinated by her discoveries.

Gray's powerful arms encircled her and pulled her near. Her soft breasts yielded against the wall of his chest, branding her with its heat and sparking unknown feelings to life. He lowered his mouth to hers and sampled her lips. She was awkward and unsure of herself but his expert guidance soon taught her. His mellow kiss deepened as his probing tongue sought out and found the sweetness that lay within.

Rachel trembled with excitement as he covered her face

and neck with hot searing kisses. She was lost in the feel of him, spellbound by his actions, unable and unwilling to stop him.

An urgency grew within Gray and he communicated it to Rachel as his lips took hers with a more demanding kiss. He untied her wrapper and slipped it off her shoulders. His deft fingers quickly unbuttoned her night rail and it, too, fell to the floor. Standing naked before him Rachel felt no shame or embarrassment, only a need to be near him. He sought out the curve of her hips and his hands anxiously climbed higher to cup her breasts. A moaning deep in his throat was the only sound heard above the storm as he lifted her slight weight into his arms and laid her upon the bed. Quickly he stripped off his few garments, tossed them carelessly aside, and stretched out his long form beside her.

Rachel's frenzied emotions flew to the winds as his lips took hers once more and his hands roamed freely over her breasts, stroking the tiny buds to life, then continued downward to seek out other treasures. His intimate caresses awoke a craving within her. Rachel's arms curled about his neck and pulled him near as she rained hot sultry kisses across his face. Passion was born within her as she boldly stroked his chest and hard flat belly, yearning for the feel of him.

The touch of such soft silken fingers against his skin sent desire racing through his veins. His throbbing manhood was anxious for relief but he held back. He wanted to prolong the passion he shared with this delicate woman. Her supple flesh was like silk, her kisses sweet but passionate, with a feminine fragrance that was uniquely hers. Her ardor rivaled his and grew until he was crazed with desire for her.

He moved atop her and Rachel drew in a quick breath as his bold manhood touched her intimately. She clung to him tightly and buried her face against his neck as the pain of their union tore through her. Then gently, easily, he began to move and his motion overtook her, tapping a well of undiscovered pleasure deep within her. His thrusts became bolder, exacting a response. She answered him in kind. They moved with a fervent rhythm until their ardor rivaled that of the storm, and their union exploded like the streaks of lightning that split the darkness. Then, like the raindrops, they fell to earth in exhausted bliss.

The brilliance of the early morning sun sent daggers of pain through Gray's eyes, increasing the pounding in his head tenfold as he stepped out on the porch of Cora's Tavern & Inn. He pulled his hat down to shade his eyes, but that only worsened the ache in his head, and he thought the thing must have shrunk from yesterday's downpour. His stomach rolled continually and his mouth tasted as if he had chewed a horse harness all night. Gray hooked his arm around one of the porch posts to steady his faltering steps. He couldn't remember when he ever felt worse.

But he was having difficulty remembering much of anything from the night before. The last thing he clearly recalled was meeting Ezra Daniels. Everything after that was but a series of fog-shrouded fragments. The only thing he could recollect with certainty was the passionate lovemaking shared with the beautiful young woman who had appeared in his bed. Their ardor had surpassed any of his previous experiences. The lithe form beneath him had stirred him with passion he had never imagined.

If only his hazy mind would come clear and reveal her identity. She seemed familiar to him, then again not. He remembered the storm, and the feel of her clothing, and those dark eyes wide with innocence. But he could not remember who she was! Gray massaged his forehead with an unsteady hand and tried to force his brain to work. But it only fumbled about uselessly inside his head, still awash with the massive quantity of ale he had consumed. He tried to reason through the situation but that was even more difficult because nothing followed a logical pattern. When he had awakened and found himself alone he had thought the woman who had shared his bed was the young scrub girl he had seen earlier. He hadn't seen her face clearly, but for a reason he didn't understand felt it was she. But when he rose and saw the bright red stains on the bed linen he knew that it could not possibly have been the widow. So who had shared his bed? Whose virginity had he taken?

The pounding in his head worsened as Gray squinted his eyes against the brightness of the sun. The streets had already come to life despite the early hour as people on foot and in carriages made their way through the mud. He had missed his meeting the night before and hoped he could arrange to see the same men today, though he hardly felt up to it.

Perhaps some strong coffee would help, he decided and turned to reenter the tavern. Just then the door opened and a couple walked out followed by their many children. Among them was a slender light-haired girl of about twelve. The girl's eyes locked with Gray's and she gave him the most flirtatious and knowing smile he had ever seen. She batted her eyelashes coyly and sauntered away to join her family.

Gray's stomach twisted into a knot as all the strength left his body and his knees threatened to buckle. *Oh, God, no! Not her! Not a child!* Surely he couldn't have—wouldn't have—taken a mere babe to his bed. If only he could remember more clearly. If only he hadn't drunk so much ale. He had experienced the most loving and passionate night of his life and now he couldn't even recall who it was with! But certainly not this—this child. *No, please, not her!*

Gray debated for a moment on whether to approach the girl's father. But what could he say? He could not confess to something that he wasn't even sure had happened. That would only serve to compromise the girl's reputation, and more likely, land him a thrashing from the man. Small beads of perspiration dampened his collar as Gray glanced once more at the girl. He tried to gather his thoughts, but his mind failed him.

Well, to hell with it!

It had been a short trip up from Westport, and he hadn't expected to find much here anyway—he had come on a whim—so why prolong his misery by staying? He would forget his business here, forget the passionate young woman, forget he had ever been to St. Joseph, Missouri. He would return to the docks at once and book passage back home to—Claudia.

Spasms rolled through his stomach as he pictured his wife-to-be scowling at him, her arms folded primly across her full bosoms. The thought reminded him of a maiden aunt with whom he had spent some time as a child and who never found favor in his actions. Gray clasped a hand across his mouth to contain the foul bile which threatened to rise, and dashed across Third Street toward the docks and forever away from Cora's Tavern & Inn and St. Joseph.

High in her attic room, Rachel sat on the trunk by the window looking down at the street. She wrapped her arms around her legs as she drew them up to her chest and rested her chin on her knees. Tears rolled freely down her cheeks and were absorbed by the batiste night rail she wore as she saw the dark-haired stranger striding across the street. She watched him until he disappeared from sight, then for many moments stared at the spot where she had last seen him.

Hers were tears of sadness but not because of what she had done. She felt no sorrow over her lost virginity and no shame for her actions. The night she had spent in the stranger's bed was the most beautiful time of her life. He was so gentle and loving, and filled with such tenderness that she could never regret joining him willingly in his bed.

All along she knew he wouldn't stay in St. Joseph. He was obviously a man of great wealth here for some business purpose. His clothing and manners were too fine to be anything less. And it was for that reason that Rachel knew he would not stay. He didn't belong in this world. His was a place of much nicer things, a place of servants and beautiful homes, surrounded by the most fetching of women. The place she had once belonged. And now she would never be good enough to vie for the attention of such a man. That opportunity had been robbed from her when her father had gambled with her future and lost. But she had had her moment with him, a time of beautiful passion, and no one could take that from her.

She opened her clenched fist and looked at the pocket watch she held. In her haste to leave his room she had picked it up with her wrapper that was lying among his clothing. She turned the watch over and read the inscription once more. Perhaps it was from his wife, perhaps not. She brushed the tears from her eyes. No matter. He had belonged to her for a few brief hours and that memory was hers to keep, even if he wasn't.

As she went about her daily chores Rachel found her mind was beset by thoughts of the stranger and their night together. She only wished she had a name to put with his handsome face. But when she checked the register she saw that no one had signed for the room he occupied, which wasn't unusual considering Cora's somewhat unorthodox bookkeeping method. She had casually questioned her cousin about the stranger but Cora was quick to say that she knew nothing of him and was glad he had left as suddenly as he had arrived. There was nothing else Rachel could do. Asking too many questions might raise suspicion, so she was left with a nameless yet handsome body to warm her thoughts.

The cold days of December were harder on Rachel than she anticipated. She was unaccustomed to the bitter cold and dampness. It left her feeling wrung out so that she would often have to nap at midday or retire to her room at an unusually early hour. Luckily there were few guests during the winter months and not much cleaning was required of her. She spent many afternoons in her room crocheting a shawl to give Cora for Christmas. She had taken some of her carefully hoarded coins from their hiding place at the bottom of her trunk and bought yarn from the mercantile across the street. Rachel worked diligently yet her eyes strayed from their task to cast a glance across Third Street; there was never a sign of the stranger.

The holiday season was a festive one. Not so grand as

her Christmases at Richfield, but neither as dismal nor bleak as those at Briarcliff. She and Cora put a small tree in the common room and on Christmas Day Liz and Jean and their families came over as well as Hannah and Seth, the owners of the mercantile. A small feast was prepared and they dined together, sang carols, and exchanged their modest gifts.

Rachel felt secure in the company of her newfound friends. She and Cora became closer and she felt a special fondness for Hannah. Though she wasn't terribly smart, Hannah helped Seth in the mercantile as much as her limited education would allow, and she was always eager to please him. A few years older than Rachel, they had been married for a short time but had no children, an obvious disappointment to Hannah. Cora predicted that Hannah's mild manners and saintlike patience would lend themselves to successful child-rearing.

The coldest of the winter months seemed endless to Rachel as she was plagued by fatigue and a variety of minor illnesses. She was either ravenous and consumed every scrap of food in sight or sickened by the mere thought of it. Her whole body was out of tune and she wondered if she would ever adjust to the cold climate. When she described her ailments to Cora her cousin recommended hot tea and rest, remedies Rachel heartily agreed with.

A brisk March wind blew along Third Street sending dust and dirt flying into the air. Rachel pulled her shawl closer as she hurried up the steps to the inn. There were few travelers, since it would be a few more months before the first wagon train pulled out, and the common room was empty. She went into the kitchen to finish her chores and found Cora seated alone at the small table working on her books.

"Seems too fine a day to be inside," Rachel observed as she hung her shawl on a peg by the stove. She felt especially chipper today.

Cora looked up from her work. "Glad to see you are feeling better."

She smiled as she tied on the long white apron. "This cold weather does not agree with me. I don't know when I've felt so bad for so long."

"Does Seth have that pot I ordered?"

Rachel shook her head. "Not yet, but he says it should be here soon." She poured hot water from the kettle into the wooden tub and stacked the dirty dishes in it.

"He's been saying that for weeks."

"You know supply shipments are unreliable during the winter," she pointed out. She turned the conversation to a happier note, anxious to share the information she had just learned. "Hannah just told me that she and Seth are going West in the spring," Rachel said as she washed the dishes.

Cora shook her head disgustedly.

"You don't think it's a good idea?"

"I've heard of too many tragedies. On the trail for months, with no steady water supply, no protection from the heat and rain except a covered wagon. If disease and wild animals don't get you, the Indians will."

Rachel shrugged off her cousin's remarks. "But it's such a wonderful adventure. Going to a new land and making a life for yourself out of nothing. Hannah and Seth are both excited about it."

"What about the mercantile?"

"Seth is going to sell it. He thinks he will have a better

chance of getting rid of it in the spring when business picks up."

"I guess everyone has got to find their own way in life," Cora commented.

Rachel finished the dishes quickly and removed her apron. She turned to leave when she saw Cora staring at her. She followed her gaze to the front of her dress. "Is something wrong with my dress?" It was a simple cotton print, a far cry from the gowns she used to wear, but it served its purpose well.

"It looks a bit . . . snug lately."

Rachel ran her hands down the sides of her dress. It was true that everything felt tighter than usual, but that was because her appetite had improved with the warmer weather.

"I can see you've been feeling better this past week," Cora said, "but is everything back to normal?"

A knot twisted in Rachel's stomach and she picked up a cleaning rag and wiped down the sideboard. "No, no, not everything. But I'm certain it's just the weather here. That's all—it's just the cold, nothing more." She scrubbed harder, turning her attention to her chore.

"When did you say Mr. Fontaine passed away?"

"Who?"

"Mr. Fontaine, your husband," Cora said softly.

Rachel swallowed hard. *No, it can't be. It can't!*

"It was a few days—a week—before I arrived here," she said quickly.

Cora rose and walked to stand by the sideboard. "Rachel, dear, you have been cleaning that same spot for five minutes."

Rachel stopped, suddenly realizing her shoulder was aching. She didn't want to hear what her cousin was going to say. She had suspected it herself, but refused to face it. She lifted her eyes to meet Cora's, knowing now that there was no doubt. Tears sprang from her eyes as Cora took her into her arms.

"It's a shame," Cora said soothingly, "and I don't blame you for the sorrow you feel, knowing your husband lies cold in the ground never to know he had a babe on the way."

Chapter 3

It had been all right when there was only herself to consider. Life in a small town and little contact with the larger, more civilized portion of the country had suited Rachel perfectly. She had found a safe haven from everything she wanted to escape. But now there was more to consider. The needs of someone else must be filled as well. A baby. *His baby.* The child of a wealthy man who would never know of the birthright that should have been his. In her mind she pictured the baby in his father's arms, wrapped in the finest of blankets, in a beautiful home, cared for by legions of servants. That's how it should have been.

Rachel stopped her pacing and looked down at the street below. She imagined a child, born to a scrubwoman, living out his life set on the edge of civilization. Tears threatened to fill her eyes but she willed them to subside; she had already wasted too much time with useless crying. She drew in a deep breath and summoned her courage. Yes, she told herself, yes, she would see to it that her babe had more out of life. Her child would have it all and she would be the one to make it possible. She sat down on the trunk and took one final look out the window at the spot where she had last seen the stranger who had changed her life. *No. No more watching the street. He's not coming back.* He was the past, and the past was irrelevant. Now she would look only to the future and do what was best for her child. It was up to her, and she would not fail as her parents had done.

She moved away from the window and rested her hand on the small bulge in her belly. Her heart mellowed when she thought of the tiny babe growing inside her. She loved him already. She would care for him and provide a good life for them both—and nothing would stop her.

The tiny kitchen in the back of the mercantile was warm and cozy and smelled of the apple pie Hannah had just placed on the sideboard. She wiped her hands on her apron and hurried to join the others seated at the rough-hewn table. There was a tension in the air that was foreign to this gathering of friends.

"We can have pie a bit later," Hannah commented and settled herself next to her husband. Cora and Rachel sat across the table from them. There was a long silence and finally it was Seth who spoke.

"You two look mighty serious, Cora. What brings you over this evening?"

"I'm only here at Rachel's request. I'll let her do the talking."

Rachel shifted in her chair and managed a thin smile. She had asked Cora to join her tonight for moral support and was glad she had agreed to come. "I'm here to discuss business."

Seth clamped down on his pipe. "Business?" His bushy brows rose in surprise.

"Yes. I want to buy your mercantile." She said it calmly but her heart raced within her.

Seth snorted and cast aside her statement with a wave of his thin hand. "That's nonsense, child."

She knew she would be in for a fight, but she was prepared. She had already argued every side of her proposal with Cora, who had been dead set against the notion as well. Rachel had convinced her finally, and in doing so convinced herself she was up to it. "It's not nonsense. I have given it a great deal of thought and I know it's the right thing to do." She spoke with a calm, even voice.

"But how are you going to run a business when you are ..."

Rached leaned back in her chair and slid her hand over the roundness of her belly. It had been a full month since she had realized she was with child and now her condition made itself known to the whole town. "This babe is exactly why I must buy your mercantile. I must be able to provide a respectable life for my child. It's all up to me, since my husband is ... gone." She managed to look sorrowful when she spoke of the late Mr. Fontaine.

Seth considered her words, then presented another objection. "You are quite young and lack the education necessary to run a business."

"On the contrary. I am quite well read and proficient with numbers," Rachel was quick to point out.

"I can vouch for that," Cora put in. "You should see the wonders she has worked with my books. I didn't realize I was doing so well until she took over."

56

"And what do you know of the mercantile business?" Seth questioned.

Rachel could not tell him that her only "qualifications" were the detailed analysis of her cousin Melvin Carmichael's ledgers she had done to occupy herself during her stay at Briarcliff and the fact that she had been with her mother to every conceivable type of shop since she was old enough to walk. Resourcefully she called on her poor deceased husband for help. He had served her well in securing her undetected escape from St. Francesville, and in keeping the town from knowing the child she carried was a bastard. Once again he would provide the means by which Rachel could accomplish her objectives.

"Mr. Fontaine and I ran a mercantile together during our brief marriage." *Another lie. Well, what harm can one more do?*

"You can't look after the place alone. There is too much work, and in your condition you will never be able to get it all done," Seth told her.

"I have already spoken to Jean's little brother. He is willing to come by and help out whenever I need him." Rachel could see Seth was running out of arguments.

"The roof leaks."

"I'll live here on the first floor."

"The storeroom is in sore need of reorganizing."

"I had planned to do that anyway."

Seth ran a hand across his narrow lips. "Rachel, honey, it's just so many things that need to be done around here."

It was time for Rachel to take the offensive. "Don't you and Hannah want to move west?"

"Well, sure we do."

"Have you had any offers to purchase yet?"

"No, not yet. But I know that will come in time."

57

"I am willing to take it off your hands immediately— as is. You and Hannah will be free to leave with the first wagon train next month." Rachel spoke in the business- like tone she had heard her father use so many years ago when she had accompanied him to the city to conduct business. A new sense of power came over her as she re- alized she had successfully turned aside every objection Seth had offered. Self-confidence surged through her as she delivered her final ploy. "I have cash."

Seth sat up straighter in his chair, and for the first time turned to look at Hannah. She had been silent, keeping to the station life had given her. "It would be the answer to our prayers," she said softly, and touched his arm.

Rachel held her breath while Seth thought over the proposition. Finally a smile broke across his face. "You have got yourself a deal," he said, and extended his hand across the table. Rachel smiled broadly as she rose and accepted his hand.

The first shafts of sunlight broke over the eastern ho- rizon, holding the promise of a beautiful spring day. But its grandeur was lost amid the noise and confusion of the wagon train staging area on the gently rolling banks of the Missouri River. Such excitement! Everyone was calling to their teams, wagon drivers swearing and shouting out last minute instructions. The animals moved about ner- vously and the noise of yokes, harnesses, and chains filled the air. Bells clanged and cattle lowed, horses pawed ner- vously at the ground.

The trip westward would take in excess of four months. The caravan might hope to cover as much as one hundred twenty miles in a week as it inched its way through the most trecherous and desolate of lands. There were so many things that could go wrong. The threat of cholera, shortages of water and food, and wild animal attacks all paled when compared to the possibility of confrontation with the Indians.

Each wooden wagon was filled to capacity with supplies of sugar, flour, salted ham, smoked bacon, ground coffee, bushels of beans and dried fruit, and sacks of rice. Added to this already considerable weight were axes, saws, carpenter's chisels, picks, spades, and shovels. There was precious little space left to bring along many personal items.

Rachel waved a final good-bye as the wagon train set out. Seth and Hannah had been so excited about their adventure, so full of plans and hopes and dreams for their new life that they had given little thought to problems that might be headed their way. Rachel felt a pang of envy as she saw the closeness of her two friends and their desire to build a life together. She could wish them nothing but the best.

She gathered the fullness of her dress and walked slowly back toward the mercantile. She chose her steps carefully, prolonging the quarter-mile walk. The month of May had brought a new influx of travelers to St. Joseph, all anticipating the departure of the first wagon train. And they had all brought one thing with them—money to spend.

Rachel had just enough time to acquaint herself with her new venture before business began to increase. Seth and Hannah had stayed to help her for as long as they could and she appreciated it all. Seth was a wise businessman and gave her much useful information. But now they were gone and Rachel had a few changes in mind for her mercantile.

Rachel stopped by Cora's to let her know that Seth and

Hannah had departed. "I still think it's a fool thing to do," Cora said as she prepared the morning meal for her already busy common room.

"I think it's wonderful," Rachel said dreamily, still remembering the expression on Hannah's face when they had said their farewells.

"That Seth is no spring chicken and Hannah is about the frailest-looking woman I ever saw around these parts— except for you, that is—and neither of them has got any business trying to make such a trip." Cora turned back to the cook stove, ending their conversation.

Undaunted by her cousin's harsh view of reality, Rachel left the tavern still feeling the excitement that had filled her earlier. Several customers had already gathered outside her mercantile as Rachel crossed the street and unlocked the front door, signaling the beginning of another day of brisk sales.

Completely lost in her work, the days and weeks rolled by uncounted. Rachel made changes to her business which included increasing the prices moderately and introducing some new lines of merchandise. She spent some of her profits on a grand new sign which proclaimed the establishment Fontaine's Mercantile. Rachel had supervised the hanging of the sign from the center of the street giving no thought to how the young widow with the huge round belly looked to passersby.

Her home was now the two small rooms in back of her mercantile which served as kitchen and bedroom. She rarely cooked, though, preferring instead to eat at Cora's when time permitted. More often than not she would see Liz or Jean appear with a tray of food sent over by Cora. The meal was also served with a stern lecture on eating properly. Rachel never meant to neglect her health and always tried to take good care of herself, but there were times when she was busy with customers or absorbed in her bookwork and she simply forgot. It warmed her to know there were others who cared about her and her baby.

The child inside her did little to slow Rachel down and many people commented on how remarkably healthy she was. Most predicted a strong boy would be delivered. In truth, Rachel was so caught up in her new endeavor she gave little notice to the aches and pains she felt. For the first time in her life she was doing something she genuinely enjoyed. And she was doing it on her own. And doing it well! Rachel liked the feeling of self-confidence running the mercantile gave her.

By late July, with the birth of her child only weeks away, Rachel was forced to slow her pace. She still insisted on opening the store early and seeing to the customers as much as possible, but she did concede to allow Jean's younger brother to help out more. Jimmy was only a few years younger than Rachel, but she felt older by decades. His fresh face and constant smile were a welcome sight and he had so proved his competence that Rachel was confident that he could handle any problems that might arise.

Rachel rose from her afternoon nap feeling troubled. She had dreamed of the dark-haired man again. That had happened more frequently in recent weeks. As always, she had dreamed that he was near her yet just out of reach. It was a maddening dream and she wished it would stop.

She rinsed her face with cool water and rearranged her simple coiffure. The baby gave a firm kick within her and a smile spread across her face. She loved the feel of him insider her; she would miss that after he was born.

The mercantile was quiet when she entered through the

curtain that separated it from her living quarters, so she moved to the other side of the store and began to tidy up the display of yard goods. She was considering expanding the types of yardage offered when a familiar voice pulled her from her own thoughts. She turned quickly seeking the source of the man who had called her name. To her surprise she saw Captain Daniels standing in the next aisle. "What a wonderful surprise," she exclaimed.

The captain strode around the copper kettles that separated them and took Rachel's outstretched hands. "Mrs. Fontaine, I was hoping I would see you again," he said warmly. "When I inquired at Cora's Tavern I was directed over here."

"I'm so glad you came," she said earnestly.

The captain looked around the room. "I see you have done quite well for yourself."

Rachel smiled modestly. "Business is booming."

"I seem to have invested in the wrong types of businesses here in St. Joseph," he said. "Sad to say, but mine aren't doing nearly as well as yours. Are you interested in taking on a partner?"

Rachel returned his teasing smile. "Not at this time, but I will keep you in mind."

For the first time he noticed the roundness of her belly and his eyes widened in surprise. "Congratulations, my dear. I wasn't aware that you had remarried."

The smile faded from her face. "I haven't. I'm a widow." She turned her left hand so the wedding band she wore would be more easily seen.

A confused frown crossed his face. "But I understood you to say that your husband had been dead for several months prior to your arrival in St. Louis."

Rachel cursed her poor memory. She had forgotten she

had told Captain Daniels a different story. The best she could do now was to try to cover up for it. "I believe your memory has failed you, Captain, or perhaps in my grief I did not explain the situation clearly. My husband passed away only a few days before my arrival here. It is his child I carry."

Captain Daniels let the issue drop and turned the conversation to a happier subject. Rachel was relieved he had believed her story. He visited for a while longer as Rachel showed him about the store, but he had to return to Westport all too soon. He was pleased to see Rachel doing better for herself and no longer scrubbing floors for a living. He bid her farewell and walked away toward the docks.

It troubled him that Rachel should be all alone at a time when a woman needed her husband. And that was another thing that bothered him. He was certain she had told him that her husband had been dead for some time. Too long a time, in fact, to be the father of the child she carried. He did a quick mental calculation. From the looks of her belly the baby's arrival couldn't be more than a month away and that would mean she couldn't have been pregnant prior to her arrival in St. Joseph. Captain Daniels shook his head. It was really none of his business if she had fallen under the spell of some young man and, finding herself in the family way, tried to pass the child off as that of her deceased husband. He couldn't blame her for trying to protect her reputation as well as that of her unborn child. He only hoped that it had been a handsome, gentle young man and not some drunken—

He stopped in his tracks as a long-forgotten vision came to him. During his last visit to St. Joseph, after he had put his friend Gray Montgomery to bed for the night, he had seen Rachel entering his room to return the water pitcher. At the time he had thought nothing of it, but now it disturbed him greatly. Gray was a worldly man with expensive tastes and not the sort of man to find solace with a scrub girl. However, Gray was so very drunk that night and it was terribly cold . . .

Captain Daniels pushed the thought from his mind. It was too ridiculous to be true. And of little significance as well since by now Gray was married and Rachel seemed to be doing fine on her own. He chided himself for letting his imagination run away with him and tried to dismiss the notion. Yet it still nagged at him and, try as he might, he could not rid himself of it.

Sitting at her kitchen table, Rachel worked faithfully on her books. She always kept them current. Every night she tallied the day's receipts and compared them to expenditures. She was pleased that her profits were so much better than she had anticipated. The new line of small household wares had proven very successful and she was tempted to try out some of her other ideas.

An urgent rap at her back door startled her; the hour was late. With lantern in hand she pulled back the curtain and saw Cora waiting. A feeling of dread came over her. Cora would not be out this time of night unless there was a problem. Her suspicions were confirmed when Cora entered the kitchen and instructed Rachel to sit down.

"There is just no easy way to tell bad news," Cora began. She looked tired and drawn.

"Cora, please, what is it?"

"It's Hannah. She came today with some of the other settlers who had to turn back."

"What happened? Where is Seth?"

"Just calm down. Don't get yourself upset. I've been

tending the sick all day and in no mood to help deliver a baby," Cora said sourly. Rachel forced herself to be patient and listen. "The wagon train was hit with cholera. Seth came down with it. He didn't survive."

Rachel's heart lurched, but she held back the tears that threatened. "I must go to Hannah. Where is she?"

Cora waved a hand to calm her. "She is staying at my place. The doctor was with her and gave her something to make her sleep. There is nothing you can do tonight."

"How horrible," Rachel murmured. "Is Hannah all right? Did she come down with it, too?"

Cora shook her head. "Doc says she will be fine. She has been through a lot and needs some care and some meat back on her bones."

Rachel recalled how happy Hannah and Seth had been when their journey had begun. She had never imagined such tragedy would befall them. "I will come to see Hannah tomorrow."

Cora patted her hand. "You get yourself to bed and rest."

Rachel placed her palm on the small of her back and tried to rub away the aching there. She said good night to her cousin and went to bed. Hannah and Seth were uppermost in her thoughts, but that night she dreamed again of her dark-haired lover; as usual, he was far, far out of her reach.

The next day she went to visit Hannah, who hardly looked like the same person Rachel had said farewell to a few months ago. Hannah was thin and frail looking, and her eyes lacked their former gleam. Rachel sat down at her bedside and tried to talk with her, but she was groggy from the sleeping potion and Rachel wasn't sure she had gotten through to her. After another week had passed there was no change, no improvement.

Rachel was struck with a burst of energy when she rose from a restless night's sleep and set about cleaning everything in her path. She thought it quite strange because she hardly had the strength to cross the street during the past week. But she didn't question it; it felt good to stir about again. The spurt of energy was short-lived, though, and by that evening she was beset with strange aches and pains, so much so that she couldn't sleep. She made hot tea for herself and walked about the mercantile. But nothing helped. She felt miserable. Finally around dawn she realized what was happening. She had to laugh at herself for being so witless. The baby was coming!

Rachel gathered a few of her belongings and explained to Jimmy that she would be at Cora's for the day. She tried to remain calm, but she was filled with a mixture of fear and excitement. At last the time had come, just when she was beginning to think she would be pregnant for the rest of her life! When she appeared in Cora's kitchen holding a bundle of her belongings, her cousin asked no questions; she knew from Rachel's face what was happening. Liz and Jean were beside themselves with excitement and anxiously helped Cora prepare for the great event. The morning meal service was completely abandoned as all three women took Rachel upstairs.

To her surprise, Rachel found herself in Room Two—this was where she had gotten into this fix in the first place! She changed into a thin night rail and settled into the bed. For the first time in months she allowed herself to think of *him*, and recall every detail of his strong body and handsome face. She wondered where he was, what he was doing, who he was with. Her mind was filled with thoughts of the dark-haired man and she longed to cry out for him. She had tried to forget him, tried to deny her emotions for months, and now, once and for all, she had to face the truth. She loved him!

Soon Rachel's mind was turned to herself as her labor progressed. Cora stayed with her, sponging her sweaty forehead and dampening her parched lips with cool water. The hours dragged by as the sun arced across the sky and touched the western horizon. Finally, when Rachel thought she could bear no more, when her whole body was nearly numb from exhaustion, Cora sent for the doctor. Liz and Jean followed Dr. Sawyer upstairs and waited anxiously outside the door. From within they heard Rachel's struggles and the calming words of the doctor and Cora. At last the thin, ragged cry of a baby was heard above all else and the women hugged each other happily. Cora opened the door to admit the baby's first visitors. Rachel lay back against several pillows, her hair damp against her face, holding her baby close. The child continued to scream as if announcing to the world in the only way he knew that he had arrived.

Dr. Sawyer cleaned his hands in the washbasin as the women gathered about the baby and his mother. "Mr. Fontaine must have been a large man," he commented.

"Who?" Rachel asked.

"The baby's father." He was used to women saying strange things during childbirth; at least this one hadn't thrown anything at him. Rachel was more interested in her child than the doctor's observations, but he spoke anyway to whomever cared to listen. "He's a big boy. Almost too large for your frame, Rachel. You had a difficult time but you both came through fine."

She pushed back the blanket that covered the wispy

dark curls of her son's head. She knew all along this baby would be a boy.

"Rachel, he doesn't look a thing like you," Liz noted.

Rachel smiled down at her son. "He looks just like his father."

The women's chatter ceased abruptly and Rachel looked up to see Hannah standing in the doorway. Her eyes were fixed on the crying child. "Come in! See my son," Rachel bade eagerly.

Hannah, still dressed in her night rail, slowly advanced to the bed. She ran her finger down the baby's soft cheek and touched his tiny hand. Immediately his fist opened and closed again around Hannah's finger. Her face lit up with a smile Rachel had not seen in a long while.

"Can I hold him, Rachel?" Hannah asked, still not taking her eyes from the child. "Please?" Rachel did not want to turn loose of her baby but reluctantly did so. Hannah cradled him and rocked him gently, and shortly his crying abated. "I think he likes me!" Hannah announced as tears of joy stood in her eyes. She sat down beside Rachel and held the tiny baby between them. The others gathered around to share in the joy this new life had brought them all.

As Rachel's recovery progressed she found that Hannah improved as well. The rocker was brought from the mercantile and placed in Rachel's room. It was Hannah who occupied it most often, sitting for hours on end rocking baby Andrew, singing and talking to him softly. Rachel was pleased to have someone sharing her joy, and doubly glad that the babe had pulled Hannah out of her depression.

When she was strong enough Rachel moved back to the mercantile. A tiny cradle was placed at the foot of her bed for Andrew. He was a peaceful baby and slept much of the time. Rachel loved the hours she spent with him, caring for his simple needs, holding him, loving him. But she could not look at him without being reminded of his father. And she no longer minded that, either. In the short time the man had been in her life he had managed to change it permanently. He had forced her to face life head-on, to change herself and her circumstances. And he had given her her precious Andrew. Yes, she liked the changes.

Rachel was torn between her duties in the mercantile and her desire to care for her son. Business was ever-increasing as were the baby's needs. There seemed to be not enough hours in the day to accomplish all her chores. Many times she would go about her job in the store carrying the baby with her. He was mild-mannered and hardly noticed the activity. Up late at night doing the books, Rachel would finally crawl into bed only to have Andrew wake up, ready to eat.

She tried to balance all her responsibilities but soon it became clear that she could not handle it all. There seemed only one option available—she would have to hire additional help. But she hated the thought of someone else taking care of Andrew. It would require lengthy interviews and research to locate the proper person. And even after all that was done she was reluctant to turn her child over to a complete stranger. The only other alternative was to find someone to manage the mercantile, and she did not like that, either. She had no desire to trust another person with her future.

As Andrew's second full month of life was completed, the strain of managing all her responsibilities began to weigh heavily on Rachel. She stood restocking her shelves with arms so heavy from lack of sleep that she could barely lift them. At her feet, Andrew lay in his basket. He had been cranky all day and she had been unable to comfort him. He squirmed about fitfully then broke into an deafening wail. "Oh, Andrew," she said wearily as she looked down at him, "please don't cry. I have so much work to do." The child paid her no heed. She gathered her skirt to climb down from the ladder when Hannah appeared beside the basket. She scooped the baby into her arms and placed him across her shoulder.

"Goodness, Rachel, I heard him crying from outside. Is he sick?" she asked as she patted his small back.

Rachel sighed with relief. "I don't think so. He has been fussy all day. But then, so have I. After being up most of the night, neither of us is having a very good day. I don't know how much longer I can keep doing this."

Andrew quieted under Hannah's gentle hand. She looked up at Rachel with wide eyes. "Let me keep him."

Rachel climbed down the ladder. Hannah was the perfect choice. Why hadn't she thought of her before? It seemed too good to be true. "Are you serious?"

Hannah rocked the babe, scarcely noticing Rachel. "I can think of no nobler task in life than the proper rearing of a child."

And so it was decided. Though Hannah was willing to care for her Andrew at no charge, Rachel insisted on paying her a small wage. The arrangement suited everyone's needs including Andrew's, who was as contented in Hannah's arms as his mother's.

Chapter 4

Would they ever stop coming, Rachel wondered as she stole a quick glance out her shop window. The streets were thick with unaccustomed hustle and bustle, people coming and going wherever one turned.

The nation was gripped with gold fever, and neither Rachel and her store nor St. Joseph as a whole had been spared. It had been little more than a rumor in the summer and fall, but in December of 1848 President Polk had made the official announcement that had rocked the nation. Gold had been discovered in California! Word spread like wildfire and within weeks there was not a ship on the Atlantic Coast not filled to capacity. Fair weather attracted prospectors by the thousands to the land route, and like the pioneers, many began their journey in St. Joseph, Missouri. Rachel sometimes wondered if it was a curse or a blessing.

Rachel kept her mercantile open from dawn until well past sunset as the frenzied buyers purchased their mining equipment and supplies. They were willing to pay any price in their rush to begin their journey. They crowded into the mercantile taking what they needed with no thought of the continually rising prices. Often two or more men would bid for the last pan or shovel in stock, unwilling to wait for the next supply shipment to arrive. Lost time here could mean losing out on the gold that awaited them in California. Rachel raked in the profits at an astounding rate. She was quickly becoming a wealthy woman, and there was no end in sight to the madness that drove people westward. The whole town was gripped with Gold Fever as the thousands who passed through St. Joseph were anxious to pay whatever the cost to get to the gold fields. But it was the merchants themselves who sat atop the real gold mines. Investors and businessmen from the East flocked to St. Joseph and other towns along the route prospecting for a different type of reward. They made the rounds to the established businesses offering to buy them out. Some accepted quickly and headed West themselves. Others stayed on, turning down the generous offers.

Rachel was approached as well and was made an offer for her mercantile of over twice what she paid for it. She gently refused. It never occurred to her to leave St. Jo. She had her family and friends here and had built a well-run business that brought in more profit than she had ever imagined. And besides, where would she go? The offers continued to come in, each more generous than the previous, but she refused them all.

The sun slipped toward the horizon and Rachel had stood all the pressing crowds she could take that day in the April warmth that made her shop feel oppressive. She asked Jimmy to close for the night as she ducked out the back way for some much needed fresh air and solitude.

The cooling breeze blew through her hair loosening several strands from the coil at her nape as she headed for the wooded area in the hills above the wagon-train staging area. She often came to this spot to sit and think. Sometimes she would bring Andrew and they would lie on a quilt and spend a rare afternoon together.

Her head buzzed with the confusion of the day's business, the voices of her patrons still ringing in her ears. Two men had almost come to blows over who would purchase the last blanket in stock. Rachel had come from behind the counter and thrown herself between the two, holding them at bay. She had threatened to throw them both out into the street if they didn't calm down. The two towered over her, yet allowed her to settle the dispute. She took a blanket from her own bed and sold it along with the new one to each man. The rugged, grizzlylike man clutched the quilt and vowed it would keep him warmer than a new one because it carried the scent of Rachel's delicate cologne. As they left the shop, she heard them arguing now of who should have gotten the used one.

There seemed to be no situation Rachel could not handle. She stood toe-to-toe with those of her suppliers who tried to overcharge her. She was faster with numbers than most men and was quick to catch their methods of cheating. Customers who chose to barter for their supplies received no favor from the young merchant. Her trim figure and soft features belied the sharp mind and tongue within.

Rachel rubbed her temples with the tips of her fingers and drew in a cleansing breath. The quiet was oh so welcome. She had been approached again today by a businessman up from Westport who made her another offer for her shop. She had turned him down cold. But now as she sat in the woods she began to wonder if she could go on at this pace much longer. She saw Andrew for only a few minutes a day now, and was truly thankful that Hannah was so adept at caring for him. But the child was hers, not Hannah's, and she wanted to be free to spend more time with him.

Rachel looked down the hill at the wagons settling in for the night. Maybe she should go West and seek an even greater fortune for herself and Andrew. She giggled aloud at that ridiculous thought. Perhaps New York or Boston would make a fine home for her son, she mused. And live among the Yankees? She dismissed the thought at once.

A notion suddenly seeped into her thoughts. She nearly disregarded it immediately as totally absurd but instead allowed it to come full force into her mind. *Charleston.* She could return to her home, to the life she had been born to, the life she had been meant for. Excitement ran through her veins as she recalled the elegant city that had once been her home. She could give Andrew the best of everything there. A good education, introduction to the finest families, a beautiful home in which to grow to manhood.

Another thought crashed into her already spinning mind, bringing her to her feet. Richfield, the plantation that had belonged to her father, could be hers as it was intended. She could purchase it and make it the home for her son. It was almost too thrilling to be true. She might after all have the life she thought was lost to her and provide everything that Andrew could ever need.

Rachel was filled with excitement over the prospect when she returned to the mercantile and began going over her books. She had already amassed a sizable amount, but much more wealth would be needed to acquire Richfield. She spent a sleepless night, but by morning her mind was made up. She would do it. She would squeeze every cent from the mercantile then sell out. She would return to Charleston a wealthy woman and regain her rightful place at Richfield. And nothing or no one would stop her.

She pushed herself even harder than before in the mercantile. She increased prices substantially, bringing groans and complaints from customers. She told them quite matter-of-factly that they could buy elsewhere if they didn't want to pay her price, all the time knowing there was no other mercantile left in town. She knew it was only a matter of time before another store opened, but until she was faced with competition she would keep her prices, and her profits, high.

Rachel told no one of her plans to leave, not even Hannah or Cora. It was her secret dream. At times she would lie awake at night and try to imagine what life would be like in Charleston again. She would once more wear lovely gowns, instead of the simple cotton dresses that were her everyday attire now. There would be no rough-looking men of questionable parentage, but finely clothed gentlemen. And she would no longer have to work hard at menial tasks. There would be a bevy of servants to fulfill her duties, leaving her time to spend with her son. She would be a great lady as her mother had been, respected, adored, and loved by everyone around her. The only difference was that Rachel would not repeat Althea's mistakes.

Weeks swept by with each day blending into the next. There was always the mad rush of patrons, streets congested with horses, carriages, wagons, and the never-ending stream of people. It all moved at a frenzied pace.

Dawn's first light found Rachel sweeping the porch outside her shop. It was the only time of day she could perform the task uninterrupted. With so much of her emphasis on selling, she still sought to provide a clean shop for her patrons. Two gentlemen climbed the steps behind her giving Rachel a start. She spun around to face them, clutching her crude straw broom. She recognized them immediately. "Mr. Basham, Mr. Pearce, I was deep in thought and not expecting anyone so early in the day," she said breathlessly.

The kindly, gray-haired Mr. Basham chuckled. "We are so sorry to frighten you, Mrs. Fontaine. It was only our desire to speak privately with you that brings us out at this hour."

"Looks like another fine day," Mr. Pearce noted, turning his heavily lined face to the eastern horizon.

"In truth, sir, the days all look the same from within these walls," she admitted, gesturing toward her shop.

The men smiled and exchanged a glance. "Perhaps, madam, you could spare a few moments for a business discussion," Mr. Pearce requested.

Rachel eyed the two finely attired men. She had been approached by them before with offers to purchase her mercantile. "Sir, we have had this same discussion on several occasions."

"Please, madam, indulge us. We have traveled up from Westport for the sole purpose of meeting you," Mr. Basham pointed out.

She considered the two. "Very well. Come inside."

Rachel led the way through the well-stocked shelves of the mercantile and offered them seating at her kitchen table, all the while pretending not to hear as the men murmured about the quality of the merchandise. Hannah was at the stove while Andrew still slept. The men greeted Hannah, who offered them coffee as they sat down across from Rachel. The steamy cups set before them, Hannah excused herself to attend to duties, leaving Rachel alone with the men.

"Let us come right to the point," Mr. Basham began. "We are here again today, Mrs. Fontaine, to make you an offer for this establishment."

Rachel looked between the two men. "I gathered that, sir, and while I am flattered by your attention I fear that once again your trip has been in vain."

"I beg of you, Mrs. Fontaine, to hear us out. We are now able to make a more generous offer with the help of eastern investors, and they are most anxious to rid themselves of a goodly sum."

Rachel appeared calm and composed as she listened to the men. Her slim shapely figure and wide brown eyes made her appear childlike and innocent. Her ivory skin held a youthful glow. All her features concealed the turmoil of excitement and anxiety that raged in her.

"Sir, I beg you to understand. This is my home and my livelihood. Mr. Fontaine, God rest his soul," she paused and touched her wedding band, "left me with only a small sum and a wee babe to raise. I must consider my future and that of my son."

"Yes, but think of this, please," Mr. Pearce pointed out. "With the money we are offering, you can provide a comfortable life for your child."

"But, sir, it is not a sum expected to last a lifetime," Rachel noted, and folded her hands in her lap.

"Then consider, if you will, the possibility of moving elsewhere to establish another business," Mr. Pearce suggested.

"You have great ability in merchandising, Mrs. Fontaine, and it would be with great ease that you could begin another profitable venture," Mr. Basham put in. The two men knew the young widow would be as difficult as usual and that different tactics would be necessary to persuade her.

Rachel allowed herself to look surprised at their suggestion, and considered it for a few moments before shaking her head. "That would mean leaving my friends and what little family I have and taking my son to some far-off land," she said doubtfully.

"But think of the benefits to your son," Mr. Basham said. "You could settle in the East where he could grow up among civilized men, not here in this rough-and-tumble town. Think of the opportunities there."

A gleam showed in Rachel's eye, giving the men confidence in their methods.

"You are quite right to consider your son's needs first," Mr. Pearce put in. "But consider not what is best for today, but tomorrow."

Rachel rose from her chair with a look of great concentration on her face. In truth, it was all she could do to conceal her amusement. The aging gentlemen had stolen from her the very argument she had intended to plead. She walked slowly to the window and peered out as if considering their words. She remained there for several moments before turning to the men. "There is much truth in what you say. You possess great wisdom, much more than a young simple-minded widow such as I."

The men blushed at the compliment. "Think of your son," Mr. Basham repeated.

"The time to act is now, Mrs. Fontaine, while property values are high and the Gold Rush is on. As yet, you have no other competition in town and that adds to the worth of your shop. Move now, madam," Mr. Pearce encouraged.

"Don't let this opportunity pass you by," Mr. Basham urged.

Rachel moved once more to the table and stood behind her chair, her hands resting on its high back. "Your arguments are very convincing, gentlemen, and I find that I cannot refuse."

Mr. Basham and Mr. Pearce suddenly lit up in amazement. It wasn't nearly as difficult as they had anticipated. But they were worldly businessmen and she was but a slip of a girl. They were about to congratulate themselves when they looked up at Rachel standing stonily above them. Her features hardened and her eyes grew cold, losing their childlike innocence. She spoke with a calculating voice and named her price for the establishment. The two men rocked back in their chairs, their faces suddenly gone white.

"But—but, Mrs. Fontaine, surely you realize you have named a figure that is impossible to meet," Mr. Basham said when he found his voice.

"Impossible? I think not, sir, when the offer is made by two such successful men as yourselves, backed by eastern investors."

"Even so, madam, surely you realize—"

"I realize I must provide for my son, and as you so ably pointed out, that will require a healthy sum," she said crisply.

"But the reality of the situation—" Mr. Basham began in a pleading voice.

"The reality is, sir, that I have the only mercantile in town and it is bringing in a profit at an astounding rate. As you noted, there is no competition here and prices are set by what the market will bear. And right now the sky is the limit."

"Madam, I would point out that we could build our own mercantile and drive you out of business," Mr. Basham stated with an edge to his voice.

Rachel tilted her head coyly. "That is certainly your option," she admitted, then hardened her tone. "Land prices here are at a premium, and building materials are in short supply. One would be hard pressed to find a capable carpenter crew willing to remain here long enough to see to the completion of the structure, with the lure of the West uppermost in every man's mind. And there is, of course, the delay in receiving goods to sell as they must come upriver for such a long journey. Which of you fine gentlemen would wish to stay in St. Joseph to oversee the project?" Rachel paused and added demurely, "But I'm certain you wise gentlemen considered all that before coming to me."

The men looked begrudgingly at each other. The widow had fooled them again, this time catching them in their own trap, turning their words into allies of her own. But they wanted the shop, and while her price was higher than they had intended to pay, they had no choice. The profit potential was too great. Mr. Basham rose from his chair. "Mrs. Fontaine, though your sum is nothing short of robbery, we are authorized to meet it."

"We will meet with you at the bank today at the noon hour," Mr. Pearce said, rising. "We are anxious to conclude this transaction."

"As am I," Rachel agreed."They say the gold in California can be found but laying about on the ground. One has only to stoop over to become wealthy. But by tomorrow, well, who can say what the future holds for any of us?"

The men departed in a huff, feeling totally dissatisfied

80

with the bargain they had struck, but with a new respect and wariness of seemingly witless widows.

Rachel was unable to contain her enthusiasm. Her pulse raced with excitement over her ability to win out over two highly successful businessmen. She danced about the room, shouting with glee.

"Rachel, what is it?" came Hannah's worried voice from the doorway.

"Oh, Hannah! I've done it! I'm beginning to think there is nothing I can't accomplish!"

"What? Tell me!" Hannah pleaded, crossing to meet her. A smile spread across her face as she joined in Rachel's enthusiasm.

Rachel took both of Hannah's hands. "We're leaving."

"What?"

"We're leaving St. Joseph."

Hannah looked perplexed. "Leaving?"

"Yes! We are going south to Charleston," Rachel said, her eyes wide with excitement.

"The Carolinas?" The smile faded from her face. "But that is so far. I'll never see little Andrew again and I'll miss him so."

"No, no, Hannah. You are coming, too!"

"Me? Go to Charleston?"

Rachel nodded enthusiastically. "Oh, Hannah, it is beautiful there in the spring. The ocean is breathtaking. And the ladies wear such lovely gowns and all the men are gentlemen. Oh, Hannah, I can't go without you. Say you will come." Hannah's face was a mask of indecision. "You must. Andrew loves you so. There is nothing to tie you to St. Joseph," Rachel pleaded.

Hannah knew her words were true. "All right, I'll do it."

They both squealed with delight and threw their arms about each other. From the cradle in the next room, Andrew announced his intention to be included in the celebration and Rachel quickly gathered him in her arms. "My son, you are going to love your new home," Rachel cooed as she stroked the dark ringlets that covered his head.

"You speak so clearly of the city, Rachel. Have you been there before?" Hannah asked.

Rachel caught herself before revealing anything of her past. She wasn't willing to have anyone know the truth, not even her closest friend. "Yes, I visited there briefly as a child."

"You must have been quite impressed to base a new life solely on one visit during your youth."

"Charleston has that effect on many people," Rachel noted and tried to sound casual. All the while her mind raced in anticipation of the life she was about to recapture.

It was a tear-filled farewell some two weeks later when Rachel, Andrew, and Hannah stood ready to board the paddleboat. Jimmy and all their friends had come to wish them well in their venture, expressing, too, their sorrow at seeing them go.

"It just won't be the same without you," Cora said, trying to hold back her tears. "When you came here you were little more than a child. Now you're a grown woman with a child of your own. I wish you happiness, honey, nothing but happiness."

Rachel's arms went around her cousin and she clung to her as small tears sprang from her eyes. She hated to think what might have become of her if Cora had turned her back on her. It was hard to leave. "Thank you for everything," she whispered as she pulled away and dabbed at her tears.

Cora shrugged off her sorrow and put on a smile. "Enough of this! We are carrying on like two old women!" she barked. "You take care of yourself and that baby. I wish you all the best."

Rachel returned her smile. "I will," she promised. She hugged Liz and Jean and Jimmy then took Andrew from Hannah and walked up the gangplank. At the top she turned and looked one last time at her home and friends. Many good things had happened to her in St. Joseph, the best of which she now held in her arms.

Hannah said good-bye to the gathering, then joined Rachel on the deck of the huge boat. The two women looked at each other, their expressions a mixture of sorrow and excitement. Then a smile parted Rachel's lips and Hannah followed suit and they waved enthusiastically to the crowd on the dock. A blast of the mighty whistle shook the air as the paddleboat slowly pulled away, taking the trio not away from something but toward it.

Charleston. Home!

The hustle and bustle of the train station, the press of people were like a fine wine quenching Rachel's hearty thirst. Grand carriages waited across from the platform as elegantly dressed men and women moved through the crowds. Negro slaves worked to transport baggage, trunks, and cargo for their masters.

"This is it, Hannah, our new home," Rachel announced from where they stood on the platform overlooking the scene.

"It's certainly—busy," Hannah commented. She held

Andrew in her arms, his blue eyes wide as he, too, took in his new surroundings.

"It seems foreign now, but we will feel at home here very quickly."

Rachel moved through the crowds with ease as she made arrangements for a carriage to take them and their belongings to the hotel. She wore a russet gown with a high collar and a cream-colored bonnet set jauntily among the swinging ringlets of her blonde hair. It was one of the many ensembles she had purchased during their stopover in St. Louis. She was not about to return to this grand city dressed as a peasant woman from the prairie. Her newly acquired wealth permitted her to purchase a complete wardrobe of the most fashionable gowns for herself, as well as fine clothing for her son. Hannah was reluctant to dress so grandly, saying that she wanted to be considered as Andrew's nanny and nothing more, and would be uncomfortable in such fancy attire.

The week they had stayed in St. Louis before going downriver to Memphis and overland by train, had given Rachel time to prepare herself for her return home. Her hands were soaked in oils each day until they lost their calloused feel, and her ivory skin took on a transparent glow when she finally got the amount of rest she needed but had not allowed herself in St. Joseph. She changed her thought patterns, too, recalling all Althea had taught her of proper etiquette and social grace. Those skills had gone unused for so many years, yet she quickly swept away the cobwebs and brought them to the fore.

Another situation that had perplexed her had also been resolved during those quiet afternoons in St. Louis when Andrew napped and Hannah busied herself with her sampler. Rachel had decided to tell no one in Charleston of her true identity. She would carry on the charade of the widow and not reveal that she was actually the daughter of Frederick and Althea Samuels, who had fled the city in disgrace three years earlier. She intended to establish herself in a business here as well as in the social scheme and wanted to be judged on her accomplishments alone, not by the memory of her parents. In time, perhaps, she would reveal the truth, should the situation warrant. But it was almost impossible that anyone would connect her to Frederick and Althea and their fall from grace. Rachel was but a child then and now stood fully a woman, so different in appearance that no one would recognize her. She lacked any of the facial features of her parents. Their looks, attractive yet not outstanding, had blended together to produce the oval face and delicate features that were hers alone. So the choice would be hers alone whether to divulge her past—and she liked it that way.

Rachel alighted from the carriage outside the lovely hotel with the assistance of the coachman and instructed Hannah to remain with Andrew, sheltered from the hot June sun while she arranged for their suite. Heads turned as Rachel swept into the lobby, her hooped skirt swaying with her hips, looking cool and refreshed despite the humid day. The young man at the desk pulled uncomfortably at his cravat and found himself tongue-tied when Rachel presented herself.

"Your reservations were for 'R. Fontaine," he said nervously. "I thought you were a man—ma'am."

"I hope you can see that your presumption was incorrect," Rachel said smoothly.

The boy's gaze fell to her bosom, then slowly moved upward to meet her dark eyes, bringing a pinkish tint to his cheeks. He cleared his throat uncomfortably and offered her the quill with a trembling hand.

Rachel signed the register with a fluid stroke. The boy's actions had greatly bolstered her self-esteem giving her renewed confidence in her appearance.

"Your suite is ready, ma'am," the young man said and signaled for help with the baggage.

It had taken two carriages to bring all their luggage from the train station and Rachel stood watching as the caravan of men crossed the lobby bearing the trunks and bags she had purchased in St. Louis. The seemingly endless stream brought whispers from the guests seated about the lobby and speculation that the young woman was as wealthy as she was beautiful. At the end of the procession Hannah appeared with Andrew in her arms and the onlookers were even more perplexed when the child held out his arms to Rachel and she eagerly took him. Seeing that she was the center of attention in the room, Rachel smiled pleasantly in a greeting before gathering her skirt and climbing the stairs.

The suite of rooms was light and airy. The two bedchambers were connected by a sitting room, all comfortably furnished. Rachel was glad she had let her banker in St. Louis make the arrangements for her. He had been kind enough to also put her in touch with a banker here in Charleston when he had arranged for the transfer of funds in her account. She planned to meet with this Mr. Bernard Wade after the noon meal.

In her room, Rachel shed her gown, heavy hoops, and corset and donned her new peach-colored wrapper. She still kept the green brocade wrapper that had been her mother's. It rested safely in one of her trunks with other keepsakes, including her family Bible and the pocket watch that belonged to Andrew's father.

Hannah and Rachel ate in the sitting room while Andrew slept. Rachel was so excited about her arrival she could scarcely eat. Hannah, on the other hand, was taking the change quite well and found much pleasure in the strange foods placed before her.

Rachel selected a different gown for her afternoon outing. It was a pale green with a shirred bodice coming to a point in the front, topped by a white lace collar and a large bow at her throat. The sleeves were shirred to the wrist where the laced cuffs matched the collar. A small bonnet of the same hue was tied beneath her chin with a soft ribbon. She swept a white triangular shawl loosely about her shoulders and descended to the lobby once more. The young man at the desk was attentive to her needs, seemingly mesmerized by her eyes as she requested a carriage. He walked with her outside, assisted her into the landau, and stood watching until it rounded the corner out of view.

She was escorted immediately into the private office of Mr. Bernard Wade, the bank president, who did his best, however unsuccessfully, to hide his surprise over the appearance of so large a depositor. The graying, rather distinguished gentleman sat Rachel across from his desk then lowered his stout frame opposite her. He fussed about for a moment straightening his desk then folded his hands and turned to the business of greeting his newest customer. "Welcome to our fair city, Mrs. Fontaine," he said, finally finding his voice. Most of the people he dealt with were men and he was quite unaccustomed to having so lovely a woman occupy the chair across from him. "I hope you have found everything to your liking."

Rachel smiled. "Charleston is very beautiful. I trust my accounts are in order."

"Accounts? Oh, yes, yes, your accounts." He searched his desktop. "Oh, yes, here it is." He glanced through the sheafs of paper and his eyebrows went up in surprise. "You have quite a sizable wealth."

"I'm seeking an investment of sorts here in Charleston. Perhaps a mercantile, as that is where my experience lies."

"A mercantile? But a woman of your obvious beauty and charm would not want to be burdened with so tedious a task. Let me suggest you occupy your time with more genteel projects. My wife would be happy to introduce you into the ladies' sewing circle and church activities."

Rachel smiled indulgently. "Mr. Wade, your offer is very kind and while such activities sound most appealing, I am afraid I am not in a position to enjoy them." She wanted to add that she would be bored to death, but managed to bite her tongue.

"But, madam, you are quite well off," Mr. Wade pointed out, unsure now of how to take this young woman.

"My late . . . husband departed this world leaving behind little money and an unborn son. I took what there was and built it into the wealth now deposited in your bank. I have my son to care for and, therefore, Mr. Wade, I cannot sit idle and hope the future will provide for him. I must make certain that happens." She spoke calmly but with a serious tone.

Mr. Wade was not unaffected by her words. "My dear child, you have had too much to bear in life already." But he could see she would not be swayed. "Very well, I will check into this right away."

"I shall also be purchasing a home."

"There are several very fine homes available only a short distance from the business district."

"Actually, sir, I was considering a home with some land. A plantation, perhaps."

"A plantation?" Mr. Wade echoed in disbelief. "But what do you know of—"

"Are there any available?" She was growing weary of his assumptions that she was frail and inept.

Mr. Wade was quite perplexed but saw in Rachel's darkening eyes that she would tolerate no more of his protests. "Nothing comes to mind, but I will check on that as well," he conceded.

Rachel rose, bringing Mr. Wade up with her. "I would greatly appreciate it if you could let me hear from you as soon as possible. In the meantime, I will check around on my own."

Mr. Wade wanted to caution her against venturing out alone but he held his tongue, realizing his words would fall on deaf ears. Instead he watched in silence as the beautiful, strong-minded widow swept out of the bank drawing the attention of the other patrons.

Rachel's heart fluttered with excitement as she strolled through the streets of Charleston. It was so good to be home again. Everything seemed familiar despite the many changes that had taken place since she had been away. The clip-clop of the horses' hooves on the cobblestones, the sweet smell of magnolias and jasmine in the air, the crowds of finely attired patrons moving from shop to shop, all brought back the fondest of memories. Rachel recalled the many times she had come from Richfield with her father and sat quietly at his side while he conducted business. Her shopping trips with Althea had all been filled with laughter and fun as she and her mother browsed through shops stocked with beautiful merchandise just in from far-off places. It seemed at the time that her parents knew everyone, as they always were stopped by people wishing to spend a few minutes exchanging news or gossip. She had thought the world of her parents—then.

With a keen eye, Rachel noted the areas of town where most of the patrons congregated. She strolled through the shops there mentally recording the goods offered, the attentiveness of the clerks, the displays that attracted customers. It was different from her mercantile in St. Joseph which catered to the more basic necessities of life. The wealthy people of Charleston wanted more, and Rachel was quick to determine how to provide that. A shop here in this city would be a new challenge for Rachel, but one she welcomed.

The following day Rachel rose early and hired a carriage to take her out of the city. She had tossed and turned most of the night unable to put the anticipated trip out of her mind. She was going to see Richfield. Creeping into Hannah's room shortly before sunrise, Rachel stood over her son's small bed and silently promised him once again that he would have what was rightfully his. The child had slept contentedly, unaware of the tears that pooled in his mother's eyes.

The trip passed pleasantly as Rachel looked out at the once familiar countryside. A breeze stirred the hot, humid air bringing cooling relief to the inside of the carriage. The trip had seemed much longer as a child. There were a few new homes along the way but none so grand as Richfield.

Her heart rose to her throat when the carriage jerked to a halt outside the wrought-iron gates of the plantation. Slowly she left the carriage and moved to stand in the shade of a giant oak as her eyes fell to rest on what was once her home. The two-story manor house of red brick was sheltered by huge oak trees. It stood as strong and tall as Rachel remembered. Smoke curled from the cookhouse behind the main structure. In the distance were the slave quarters, barns, and outbuildings.

Yet it wasn't exactly the same as Rachel recalled. Althea's much fussed-over lawn and flower garden were overgrown and dotted with weeds. Some of the buildings were in disrepair and all needed a fresh coat of whitewash. The vegetable garden was only half its necessary size and some of the fields, once white with cotton, now lay bare.

Rachel pressed her lips angrily at the sad state of her home. Evidently the new owner had not the slightest idea of how to run a plantation. It should be self-sufficient, producing all things necessary to sustain itself and enough again to gain a profit at the marketplace. Her anger grew, twisting her stomach into a knot until she could not stand it anymore. She must get Richfield back—now! She couldn't abide the thought of it being abused so. The present owner should be pleased to be rid of it as it could not possibly be bringing in much money, she figured. With determined mind, Rachel instructed the driver to take her to the bank at once. She settled back in the carriage, her mind whirling with plans for the future when Richfield would be hers again.

The full heat of the midday sun bore down on the city as Rachel's carriage stopped in front of the bank. It had been a long, airless return to Charleston and the excitement and anxiety over Richfield quickened her pulse. Hurrying from the carriage her mind was filled with a thousand details when she ran headlong into a man exiting the bank. Embarrassed by her clumsiness, she looked up to offer a profuse agology, but instead the words caught in her throat and she stood rooted to the spot.

Dark blue eyes shaded by a wide-brimmed white hat looked down at her. Black curls framed the square jaw and straight nose as a mellow voice spoke out to her. The words were unintelligible, heard but not able to penetrate her frenzied mind as it tried desperately to comprehend. Two strong arms reached out to steady her and the touch of those hands brought reality to her muddled thoughts.

You!

Chapter 5

She was floating, suspended in midair by a touch that sent her feelings soaring. Strong hands on her arms, burning her flesh. A heady masculine scent. Her soft breasts yielding to his rock-hard chest. Deft fingers intimately caressing her. A storm raging around them whipping up a fury equal to their rising ardor. Black hair ... slate-blue eyes ... Andrew?

The pungent odor of smelling salts penetrated the fog that enveloped Rachel. Her eyes blinked open. Andrew's father!

"Lie still." He gently pressed her down. The leather of the sofa creaked beneath her.

Her heart pumped rapidly. It couldn't be true!

"You fainted."

His words pelted her frenzied thoughts as his steady gaze upon her raked her emotions. It was he ... the stranger ... Andrew's father. She tried to speak but no sound escaped her tight, dry throat.

"You must rest, madam," he instructed.

I shared your bed.

"You will feel better momentarily."

You made love to me. Her eyes widened as her thoughts spun crazily. *I bore your child ... a beautiful boy.*

"Do not be frightened, madam. You are quite safe here."

Don't you remember? She searched his face. Yes, there was concern and attentiveness showing there. But recognition? Her heart was squeezed nearly to a stop by its aching. *No, you don't remember.*

Rachel pushed herself to a sitting position. The room tilted with her movement and instantly he steadied her. His touch burned the bare flesh of her arms and she gasped.

"It's all right. Just relax," he said softly as his eyes met hers.

"It's this dreadful heat. One simply cannot be out in it," a woman of about fifty years announced as she batted the air with her fan. "Bernard, do bring a sip of cool water for this dear girl."

Rachel recognized Bernard Wade rising from his desk across the room and realized she was in his private office. He complied with the request instantly and pressed the glass into Rachel's hand. She drank slowly and set it aside, her eyes riveted to the man who had caused her to swoon now kneeling by the sofa where she sat. *Why are you here? I thought I would never see you again.*

"There, she looks ever so much better," the woman declared with a broad smile.

Dragging her eyes from him, Rachel touched her brow.

"I'm sorry to be such trouble," she apologized, looking at the concerned faces that surrounded her.

The woman lowered her wide frame to the sofa beside her. "Nonsense, dear, this is quite a common occurrence here."

"It was my pleasure to assist you in this small way." His voice shook her emotions and she fought to control her trembling hands.

"Perhaps now proper introductions can be made," Bernard said. "My wife, Charlotte, and my nephew, Gray Montgomery. This is Mrs. Rachel Fontaine. Mrs. Fontaine arrived only yesterday from St. Louis, I believe. Is that correct?"

Rachel didn't catch Bernard's error as she struggled to calm herself. Thankfully, Gray had retreated across the room. Yet she felt his eyes constantly upon her, unnerving her further.

"Such a greeting to our city!" Charlotte declared. "My dear girl, where is your husband? Shame on him for letting you out alone like this."

"My husband is . . ." Her eyes turned instinctively to Gray before returning to the woman. " . . . deceased."

"You poor, dear child," Charlotte exclaimed and draped a sympathetic arm about her shoulders. "And you are so young. Oh, my, my. Do you have family here?"

She shook her head. "No."

"Then we shall have to see to it that you are not lonely. Bernard!" Charlotte thrust out her hand and obediently her husband assisted her to her feet. "I insist you join us for supper tomorrow evening, and I simply will not let you decline."

"Thank you. That is very kind," Rachel heard herself say as the man across the room still riveted her attention.

"I will send my driver for you. We shall have a lovely evening," she predicted. "Now I must be on my way. Gray, do walk with me."

Gray pulled his eyes from Rachel long enough to assure his aunt he would be right with her. Charlotte spouted detailed instructions to Bernard as he followed her from his office. Gray turned his full attention once more to the young woman who sat across the room. Something about her was familiar. What was it?

Rachel could no longer bear his gaze upon her, setting her nerves on end. She rose, smoothing her wide skirt, then raised her eyes to look at him. She wanted to rush to him and throw her arms about him and confess her love for him. She wanted to tell him of Andrew. But how could she suddenly blurt out such news? What would he say when presented with such a story from a total stranger? Would he simply accept it as fact? Would he suddenly declare his love for her and her child? No, never. And either way the result would be a devastating blow to her reputation and leave her son branded a bastard. That, she would never allow. She would have to play out the hand she had dealt herself and continue the charade; it was the only course open to her.

"Thank you for your assistance," Rachel said, breaking the heavy silence in the room. "I am really quite embarrassed."

"You needn't be, madam." He crossed the room and stopped before her, looking perplexed as he searched her face.

Rachel felt her cheeks pinken. "I fear my fainting spell has left me quite a mess," she said, and touched her hair.

"Oh, no, madam, your appearance is quite lovely," he assured her as his eyes scanned her ivory complexion and blond hair, then swept her figure from head to toe. A smile played about his lips. "Quite lovely, indeed."

Bernard reentered the office. "Gray, your aunt is anxious to be on her way."

Gray's eyes caressed Rachel's face once more. "Perhaps we shall see each other again soon."

"Perhaps we shall," Rachel said as her heart fluttered. Gray strode from the office, leaving Rachel to stare after him for a long moment. Finally, Bernard's throat-clearing brought her out of her spell.

"There is a matter I want to discuss," Rachel said, and seated herself across from him at the desk. "I have found some property I wish to purchase. A plantation, actually. The name by the gate read 'Richfield.' " She had been glad to see that the name given the land by her father had remained.

"A plantation! Madam, I beg you to reconsider. It is a massive undertaking to run a plantation," Bernard exclaimed.

"I have every confidence that I can handle it."

"But, but, you are a woman—"

"Would I be correct in assuming that the present owner is a man?" she asked crisply.

"Well, yes, of course," he answered, unsure of the relevance of her question.

"And it is your contention that a plantation could not be run as well by a woman as a man," she stated as if clarifying his position on the subject.

Bernard nodded emphatically, relieved that the young woman had finally come to her senses.

"Then may I say, sir, that the present owner of Richfield—a man—is doing a very poor job of managing it. I was there only briefly this morning and in those few moments I could readily see the run-down condition of the buildings, a garden which will not produce sufficient vegetables, fields neglected and not yet planted. There is little hope that the plantation is producing much of a profit. And so, sir, I fail to see how you can substantiate your claim that men are superior to women in such matters." Rachel delivered her logic in a cool, direct tone, then waited in silence for the banker's response.

Bernard, unprepared for this outpouring, sat overwhelmed for a moment. When he finally found his tongue he could do nothing but agree. "Mrs. Fontaine, I must admit that your assessment of the plantation is accurate. Richfield has not had a full-time master in a number of years. It was completely unattended for many months—I'm not certain of the details there—then was purchased as a wedding gift for a bride-to-be. Unfortunately the wedding was, well, shall we say, called off. The new owner made only a halfhearted attempt at making it profitable, never lived there permanently, choosing instead to seek other ventures elsewhere. I suppose he might consider selling."

Rachel's face brightened. "Then I must speak with him immediately. We must discuss terms of the sale at once. Who is the owner? When can I meet him?" she asked excitedly.

Bernard chuckled. "You have already met the owner. He is my nephew, Gray Montgomery."

Rachel sat before the mirror of her bureau making a third attempt at styling her hair. Her fingers moved awkwardly, lacking their usual dexterity, and succeeded only in leaving her hair in a tangled knot. She drew in a deep breath and ran the brush through her hair absently. She studied her reflection in the mirror but her mind was consumed by something else. The same thing that had occupied so much of her thoughts while in St. Joseph.

Gray Montgomery. At least now she had a name to put with those fond recollections, and that brought her some comfort. She had tried for months to put him out of her head and had been hopelessly unsuccessful. He had invaded her dreams and popped into her conscious thoughts as if he willed it so himself, leaving her with no control over the situation. And after meeting him yesterday at the bank, she had tried even harder to forget him, but it proved to be a totally wasted effort. She had long ago resigned herself to the fact that she would never see him again. Yet he had appeared before her and in that split second had dashed all her efforts to forget him. Now she realized that it would be impossible to do that.

Rachel rose from her chair and paced about the room. If she could not forget him she would have to learn to live with seeing him again. At first she had been hurt that he hadn't recognized her, but later was glad he could not recall their evening of lovemaking and, therefore, could place no claim on her child. She would not tolerate such a blow to Andrew's reputation if word got out that he was illegitimate. So, it was better that things continue on as she planned. She would only have to see him a few more times while they concluded the transaction for Richfield and, though it would be difficult, she would find the strength to pull it off. She thought of her mother and her cousin Annora who had trusted their futures to a man. No, no, she would not make that mistake. She would see to her own fate and that of her son. And nothing would interfere with that.

There came an urgent rap at her door before Hannah stepped inside. Her eyes grew wide. "Rachel, the Wades' carriage has arrived and you are not even dressed."

"I was deep in thought and didn't realize it was so late. Hannah, please help me do something with my hair. I'm all thumbs tonight," Rachel begged, and sat down before the mirror.

Hannah took the brush and swept Rachel's hair into a mass of loose curls atop her head. She assisted Rachel into the honey-colored gown she had selected, then stood back to inspect the finished product as Rachel stepped into tan slippers.

"Do I look presentable?" Rachel asked nervously as she smoothed her skirt and adjusted the gown's low-cut neckline.

Hannah dismissed her concern. "You are beautiful. Too pretty to spend the evening with only the elderly Wades eyeing you."

"Oh, Hannah, what would I ever do without you?"

Hannah gave her a small hug then pinched some color into her cheeks. "You just enjoy yourself and don't give me or Andrew a thought," she instructed.

Rachel smiled her thanks and hurried down to the Wades' carriage, stopping only long enough to give her son a good-night kiss.

The Wades lived in a lovely two-story house a short distance from the hotel. Rachel felt at home immediately as she and Charlotte chatted about a variety of subjects. Bernard seemed to have come to terms with Rachel and accepted her as she was. He proved to be a very cordial host.

After dinner the three moved to the piazza which overlooked a carefully tended garden at the rear of the house.

100

They sat in the cool night air, the ladies sipping sherry while Bernard enjoyed a more potent drink. Just as Charlotte was about to launch into one of her usual detailed accounts of a party she had recently attended, she was called away to settle a minor crisis upstairs leaving Rachel and Bernard alone.

"It is so kind of Charlotte to take an interest in my acclimatization to the city," Rachel said, seated in a wicker chair beside him.

Bernard swirled his brandy glass. "Charlotte is quite big-hearted and genuine in her desire to help others," he agreed.

Bernard looked past her and in the dim light Rachel saw his brows go up in amazement. "This is a surprise. Come in!"

Rachel turned in her chair and her heart lurched as Gray walked onto the porch. He wore crisp white shirt and trousers, blue waistcoat and jacket, and black cravat. The fine clothing served only to make him more handsome, outlining his broad shoulders and narrow hips. A gentle smile curved his lips as his eyes fell to rest on Rachel. Her heart pounded wildly and she thought once more that he was the most handsome man she had ever seen.

He approached slowly, almost cautiously, turning his hat over and over in his hand, and stopped between the chair where Bernard and Rachel sat. "Good evening, Mrs. Fontaine," he said stiffly.

"Mr. Montgomery, it is nice to see you again." It took all her willpower to speak calmly and control the swirl of emotion she felt.

"Would you care for a brandy?" Bernard asked.

Gray shook his head. "No, thank you."

"I haven't seen you take a drink in months. Sworn off the stuff for good?"

"Let's just say I prefer keeping a clear head," Gray murmured. He moved past Rachel and took a seat opposite her. His presence dominated the porch and filled Rachel's senses. She placed her sherry on the table for fear her trembling hands would upset it.

"Mr. Bernard," came a voice from the house. They turned to see one of the servants outlined in the light of the house.

"What is it, Phoebe?" Bernard asked impatiently.

"Miz Charlotte says for you to come. She be needin' you," the young girl said, then disappeared. Grumbling, Bernard excused himself and followed her.

The once quiet evening suddenly came alive for Rachel. She now heard the chirp of the crickets and the call of birds from high in the trees. The sweet smell of the flower garden filled the cool night breeze. Above, the black sky shone with thousands of twinkling stars. She wondered why she had not noticed all these things before. Her gaze fell on the man seated across from her and she realized that his presence brought all things to life for her.

Gray studied her lovely oval face as the dim light made her flawless skin seem to glow. He searched every detail of her wide eyes, small, straight nose, and gently curving mouth. She was intriguing. There was something special about her. Something he didn't understand—yet.

Together they realized that many moments of silence had passed as they had both been content to stare at each other.

"I trust you are acquainting yourself with the city,"

Gray began and leaned forward, resting his elbows on his knees as he continued to fumble with his hat.

"Yes." She concentrated on her words, trying to calm her jangled nerves. "I am planning to open a business soon."

"Indeed?" He sat back and laid his hat aside. "And what type of business will you try your hand at?"

"It shall be more than merely 'trying my hand,' Mr. Montgomery," she pointed out. "I ran a mercantile—a rather successful mercantile, I might add—prior to my arrival in Charleston. It is my intention to continue in that vein."

A woman running her own business? Gray was startled by the thought. "And for how long did you run your mercantile?"

"Long enough," she responded, now mildly irritated by his attitude.

"Then will it not be a rather long journey for you traveling from Richfield to Charleston each day?" he asked casually.

"I see Bernard has already spoken to you regarding my interest in ... your plantation." She spoke slowly, trying to keep all emotion from her voice.

"Yes, he has. Unfortunately, madam, I have no desire to sell."

Irritation grew in Rachel but she held her voice steady. "I should think, sir, that in view of the circumstances you would be more than happy to rid yourself of it."

"Circumstances?"

"Your uncle mentioned that you had purchased Richfield as a wedding gift but that the marriage was called off. I would think the plantation would serve as an un-

103

pleasant reminder of the woman who rejected your proposal," she explained.

"I am afraid you were misinformed," he said flatly.

She was beginning to find his calm and casual attitude as irritating as his refusal to sell. "Then perhaps, sir, if that be the case, you could set the record straight," she requested.

"My personal affairs are not a matter of public record."

Anger began to spread through Rachel as Gray seemed to toy with her. He watched her every movement, waiting for a reaction to his words.

Rachel held her tongue and rose from her chair. She walked sedately to the porch railing and gazed out into the darkened garden. She heard him rise from the creaking wicker chair and move to stand behind her.

"However, it is certainly no secret. In fact, there are those who still enjoy retelling the tale, though it is months old now." Gray's voice softened as he spoke to the back of her head. "You see, it was not the lady who rejected my proposal. It was I who broke off our engagement."

Rachel's heart pounded against her ribs, racing with excitement. It was he who could not go through with the wedding! Could it mean that unconsciously he remembered her? Cared for her? Possibly loved her?

She stopped her runaway thoughts. Such a notion was meaningless. He didn't even know it was she whom he bedded that night so long ago. "Even so, sir, it would seem that you have no use for a plantation," Rachel said calmly, returning her thoughts to the business at hand.

Gray leaned a hip against the balustrade and crossed his arms casually across his generous chest. He studied her profile as she stood a few feet from him. "Actually, Mrs. Fontaine, I do have need of Richfield."

Rachel turned away and moved down the porch feeling more comfortable with some distance between them. "I have seen Richfield and, if you will forgive me, I must say that it is in need of a full-time master, something it obviously lacks now," she pointed out as tactfully as her rising temper would allow.

Gray considered her words as he strolled to her side once again. "I see the lady is not only a successful businesswoman but an expert on plantations as well," he commented as a playful grin curled his lips.

"Mr. Montgomery, one need not be an expert to recognize unplanted fields and caved-in roofs," she shot, anger showing in her dark eyes.

His lazy gaze took in her tightly pursed lips and set jaw. A woman with spirit! What a refreshing change.

How could this man keep sending her emotions to such extremes, Rachel thought. One minute she wanted to melt into his arms, and the next she was thoroughly irritated by him. What was happening to her? Rachel spun away and moved to stand behind the wicker chair. She must get a hold on herself.

"If it will ease your mind, madam, let me say that Richfield will have a full-time master. I have decided to take up residence there and devote my full attention to its operation."

And prepare it for another bride, Rachel thought resentfully. The place lay unattended for months and when this man learns of her interest in it he suddenly has a desire to occupy it. A handsome man such as he would not be willing to live a secluded life for long. Surely he had some plan for yet another wife and, of course, children to follow—lots of children. But Richfield belonged to her, and to her son—their son . . .

Rachel's thoughts raced on, threatening to overtake her common sense. She must calm herself. She took her sherry glass from the table and gulped its contents down quickly.

Suddenly, her mouth, throat, and stomach blazed with fire. She wheezed loudly as the evil liquid took her breath away. She swayed in the tilting room as her legs threatened to buckle under her.

Gray's strong arms encircled her and held her against his chest for support. He took the glass from her hand and held it up to the light. "Really, Mrs. Fontaine, brandy is much better when sipped," he pointed out, unable to keep the amusement from his voice.

"Brandy!" she croaked.

Gray set the empty glass aside and patted her back, gently pulling her closer against his chest.

Rachel's breath returned only to have it stop completely when she realized that she was pressed against him, their bodies touching intimately. The hand that had helped restore her breathing now rested firmly on the small of her back. She lifted her eyes to his face and saw the look of desire in his gaze as it fell to devour her breasts crushed against his chest, nearly spilling over her bodice. As his fingers slowly traced the line of her jaw, her body tingled under his touch and her senses came to life.

Gray drank in her beauty and the softness of her curves which sent desire coursing through his veins with an intensity he had not experienced since . . . since when?

There it was again, an obscure fragment that haunted his thoughts. What was it? His brows drew together as he feverishly searched his memory. It had plagued him since yesterday but would not present itself in full.

Seeing the concentration on his face, Rachel retreated from his grasp. She forced her heart to slow to its normal pace.

"Gray, it is so good of you to keep Rachel entertained," Charlotte called as she returned with Bernard trailing in her wake. "These servants! My, but what problems they can create."

"A firm hand, Charlotte, a firm hand," Bernard advised as he sat down. He lifted his brandy glass to his lips only to find it was empty. Perplexed, he set it aside. Gray and Rachel exchanged a guilty look and stifled a smile.

Gray picked up his hat. "If you will forgive me, I must be on my way."

Disappointment spread unexpectedly through Rachel.

"Must you go so soon?" Charlotte asked as she settled into a chair by her husband. "It seems we rarely see you."

"Sorry, Aunt Charlotte, but I have to meet with some men," he apologized.

"Then come to supper tomorrow night," she requested.

"Actually," he said slowly, and turned to Rachel, "I was about to ask Mrs. Fontaine if she would care to join me for supper tomorrow night."

His invitation caught her by surprise. She wanted so desperately to say yes. It would have been so easy. But the easy way, in this case, was not the best way. "It is very kind of you to ask, Mr. Montgomery, but I am sorry to say I have a previous commitment." It was a lie.

"Perhaps, then, another time."

"Perhaps," she responded, noting that he did not appear overly disappointed at her refusal of his invitation.

Gray said good night to his aunt and uncle and departed.

"That boy! I just don't know what has gotten into him." Charlotte wailed.

Rachel sat down across from her and tried not to appear overly interested in this topic of conversation.

"He will be fine," Bernard assured her.

She pressed a lace kerchief to her lips. "Everything seemed to be going smoothly. He was successful and happy, engaged to a beautiful girl. Then, suddenly, without cause, he simply broke off the engagement with no satisfactory explanation to Claudia or her father."

"The boy owes no one an explanation," Bernard said.

"Claudia is a lovely girl. She would make a perfect wife."

"Perfect?"

"Well, adequate," she conceded.

"In truth, my dear, you must admit that you hardly liked the girl," Bernard said.

"Yes, yes, Claudia and I had our differences, but that is not the point," Charlotte said quickly. "She would have been the right type of wife. And now instead of being happily married and raising a family, Gray is galloping all over the country in search of some vague and obscure business deal. He has been at loose ends for months and months."

"He will find himself," Bernard predicted.

Charlotte turned to Rachel. "He is my sister's son and it is my duty to watch over him," she insisted.

"He is a grown man," Rachel pointed out.

"You will understand when your son is grown," Charlotte said wisely.

"I suppose you are right." She did agree that the behavior Charlotte described was rather unsettling.

The long evening was beginning to wear on Rachel. The emotional ups and downs of seeing Gray left her feeling drained. "I'm afraid I really must be on my way," she said.

"Of course, dear, I know you have a great many things to do," Charlotte said. She struggled briefly to climb out of the low chair.

Rachel rose. "I plan to spend tomorrow looking for a home to purchase."

Bernard stood with the ladies. "Gray was not receptive to your offer of purchasing Richfield?" he asked, surprise evident in his voice.

She shook her head. "It seems he plans to take up residence there permanently."

"Now, there . . ." Charlotte said pointedly. "There is just another example of his most peculiar behavior. Oh! I am so glad my dear sister isn't here to see how her son's life is turning out."

"Nonetheless, that leaves me searching for a home," Rachel commented.

"A hotel is no place for a baby. We must find you a house at once," Charlotte declared. She pursed her lips in concentration. Suddenly her eyes opened wide. "I know the perfect home."

"Tell me," Rachel said anxiously.

"A couple—the Merriweathers—moved down from Boston but stayed for only a few months. They were nice enough people, I suppose, but Mrs. Merriweather could not adjust to our climate. So they simply left. The house is vacant and fully furnished. Bernard, I am surprised you did not think of it yourself. You are supposed to be trying to sell it for Mr. Merriweather."

"I expect I would have had I been given a moment to think," he said defensively.

The trio moved into the drawing room as Charlotte described the house, the furnishings, and the Merriweathers in great detail. Rachel took in the beautifully appointed room as she waited for her shawl. Her attention was drawn to a small portrait of a mother, father, and small child. Rachel looked closer. The boy looked exactly like Andrew. "Who is this?" she asked quickly, interrupting Charlotte's description of the house's gazebo.

The older woman joined Rachel and eyed the portrait. "That is my sister and her husband."

"And the child?"

"That is Gray."

Charlotte pressed on with a detailed account of their wedding, life, and untimely death, but Rachel didn't hear. All she could think of was Andrew and his strong family resemblance to Gray and Gray's father. It was shocking. They all had the same facial features, blue eyes, and dark hair.

Now she was presented with a new problem, one which seemed almost insurmountable. Her child bore a striking resemblance to Gray Montgomery. How could she explain that away? The only option open was to keep Andrew away from Gray and the Wades and pray that as Andrew grew older he would develop more of her own features. It was a slim thread of hope, but it was all she had.

Rachel said good night to Charlotte and Bernard and

promised faithfully to meet Charlotte the next day to look at the house. Riding alone in the carriage she analyzed her feelings for Gray. He turned her emotions upside down tonight as he had done on their other meetings. But she could not allow that, she reminded herself. She would have to remain unaffected by his presence, should she see him again, and there was little chance of that since he had refused to sell Richfield to her. If by some coincidence they would meet again she would be cold and aloof—somehow. She would make herself do it, she vowed. She had her future to prepare for and Gray Montgomery did not fit into that future.

Chapter 6

"Good morning, Mrs. Fontaine."

Startled, Rachel gasped, knowing instantly who was beside her. Quickly, she reminded herself of her vow of the night before. "Good morning, Mr. Montgomery," she said coolly, stealing a glance at him. He was smartly attired, as always, in emerald waistcoat and tan trousers, and looked incredibly handsome.

"May I say, madam, that you present a very lovely sight this morning," Gray said lazily as his eyes roamed the pale-blue gown she wore.

Rachel steeled her feelings. "If you will excuse me, sir, I must be on my way," she said primly and stepped off the curb onto the cobblestone street outside her hotel. She knew she must get away from him, but to her dismay he appeared beside her once more. She walked faster, but his long legs easily kept pace with her.

"My, but you do seem to be in a hurry this morning," he commented as they stepped onto the opposite curb.

Rachel stopped abruptly and turned to face him. He walked on a few steps before realizing she had stopped, then came back to where she stood. "I have several important matters to attend to, Mr. Montgomery, so if you will please excuse me I will be on my way."

"Business matters?" A smile played about his lips.

"Yes, business," she assured him, then walked on only to see him beside her again.

"Since we both seem to be headed in the same direction, do you have any objections to my walking along with you?"

She stopped again, as did he. "Surely you must have something to attend to this morning."

"Nothing that can't wait while I enjoy the company of a beautiful young woman," he said softly.

Rachel tossed her head indifferently. "It is a public street. You may walk where you choose," she said crisply, and brushed past him.

He was at her side once again. "And I choose to walk with you," he told her as he studied the delicate features of her profile.

"Suit yourself."

"I always do, Mrs. Fontaine."

Rachel glanced at him, then quickly turned her eyes straight ahead. He was making it very difficult for her to remain cold and uncaring.

Gradually she slowed the rapid pace she had set, since Gray, who was not subjected to the confines of a whalebone corset, seemed unaffected. While it was considered a sign of good breeding to swoon, Rachel had no desire to collapse into the man's arms. At least not under these circumstances.

Gray was contented to stroll beside her in silence, taking in her feminine fragrance and enjoying the sight of her. He dared not tell her it was more than mere chance that he was outside her hotel this morning at the exact moment she appeared. She was different from the other ladies he knew, who could do little more than giggle and bat their lashes, feigning innocence. Rachel demonstrated the grace and poise of a well-bred woman and was certainly as beautiful as any other he had met. But her determination and independent thinking set her apart from all the rest. He liked that.

Rachel stopped and turned her attention to a small shop across the street. It was a general merchandise store, plain in comparison to the shops that surrounded it, and had far less patrons. It had caught her eye during her walk the previous day. Gray followed her gaze and studied it as well, then turned to her, finding her face a more pleasing sight.

She felt him staring at her and found it quite unnerving. "Really, Mr. Montgomery, you make it very difficult to concentrate," she said tersely.

"Oh?" he responded hopefully.

Rachel managed to hold her emotions in check. "I am considering buying this business. This is not a game to me."

Gray looked at the shop and turned to Rachel again. "I was not aware it was for sale."

"It's not," she admitted. "But I intend to find out who the owner is and make an offer.

Gray frowned. "On this? Really, madam, this is hardly a booming business. Perhaps my uncle or myself could offer you some guidance before you make such a purchase."

"I am not in need of anyone's guidance," she informed him and struggled to control the aggravation the man always seemed to bring out in her.

"I happen to know that this shop does little business—"

"That is apparent."

"In fact, I happen to know it has been losing money."

"I suspected that as well."

"Good God, woman, why would you want to sink your money into a losing proposition?" He was becoming more than a bit perturbed by her hardheadedness.

"I can assure you, Mr. Montgomery, that once I take charge of this shop it would cease to be a losing proposition," she told him angrily. Who was he to question her abilities?

"And just what is wrong with this shop now that you could correct, Mrs. Fontaine?" he challenged.

"First of all, it is dreary and dark inside. The merchandise is not keeping pace with the tastes of the patrons. The storefront is unappealing and could not possibly be attracting anyone to come in and browse." Rachel rattled off the list of deficiencies in rapid fire succession, then turned to Gray smugly.

He was astounded by her assessment of the situation. "You determined all that by looking at the shop?" he asked as he glanced back and forth between the store and Rachel. She nodded her head. "And you know how to remedy all those ailments?"

"As I told you, I have a great deal of experience in the merchandising business."

Gray stroked his chin thoughtfully. "So you plan to purchase this business, make your improvements, and turn a handsome profit?"

"That is exactly my plan. All I have to do is contact

the owner. I feel certain he will be glad to have the shop off his hands."

"Perhaps not," Gray said as his lips curled into a small smile.

"Do you know the man?" she asked suspiciously.

Gray nodded slowly. "Yes, as a matter of fact I do. You see, madam, this shop belongs to me."

Anger raced through Rachel. He had stood there, goading her on, while all along knowing the shop was his. What an arrogant man! "Well, sir, I can see that you are as proficient at running a mercantile as you are at managing a plantation," she shot.

Gray chuckled. "Please, madam, calm yourself."

"I am glad you have found this so amusing. But unlike you, I am not free to skip about making feeble attempts at running businesses. I have a son to secure a future for—"

"A son?" Gray asked quickly, the smile suddenly leaving his face. Why had no one told him she had a child?

Rachel pressed her lips together firmly, angry now at herself for mentioning Andrew. She had let him push her into things she should avoid.

"You have a son?" Gray repeated.

"I am a widow," she reminded him.

"Then why is it I have not seen him with you?" he asked.

"He is a small baby," Rachel said softly, and could not help but notice the change that had come over Gray. But she had no desire to let this conversation continue. "Will you consider my offer to purchase this shop?"

Gray nodded. "I will consider it," he said softly.

"Why, Gray, my darling" came the sultry cry of a feminine voice.

116

Rachel turned to see a dark-haired woman a few years older than herself saunter over to join them. The woman immediately slid her arm around Gray's and clung to him intimately.

"What a surprise to see you in town today. What are you doing here? I know. You are buying me another gift, aren't you?" she purred.

"Claudia," Gray said, "I thought you were in Atlanta."

Her lashes fluttered as her mouth formed a well-practiced pout. "I just could not go," she told him.

The woman had purposely ignored Rachel and chose now to turn her full attention to the younger, slimmer girl, quickly taking in her fine gown and obvious beauty. Rachel returned her critical gaze calmly. Dislike for each other sprang up instantly.

"Claudia, I would like you to meet Mrs. Rachel Fontaine," Gray said cordially. "Mrs. Fontaine, this is Claudia Danforth."

"Mrs.?" Claudia asked, and some of the hatred left her face.

Rachel recognized the name immediately from her conversation with Charlotte Wade. This was the woman Gray had been engaged to wed. "I am a widow, *Miss* Danforth," Rachel said sweetly, stressing Claudia's marital status, or lack of it.

"Oh, Gray, you simply must come see this most divine new bonnet at the millinery store," Claudia pleaded. "I just don't know whether to buy it or not. I need a man to tell me what I should do."

"Actually, Claudia, I have some business to attend to," he said, glancing uncomfortably at Rachel.

Claudia clung determinedly to Gray's arm, pressing

her full breasts against him. "Please, I need your help. You have the most exquisite taste in women's apparel. All of the things you have bought me have been so lovely," she insisted and was careful to speak loud enough for Rachel to hear every word. "I will not take no for an answer," Claudia told him, and pulled him along the street with her.

Helpless to escape her, Gray tipped his hat to Rachel. "We will discuss the situation at a later date," he called.

A mixture of jealousy, envy, and hatred ran through Rachel as she watched the two of them walk away. Tears threatened to fill her eyes. Why must life be so hard for her? Others seemed to have everything they wanted, their slightest whim answered, while she had to work hard and fight for everything she wanted. And to have lost her heart to a man whom she could not claim was—

Rachel pushed the thought from her mind and forced back her tears. She would have to be strong. There was no rhyme or reason for her life turning out as it had, at least none she was yet aware of, but it was up to her to make the best of what she had. Her feelings for Gray would have to be buried since he could not possibly figure into her future. That was becoming the most difficult part of the burden life had given her to bear.

Rachel continued about her business, her mood now matching that of the gloomy, overcast day. At the bank Bernard reported that there were few business investments suitable for her. Rachel pressed him for details and reluctantly he provided her with a list of names and addresses. She was unfamiliar with them but wanted to check into them herself since it now seemed unlikely that she could purchase her first choice.

As previously arranged, Charlotte met Rachel at the

bank and the two ladies went to inspect the house Charlotte had raved about. The prospect of a real home of her own brightened Rachel's outlook considerably; at least if that much could be accomplished she would feel like she was getting somewhere. The hotel suite was comfortable but getting smaller by the day. Andrew had begun to pull up and walk about the room using the furniture to steady himself; it would not be long before he would be off and running on his own.

Rachel rode in silence listening as Charlotte rattled on and on covering a variety of subjects. It seemed the woman knew everything about everyone in the city. The carriage finally stopped before a three-story brick house on a quiet, tree-lined street. Like so many others in the city, the narrow front faced the street while the house ran deep into the lot. Large, arched windows on all three stories dominated the facade looking down on the many trees and shrubs that surrounded the house. It was bounded by a tall brick and wrought-iron fence offering a good degree of privacy.

Many of the furnishings remained, now shrouded with white cloths, and would be sold with the house, Rachel learned as Charlotte led her through the first floor. There was a parlor, an oval-shaped dining room, and a small study. The second story held the bedchambers, and the third housed the servants, who were also included in the price of the house. Rachel was pleased with the layout of the house, the fine craftsmanship exhibited in the hand-carved woodwork, and the good quality of the furnishings. But what convinced her that this house should be her new home was the beautiful garden in the rear. It was surrounded by an eight-foot brick wall, perfect for corraling a small, active child. There were all sorts of sweet-smelling flowers and tall trees shading it from the hot summer sun. And in the far corner was a white latticework gazebo, an ideal spot for Rachel to lounge at day's end and watch over Andrew as he played.

"I knew you would love it," Charlotte exclaimed when Rachel told her she wanted it.

"It will be perfect for us," Rachel agreed.

The two women discussed the house, its furnishings, and the necessary changes and additions Rachel wanted to make as they rode back to the bank. Bernard was only too happy to handle the details of the transaction.

Rachel returned to the hotel and told Hannah all about the house. Hannah was excited over the news and especially glad to hear about the garden Andrew would have to play in. Since their arrival in Charleston, Hannah had taken the baby for a stroll to the park as part of his daily routine. But with his newly found freedom he was less and less happy in the confines of the baby carriage.

In bed that night, Rachel tried to focus her mind on her accomplishments of the day. She had found a home for them and had obtained a list of possible investments that she would begin checking into the following day. Yet her thoughts kept straying to Gray, and she recalled over and over his oh so very handsome face and masculine physique. He made her pulse race when he was near and it was almost impossible to remain uncaring in his presence. She even dared to hope that he found her interesting in some small way since he had wanted to walk with her this morning. Even though she was rude, he still insisted on being near her. Rachel's heart had ached when Claudia Danforth had shown up, as sickening sweet as molasses, and taken Gray away with her. It was evident that though their engagement had been called off, the two of them still kept company. That bothered Rachel a great deal, more than she wanted to admit to herself.

The next morning Charlotte appeared unexpectedly at Rachel's suite. "I do hope I'm not interrupting," Charlotte said as she seated herself on the sofa.

"Of course not. I'm so glad you dropped by," Rachel said as she nervously glanced toward the open bedroom door where Andrew now played. The last thing she wanted was for Charlotte to see the baby and recognize the family resemblance. "What brings you over?" She eased across the room and glanced inside. Hannah held Andrew on her lap reading one of his favorite stories. They were both completely absorbed in the story and never noticed when Rachel quietly shut the door.

"I want to extend to you an invitation," Charlotte announced.

"Oh?" Rachel sat down across from her.

"I am planning a small party tomorrow evening and I would like for you to be there. It will be an excellent opportunity for you to meet some of the people in our city," Charlotte explained.

"That would be very nice. Thank you, I would love to join you," Rachel said.

"Good," she said, then turned to a new topic. "Now, I must see that baby of yours. Where is he?"

"Oh, well, actually, Andrew is—" Rachel searched her mind for a good alibi. "Andrew is not well today."

Charlotte looked troubled. "Is it serious?"

"No, no, it's not serious," she assured her quickly. "You know how children seem to catch everything."

The older woman nodded knowingly, then plunged into a detailed accounting of her six children's illnesses.

121

Rachel was quite relieved when the story was finally concluded and Charlotte was on her way.

That afternoon Rachel went shopping for items for her new home. Since she had offered to meet the price asked by the owners, and it was a bargain at that, all that was necessary to complete the transaction was for Bernard to prepare the paperwork for her signature. That should be done in a few days. In the meantime, Rachel was anxious to get some of the needed items and be ready to move as soon as possible.

She shopped leisurely, selecting only the finest of goods. The merchants, seeing her obvious wealth, were attentive to her every need. She was enjoying her shopping greatly when suddenly Gray appeared.

"Good afternoon, Mrs. Fontaine," he greeted with a slow smile. "As always, you are the picture of loveliness." His eyes quickly took in the ecru gown she wore.

Rachel tried to still her runaway heart. "I am surprised to see you," she said nervously, then remembered how quickly he had left her when Claudia needed assistance in purchasing a hat. "I thought you spent most of your time in the millinery shop," she said tightly, and moved down the aisle, casually looking over the merchandise.

Gray stifled the grin that betrayed his amusement. "Selecting ladies' hats is only one of my talents. Perhaps I could aid in your purchase?" he offered.

"That is not necessary. I have no trouble making my own decisions," she assured him coolly. Why didn't he leave her alone? He was making things so difficult for her.

"An admirable quality," he admitted. "But don't you find that a bit lonely?"

Rachel looked up at him and for a moment her eyes locked with his and she was lost in the depths of their blueness. If he only knew how lonely she had been. If she could only tell him of the many nights she lay awake thinking of him and of the nights when he filled her dreams. She wished he knew the emptiness she had felt when she had given birth to his son and had not had him there to share it.

She pulled her eyes from his and turned her attention to the display of yard goods beside her. "No," she said softly.

Gray's brows drew together in concern for this young woman who seemed to have the weight of the world on her small shoulders. Yet she was so determined to do it all by herself, so bullheaded that she would accept no help or guidance from anyone. For a brief instant he had seen vulnerability show in her dark eyes and more than anything he wanted to help her. If only she would let him.

"I insist," he said lightly.

For the life of her Rachel could not remember what she had been shopping for. How unlike her to lose her concentration, she thought, then berated herself for going all to pieces each time Gray came near her. "I am picking up a few things for my new house," she told him.

Gray followed her down the aisle. "Where are you moving?"

"It's the house your aunt told me about."

"Yes, I know the place. It's quite lovely." But his mind was not on houses or shopping.

"Now all that remains is to find a proper business to invest in," Rachel said, and turned to face him. "Have you made a decision to sell me your mercantile?"

Gray rested his finger against his jaw thoughtfully. "Actually, I was hoping we could discuss it further."

"My offer was straightforward. I do not know what there is to discuss."

"Many details come to mind," he told her. "I suggest we have supper together this evening and attempt to work them out." A quiet, candlelit evening alone with the young widow sounded very appealing to him.

Oh, yes, yes. You have no idea how I've longed to hear you say that.

"That is out of the question," she said abruptly. "I have a sick child to attend to. Please excuse me." She brushed past him and disappeared out the door before Gray could protest, leaving him to stare after her.

The Wades' home was warmly lit, bidding a welcome to their guests the following evening. Rachel left her carriage and walked onto the porch feeling excited and nervous about attending the party. She recalled her mother telling her about these social events when she was but a child and too young to attend. Back then she had wanted to be just like Althea and take part in the lovely gatherings her mother had described in vivid detail. And now Rachel was doing just that. She had not arrived at this point in her life in the manner she had expected to, but she was here nonetheless. It was important that she be accepted by the prominent families in Charleston, some of whom would be in attendance tonight. Not only for herself but for the sake of Andrew's future as well.

Charlotte met her at the door. "My dear, you look lovely tonight."

Rachel murmured her thanks, glad that she had worn

her most elaborate gown, a delicate peach with ecru trim. The "small party" Charlotte had invited her to filled the house with at least twenty people, all dressed in their finest attire. Servants moved through the rooms offering refreshments before the meal was served.

Charlotte escorted Rachel through the festive party atmosphere introducing her to the other guests. They were all quite cordial, asking their usual questions about her background as tactfully as possible. She knew she would be carefully scrutinized before being accepted into their circle and had prepared responses to their inquiries. Rachel didn't like to lie, but there were few other options open to her, and it was for a good cause, she reminded herself.

As Rachel moved about the room there was much talk among the ladies of the latest imports from abroad and speculation on the newest of styles. When introduced to the men, she overheard their discussions on the slavery issue, comments on President Taylor's administration, and talk of the Gold Rush. Rachel felt equally at ease with both groups and offered her comments on the subjects at hand. She had to remind herself that women who were too outspoken on issues typically discussed by men were not considered to be ladies, and on several occasions found it difficult to hold her tongue.

As mealtime approached Rachel found herself scanning the room for the tall, handsome nephew of her host and hostess. She had expected he would be in attendance tonight, yet at the same time hoped he would not. She was mentally scolding herself for allowing Gray to occupy her thoughts when he strode casually into the room. He looked as dashing as ever in russet jacket and cream trousers that clung to his muscular thighs. Rachel turned

125

away hoping he wouldn't see her among the other guests, but to her dismay he appeared by her a few seconds later.

"Good evening, Mr. Montgomery," she said in response to his greeting. With the other guests surrounding them she could not afford to display anything less than her very best manners.

Gray's eyes roamed the loveliness of her face and the gown she wore. Although she sounded pleased to see him he could tell she was no more glad to be in his company now than on the occasions of their other meetings. He was at a loss to understand why she had such an aversion to him. While so many other women in Charleston were most anxious to be seen with him, this one would hardly give him the time of day. He found her most attractive and was eager to learn more about her; he did not intend to be cast aside so easily.

"May I get you something to drink?" Gray offered.

"No, thank you," she said quickly. Maybe if she was cool with him, without being openly rude, he would seek the company of some of the young ladies whose eyes had hungrily followed him across the room.

"Perhaps a brandy," he suggested brightly.

A bubbling giggle escaped from Rachel's lips. 'No, never again," she told him.

Gray soaked in the beauty of her smile and shared her laughter. She seemed special to him in a way he didn't understand. But he did intend to unlock the mystery that surrounded her and get to know her much better.

"How is your son feeling?" Gray asked.

"He is fine," she assured him.

Gray looked puzzled. "I thought he was sick."

Rachel had forgotten that a trumped-up illness had been her excuse for leaving Gray so quickly the day before. "Well, yes, he was sick, but now he is better. You know how it is with children."

"Actually, I don't," he said softly. "But I would like to know."

Just then Charlotte stepped between them and announced that supper was served, much to Rachel's relief. A discussion of children was the last thing she wanted to engage in with Gray Montgomery.

Rachel took her designated place at the table between the aging Mr. Padgette, a local merchant, and Mrs. Evanston, the wife of a planter. The meal began with a soup and was followed by a portion of beef and vegetables. Rachel ate a fashionably modest amount and made small talk with those guests seated around her. Gray was seated across from her, and she felt his eyes upon her throughout the meal. When she dared to look his way, she always met his gaze steadfast upon her. At first she found it nervewracking, then calmed herself and found that she enjoyed his attention.

When the meal was concluded, the gentlemen retired to the library for cigars and brandy while the ladies settled themselves in the drawing room. Rachel excused herself for a moment and slipped out onto the rear porch for a breath of air. The night was cool and clean and scented with the blossoming flowers of the garden. Rachel stood by the balustrade enjoying a respite from discussions of stitcheries and menu selection. It seemed that socializing was not going to be as easy for her as it had been for Althea.

The solitude of the moment was interrupted as the creaking of boards drew Rachel's attention to the guest who had just stepped onto the porch. In the dim light she saw it was Gray and her heart fluttered.

"Lovely evening," he commented as he stopped beside her and gazed out into the darkened garden.

"I thought you would be in the library with the men," she said, and stepped farther away from him.

Gray chuckled. "And you should be with the ladies discussing hats and sewing and the like," he pointed out and took a step closer to her.

"I just needed a breath of air," she said defensively.

"More likely you were bored silly," Gray said knowingly.

Rachel smiled, unable to deny the truth of his words, and strolled casually down the porch. "And are the men equally boring?" she asked, and cast a glance at him over her shoulder.

"Not usually," he said, and followed her path. "But this evening I can't keep my mind on the discussion," he admitted.

Gray reached out a hand to touch her shoulder, but Rachel saw it coming and whirled away, moving quickly to put the wicker chairs between them. "Good God, woman, why do I get the impression that you are always trying to outdistance me? I feel like a hound pursuing a rabbit each time I am in your company." He came to her side and softened his voice. "Do you find me so unappealing? Have I offended you in some way? Please, Rachel, tell me what I have done wrong."

Hearing him speak her name for the first time sent shivers up her spine, and her stomach twisted into a knot as her feelings raced.

Gray captured her eyes and held them. "I find I am very attracted to you," he said, and his mellow voice weakened her knees. "If you care nothing for me, tell me now and I will leave you," Gray said. His large, warm hands took hers then slowly traveled up the flesh of her arms and shoulders sending waves of pleasure through her trembling body.

Rachel looked into his eyes. She should tell him now to leave her alone. This was her chance to be rid of him and the threat he placed on her future. She tried to speak, but the words refused to form. Her throat tightened, allowing no sound to escape. She could not do it. Her mind screamed out the sensible thing to do, but her heart refused to let her obey. She was held captive by her own feelings for the man and a love she could not deny.

Ever so gently, Gray pulled her into a close embrace, his powerful arms encircling her. His lips sought hers and caressed them easily, cautiously, caringly. Under his expert guidance, Rachel's lips moved with his until their mouths melted together in a deep, satisfying kiss. Gray's hands softly rubbed the back of her neck and ached to delve into the depths of her thick blond tresses. Her rigid body soon came full against his as the sweetness of their kiss robbed her of her strength.

His heady masculine fragrance and sheer strength overpowered Rachel as her senses were filled by Gray's kisses and the touch of his hands. The rest of the world was lost to her as Gray consumed her thoughts and emotions. She was his, totally and completely, now as she had been on that special night so long ago. As then, she was helpless against him, desiring to share herself with him completely.

Slowly their lips parted and Gray reluctantly released her from his embrace. Their ragged breathing evened out as they stood in silence facing each other.

"I think I could use that brandy now," Rachel whispered hoarsely.

Gray chuckled. "I find, madam, that you leave my head spinning more than any libation I have ever consumed."

His eyes caressed the gentle curves of her face and came to rest on her sweet lips. How he wanted to explore them further! With great willpower he held back.

"I think we should return inside before we become the talk of tonight's gathering," Gray said, and offered his arm.

Rachel accepted his assistance and they reentered the house. Reluctantly he left her at the entrance to the drawing room and proceeded to the smoke-filled library where a debate over the advisability of foreign investments was going on between his uncle and another banker.

Gray stood in the back of the room totally oblivious to the discussion. His mind was filled with Rachel and the surge of passion she had just evoked in him. He had not experienced such an instant attraction to any woman since ... There it was once more, that mysterious fragment which was so elusive. He tried to concentrate on it, but the memory of Rachel's soft yielding body in his arms soon dispelled all other thoughts. Yet he did think it strange that her kisses, delightful though they were, showed a distinct lack of experience. After all, she had been married and had borne a child, and most certainly should be knowledgeable in such matters. But perhaps her husband had not adequately shown her the ways of a loving couple. Gray himself could certainly do that, and with much pleasure, he thought. For even with her obvious lack of experience her kisses were sweet and warm and her body had come against his willingly, sending a warmth through his loins.

Gray shook his head and forced himself to pay attention to the debate that had heated up considerably now. Dwelling on such thoughts would do little more than give him a frustrated, fitful night's sleep.

In the drawing room Rachel was having equal difficulty keeping up with the rapidly changing topics of conversation. Her thoughts of Gray warmed her and left her with a feeling of excitement. Was it possible she could have a future with him? Did he want to be part of her life? She couldn't answer those questions now. All she could do was to continue on with her life and let things fall where they might where Gray Montgomery was concerned. That was as much of a deviation from her plan as she was willing to make.

A sewing bee. Rachel smiled to herself as she waited in the carriage outside the home of Charlotte Wade and thought how proud her mother would have felt that Rachel had been invited to take part in a sewing circle, especially one that was to be held at the plantation home of the Williamsons along the banks of the Ashley River. Her mother had set such store by those things. It had caused Rachel a bit of concern that her skill with needle and thread might not be as accomplished as the other ladies since she had spent little time sewing over the past year or so, but she had already accepted Charlotte's invitation and could not possibly back out.

Finally Charlotte appeared in the doorway of her home and made her way down the walkway to the carriage. The driver assisted her laboriously inside and she dropped onto the seat at Rachel's side.

"Good morning, good morning." She nearly sang her greeting.

"How are you this morning, Charlotte?"

"Wonderful, simply wonderful. I am so looking forward to today," she declared, and adjusted herself in the seat. "The Williamsons are delightful people and I am very anxious for you to meet them."

Rachel had to slide over to give Charlotte the room necessary to accommodate her wide frame. "I'm glad you invited me. Tell me about the Williamsons." She knew such a request wasn't really necessary.

The carriage lurched forward just as Charlotte drew in a deep breath to begin what would no doubt be a lengthy discussion of the family in question, but halted again almost immediately. As Rachel peered out the window trying to determine what had caused the holdup, the face of Gray Montgomery appeared before her.

He favored her with a lazy smile and tipped his hat as he reined in his horse. "Morning, ladies."

A hailstorm of emotions pelted Rachel. How could she remain detached when Gray kept appearing from nowhere? And looking so handsome, to boot? She curbed the rush of warmth, clamped her jaw tightly, and sat back in the seat turning her eyes forward.

Charlotte made no effort to hide her pleasure. "I wasn't expecting you this morning."

"I saw Bernard at the bank a few minutes ago and he told me of your outing. If you have no objections, I would like to join you," he said.

Rachel drew in a sharp breath. She could neither travel a great distance confined in the same carriage with him, nor tolerate an entire day in his company. It was too much for her to attempt. Perhaps he wasn't really serious, she thought, and said a silent prayer.

"No objections, I hope, Mrs. Fontaine," he said.

"I had no idea your talents included sewing," Rachel said, and eyed him coolly.

His blue eyes twinkled. "I have a great many talents, madam. Perhaps one day you will become acquainted with them all."

She was already acquainted with far more of his talents than he imagined, and the thought brought a blush to her cheeks.

"This is divine," Charlotte declared.

Gray gave his horse to the servant and climbed inside and sat down across from the ladies. He rapped on the roof and the conveyance got under way. He tossed his hat aside and stretched out his long arms along the back of the seat making himself comfortable. Though he would have preferred to sit next to the comely widow, at least this vantage point offered an uninterrupted view to her, which to his way of thinking was the next best thing.

"I was planning to visit Henry Williamson one day soon," Gray explained. His gaze swept over Rachel and the fetching pale-blue gown she wore. "And when I heard you two were making the journey, I felt this would be the perfect day."

"We are so glad you did, aren't we, Rachel?" Charlotte assured him.

Her eyes had roamed any and every part of the carriage to keep from looking at Gray but finally gave up knowing that it was impossible to avoid him. She forced herself to smile. "Of course."

"I didn't recall that you and Henry were such good friends," Charlotte noted. "In fact, I thought you didn't like him."

"I can tolerate Henry as long as we don't see each other more often than every six months," Gray said. He directed his comments to Rachel. "Henry tends to be a bit arrogant."

"But the rest of the family is lovely. Let me tell you about them." Charlotte immediately began to share her extensive knowledge of the Williamson family.

Rachel knew there would be no opportunity to get even one word in between Charlotte's so she sat back and resigned herself to listening. And looking. No, she wouldn't look. She didn't want to look. She looked anyway. Her eyes betrayed her heart's yearning as they continually stole glances at Gray. Why could she never control herself around this man?

He seemed to realize that he and Rachel were both in for a long discourse on the Williamson family as he casually crossed his ankle over the opposite knee. The motion caught her attention and she sat nearly spellbound by the rippling, hard muscles of his thighs outlined by his snug trousers. She knew those thighs and those long, powerful legs. She remembered how they had felt against her soft flesh, the ease with which his body fit against her, the feelings he had awakened in her. Her eyes caressed him, moving slowly over each facet, each fiber. Then, feeling guilty for her bold ogling of his thighs and legs and whatever, she lifted her eyes. Gray had propped his hand against the back of his head and was watching her watch him. She quickly offered a prayer that the other talents he had bragged of did not include mind-reading and turned her attention to the passing scenery.

Since he had left her in St. Joseph she had wondered what would happen if they should meet again. It had never occurred to her that he would not recognize her. There was no chance he would remember her now. Gray never showed the slightest signs of recognition or asked if they had ever met before. It seemed he accepted her for what she was, or what she was pretending to be. She considered telling him the truth, but what could she say? *I'm the little tart who hopped into your bed even though you didn't know me, and I didn't even know your name. Oh, and by the way, I bore your son, whom I have passed off as another man's child and have kept hidden from you.* There was no way she could tell any of it.

Other times Rachel wondered how Gray would react if he saw Andrew. The child looked so much like his father that surely Gray would notice it. She could avoid that easily enough, simply by keeping Andrew away from everyone. Since he was just a baby she could keep him hidden for months to come, and by the time Gray or the Wades saw him they would think little of it, hopefully, because they would have accepted Rachel and all her lies as fact.

The carriage continued onward, and Charlotte's monologue was nowhere near an end. She had not yet stopped to draw breath, and Rachel's gaze returned to Gray. He looked as bored as she, and they shared a knowing smile.

Sometimes, like now, when he looked so handsome and she could almost feel his strong arms around her again, Rachel wished that she could make him remember her. She had read accounts of memories suddenly lost or regained by a blow to the head. She stole a sideways glance at him, considering. Perhaps if she could lay her hands on a blunt object and deliver such a blow on the exact spot ... Rachel dismissed the idea. With her luck she would either kill him and spend the rest of her days in prison, or render him a blundering idiot. She sighed resolutely and turned her attention to Charlotte.

" ... and then about six years ago—"

"Is it much farther?" Rachel asked, interrupting her.

Gray sat up quickly, grateful for a break in his aunt's speech, and looked out the window at the forest of tall pines that lined the road. "We should arrive soon," he told her. But he didn't care if they ever arrived. It brought him such pleasure to look upon Rachel that he could do it for hours, though he was not certain how much longer he would be content only to look. It would do for now, he decided.

By the time the carriage reached the grand manor house, Rachel was well acquainted with the history of the Williamson family. A woman she knew must be Virginia Williamson was waiting on the portico when their carriage halted. She was trim, with dark hair peppered with gray and a calm, sedate manner.

"I am so pleased you have come," she called as her guests joined her. "It gets terribly lonely in this big house at times."

"With a home as lovely as this, I'm not sure how that is possible," Rachel said graciously.

"You must be Rachel. I have heard so many complimentary things about you," Virginia said warmly.

"And all of them quite true," Gray put in as he joined the ladies.

His words surprised her, and Rachel cast a sidelong look at him. His appreciative smile confirmed his comments.

"Charlotte, it's so good to see you again. And, Gray, you rake, you grow more handsome each time I see you," Virginia said in motherly fashion. "Why don't you come around more often? Gilbert and I enjoy your company."

"Madam, you know very well that I can abide your

son for only brief spells," Gray told her with a teasing smile.

"But during those brief spells you two create a good deal of mischief," she pointed out, then rolled her eyes. "That Henry, I don't know what I am going to do with him. Gilbert is in Richmond and Henry has become almost impossible to live with. And if that wasn't enough, Anna is with child and you would think by the way he carries on about it that Henry was having the babe himself!"

They all laughed as they entered the house and made their way to a small sitting room in the rear. Gray excused himself to join Henry at the stable. Rachel seated herself on the end of the sofa near the window and her eyes followed him down the path.

Presently Virginia's daughter-in-law joined them. Anna had pleasing features and soft brown hair. She was about Rachel's age, and her full smock top hung loose over her rounded belly. Jessica was Virginia's daughter, a plain but not unattractive girl of about thirteen years. She shared the couch with Rachel as the other ladies took seats to form a circle. Introductions were made and Rachel soon felt at ease among the strangers.

Their first topic of conversation was, of course, Anna's babe, and they discussed it at length as their sewing began. This was her first child, and Rachel understood the worries Anna was experiencing.

As Rachel had feared, her sewing skills proved quite rusty as she awkwardly manipulated the needle and cloth. She glanced around at the other ladies, including young Jessica, who wielded their needles expertly. She wondered if the families for whom the garments were intended would really want anything of such questionable quality as she had sewn. But she pressed on diligently, though she had already pricked her finger twice and had unraveled as many erroneous stitches as she had sewn correct ones.

She was much relieved when they laid their work aside for the noon meal, but felt oddly disappointed when a servant brought word that Gray and Henry would not join them. But the food was good and the company enjoyable as the ladies dined. A special kinship developed between Rachel and Jessica, who seemed restless and bored by the day's activities. When the chance arose, the two discussed anything but sewing and babies and charitable work. Jessica's mind seemed always to be reaching out for other things.

Much too quickly to suit Rachel, the ladies returned to the sitting room and took up their chores once more. They were progressing nicely and many items had been completed, though Rachel lagged behind the others in that category. She wondered how women could spend so much of their time at so boring a task. Yet she gritted her teeth and pressed on, engaging in conversation that ranged from idle gossip to the latest fashions in hats. It proved to be a long afternoon.

Gray and Henry burst into the room bringing the roar of their laughter into the quiet, dignified setting. Henry slapped Gray on the back knocking him offstride, and their deep guffawing began anew.

As one, the ladies turned to stare.

"Would you gentlemen care to share your amusement with us?" Virginia asked.

The two men straightened up quickly and swallowed their laughter.

"No, ma'am," Henry said earnestly. He and Gray exchanged a knowing smile, and one final snicker before bringing themselves fully under control.

"How is your work progressing?" Gray asked the group as he strolled across the room to stand near the sofa.

Rachel was so glad to see him she almost stood up and cheered. She couldn't remember when she had spent a more boring day. Her skills had improved little since the morning and she had injured herself with the needle more times than she could recall. Perhaps with the addition of the men the conversation would be more stimulating, or at least she could go home soon.

"Very rewarding," Charlotte declared.

Henry stood at the back of his wife's chair, and his gaze swept the circle. He looked to be about Gray's age, was slimmer, and not quite as tall. "It is rewarding to see the ladies working so diligently, contented with their God-given place in life."

Rachel's eyes came up quickly, and bored into the man. His condescending tone of voice struck a nerve.

"I do not recall the scriptures stating that a sewing circle was a ladies' place," Jessica told her brother.

He ignored her remark. "It has always amazed me that women can find joy in the most menial of tasks," he said to Gray.

"I hardly think sewing clothing for needy, unfortunate families could be classified as a menial task," Rachel pointed out in a tight voice.

Henry's eyes fell to rest on her. "I am sorry, madam, I don't believe we have met."

"This is Mrs. Rachel Fontaine," Virginia said. "My son, Henry."

"It's a pleasure to make your acquaintance, Mrs. Fontaine," Henry said. "Perhaps on your next visit your husband could join you."

"Mrs. Fontaine is a widow," Gray explained, and poured himself a glass of lemonade from the pitcher on the table behind him.

"I am very sorry." Henry offered his condolences and turned to Gray. "A lady's drink?" he inquired with raised eyebrows.

"Certainly," Gray said, and lifted the glass in a salute to his host. "A lady's drink so that I may sit among the ladies." He smiled rakishly and seated himself on the sofa between Rachel and Jessica. The younger girl smiled nervously.

"Your life must be very empty without your husband," Henry said to Rachel.

"Not at all," she informed him, and attacked her sewing with a vengeance. "My . . . husband has been dead since before my son was born and I—"

"A son? What a burden for you to shoulder alone," Henry said sorrowfully. "A woman was not meant to raise a child alone. It's not natural."

Rachel's temper was rising rapidly and she fought to control her tongue as she jabbed the needle into the cloth.

"Mrs. Fontaine is managing quite well, Henry," Gray told him as he caught a glimpse of her hostile sewing technique.

"But who provides for her and handles her affairs?" he asked.

Rachel's simmering temper threatened to boil over.

"She provides for herself and handles her business matters," Gray explained.

Henry chuckled. "She conducts her own affairs?" he asked skeptically.

"I understand Rachel ran her own mercantile before coming to Charleston," Gray continued.

Rachel seethed with anger. They were discussing her as if she wasn't in the room!

"You did?" Jessica exclaimed, her eyes wide. "You ran your own business?"

"I plan to do the same here in the city," she said, managing to keep a cordial tone in her strained voice.

"That is exciting!" Jessica said. "When your store is open, could I come to see you? Perhaps get a job? I'm very good with figures and—"

"Now just a minute, young lady," Henry interrupted. "You will do no such thing."

"Every time Papa goes away you get the mistaken idea that you are running the house," Jessica told him angrily.

"Children, please." Virginia said, and quieted her offsprings. "I see nothing wrong with a woman making the best of a difficult situation, even if that does include running a business. One must provide for oneself. I'm sure, Rachel, you did only what was necessary to survive."

"I maintain that a woman's place is at home," Henry said as his hand fell to rest on his wife's shoulder, "doing what God intended women to do, bearing children for their men."

Rachel pressed her lips together tightly to hold back her comments.

"But if a woman has the mental capability to do more, and the situation demands it, as in Rachel's case, I don't think a woman should shy away from using her full capacity," Anna said.

"A woman using her mental powers to successfully

fend for herself?" Henry questioned. He shook his head uncertainly.

Rachel would not sit quiet another moment. "If God had not intended for a person to use his or her brain, why do you suppose He bestowed it in the first place," she asked, then mumbled caustically, "those of us who have a brain, that is."

Gray heard her barb directed at Henry and he was barely able to smother his laughter. He glanced at Rachel and saw thinly veiled anger flashing in her deep brown eyes.

"What do you say to that, Gray?" Henry asked.

All eyes turned to him and he felt Rachel's glower. This was a hell of a time to be called on for a comment! "I, for one, am quickly bored with dull, witless women. It seems that in this instance God has given Rachel not only a place in the sewing circle but a place in the business community as well." Gray cut his eyes to the knotted, tangled mass of thread and fabric in her lap. "And it's a good thing, too," he whispered to Rachel. Her eyes met his and turned from angry to angrier to indignant.

"I still say—" Henry began.

Gray set his glass aside and jumped to his feet. "With your permission, Mrs. Williamson, I would like to show Mrs. Fontaine your lovely garden. Aunt Charlotte bragged about it our entire trip this morning and I wouldn't forgive myself if I didn't make certain Rachel viewed it."

"Why, of course," Virginia responded with an appreciative smile.

But Gray had already pushed aside the garment, or whatever it was, that Rachel had vented her wrath upon and pulled her off the sofa. He grasped her elbow firmly

142

and propelled her out of the room and onto the back portico.

"That arrogant, conceited ..." Rachel held back a more colorful description.

Gray walked with her down the steps and along the path. "In my opinion you are being too kind," he commented.

"You are no better than he is," she declared.

"What? What did I do?" Gray wanted to know. He never knew what this woman was thinking.

"You and our gracious host were discussing me as if I was a two-headed cow," she complained.

"A what?"

"A freak, a monstrosity, a—"

"I was doing no such thing. I was simply stating the facts," he told her. "I was defending you."

"I don't need you to defend me, or anyone else for that matter. I am perfectly capable of speaking for myself," Rachel informed him hotly.

"I, too, am capable of speaking for myself and I wanted my views on the subject to be known," Gray replied, annoyed that his attempts to do the right thing had so angered the lady.

Rachel tossed her head. "Humph! I would like to see Mr. Henry Williamson or you, Mr. Montgomery, sit through an entire day of insignificant chatter about colicky babies and hat feathers and who-wore-what-when, and have to sew on top of that. Look at my hands!" She held her fingers out in front of her. "Look at the injuries I have suffered. You men, you wouldn't do it—any of it—for an instant. Yet you don't hesitate to stand in judgment, and heaven forbid, allow a woman to venture from her 'place.' "

"How did I get categorized with the likes of Henry Williamson? I wasn't saying those things, he was," Gray exclaimed.

"You men, you're all alike," Rachel declared distastefully.

By now they had entered Virginia Williamson's formal garden. It was a maze of brick walkways winding through carefully sculptured shrubs, blooming plants and flowers, and dotted with graceful statuary. A tall hedge surrounded the garden keeping it hidden from the rest of the estate grounds as a paradise all to itself.

"All you men think of is—"

Rachel felt Gray's strong hand close over her elbow, and he spun her around to face him. His lips claimed hers, silencing her tirade. She struggled for a moment before giving in to the warmth and pleasure of his sensual kiss.

He drew her closer and his mouth took hers intimately, turning his knees to liquid. God, he had wanted to do this all day. She tasted sweet and fresh and he couldn't stop himself. But the warming in his loins finally registered in his brain and he reluctantly broke off their kiss. Rachel's cheeks were flushed as he looked down on her with passionate eyes.

"Oh, my," she mumbled, backing away from the heat of his body to collect herself. His nearness did things to her, things that she remembered from the night she had shared his bed, things she did not understand then or now.

If he had not been so aroused he might have found humor in her pinkened cheeks and wide, innocent eyes. She looked embarrassed or frightened, or, well, he couldn't say just what the look was. Had his kiss been too bold, too intimate? She had been married and surely was no stranger to such familiarity between a man and a woman. But the naiveté in those big brown eyes made him feel he had violated her and brought from the depth of his subconscious an image of—

Gray blinked and shook his head. Whatever the thought may have been was too quick to be captured. He let it go without a struggle and focused his attention on the small, delicate woman before him.

She just wanted her heart to stop pounding. If only it would, maybe she could compose herself, and maybe, one day, look Gray Montgomery in the eye again. What would he think if he knew how his kiss affected her? Certainly none of the ladies in the sewing circle would ever allow themselves to feel such things!

"Since your day has been so uninteresting perhaps we could find something more stimulating to occupy your time," Gray suggested.

Rachel's cheeks flamed.

He chuckled. "I was referring to some meaningful conversation."

Now she was doubly embarrassed. She turned away. *Swallow me up, sweet earth!*

Gray peered around her shoulder with a boyish smile etched in his handsome features. "Conversation not to your liking?"

Her heart melted at the sight of him. "Just don't ask me to sew you anything," she begged, and began to giggle.

"Fear not, madam, you shall never hear that request from me," he assured her, and joined in her laughter.

They strolled through the quiet garden, and Gray took her small hand in his.

"Thank you for defending me," Rachel said.

"I was only stating my point of view," he said quickly. She had just calmed down and he wasn't about to get her riled up again. "It was simply a coincidence that my opinion favored you."

"I tend to be a bit outspoken, don't I?" she said.

There was no way in hell he was going to answer that question. "Don't you love what Virginia has done with the azaleas?"

Rachel laughed. "You are a wiser man than I had realized, Gray Montgomery. All right, we will talk about something else. Will you sell me your mercantile?"

He groaned. "Rachel, that store is a terrible investment."

"In your opinion," she pointed out.

"I know it for a fact."

"You are not realizing the shop's full potential."

"Let me help you find a proper investment," he begged.

"I don't need any help," she informed him crisply.

Why was this woman always so difficult! "Is it too late to answer the question concerning your outspokenness?" he demanded.

"Yes," she said decisively. "Will you sell to me, or not?"

He eyed her sharply as he wrestled with her question. "I will think about it," he informed her.

"You have been thinking about it for ages. No wonder the shop isn't making any money if it takes you this long to make a decision," she scoffed.

"All right, back in the house with you!" he threatened, and pulled her in that direction. "I'm sure the ladies are engaged in an in-depth discussion of hair nets, and I know you won't want to miss a word."

She pulled against him, but his greater strength swept her along easily. "No, Gray! Please! I'm sorry!" she cried. "Don't make me go back."

He stopped and looked sharply at her. "No more talk about that mercantile," he dictated.

She faced him squarely, clinging determinedly to her pride despite the fact that he held a decided upper hand. "Very well," she agreed. "But you will think about it, won't you?" His eyes narrowed threateningly. "I will take that as a yes," she announced with a quick smile. Gray grumbled something she couldn't understand, and she felt that it was probably for the best.

This time they walked about the garden in earnest. They talked little and both enjoyed the quiet atmosphere before returning to the house. Much to Rachel's relief the sewing had been put aside and the ladies were preparing for their leave.

Twilight had settled upon the land before all the well wishes and good-byes were said. Charlotte lingered on the portico talking to Virginia as Gray assisted Rachel into the carriage and climbed in behind her. This time he took the seat next to her. The older woman joined them a few moments later, and the carriage pulled away. Conversation between the three of them died out quickly as darkness closed in and the sway of the conveyance lulled them into a state of relaxation.

"I believe your aunt is asleep," Rachel whispered. Charlotte had been silent for far too long to be in any other condition while still breathing.

"My uncle says that sometimes she even talks in her sleep," Gray said softly.

"I can believe that."

Gray stretched out his arm along the back of the seat behind Rachel's head and stifled a yawn. "I'm rather tired myself," he admitted.

Rachel rubbed her eyes. "It was a tiring day," she agreed. "A dull, boring, uninteresting, tiring day."

He pressed her back against the seat. "Rest."

She wasn't certain if he was referring to her person or her topic of conversation but she took his instructions to heart. It was odd, but she no longer felt nervous around him. She didn't want to push him away anymore or try to discourage the attention he gave her. Rachel even dared now to hope that something might come of their relationship. But even if it didn't, she enjoyed his company. For the most part, he was comfortable to be with, except when he kissed her and looked at her with those smoldering blue eyes that would forever be etched in her memory. As her eyes fluttered closed, she was thinking how it felt good and right to be with him.

"Rachel." His mellow voice was soft in her ear and she could feel his warm breath against her skin, sending a tingle through her. She realized then that she had fallen asleep and had no idea how long she had dozed, but she was leaning against Gray and her head rested on his shoulder.

"While I do enjoy boldness in a woman," he continued in a low voice, "I should caution you that your actions may land you more than you bargained for."

His words drove the hazy film of sleep from her thoughts, and to her extreme embarrassment she realized that her hand was resting on his thigh with her little finger against the bulge of his manhood. A sickly squeal sounded in her throat and she pulled her hand away as if it had been scalded and clutched it to her breast. Her cheeks burned. She threw herself to the opposite side of the carriage, as far from Gray as she could manage, and stared out the window, fervently hoping she would drop dead on the spot. His soft chuckling only increased her mortification but kept her wide awake for the remainder of their journey. And once in her own bed that evening the memory of his hard, muscular thigh beneath her hand prevented her from sleeping for the rest of the night.

Chapter 7

She looked at the list again. There was another shop a few blocks farther down. For a moment she was undecided. She had left her carriage at the hotel and proceeded to walk off the energy that had kept her wound tight as a clock since last evening. Well, she had come this far and she might as well complete the task. She would hurry and be sure to get clear of this area before darkness fell.

Quickening her pace, Rachel accomplished the distance in record time. And realizing the area of town she was in, it was easier to move faster.

After seeing the other shop that was for sale she was sorry she had come all that way as it was not a fit place for a decent woman. Rachel turned back. Darkness began to close in and she suddenly became aware of the unsavory element that inhabited this part of town near the waterfront. Gaily dressed women with rouged cheeks appeared on the street corners; shabbily dressed men sat beside buildings drinking from bottles; sailors clutching each other for support flowed in and out of the taverns. The sounds of laughter, poorly tuned pianos, shouts, screams, and curses filled the air.

From across the street two men whistled and called to Rachel. She ignored them and tried to appear calm as she walked faster, her heart pounding wildly. How foolish of her to come here alone, she thought angrily, and vowed that if she got out of this alive she would be wiser in the future.

Turning the corner quickly, Rachel glanced behind her to be sure that she wasn't being followed, and she ran head-on into someone. Suddenly terrified, Rachel screamed and fought to be free of the strong hands that held her shoulders.

"Rachel?"

A familiar voice cut through her fear. Gray!

"Thank goodness it's you," she said with relief as she tried to restore her breathing to its normal pattern. She was never so glad to see anyone in her life!

"Are you all right?" Gray asked with concern. His eyes searched her face.

"Yes, yes, I'm fine."

"What are you doing here?"

"I was looking for shops."

"Shops?"

"Shops. To purchase. Your uncle gave me a list." Rachel showed him the paper, now mangled and torn.

"And you came down here alone?" he asked. His voice was tinged with anger.

"I wanted to see what they looked like," Rachel explained meekly, sensing his displeasure.

Gray snatched the list from her hand and hurled it to the ground. "What in God's name do you think you are doing?" he bellowed, then proceeded on before she could answer. "This isn't a fit place for you! Don't you know what kind of people populate this area?"

"I do now," she said quietly.

"I cannot believe my uncle sent you here," Gray said in disgust.

"I came here on my own. I made him give me the list even after he advised against it," Rachel admitted.

"Don't you have a brain in your head!" he thundered. "The unseemly lot of men here would waste no time in claiming you. Couldn't you see what you were walking into?"

Now Rachel was growing angry. "You needn't stand there preaching to me and pretending you had no hand in the matter," she informed him.

"Me!" Gray exclaimed, his deep blue eyes wide with astonishment. "Pray tell, madam, what had I to do with this?" he challenged.

"You refused to sell me your mercantile," Rachel said accusingly.

"My mercantile?" he repeated, unable to follow her thinking.

"Although I fail to see why you so determinedly cling to that losing proposition." She couldn't resist throwing that in.

Gray let her comment pass. "What has my mercantile got to do with you being foolish enough to walk the streets of this neighborhood after dark?"

"Did you think I would simply give up the search for a mercantile to purchase when you refused to sell yours?" Rachel wanted to know.

"Is that what this foolishness is all about?" he raved.

"It is not foolishness!"

"Then you can have the damned store!"

"What?"

"It's yours! As of this moment!"

"You're not serious," Rachel said, shocked by his words.

"The mercantile belongs to you," Gray repeated. "But only on one condition."

Rachel's eyes narrowed suspiciously. "One condition?"

"That you promise never—ever—to do such a stupid thing as this again," he demanded.

Rachel considered his words for a moment. She had already decided never to come here again anyway so she might as well agree to his condition. So what if he thought it was his idea? "You have my word," she said.

Gray heaved a sigh of relief. "Congratulations, madam, you own a mercantile."

Rachel's face brightened. "Really, Gray? You will really sell it to me?" she asked anxiously.

"Yes," he told her as he still tried to look angry. "Though I can't imagine why you are so determined to purchase such a losing proposition," he added sourly.

"Oh, thank you!" She looked like a child just presented with a new toy.

"You just remember your promise," he told her, unwilling to give up the modicum of control he held over her.

"I will remember," she assured him. Rachel's mind had already moved ahead. "First, we will have your uncle draw up the papers, then—"

"First, we had better get out of here," Gray said as he glanced around to see that they had attracted a rather unsavory group of onlookers. "I don't relish the thought of fighting half the sailors in port tonight to preserve your honor.''

Rachel was quick to agree. Accepting Gray's arm, they walked hurriedly to a safer part of town.

"Now I must insist you join me for dinner," Gray said when they had reached a more respectable neighborhood.

"I don't think I should, Gray."

"I insist," he told her. "To seal our business deal."

Rachel smiled. "Well, I suppose that would be all right."

Gray took her to a nearby restaurant that was quite elegant and Rachel wished the gown she wore was more appropriate for the occasion. But Gray seemed not to notice as he proudly introduced her to several friends seated together, then took her arm and escorted her to their own table. She couldn't help but notice the ladies who followed Gray with appreciative eyes.

When they were seated at a quiet corner table a bevy of butterflies flew into flight inside Rachel's stomach. This was the first time she had ever been out in public with a man. And this was not just any man, this was Gray Montgomery, the man who could set her wits on end just by looking at her. She drew in a deep breath and tried to gather herself. But her heart raced uncontrollably, both from sitting at the same table with him and because he had finally agreed to sell her the mercantile she wanted so desperately.

"I can't thank you enough for selling me your store," she said, and her elation was evident in her expression.

"I only hope you will continue to thank me when the place leaves you penniless," he told her.

She disregarded his skepticism. "Though you may have no faith in my ability, I am quite confident I can make a small fortune from the place. Then you will be the one feeling sour because you sold it before its full potential was realized."

Gray smiled. "I wish you much success," he offered graciously. He gave their order to the serving girl, then turned his full attention to Rachel. She was so full of enthusiasm that he somehow knew she would succeed at anything she put her mind to.

"I have so many things to do," she said excitedly. "I'll have to arrange for a carpentry crew, and secure the proper merchandise. I will need a wagon for deliveries and a good team of horses. Could you suggest a reputable horse farm?"

"Jonas Peabody raises the finest horses in the county, without a doubt," he told her.

"Jonas Peabody," she repeated to herself. "I will need a team for my personal carriage. I suppose he could help me with that, too."

"Old Peabody will help himself to your money and leave you with four broken-down old nags, if you're not careful," Gray cautioned.

Rachel's mind was filled to overflowing with plans and she didn't want to hear anything that would interfere with them. "I'm certain I can select four sturdy steeds that will suit my needs," she assured him.

"Really, madam?" he challenged. "And when was the last time you purchased a horse, if I may ask."

She leveled her brown eyes at him. "I suppose you are going to tell me that men are much better than women at evaluating horses."

At last she was saying something that made sense. "That is my point, exactly," he said.

She smiled sweetly. "The same as running a plantation and owning a mercantile?"

A scowl crossed his face, then turned quickly to a boyish grin. Her mind was sharp, and he would not misjudge her again.

"Enough talk of business," he decided. "Tell me about yourself, Mrs. Rachel Fontaine."

The butterflies in her stomach seemed to suddenly have grown stone wings. What of her past could she tell him? Nothing!

She smiled demurely. "I'm certain that my simple upbringing pales in comparison with a life such as yours. Have you not traveled to beautiful cities and far-off lands?"

Gray told her of the many places he had visited in America and Europe. He spoke eloquently, vividly detailing the spectacular landscapes and elegant cities, the warm people he had met and their unusual customs. Rachel's eyes grew wide as she listened and they sparkled in the candlelight. She pictured each scene as he spoke and imagined that she had been there with him. Rachel was enthralled by his descriptions and asked many questions. Gray had seldom enjoyed such an intent audience and took great pleasure in sharing his experiences.

"It sounds so thrilling. I should like to see those places one day," she said as their meal was served. "I have never been anywhere as beautiful as you make them sound."

"You have not traveled much?" Gray asked.

"I have lived in a few places but never visited a city for the sake of going there," she explained.

"Not even a honeymoon trip?"

The fork slipped from her grasp and clattered against the china plate. As the smile vanished from her face she cast her eyes downward. Could she never have a moment's peace from the lies she had told?

Gray froze seeing her ashen face, then silently cursed himself. "That was a callous remark. Stupid and insensitive." He reached across the table and folded his hand warmly over her slim fingers. "I'm sorry."

She looked up and her eyes locked with his. In the depth of their blueness Rachel saw concern and worry and shame for what he had said. *Don't apologize! Don't be nice! I've taken your son from you! I don't deserve your kindness.*

A faint smile twisted his lips. "Forgive me? Please."

He looked like a little boy—like Andrew—and Rachel couldn't resist that grin on either of their faces. She smiled back at him. "Please, don't apologize."

"But what I said was—"

"Not another word," she insisted graciously. *Please!*

Gray gave her hand an affectionate squeeze before releasing it. He watched her as they dined and caught himself wondering about her life, her marriage, her late husband. A quick, sharp jab pierced his heart and for an instant he felt envious of a man he had never known.

Their meal concluded, Gray and Rachel strolled arm in arm to her hotel. The crisp air was refreshing and the stars overhead twinkled with a brightness Rachel had never noticed before. They chatted easily, finding a new level of comfort in each other's company that was pleasing yet at the same time exhilarating and frightening.

"Could I come in?" he asked, standing outside the door to her suite. "I would like to see your son."

"I'm afraid that is not a good idea," she said quickly. To her dismay Andrew grew to look more and more like

157

his father with each day that passed, so she certainly was not going to let Gray see him. "He is sick."

"Sick? You told me yesterday that he was well." He looked concerned. "Have you taken him to a doctor? I know several excellent—"

"That is not necessary," Rachel assured him. She was going to have to come up with better excuses in the future. "It's just one of those childhood illnesses," Rachel explained. "I'm sure he will be perfectly well very soon."

A burst of laughter, gurgles, and coos came from within the suite, lending little credence to her claim of illness. Gray eyed her skeptically. "You see, he's better already," Rachel announced brightly.

"Then I can see him," Gray assumed.

Rachel slid her body between Gray and the door, blocking his path. "Hannah is with him and I am sure she is not properly attired to receive company at this late hour," she said, and was thankful she had managed to sound convincing.

"Very well, I can see him another time," Gray said, mildly irritated.

"Thank you for dinner. It was lovely," Rachel said sincerely.

He smiled. "You were lovely," Gray corrected.

He slipped his arms about her, and as Rachel's arms encircled his neck their lips met in a warm, generous kiss. Gray wanted to hold her forever in his embrace. Her body felt so right against his. Reluctantly he released her.

"Good night, my dear," he said with a husky voice.

"Good night," she whispered, her breathing uneven as she disappeared inside the suite.

Gray placed his hat jauntily on his head and whistled softly as he descended the stairs into the lobby. He was feeling especially pleased with himself. Dinner with Rachel had been better than he had anticipated. She was warm and caring, pleasant to be with, and possibly—no, definitely—the most beautiful woman he had ever met. Beneath her cool exterior he had found a very charming woman. Yet she had looked almost like a child when he had told her the mercantile was hers. If he had known that simple act would bring her closer to him he would have agreed to the sale when she first suggested it. Instead he had put her off, using it as an excuse to see her again.

The night air was cool as he crossed the street and turned back to look up at the lighted rooms on the hotel's second floor. He didn't know which room was hers, but he felt strangely content knowing Rachel was there. An elusive memory darted quickly through his mind. He tried to seize it and analyze it, but it was gone as swiftly as it had come. Gray shook his head, irritated with himself for not being able to identify the intangible piece of his past that had haunted him lately. He took one final look at the hotel and, sighing wantingly, continued on his way. Another night, he thought, perhaps another night.

The carriage bounced over the rutted road, and Rachel had no choice but to have faith that the driver knew where he was going because this section of farmland was completely foreign to her. The morning dew still clung to the lush green fields that bordered the trail as the early-morning sun caressed the magnolias and azaleas that dotted the countryside. Patches of tall pine and oak interrupted the landscape. Within the carriage, Rachel sat nervously tapping her toe, trying to remember everything the blacksmith had told her this morning during their brief discussion, trying to recall the details of the many similar trips that as a child she had made with her father. Her credentials left a good deal to be desired, she readily admitted, and she was short on experience as well. But like so many other times in her life she had no one to turn to for assistance.

Well, not exactly, she begrudgingly conceded as she watched the countryside go by. She could have asked Gray Montgomery. He would have done it. Happily. And taken great pleasure in demonstrating to her that his talent for purchasing horses was far superior to her. Perhaps if he wasn't so arrogant she might have asked for his help. Maybe if the man wasn't always so all-fired sure of himself, her pride wouldn't have gotten in her way and she would have asked for the help she desperately needed to purchase these horses this morning.

Rachel sat back and sighed. She could lie to all the world about her past and her child and the late Mr. Fontaine, but she couldn't lie to herself. It wasn't Gray's arrogance that kept her from requesting his assistance. Nor was it her pride—not entirely, anyway. It was her heart, her own heart, hopelessly lost to the man that sent her on this mission alone. She was so drawn to him, so in love with him, that she was allowing herself to become too close. She must hold her feelings and emotions at bay and continue on with her own life. And for Gray Montgomery's place in her life? Well, it was nothing that she could count on.

The carriage jolted to a halt before a large white frame house. The grounds were well kept and showed attention to detail, as was common for a family of modest means such as the Peabodys. The driver helped Rachel to the ground and she drew in a determined breath. She wasn't certain what to expect from this Jonas Peabody; the black-smith had suggested she be very cautious of him, as had Gray the night before. The man made his living by selling horses and she expected he would drive a hard bargain. She did hope he would not try to take advantage of a young widow's lack of knowledge and sell her an unsuitable team. All she could do was hope, because it was too late to back out now, she realized as a white-bearded man emerged from the house and crossed the long portico leaning heavily on a walking stick. He made his way awkwardly down the steps and met Rachel on the walkway.

"Morning, ma'am," he greeted, eyeing her warily.

"Good morning. I am Rachel Fontaine and I am hoping to see Mr. Jonas Peabody." The nervousness that shook her innards was well hidden beneath her poised and dignified demeanor.

"I am the man you seek." He squinted his eyes in the bright morning sun.

"I was told, sir, that you raise the finest horses in all the county. If that be true, I hope we can conduct a bit of business," she explained.

Jonas looked troubled. "Business?"

"I am in need of two teams of horses," she said. Rachel had seen that look before and knew what was coming next.

"Send your man over. Then we'll do business," he grumbled, and turned to leave.

"That would be impossible, though nothing would please me more," she said. Jonas stopped and turned to face her again. Rachel sighed; it was time to drag Mr. Fontaine out once more. "My husband is dead, Mr. Peabody, and the only other man in my life is my son, who has not yet reached his first birthday. So you can see, sir, that I have no choice but to speak for myself. There is no other to do it."

The hard line of his mouth relaxed. He didn't like doing business with a woman, especially one as young and pretty as this one. But the sadness he saw in her big brown eyes and the woeful tale she related caused him to rethink his position.

"A widow, huh?" he grunted. She nodded. "My ma was left a widow when I was just a boy."

"Did you and she have to go without horses because of it?" she inquired.

Jonas snorted. "No, I don't reckon we did." A smile broke over his craggy face. "Come along to the stable, Mrs. Fontaine, let me show you my darlings. Now, what kind of horses will you be needing?"

The two made their way around the house and down the path to the stable. Jonas moved slowly, hindered by his problem leg, and Rachel strolled beside him at an unhurried pace. She told him what she needed the horses for. He listened intently until they reached their destination.

The big red stable was surrounded by different corrals, holding a variety of horses. There were wagons and haystacks and tools about, and it smelled of leather and feed and the horses themselves. Rachel, in her wide-brimmed straw hat and pink print muslin gown, looked very much out of place.

A bay mare hung its head over the fence and Jonas stroked its velvety muzzle. "This little lady is a fine animal," he praised. "In fact, all my ladies are fine. My gents, too."

"They are all beautiful." Rachel agreed.

"Especially this boy coming here."

Rachel followed the man's line of vision to the far end of the pasture where a dark horse carrying a rider had just emerged from the woods. The expert touch of booted heels urged the animal into a canter and its long, muscular legs settled into stride, sending clods of grass and dirt flying into the air with its sharp hooves. The rider's deft hands held the reins, firmly controlling the stallion, then loosened and gave the horse its head. It lunged forward and the rider expertly kept his seat as the horse's powerful legs carried them toward the stable at a full run. Man and beast moved together in perfect harmony. They neared the stable and the rider made no attempt to slow the horse. Rachel held her breath as the stallion approached. His ears pitched forward as he turned his concentration on the fence. With no apparent command from the rider, the horse's muscles bunched and he sailed effortlessly over the fence a few feet from where Rachel and Jonas stood.

"Hot damn!" Jonas swore, his eyes dancing with merriment as he watched the black stallion touch ground gracefully.

The rider reined him in and the horse tossed his head in protest. But the man brought him under control and wheeled him about.

"Isn't he a dandy!" Jonas praised.

"He is wonderful," Rachel agreed. Her heart was beating fast from the expert display of horsemanship she had just witnessed.

With flared nostrils and prancing hooves, the powerful stallion made it known that it was anxious to go again. But the rider held him with a firm hand and brought him to a stop in front of Jonas and Rachel. She looked up and was shocked to see that it was Gray Montgomery aboard

163

the stallion. Determinedly, she turned her attention back to her host.

"Now here is a gent who knows how to keep the ladies happy," Jonas declared.

Rachel's head snapped up and her eyes locked with Gray's. An amused, arrogant smile flashed across her face. Rachel's cheeks reddened profusely and she pulled her eyes from his as she realized that Jonas was referring to the horse.

Gray swung to the ground and walked to the horse's head. "He is a fine stallion, Jonas. I'm going to talk him away from you one of these days."

"You and every other man in the county," he scoffed. "But I'll be back on him soon. As quick as this damned knee of mine—" Jonas turned to Rachel. "Begging your pardon, ma'am."

"That's quite all right," she muttered.

"Forgive me my manners, as well, Mrs. Fontaine," Jonas apologized. "Are you acquainted with Mr. Montgomery?"

Well acquainted, thank you. Rachel cast off her embarrassment and pulled her composure together, eyeing him coolly. "We have met," she said crisply.

Gray touched the brim of his hat. "As always, Mrs. Fontaine, it is a pleasure to see you, and, as always, under the most unexpected circumstances."

"Mrs. Fontaine is here to purchase some horses," Jonas explained.

"Really?" Gray asked with mock surprise.

Rachel fumed silently. What was he doing here? Could she not make a move in this city that Gray Montgomery wasn't underfoot?

The stableboy took the reins from Gray and led the stallion away.

"I was about to show Mrs. Fontaine the horses in the lower corral. There are several there to suit her needs," Jonas said.

"Don't trouble yourself," Gray said cordially. "I will walk the lady down so that she may evaluate the horses and make her expert decision. Go rest that leg, Jonas."

"Very well," he relented, and hobbled back toward the house.

Gray turned to offer Rachel his arm only to see that she had headed down the path without him. Biting his lower lip to contain his laughter, he hurried to her side.

"Mr. Montgomery, I don't know why you insist upon intruding into my affairs time and time again," she said tightly.

"Intruding upon your affairs? Madam, it is but simple coincidence that finds us both at Jonas Peabody's farm this morning," Gray insisted. But, in fact, he had known without a doubt that she would be here this morning to purchase her horses, too bullheaded to ask anyone for help. Peabody was a hard man, a tough horse trader, ruthless at times, and Gray didn't want to see the young widow taken advantage of.

"I have no attention of interfering with your selection in any way," he assured her. "I am certain you are quite knowledgeable in the subject."

"Thank you," she said crisply.

Rachel cursed her luck. She had counted on Mr. Peabody steering her in the right direction. Her pride would not allow her to admit to Gray that she had such little knowledge of horses, especially after the things she had said to him at supper last night. Who knows what she would end up with if she picked out the horses herself!

"I had no idea that you enjoyed horses so much," Gray commented. "Do you ride?"

"On occasion," she said, but didn't mention that the last such occasion was when she was twelve years old.

"But not as often as you would like," he assumed.

"Yes," she murmured as she carefully picked her way along this rocky section of the path.

"Then we shall go riding together tomorrow," Gray declared.

"What?" she exclaimed, looking up at him suddenly.

"We shall go riding tomorrow," he repeated.

"But—but don't you have something else—something important—which requires your attention? I wouldn't dream of interfering—"

"It would be my pleasure," he assured her.

Now what had she gotten herself into! She hadn't been on a horse in years. How could she possibly go riding tomorrow with Gray? There was no graceful way out of it, she had no choice but to go.

At the lower corral Gray rested his arm casually on the top board of the wooden fence and gazed out at the field of horses.

"Didn't I tell you Jonas had the best horses in the county?" he asked.

Rachel looked out at the horses, though she was barely tall enough to see over the fence. "Oh, yes, you were quite right," she agreed.

"Of course there are a few poor ones in the bunch," Gray mentioned.

There were? Except for size and color they all looked

alike to Rachel. She pursed her lips nervously. "Isn't that the way it always goes," she said wisely.

He looked back at her. "Well, madam, which ones have you chosen?"

Rachel gazed at the animals thoughtfully as she feverishly searched her memory. What had the blacksmith told her to look for? It was something to do with legs, wasn't it?

"The brown one looks nice," she ventured.

Gray appraised the horse she had pointed to. "He has a capped hock," he said with concern. "Take a closer look."

Capped hock? What was that? Should she be commenting on it, let alone looking at it, in mixed company?

Gray leaned back against the fence focusing his attention on Rachel. She was a much more fetching sight than the corral and he studied her leisurely as Rachel gazed at the horses. When they had discussed this purchase at supper last evening he had hoped she would ask for his help. But like everything else, she was hell-bent on handling it herself. Did she really not want anyone else's opinion? Would her pride not allow her to ask for help? Or had she been hurt by someone she had trusted, hurt so badly that she would trust no one again?

"I like the black one," Rachel decided. "The black horse with the white markings on his feet."

"Feet?"

Her cheeks reddened. "Hooves."

Gray stepped from the fence, arms akimbo. "You don't know anything about selecting horses, do you?" he accused.

"What concern is it of yours?" she shot back. She

hadn't asked him to come here, hadn't wanted him here or any place else in her life.

"Concern?" he echoed. What an exasperating woman! "Is it so terrible a thing to want to help you? Is it so terrible a thing to need help?"

"I can't—I won't—depend on another living soul who will be here one day and gone the next." Her voice trembled and visions of her parents and cousin flashed through her mind. She had trusted each of them and they had all abandoned her. She had vowed long ago that no one would ever do that to her again.

His irritation with her fled at the sight of tears standing in her eyes. She had been hurt by someone or something and he hated them for it. Suddenly he wanted to take her in his arms and hold her, shelter her from the world. But when he stepped forward she drew away and fought back her tears. His heart ached seeing her in such pain.

"Let me help you, Rachel." He extended his arm, offering his hand.

She wanted to turn and run and never have to face Gray Montgomery again. But she was so hopelessly in love with him that despite no promise of a tomorrow she stayed, as she had done before. She placed her hand in his and he squeezed it warmly.

"I will educate you," he said, pulling her to his side, "so that you may choose your own horses. I believe that is a compromise which even you can live with, Rachel Fontaine."

They shared a smile and he gave her a wink before beginning his lecture. She listened intently as he talked and proved an able student. She selected a matched pair of bay Morgans with blaze faces for her carriage horses, and stocky, muscular Belgian draught horses to pull the wagon for her store. Gray climbed the fence and made a closer inspection on their hooves and checked their shoulders and chests for harness galls. Satisfied with the horses, they returned to the house and found Jonas in his rocker on the front porch.

"See anything you like, Mrs. Fontaine?" the old man asked.

Rachel seated herself in a wicker chair. "You have many beautiful horses," she praised.

"Finest in the state," Jonas agreed with pride.

Gray sat down on the porch railing, a location that offered an unobstructed view of Rachel. She looked especially pretty this morning, he decided. In fact, she looked better each time he saw her. Strange, but he had never noticed that about any other woman. Jonas and Rachel discussed their transaction, but Gray wasn't listening. He was attempting to mentally compare Rachel's beauty with that of other women, only to find that he could not clearly picture the face of any other woman he had known.

Gray was suddenly yanked from his daydream when he heard Jonas name the price he wanted for the four horses. He couldn't believe his ears. The price was ridiculously low. And he was even more shocked by Rachel's reply.

"Mr. Peabody," she began, her delicate brows drawn together in a troubled fashion, "is that the best price you can give me?"

Gray very nearly cut in to their negotiations to tell Rachel that she was practically stealing the horses as it was. He didn't want her to anger Jonas with so low an offer that he raised the price considerably or, worse yet, refused to sell to her at all. And Jonas Peabody had been known to do just that.

Jonas rubbed his chin thoughtfully and twisted his face

169

as if he was in great pain. "Well, Mrs. Fontaine," he finally decided, "seeing as it's you that's asking, I guess I could knock another fifty dollars off the price."

Gray nearly fell off the railing. He would not have believed it if he hadn't heard it with his own ears. Jonas Peabody never sold a horse so cheaply in his life. Gray rose, thinking the negotiations closed, but stopped suddenly when he saw Rachel still chewing her bottom lip pensively. Good Lord, she wouldn't, surely she wouldn't.

"Oh," she said dejectedly. "Only fifty dollars?"

Jonas pulled on his beard. "Well, all right, let's make it seventy-five."

"And does that include the harnesses?" she inquired.

Gray turned away and covered his face with his hand.

"Yeah, I guess I can throw in the harnesses," Jonas said.

Rachel smiled brightly. "Then I believe we have a deal, Mr. Peabody." She rose and caught Gray's stunned expression out of the corner of her eye. "I will have the horses picked up in a few days."

Jonas got to his feet. "Pleasure doing business with you, ma'am," he said as Gray and Rachel left the porch. "And when that boy of yours is ready for a horse, you come back and I will fix you right up."

"Thank you, Mr. Peabody," Rachel called. She looked up at Gray's troubled face as he walked with her toward her carriage. "Is something wrong? Wasn't that a good price?"

"It was so good, madam, I fear you could be considered guilty of horse theft," Gray said sourly. "I've never gotten old Peabody to knock one single cent off anything I ever bought from him."

"I have bought and sold many things, and I have found

the price is usually set long before negotiations begin," she said wisely.

"Meaning that because you walk in here wearing this fetching pink frock you would get a better price than I?" Gray wanted to know.

She looked up at him coyly. "I don't recommend that you try it yourself, sir. Pink, I fear, is not your best color."

Gray had to laugh. "At any rate, madam, you got an excellent price on the horses. If this is an indication of your skill in merchandising I have no doubt that I will be very sorry I didn't insist on a partnership instead of selling you the mercantile outright." He opened the carriage door. "Though shopping at your store may prove an interesting experience."

Rachel smiled. "Thank you for your help today."

"My pleasure," he said, and assisted her into the carriage. "I will see you tomorrow morning."

"Tomorrow?" Rachel asked through the window.

He closed the door. "For our ride. Remember?"

She forced a smile. "I am looking forward to it." She waved her good-bye as the carriage lurched forward and started down the drive.

Gray turned on his heels and headed back toward the house, a new confidence surging through him. "Now, Jonas, about that stallion . . ."

Chapter 8

Was it too late to run away? No, she would have to come back sooner or later. Maybe she could say Andrew was sick. Darn, that excuse had been overused as it was.

Rachel paced fretfully across the hotel lobby, then plopped down on the sofa. Riding! She had no business on a horse. She hadn't been on one in years, she was out of shape—she had had a baby since then! Gray Montgomery, she silently fumed, that man had a way of thrusting her into the most awkward situations. Well, there was no way out, though she had lain awake until late last night trying to come up with a reasonably believable excuse, so she would just have to make the best of it.

Rachel looked down at the toes of her boots peeking out from under her long black riding skirt and wondered if anyone had ever been seriously injured falling from the mounting block. She closed her eyes and prayed that she could get through the day without making a complete fool of herself. When she opened her eyes again she saw Gray crossing the lobby toward her. He looked handsome in tall, shiny black boots, tan riding trousers, crisp white shirt, and deep brown jacket, so handsome that for an instant Rachel was glad to be going.

"You must be anxious to go," he noted with a broad smile.

She couldn't tell him that she was down here so he would not come to her room and possibly see Andrew. "Actually, Gray," she began, and stood up slowly. "I am a little nervous about this. I—I haven't been riding in a—a . . . while."

"Don't worry, it will all come back to you quickly," Gray predicted. He closed his hand around her elbow and propelled her across the lobby. "I have selected a delightful mare for you; she will be an easy ride."

The horse tethered outside the hotel was easily seventeen hands high and when Rachel laid eyes on it she dug in her heels and wouldn't take another step. "But, Gray, it's huge. I can't possibly ride—"

"That is my horse, Rachel." She swayed against him and heaved a thankful sigh. "Your horse is over here." He led her to the other side of the bay stallion to where a small, dainty white Arabian mare stood. "She is mild-mannered and good tempered. I had to wake her from a nap just so you could ride her this morning," Gray said with a grin.

Rachel stroked the mare's forehead and they spent a few minutes getting acquainted before Rachel gathered together her courage and pulled on her riding gloves. Gray placed his hands around her small waist and easily lifted her into the side saddle, then remained there while she got her balance. He checked the stirrup length and the girth before presenting her with the reins.

"Comfortable?" he asked. She nodded and he untied his own horse and swung into the saddle. "You go first. I want to keep an eye on you for a while and be certain you know what you're doing."

But it was hardly her riding ability that Gray noticed as he rode along behind her. Her riding ensemble was most appealing, with its long-sleeved jacket that came to her waist, the lacy white blouse underneath, and small bonnet set on the side on her head. She looked quite fashionable, but that didn't draw his attention, either. Instead, his eyes were riveted to the seat of the saddle where her round bottom rose and fell in step with the horse. He grew warm, warmer than the morning sun should have caused, and his breathing became slightly uneven.

"Is everything to your satisfaction?" Rachel called back to him.

A roguish smile curled his lips. "Ah, madam, very much so." Then he realized she was referring to her riding ability. "Yes, yes, you are doing fine," he said, and reluctantly brought his horse up alongside hers.

They rode south through the busy streets of the city. The little mare responded obediently to Rachel's commands, and by the time they reached the edge of town she felt more at ease. Soon she became accustomed to riding again and began to enjoy herself as she and Gray talked. Presently they turned the horses inland and urged them to a faster gait. Rachel was having a marvelous time as they rode through meadows and stands of pine and oak. The sun had reached its zenith when Gray took the lead seeking water for the horses. They emerged from the forest near the Ashley River and found a low bank where the horses drank their fill.

Gray dismounted. "We had better let the horses rest a bit," he said, and lifted Rachel to the ground.

She watched as he led the animals toward the trees a short distance away. It felt good to have her feet on the ground again, and she stretched her legs before sitting down on the grass at the water's edge and removing her gloves. This section of the river was uninhabited, except for the birds that flew overhead and an occasional squirrel that might venture from the woods. It was a quiet, relaxing spot. But the heat of the sun soon bore down upon her, so she unpinned her hat and laid it by her and took off her jacket. Somehow her lace handkerchief fell from the pocket and the gentle breeze deposited it in the shallow water. She got to her hands and knees quickly and stretched out her hand to capture it before the current carried it away.

Gray whistled softly to himself as he tethered the horses in the shade of the tall pines, but he nearly choked on his own tongue when he headed for the river and saw Rachel on her hands and knees with her bottom in the air. He approached her slowly, ungentlemanly though it was, savoring the sight.

She sensed him behind her and sat up. "Oh, Gray, my handkerchief."

He saw it floating a few feet from the bank, too far out for him to reach, either. "Too bad," he said, and shrugged his wide shoulders.

"I want it," she pleaded.

He never understood the value women put on fans and handkerchiefs and parasols and the like. "It's only a handkerchief," he pointed out.

"It is not!" she declared angrily. She was not about to sit idly by and let her mother's handkerchief—one of the

175

few of Althea's possessions she had—be forever lost in the depths of the Ashley River. Quickly she pulled off one boot.

Gray's eyes grew wide. "Rachel, what are you doing?" he exclaimed.

Nor was she going to let mere modesty or a rigid code of decency prevent her from getting the handkerchief. Besides the man had seen a great deal more of her than her feet and ankles, and if he hadn't been so drunk that night he would realize it.

"I am getting my handkerchief," she informed him irritably, and pulled off her other boot.

"Rachel, I will buy you another one," he said, trying to reason with her.

"I don't want another one! I want that one!" She pulled off her white silk stockings and tossed them aside.

There was just no reasoning with her. "Oh, all right, I'll get your handkerchief."

"Never mind! You are as slow as a plow mule! The handkerchief will be in the Atlantic before you make up your mind to do something," Rachel shot as she gathered up the hem of her skirt.

"Mule! Mule! You! You are calling me a mule!" Gray jerked off both boots. "Woman, you are the most mule-headed person I have ever known—bar none!" He peeled off his socks and rolled up the legs of his trousers. "Get back over here! I'll get the damned handkerchief!"

"Don't trouble yourself," she called as she waded into the water. "I am perfectly capable of handling this myself."

"Women!" he swore, plunging into the water after her. It was cool against his bare flesh and the river bottom was soft under his feet. But he caught up with her quickly and

176

grabbed her arm. "Just go sit on the bank. I'll take care of this," he grumbled.

"You go sit on the bank!" she said, and continued on.

There was just no dealing with this woman! Gray quickly moved past her and waded out until he was nearly calf-deep in water before he scooped up her treasured hand-kerchief. Clutching it in his fist, he whipped around. The river bottom shifted beneath him as he turned and he fell backward, sitting down in the water with a splash.

Rachel gasped and covered her mouth with her hand. And then, inexplicably, a giggle bubbled up. Then another. He looked so ridiculous sitting waist-deep in water, his knees poking up above the surface, holding her mother's lace handkerchief, that she could not stop herself. Her giggles became gales of laughter and tears spilled onto her cheeks until she could hardly stand upright.

At first, he was too shocked to utter a sound. Then he gathered his wits. "If you find this so amusing, madam, surely you would enjoy a swim yourself," he threatened with a sardonic smile. He bolted upright and charged toward her.

The meekest squeal was the only protest she presented before she dropped her skirt and dashed for the safety of the riverbank. But Gray was much swifter than Rachel and all she could do was shriek as he swept her into his arms. She kicked her feet wildly but he held her easily.

"Gray! You—you wouldn't!"

He waded deeper into the water. "Just watch and see!" He jolted her as if to toss her in and she threw her arms about his neck and held on tightly. They both fell into a fit of laughter as Gray carried her onto the bank. He dropped to his knees and laid her gently in the green grass, then collapsed beside her. Their laughter subsided and slowly their breathing returned to normal.

"What are we going to do?" Rachel said as she sat up and examined the wet hem of her skirt.

Gray rolled onto his back and locked his fingers behind his head. "We will stay here until we dry. I certainly cannot go back into town like this."

She glanced down at his trousers. The sodden cloth clung to him boldly, outlining his manhood. Rachel blushed, covered her eyes, and fell back onto the soft grass. No, they definitely couldn't go back to town yet.

Gray chuckled at her reaction. Yes, she was a lady and not supposed to look at such sights, but given that she had been married he thought her profuse embarrassment was surprising.

Rachel couldn't lie here next to him, with his trousers plastered against his—. She sat up quickly, determined to busy her fidgeting fingers, and pulled the pins from her hair, hoping to restore some order to her coiffure, all the while staring intently at her own lap. *Don't look . . . don't look . . .*

Her blond tresses fell down her back in a riot of curls. Instinctively he reached out and coiled one flaxen curl about his finger. It felt like silk. His eyes moved greedily down her trim back to where her derriere rested on the soft grass.

Don't look . . . don't— Merciful heaven above, she had looked! What was the matter with her! She was supposed to be a lady and conduct herself accordingly. And a lady most certainly did not look at a man's . . . . a man's . . . Rachel threw herself back onto the grass and stared up at the blue sky. The things this man caused her to do were unspeakable!

Gray raised himself up on one elbow and rolled onto his side toward her, studying the classic line of her profile. With a will of its own his mind replayed the scene of a moment ago when he had carried her in his arms and she had held so tightly to his neck. Her weight was nearly nothing, and he had gotten the slightest indication of the delicate frame hidden beneath her layers of clothing.

The evasive bit of memory that had flitted in and out of his mind for days suddenly presented itself again and, as always, stayed only a trifle of a second to taunt his power of recollection. It was only a fragment of a shadowy vision that brought impressions of excitement and danger and, at the same time, contentment and harmony. The memory was a contradiction in itself, a riddle screaming out to be solved, but too quick, too elusive to be caught by his conscious thought. Try as he might, Gray was forced to give up the pursuit.

She felt his gaze upon her and turned her head to meet his gaze. *Why can't you remember?*

"Did I tell you that I was moving to Richfield permanently?" The change in his avenue of thought took him by surprise.

"I believe you mentioned that was your intent."

"I have all sorts of plans for the place. Listen, and tell me what you think." Suddenly, Gray had to share everything about his home with her. He told her of his plans to redecorate, and described the rooms, asking her for her opinion on fabrics and colors. Rachel took great delight in offering suggestions, for he sorely needed some womanly advice on the subject. At the same time she recalled how her own mother had devoted many hours to painstakingly arranging the manor house. Althea had exquisite taste and bought only the very finest of everything, never knowing—or caring—of the price tag each item bore. She held true to her position in the family and left it up to the man of the house to handle the financing of her extravagances.

Then Gray told her of the planting that had been done, the vegetable garden, the crops, the orchards. He talked about the livestock and the barns, the stable and outbuildings. He wanted to share every bit of it with her. And she understood all that he said, asked intelligent questions, and pointed out an option or two that he had not considered. He had no way of knowing that she had walked or ridden over every inch of Richfield many times at her father's side while he talked incessantly of the intricate workings of the plantation. She had found it fascinating then and still did. Perhaps more so now because Gray was so excited about it, like a child with a new toy who wanted to share it with his best friend.

Without knowing he was going to, Gray stopped in the middle of his plans for the landscaping, leaned over, and kissed her. It seemed like the most natural thing to do. His lips covered hers and moved slowly over them, savoring their sweetness. Their mouths moved together in an easy, harmonious blend, striking a melodious chord that crescendoed into a symphony of delight. At that moment he wanted no more than her kiss and she gave that willingly, parting her lips to allow his tongue to also partake of their pleasure. The sweetness of her mouth twined through him, touching senses and feelings he hadn't known existed, filling him with contentment that only hinted of lustier, more passionate wants.

Rachel's mind swirled with a riot of feelings that merged easily with treasured memories. And when his lips were pulled away from hers, she was left with not an emptiness but fulfillment, wondrous and new. They looked at each other for a long moment, savoring the closeness that enveloped them, until the whinnying of the horses interrupted them and the world intruded upon them.

Neither spoke as Rachel pinned her hair atop her head and they made themselves presentable. The sun was touching the horizon as they mounted their horses and rode in companionable silence back to town.

It was only a kiss! One kiss! Nothing more! He had kissed dozens of women—several dozen, perhaps, in his lifetime. He had been to the far corners of the country and abroad, and his travels had taken him to the door of women of all types. He had been indiscriminate in his selection—blonde, brunette, even a redhead or two. None had been immune to his considerable charm. Yes, Gray had known many women, to varying degrees of intimacy, but none of them had affected him as powerfully as Rachel. With only one kiss!

Gray folded his arms across his wide chest and leaned against the red brick wall of the tobacco shop, thinking. So if it was only a kiss, why had the memory of it kept him awake most of the night? And why had he been standing across the street from Rachel's hotel for the last half hour?

He was acting like a schoolboy, Gray decided irritably, not a grown man—a worldly grown man, at that. The kiss itself meant no more than any other kiss, he told himself, and it only seemed incredibly significant because he had not been with a woman in quite some time. That was a situation he could relieve any time he chose, with nearly any woman he chose. He simply had not happened upon the right woman in the right circumstances lately; and the reason no one seemed appealing anymore hadn't quite been pinned down yet in his mind. Actually, he had given it little or no thought.

He was behaving stupidly, Gray concluded and silently berated himself with an unflattering oath. He had wasted enough of his valuable time mooning like a lovesick puppy. He would simply cross the street, go into the hotel lobby, leave a brief message at the desk, and be on his way. Gray snorted irritably at himself and moved from the shadow of the tobacco shop building. How silly he had been to—

Gray stopped suddenly, his eyes affixed to the hotel's entrance. A woman pushing a baby buggy emerged and carefully took the carriage down the steps onto the walkway. She stopped, adjusted the white bonnet that covered the child's head, then continued down the street. Gray watched until the woman disappeared around the corner. By that time his palms had started to sweat and light beads of perspiration dampened his temples. That was probably the woman who cared for Rachel's baby, he reckoned, and she was obviously taking the child for an outing, so it would logically follow that Rachel would be left alone in her hotel suite. All alone.

A familiar stirring warmed Gray's loins. Yes, it had been only one kiss, but seething beneath it had been a volatile inkling of so much more. When its memory had finally allowed him to sleep last night, his dreams had taken over where the simple touching of lips had ended and his mind had played out a fantasy that would have caused the saltiest sailor to blush.

Gray stood rooted to the spot, indecision seesawing its way through his mind. He glanced at the hotel entrance, then looked down the street at the corner where the woman and carriage had disappeared. *Alone ... totally alone ...* He turned back to the hotel's entrance and licked his suddenly parched lips. Should he obey his gentleman's code of integrity? Or should he respond to his baser instincts? Gray drew in a deep breath, pulled his hat down firmly, and left the sanctuary of the tobacco shop's shadow.

The window stood open to welcome the cool morning breeze, and the sheer drapes bellowed gently. The sofa in the suite's sitting room faced the opening and made an ideal spot for reclining. Or recouping, as was the case this day.

Rachel lay perfectly still on the sofa, for the slightest movement sent agonizing pain through every fiber of her body. And she hadn't known there were so many fibers to ache, so many muscles to hurt. A small pillow was beneath her head and her feet were thrown onto the arm of the sofa. A cool towel was draped over her face and she had pulled her wrapper up to her knees to reap full benefit from the breeze. But that was the only motion she had allowed herself. Indeed, any other movement was all but impossible.

She knew yesterday that she was making a mistake. Yet she had no idea that the ride would evolve into a colossal mistake until she had attempted to get out of bed this morning and found her limbs rebelling with waves of excruciating discomfort. Everything hurt. Hardly an inch of her body was spared. Her knees wouldn't allow her to stand, while her derriere refused to let her sit and her thighs anguished over either motion. Her arms and shoulders were so pained that she had not even been able to put up her hair. Somehow she had managed to get into a hot tub and soaked until the water cooled, thinking that would bring her some comfort. And it might have, but the water's healing effects were negated when she had had to climb out of the tub and the aching had returned. So she had sent Hannah to the park with Andrew and had fallen onto the sofa to suffer her misery in solitude.

There came a light rapping at her door. "Come in," she moaned. It was only the hotel's serving girl bringing the lemonade that Hannah had requested on her way out. Rachel had no intentions of rising from the sofa for any reason short of open fire or direct threat on her life.

She heard the door open, then close, and muffled footsteps on the rug that stopped at her feet. "Put it on the table and leave," she said sourly. Today she had no patience for the serving girl, who usually liked to chat. But when Rachel didn't hear the rattle of the tray or clinking of crystal glasses and pitcher, she realized something was amiss. She lifted the edge of the towel and peeped out. Good Lordy, it was Gray! And here she was reposing upon the sofa like a cheap strumpet flaunting her wares! Rachel jerked the towel from her face and sent it flying across the room, then yanked her wrapper over her exposed legs and jumped to her feet.

"Gray! What a—nice surprise!" She forced a smile and tried to look composed as she nervously tightened the sash of her wrapper and drew the garment together at her bosom.

"Have I caught you at an inopportune moment?" he inquired, and tried to make his wandering eyes focus on her face.

"Oh, no, no, of course not. It's only that I thought you were a girl."

His brows drew together. "I beg your pardon?" This was definitely not the response he had hoped to evoke in her!

"No, no. I meant that I was expecting the serving girl," she hastened to explain. Rachel ran her fingers through her hair trying to restore some order to the loose mass of curling tresses.

Gray's gaze swept her from head to toe. "Are you ill?" he asked with concern.

At once she was aware of the renewed aching in her muscles this sudden spurt of activity had brought on. She gritted her teeth and stretched her lips into a smile. "Oh, no. I am quite well." She was not about to tell the man that her behind hurt too much to sit down.

His eyes roamed the length of her once more, silently questioning her state of dress at this late hour, so Rachel fell back on her most durable, though overworked, excuse. "I was up with Andrew during the night," she said.

"Was he ill again?" he wanted to know.

Why wouldn't he just let it drop! Now she needed another lie to fortify the first. "It was a bad dream. He went right back to sleep, but I did not," she said, attempting to minimize her fabrication as much as possible.

"I had difficulty sleeping, too," Gray commented.

"It must have been the excitement of our ride yesterday," Rachel suggested.

For Gray, the excitement had been watching Rachel's soft, round bottom bouncing against the saddle, and he smiled broadly in response to her comment. "And I should certainly enjoy repeating that excitement."

A brief silence fell between them as Rachel fervently prayed that he would leave. She was standing perfectly still so as not to agitate her sore muscles, but her knees were screaming at her to sit down.

Gray laid his hat aside and her hopes fell. "I brought you something," he said, and reached into his pocket.

She managed a smile. "You shouldn't have," she insisted. *You should go away and let me suffer in private!*

He held up her lace handkerchief that he had fished out of the Ashley. "We became occupied . . . talking yesterday and I completely forgot to give this to you."

A genuine smile brightened her face. "I had forgotten it, as well. Thank you." She lifted her aching arm and took it from his hand and slipped it into her pocket. "How silly of me to forget after all you went through to get it back for me." They laughed together at the memory of their escapade in the river.

Gray drew in a deep breath. That memory reminded him of the lustful thoughts that had brought him to her suite, and the sight of her dressed in her wrapper did little to squelch his desires.

Obviously he intended to stay, though why he wanted to be in her company when she looked so awful was beyond her powers of reasoning. She had no choice but to be civil. "Would you care to sit down?" she inquired, inclining her head toward the sofa; it was the only part of her that didn't hurt.

"Yes, thank you," he replied, and moved to the sofa. He turned to her expectantly.

Rachel mentally kicked herself. Now look what she had done! A gentleman would never sit until the lady was seated first. She was her own worst enemy. Slowly, gingerly, she lowered herself onto the sofa and managed to keep her face expressionless as her limbs cried out in protest.

He watched her careful descent. "Rachel, are you sure you are all right?"

She looked up at him quickly. "Fine. I am fine."

He was much relieved to hear that and sat down next

to her. "I was by the bank earlier. My uncle will have the sale papers for the mercantile ready in a few days."

A knock sounded at the door. Rachel ignored it. "Good. I planned to see Bernard soon."

The noise at the portal was repeated with stronger intensity.

"I want to check on the documents for the purchase of my house," she continued, oblivious to the sound that was repeated a third time.

"Rachel, there is someone at your door," Gray felt compelled to say.

"Oh?"

"Don't you want to see who it is?"

There was no way on God's green earth that Rachel was going to get up and walk to the door with Gray ogling her every awkward movement. Absolutely no way! "Perhaps I can sign all the papers at once."

What got into this woman at times! "Rachel, someone is at the door," he repeated, speaking more slowly this time.

"Yes, I know." She looked straight at him, refusing to acknowledge the knocking that sounded again. "I believe I will ask Bernard if he can arrange that."

Gray slapped his hands on his knees and stood up. He would answer the damned thing himself! He strode purposefully across the room, opened the door, and allowed the serving girl bearing glasses and a pitcher of cold lemonade to enter. She placed the tray on the table in front of the sofa and left the room quietly.

Rachel winced. Now she would have to pour. What else could go wrong? "Lemonade?" she asked sweetly.

He stood at the end of the sofa, his fists resting on his narrow hips, contemplating her. He never knew what to expect next from this woman. One minute she was stubborn and pridefully determined to do things herself, and the next she was soft and vulnerable and very much in need of someone to take care of her. Sharp-witted, bold, funny, but with an underlying innocence that made his heart reach out for her.

Rachel looked up at Gray and saw his blue eyes darken with passion, and she realized just exactly what else could go wrong. She stood quickly, despite the pain it brought her. "It was so nice of you to come by. Good day."

He showed not the slightest intention of leaving and walked toward her instead. His hand took one of hers and with the other he brushed a stray lock of hair from her face. "You are a beautiful woman, Rachel Fontaine," he said softly. His fingers lingered to stroke her blond hair, then dug beneath those voluminous tresses to work their magic upon her nape.

His touch robbed her strength. She was vulnerable to his caresses, his nearness, and overpowered by his masculinity. For so long she had dreamed of his warm gentle hands against her skin that she had no will to stop him as he tilted her face upward and slanted his mouth over hers. His lips covered hers hungrily and his tongue pushed past her teeth. His kiss became more demanding and his hand dropped to her waist and eased its way upward to cup her breast. Rachel's blood turned white-hot as his stroking thumb brought her to life. She lifted her arms to encircle his neck, drawing him nearer.

His hands moved to her back and slid downward over her hips to the curve of her derriere. The softness of her flesh sent desire pumping through his veins and he pulled her closer, molding her against him, pressing her nearer.

Rachel suddenly cried out. He released her instantly

and looked at her with wide eyes. Never had a woman in his arms sounded pained. How had he injured her? "Rachel, I didn't mean to hurt you," he apologized, and his eyes ran the length of her trying to determine exactly where the damage had been inflicted.

"It's not your fault." The agony she was experiencing showed plainly in her expression and her hand went instinctively to her bottom. "I am just a little . . . stiff, that's all."

He watched as she slowly made her way toward the sofa. "Stiff? You can hardly walk, woman. What is wrong?"

"Nothing. I am fine." Couldn't she be spared this humiliation?

It was obvious that she was not fine and Gray grew angry at her prideful insistence. "Did you fall? Did you injure yourself? You were all right during our ride yesterday."

She looked up at him with guilty eyes and he realized what the problem was.

"Damn," he swore under his breath. Now he was angry at himself. "It is all my fault. I should have known better than to take you out riding all day. What was I thinking of? How stupid of me."

"Oh, stop grumbling," she scolded. "I will recover and no permanent damage has been done. I had a wonderful time yesterday and I would do the same thing over again, despite my current condition."

He considered her words. "Do you mean that?"

Rachel looked at him squarely. "Yes, I do," she told him. "Though I do admit it wouldn't bother me to know that you were suffering, too."

"I am suffering, madam," he assured her. "Perhaps

not in the same way as you, but believe me, I am suffer-ing."

Well, his plans for the afternoon were shot to hell. He took Rachel's arm and gently lowered her to the sofa, then lifted her small ankles to stretch out her legs. He placed the pillow behind her head. "You stay there," he in-structed as he looked down on her. She looked so pretty that for an instant his thoughts betrayed his baser needs. Guiltily, he pushed his desires aside. "Rachel, you should have told me you weren't well."

Her eyes widened indignantly and she informed him, "I was not about to tell you that my—" Color rose in her cheeks and she looked away.

Gray chuckled. Perhaps that was asking a bit much. He knelt down beside her and took her hand. His eyes cap-tured her. "Too much pride can be a bad thing," he pointed out wisely.

She smiled. "I shall consider your advice."

Somehow, he doubted that she would. Gray placed a soft kiss on her forehead, and after making her promise to rest, he took his hat and left the suite.

Chapter 9

Her guests were milling about happily chatting with one another, and Charlotte Wade was pleased by the turnout this afternoon. One never knew what to expect on an occasion such as this, so she had prepared for a large gathering and was glad now that she had. She scanned the faces in her parlor noting who of the guests she had expected had not yet arrived, and to her surprise saw her nephew appear in the doorway. She was even more surprised to see Claudia Danforth on his arm.

"Gray, I am so pleased that you came," Charlotte said as she approached the couple. "To tell you the truth, I was afraid you wouldn't be here."

He kissed her cheek. "How could I refuse your gracious invitation that threatened me with my own life if I didn't?"

Charlotte smiled. "Oh, Gray, you are such a tease." She turned her attention to Claudia, who had been busy taking in the crowd. "It's so nice to see you again, dear. We haven't seen each other in much too long."

Claudia cast a sultry smile at Gray. "I expect that will be changing," she predicted. She squeezed his arm. "Please excuse me, darling, I must go speak to Rosemary Michaels." Claudia sauntered away.

An expectant smile showed on Charlotte's face.

"Don't jump to conclusions," Gray warned quickly, and passed his hat to the waiting servant. "Claudia's carriage arrived just as I rode up and we simply walked in together."

"Oh, Gray," she fretted. "I hate to speculate on what your dear mother must think of me."

He patted her hand consolingly. "Now, now, Aunt Charlotte, don't worry yourself so. You have tried your level best to get me to the altar, but I have not cooperated. Perhaps your matchmaking talents would be better spent on someone else."

Her face brightened. "I believe you are right. As a matter of fact, I expect to see some results this afternoon."

Gray followed his aunt's line of vision to the center of the room where three men stood surrounding Mrs. Rachel Fontaine. "What is this?" he wanted to know.

Charlotte looked altogether pleased with herself. "Rachel has been in Charleston for weeks and has not met one eligible man. So, I took it upon myself to invite several young men here this afternoon to meet her."

A scowl crossed his face. "But, Aunt Charlotte, she is a widow."

"She is also a very beautiful young woman. Besides, her husband has been dead since before her son was born and the lad is nearly a year old." She nodded knowingly. "Some man will snatch her up quickly, mark my words."

"Does she know you are doing this?" he wanted to know.

"Of course not. That would take the fun out of it."

The whole idea made Gray very uncomfortable. "Just who are these . . . men?" He glared at the group. "Isn't that Ben Whittington, the clerk at Bernard's bank? Good God, Aunt Charlotte, he is only a boy."

"Gray, your language," she scolded. "Ben is a year or so older than Rachel, and your uncle says he is a very dedicated employee."

"He is much too young to take on the responsibility of a wife," Gray insisted. "Besides, what woman would want redheaded children?"

"Gray, please, there are ladies present," she whispered. "Is that Adam Greely?"

"Oh, yes. Wouldn't he and Rachel make a most attractive couple?"

"No," he said sourly, eyeing the stocky, brown-haired man. "Since he took over his father's gunsmith shop last year the family is nearly bankrupt. He's got no manners, no couth—he belches out loud in public. Really, Aunt Charlotte, you don't think Rachel would be interested in him, do you?"

"Surely you don't think she will go through the rest of her life alone."

Those words struck Gray hard. Actually, he hadn't considered that she wouldn't.

"Do be a dear, Gray, and behave yourself when the music begins," Charlotte requested.

Gray gave his aunt his assurance that his boyhood antics would not be repeated, and after she had gone to attend to other matters, turned his attention to Rachel once more. The three men were still gathered around her, and they were all talking and laughing and appeared to be greatly enjoying themselves. That, in itself, irritated

193

him for a reason he couldn't pin down. Then he suddenly recognized the third man in the group to be Phillip Newbury, the swarthy-looking heir to the prestigious Newbury Hall plantation. His wealth was considerable, or it would be when old man Newbury died, and Phillip was considered handsome, though Gray never understood why. He was a true ladies' man, dashing and bold, able to steal a woman's heart with his charms, a rogue who made a game of acquiring women. Gray had heard rumors that Phillip had pursued Claudia while they were engaged and Gray was away on one of his many business trips, and he had suspected that Claudia had encouraged him, as the wealth of the Newbury family would have appealed to her; he never found out whether Phillip had caught her or not. But certainly the man was far too experienced for Rachel. It would be child's play for him to ease himself into her heart—and her bed—and leave her, as he had so many others once his conquest was achieved. And Gray was not about to stand by and let that happen.

Gray walked over to their small circle. "Good afternoon," he greeted.

Rachel eyed him coolly. "Good afternoon, Mr. Montgomery."

The men exchanged a greeting, though none of the three seemed anxious to have yet another possible suitor join their ranks. When they failed to step aside and allow Gray into their circle, he slipped his shoulder between Rachel and Ben Whittington and forced his way in.

"I believe these other gentlemen will agree that your appearance here today brightens this occasion for all of us," Gray told her as he appraised the blue print gown she wore.

"Thank you," she replied crisply, and turned her attention immediately to Ben. "Please go on with the story you were telling before we were interrupted," she urged. But she didn't listen to a word the auburn-haired man said as she fumed angrily over Gray's presence beside her. What nerve he had! She had seen Gray come in with Claudia stuck to him like flypaper, and now here he was standing next to her. What sort of game was he playing? Whatever he was up to, Rachel wanted no part of it—or him.

She realized Ben had ended his anecdote when she heard the others laugh, and quickly she joined in.

"Mrs. Fontaine, I haven't seen you at one of these functions before," Adam said. "I am certain I would have remembered you."

She turned her most charming smile on the broad-chested man. "This is the first I have attended since my arrival in Charleston. I do enjoy good music."

"I am afraid, my dear, you will find there is little here that resembles good music. After all, this is a piano recital," Phillip said, and they all laughed.

"Nonetheless, I am very pleased that Charlotte invited me. It has put me in the company of such interesting gentlemen." Her gaze swept the three men, pointedly ignoring Gray. "But if the music is so bad, why do you come?"

"Why, to meet beautiful ladies, of course," Phillip said, his eyes raking over her.

Rachel laughed gently. "Mr. Newbury, you say the most outlandish things," she declared.

Gray was ready to put his fist through Phillip Newbury's outlandish mouth when Charlotte announced that the recital was beginning. Instead, he offered his arm to Rachel. "Shall we be seated?"

She turned her frosty gaze on him. "I believe you have an escort, Mr. Montgomery."

Adam butted between them and led Rachel away on his arm.

Gray could do nothing but stand there and watch as Phillip fell into step beside her and Ben hurried along behind. Nothing, that is, but silently curse his luck and himself for giving the impression that Claudia was his escort this afternoon.

The straight-backed chairs were arranged in a semicircle around the piano, and Rachel seated herself a few chairs from the end. There was considerable scrambling among the men, and when it was all settled Ben Whittington was on her left and Adam Greely was seated on her other side. Phillip was relegated to the spot beside Adam, much to his displeasure.

"Let's be seated, dear," Claudia crooned as she slid her arm through Gray's.

He was occupied watching Rachel and had not noticed Claudia's approach. Since he could not be openly rude to her in public, he allowed himself to be taken in tow.

"No, Claudia, let's sit over here," Gray said when Claudia stopped by the seats she had selected. "The acoustics are much better."

She looked at him in surprise. "Why, darling, what do you care of acoustics? You don't even like these recitals." He raised a doubtful brow at her and she responded with a knowing smile. "I know of a great many things you do like. Remember?"

Gray ignored her remark and moved on to the seats he preferred. Claudia sat down with him. As he had planned, he was directly across the semicircle from Rachel.

What an ego! To position himself so she would have no

choice but to look at him, Rachel fumed. She would not give him the satisfaction, she vowed and lifted her chin regally turning her attention elsewhere.

Miss Marshall, who had taught music in the county for more years than anyone cared to count, stood and an obedient hush fell over the gathering. Her white hair was drawn back in a severe knot and her tight lips left no doubt as to who was in charge of both the musicians and the audience. She delivered a lengthy opening welcome before introducing the first student, a young girl of about nine years. The child took her seat at the piano and began to play a plodding, lifeless piece that gave every indication that a long afternoon lay ahead.

Despite Rachel's best efforts, her eyes wandered back to look at Gray. Well, she could hardly help it since the arrogant so-and-so had placed himself in front of her. He was already watching her, and Rachel cut her eyes away quickly, renewing her vow to ignore him. After a few moments her gaze was drawn back to him and he smiled and gave her a flirtatious wink. A wink! There he sat with Claudia practically in his lap, and he had the gall to wink at her!

Rachel drew in a determined breath and turned her attention to the other guests. It had been a quarter hour with the same little girl still at the keyboard, and an untold number of students were still to perform. She scanned the faces in the audience and with the exception of Claudia, who seemed enthralled with the proceedings, everyone appeared quite bored already.

Her line of vision found its way back to Gray. Their eyes locked just as a sour note sounded and Gray winced in response. He looked so comical that Rachel nearly laughed aloud. As the next two students proved to be even less talented than the first, Gray's antics continued, much to Rachel's amusement. He made funny faces and rolled his eyes, and as a particularly awful piece of music continued to worsen, he fashioned his fingers into the shape of a gun and pretended to shoot himself in the head, causing Rachel to bite down on her lip to keep from laughing. Claudia glanced his way once or twice and each time he instantly wiped the playful grin from his face and stared intently at the piano, like a schoolboy nearly caught by his teacher in some mischievous act. Then he would turn to Rachel again and they would share a conspiratorial smile. The show that Gray was putting on for Rachel was much more entertaining than the recital, and he seemed to be thoroughly enjoying himself. That is, until Charlotte suddenly appeared behind him and tapped his shoulder. Rachel saw the grin fall from his face as he looked up and saw his aunt scowling at him. Her silent reprimand caused him to lower his eyes guiltily, and he sat up straight in his chair and turned his attention to the music in earnest. After he was sure Charlotte had returned to her seat, he stole a glance at Rachel. She had covered her mouth with her hand to muffle the giggles that refused to be suppressed. He captured her eyes and he began to laugh with her, and it was only the timely ending of the music and round of applause that saved them both from public embarrassment.

When the last student had concluded her performance, the guests adjourned to the back portico and garden where refreshments were being served. An odd wave of disappointment washed over Gray as he saw Rachel accept Ben Whittington's arm and leave the parlor.

By the time Gray had endured his aunt's stern lecture, offered his profuse apology, then escorted her to the portico, Rachel was already seated on the wicker sofa flanked by Ben and Adam.

"You see, Rachel has attracted several men already," Charlotte said with a note of triumph in her voice.

Gray snorted. "I don't think you should be interfering with the lives of other people."

"I have done all the interfering I intend to do. Now, we shall just stand back and let fate take its natural course." Charlotte moved on to mingle with her guests.

He didn't like it, not one bit. The freckle-faced Ben was nearly drooling all over Rachel with lust, and Adam Greely, the big lummox, wouldn't know how to treat a lady if his life depended upon it. And that bastard Newbury was watching her from across the portico like a spider waiting for the fly to fall into his trap. The more Gray looked at Rachel, the more his gut ached. She was all wrong for any of them, too young, too vulnerable, too inexperienced. She would only end up getting hurt. Gray could not let that happen. She was his friend, right? Well, all right, he admitted to himself, maybe she was more than a friend. A good friend. No, that wasn't right, either. A special friend? He thought of the times he had held her delicate form in his arms and kissed her sweet lips, and the memory increased the gnawing inside him. Then he felt annoyed with himself. No, she wasn't a special friend, or a good friend, or anything more than a friend. Just that. A friend. And, as a friend, he owed it to Rachel to protect her from these three men who were each totally wrong for her. As his aunt had said, fate would take its natural course, and Gray intended to see that it did just that.

He casually strolled to the refreshment table where Rosemary Michaels stood. She and Claudia had been close friends since childhood, and Gray knew that whatever one learned, the other knew of in a matter of moments.

"Good afternoon," he greeted. Gray had fallen out of favor with Rosemary when he broke off his engagement to Claudia, but gradually over the last few months she had come to be a trifle more than civil to him.

"I was shocked to see you here today," Rosemary commented. "Especially since you used to refuse to attend these functions with Claudia."

Gray ignored her barb. "I am glad I came today. To tell you the truth, I hadn't believed all those rumors. But seeing it with my own eyes made a believer out of me."

Her eyes flashed. "Rumors? What rumors?"

"The rumors that Phillip Newbury is infatuated with Claudia. It's all over town. Come now, Rosemary, surely you have heard."

She looked surprised. "Oh, well, yes, of course I have heard."

"That is why Phillip came to the recital. He hasn't taken his eyes off of her all afternoon. Did you notice that?" Gray leaned down and spoke softly. "I overheard him say that he wanted to take Claudia home."

Rosemary's eyes grew round as saucers. "Really? Phillip Newbury?"

Gray nodded discreetly. "Don't tell anyone where you heard that."

"I won't," she vowed, and headed directly to the garden where Claudia stood.

"Phillip, you never cease to amaze me," Gray swore as he joined the man on the steps. "I don't know how you do it, but you manage to charm away the heart of every woman you meet."

He smiled. "I suppose you are referring to the lovely Mrs. Fontaine."

"Who?"

"Mrs. Rachel Fontaine," he said, nodding toward the sofa where she sat.

"Her? That skinny girl?" Gray questioned. "No, I was speaking of Claudia Danforth."

Phillip's eyes warmed as he turned to gaze at her full, round curves. "She is quite a beauty. Maybe not so beautiful as Mrs. Fontaine, but beautiful in her own way."

Gray knew exactly what Phillip was thinking. "It's no secret that she is quite taken with you," Gray divulged. "I overheard her telling someone that she hoped you would offer to drive her home. There was some mention of a buggy ride along the river, but I didn't catch what that was all about. How do you do it? Tell me your secret." Gray was relieved when Phillip walked away without another word.

"Excuse me," Gray said when he stopped at the sofa where Rachel sat. "Ben, could I see you for a moment?" He looked at Rachel. "So sorry to interrupt."

She had noted that same devilish look in Gray's eye when he was carrying on so during the recital and she wondered now what he was up to. She watched as the two men moved a short distance away and talked quietly for only a moment. Ben looked suddenly disappointed and Gray gave him a consoling pat on the back before the younger man disappeared into the house.

Gray returned to the sofa. "Ben asked me to give you his apologies. He just received word from Bernard that he was needed back at the bank on an urgent matter."

"But your uncle gave him the afternoon off," Rachel said

Gray shrugged his wide shoulders. "That is the life of a clerk, I suppose."

"Too bad," Adam said, none too sympathetically, easing his big frame closer to Rachel.

"Mrs. Fontaine, you look parched. May I have the honor of getting you a glass of punch?" Gray asked chivalrously.

"Yes, thank you."

"Don't get up, Adam. Let me fetch it for the lady," Gray said.

Adam was on his feet immediately. "I'll get it for the lady."

"Whatever you say," Gray conceded. He gave Rachel a small smile and followed Adam to the refreshment table. "That Mrs. Fontaine is something else, isn't she? I mean, of course, for a woman her age."

Adam scoffed. "She is just a young thing."

"That is what I thought, too," Gray admitted. "Someone told me she was nearly thirt—Well, it's not my place to spread rumors. But I suppose she has a few years on her. After all, she has those four children."

"Four?" Adam exclaimed. "She doesn't look like she has borne four children."

"Isn't it amazing what a good corset can do for a woman?"

Adam sank deeper into his own thoughts. "Four children, huh?"

Gray laughed. "And all of them girls. Can you believe it? They must all favor her late husband because they are the homeliest children I have ever seen." He slapped Adam on the back. "Don't you pity the poor fool who marries her? He will be supporting those girls until his dying day."

Adam glanced back at Rachel. "Yes, a real pity," he muttered. "Listen, Gray, I have left the shop for too long already. Could you give this punch to Mrs. Fontaine for me?"

"Hum?" Gray asked. "Oh, well, certainly." He took two glasses and returned to the sofa, noting that Phillip and Claudia were nowhere to be seen. He presented Rachel with the beverage and sat down beside her.

She took a sip. "Where is Adam?"

"Who?"

"Adam. Adam Greely. The man you were speaking with a moment ago."

"Oh, Adam. He had to leave."

"So suddenly?"

Gray sampled the punch. "I suppose he is not much for social functions."

"He didn't even say good-bye."

"The man has no manners at all," Gray told her.

Rachel set her glass aside. "Speaking of manners, don't you think it's rude for a gentleman to ignore his escort?"

"Absolutely," Gray said. "But, as I said, he has the social graces of an ox."

She looked at him pointedly. "Then shouldn't you be sitting with Claudia?"

Gray's eyes locked with hers over the rim of his glass. He couldn't tell her that the reason he wasn't with Claudia was because he had used her to get rid of Phillip Newbury. "Claudia is not here," he said simply.

How nice! When his precious Claudia leaves, then he comes over to sit with her. "I see," Rachel responded, and with maximum effort managed to keep all emotion from her voice.

Gray put his glass on the table. He should explain to her about Claudia before she got the wrong idea. "Claudia and I—"

Rachel stood up quickly. "I have got to be going," she said. She absolutely refused to sit and listen to anything about Claudia Danforth.

"What a coincidence," Gray said, and got to his feet. "I was just leaving, too."

"That is a coincidence," Rachel agreed skeptically.

Gray took her arm and together they found Charlotte. She looked disappointed to see them.

"Where is Mr. Greely?" she wanted to know.

"Gone," Gray said quickly. "We are leaving, Aunt Charlotte."

"And young Ben?"

"He was called back to the bank," Rachel explained. She had never known a hostess so concerned over her guests.

She looked annoyed. "Bernard specifically told me Ben could have the afternoon off. I shall speak with him on the matter immediately."

"No, don't do that," Gray told her. Rachel and Charlotte both eyed him sharply. "Ben wanted to go back to work. You know what a dedicated young fellow he is."

"But, Gray, you told me Bernard sent for him," Rachel said.

Gray cleared his throat nervously. "Did I say that?" He ran his finger along the inside of his shirt collar; the thing seemed to be growing smaller under the two women's close scrutiny. "I think Ben is too young to know where his priorities lie," he said wisely. "Good-bye, Aunt Charlotte."

Rachel said a brief farewell before Gray took her arm and escorted her to the foyer.

"It's a lovely afternoon. Why don't we walk to your hotel?" Gray suggested as the servant presented his hat.

It was a fine afternoon and she would enjoy being in his company. "It's a lovely idea," she agreed with a smile.

Gray instructed the servant to send Rachel's carriage back to the livery and they left the Wades' home.

"I am glad to see you have recovered from our ride," Gray commented as he pulled on his hat.

Rachel couldn't help but laugh. "I am quite well, thank you." She didn't mention that it had taken the two full days since she had last seen Gray before she could sit comfortably.

"Then you are ready to go riding again," he assumed as they descended the steps of the front portico.

"No! I'm afraid my riding days were over long ago," she told him.

He smiled down at her. "Nonsense. You are an excellent rider and I know you enjoyed yourself. We will go again. But you have to promise not to push me in the river again."

"I did not push you in, though perhaps I should have," Rachel said as they strolled down the walkway. They both laughed.

Just as they reached the curb, Adam Greely rode up and dismounted. "I want to talk to you, Montgomery," he said, and jabbed a threatening finger in Gray's direction. He stopped in front of the couple. "I saw Bernard Wade just now, and he claims no one from the bank ever sent for Ben Whittington."

Gray glanced at Rachel then turned to Adam. "Thank you for coming to tell us that. Good day."

Adam stepped closer and blocked his path. "I don't believe anyone from the bank sent for Ben. Nor do I believe Phillip Newbury just happened to leave when he did.

And I sure don't believe all those things you said about Mrs. Fontaine."

"What things?" Rachel wanted to know.

"Calm yourself, Greely. We will discuss this later, after the lady has left," Gray said. *A lot later.*

"What things?" Rachel repeated.

"I believe you made it all up," Adam said angrily.

"This is not the time," Gray insisted.

"What things!"

"Did you think I was dumb enough to believe Mrs. Fontaine was thirty years old?" Adam wanted to know.

"Thirty!" Rachel exclaimed.

Gray glanced back and forth between Rachel and Adam. He would deal with Rachel's anger later. Right now Adam, who wasn't as tall as Gray but overshadowed him with sheer bulk, was much more of a threat.

"Bernard Wade told me she has only one child, not four, like you told me."

"Four! You told him I had four children!"

"And it's a boy, not four ugly little girls."

"Four ugly girls!" Rachel echoed.

"Let's all calm down," Gray urged. "I can explain—"

"I should have known you were lying, no matter what you said about her corset," Adam growled.

Rachel's cheeks flamed. "My *what!*"

"Adam, just hear me out—"

"You tried to make a fool of me, Montgomery, and I won't take that from any man. I demand satisfaction," Adam said heatedly. "I am challenging you to a duel."

Only an idiot would agree to duel with a gunsmith! "Adam, let's talk this out like gentlemen," Gray urged.

"I have heard enough of your smooth talking. Will you accept my challenge like a man?"

Adam's cold, hard eyes bored into Gray, and Rachel realized that he was dead serious. Though Gray deserved to suffer for the things he had said about her, Rachel didn't want Adam to shoot him. She would rather do that herself.

Rachel pushed her way between the men, drew back her hand, and slapped Gray's cheek. "You cad!" she spat angrily.

Stunned, he looked down at her blankly.

"I told you those things in confidence, and now I find that you are telling everyone of my four unfortunate daughters," she said indignantly. "You, sir, are not the gentleman I thought you were."

Gray rubbed his reddening cheek. "A thousand pardons, madam."

Adam Greely looked dumbfounded. "You mean it's true?"

"Thank you for your concern," Rachel said to him and held her head up proudly. "Do not waste your honorable intentions on this man. A duel would be meaningless."

"Yes, ma'am, I can see that." Adam mounted his horse and rode away.

Gray chuckled. "I am forever in your debt, Rachel. But was it necessary to put in so much realism?"

She whirled around, her eyes ablaze, and slapped his face with such force that it sent his ears to ringing. "Don't you *ever* speak to me again," she hissed, and flounced away.

By the time Gray collected his scattered wits, Rachel was halfway down the block and pulling away at a rapid pace. "Rachel, wait!" he called, and hurried after her.

He appeared beside her, but she kept her eyes determinedly forward. She was furious. Never—ever—had she been so angry.

"Rachel, wait, please. Listen to what I have to say," Gray begged.

"I think you have said quite enough for one day, Mr. Montgomery," she informed him.

Unlike most women who pouted and whined and caused a man to have to guess if they were upset or not, this one, by God, left no doubt in anyone's mind. Gray had no one to blame but himself. "I can explain," he said.

She tried with all her might to hold it in, but her anger burst forth like a volcano spewing hot lava. "Thirty! You told everyone I was thirty!"

"No, I didn't."

"Yes, you did!"

"I didn't tell everyone, only Greely," Gray explained.

"And am I supposed to thank you for that?" She still refused to look at him, but from the corner of her eye she could see him hurrying along beside her trying to make her acknowledge his presence. She wouldn't.

"Just stop for a minute and hear me out," Gray requested. He had no idea a woman so small could move with such speed.

"Four children! Girls! Four ugly girls!" she fumed. What had come over this man? Why on earth had he said such outrageous things about her?

"I had your best interests in mind when I said those things," he pointed out.

"What!"

"Greely was all wrong for you, as was Ben Whittington and that Newbury bastard," Gray told her.

Rachel was too upset to notice Gray's profanity. In fact, a few choice words were dangerously close to the end of her own tongue. "So you contrived to get rid of the three of them?"

"Yes, I did. But only because none of them was the right man for you," he explained.

She slowed her pace as she mulled over his words. Could this mean he truly cared for her? She stopped and faced him, and her hard expression softened. "And for what purpose have you appointed yourself my guardian angel?" she asked.

His hopeful blue eyes revealed the uncertainty in his soul. "Because . . . because I didn't want you to be hurt."

"Oh?" Her anger cooled.

He had finally gotten her attention and now he couldn't think of a damned thing to say. Why had he done and said such stupid things? Why had he been so concerned over her welfare? Why hadn't he wanted her to become involved with any of those men? Gray's throat felt suddenly dry and he shifted his feet nervously. "I didn't want you to be hurt because. . . . " Suddenly it came to him. "Because I look upon you as a sister."

Rachel ground her teeth and her eyes ignited with renewed fury. In a flurry of skirts and petticoats, she stomped away.

Good Lord, he had done it again. Gray raced to her side. "But—but not *my* sister," he explained desperately.

"I should have let Adam Greely shoot you!" Rachel didn't know what to think. First, he shows up with another woman. Then, he schemes to get rid of every man who shows the tiniest inkling of interest in her. Next, he wants to walk her home, only to reveal that he considers her a sister. A sister!

Every time he opened his mouth he only made things

209

worse. What was wrong with him? "Stop for a moment and let me—"

"Go away."

"Rachel—"

"Go away!"

"I will not go away. I am going to walk here beside you," he told her firmly.

"I don't care where you walk. Beside me, in front of me, across the street, *in* the street, it makes no difference at all," she told him.

Gray fell silent, knowing that anything else he said would only enrage her further. She needed some time to cool down.

Rachel could not believe they had reached her hotel so quickly. She was about to climb the stairs when Gray caught her arm and stopped her; she tolerated his touch only because she didn't want to make a scene in so public a place.

He searched her face for a modicum of forgiveness. There was none. "Didn't you ever tell a well-intentioned lie that was meant to save another person from heartache?" he asked.

Rachel felt like he had slapped her face. All the fight, all the anger went out of her and she was ashamed of herself for the way she had acted.

"I am sorry," Gray said softly. "I should not have done and said those things. I only did them because ... Well, I don't know why I did them. But I am sorry for them and I hope you will find it in your heart to forgive me." He turned and left her feeling very much alone.

Slowly, Rachel entered the hotel and climbed the stairs to her suite. Hannah greeted her at the door with Andrew in her arms.

"How was the recital?" she asked cheerfully.

"Dreadful." Rachel unpinned her bonnet and tossed it aside, then took Andrew into her arms. Even the baby could not improve her glum disposition.

"Was Mr. Montgomery there?" Hannah asked suggestively.

"Don't get any ideas about Gray Montgomery," Rachel said as they walked into the sitting room.

"Sounds like you two quarreled."

Rachel plopped down on the sofa and put Andrew among his toys on the floor at her feet. "Yes, I suppose you could call it a quarrel."

"Tell me what happened," Hannah instructed, and took the chair across from her.

Rachel sighed heavily. "I have no idea what came over him. It was all his fault."

"I'm certain it was."

"I was in the company of several other gentlemen, and Gray made up ridiculous stories to drive them away from me. Can you imagine? He told Mr. Greely I was thirty years old and had four children. Four ugly daughters. Why would he say that?" She tried to find some of her anger but could not.

Hannah began to laugh. "Has your husband been dead for so long that you have forgotten a man's way?"

That was the crux of the whole problem. Maybe if she had really been married, or at least courted, she would understand what went on in a man's mind. At any rate, Rachel did not share the humor Hannah had found in her situation. "Could you please tell me what is so funny?" she asked sourly.

"It's so obvious, Rachel. Mr. Montgomery was jealous."

"Jealous?" The notion had never occurred to her.

"He must care for you a great deal to go to such extreme measures," Hannah noted.

"No, I can't believe that," Rachel replied, though she would have liked to. "He told me he thinks of me as a sister."

Hannah nodded wisely. "Mr. Montgomery cares a great deal for you. Perhaps he doesn't realize it yet, but he cares."

Rachel didn't want to think about it. To be told, on the one hand, that Gray thought of her as a sister, and, on the other, that he was jealous and really cared a great deal, were extremes that her mind could not come to terms with. Besides, Gray's remark about well-intentioned lies had hit home with her.

She looked down at her dark-haired son. "Four daughters, indeed," Rachel muttered.

"Four ugly daughters," Hannah corrected, and began to laugh again.

A small smile chased away the frown from Rachel's face. "It is rather humorous, isn't it," she agreed and began to laugh in earnest. "And Adam Greely believed every word."

"Then perhaps Mr. Montgomery did you a favor by driving the man away," Hannah pointed out. The two women laughed together, and Andrew joined in with giggles of his own.

Presently Rachel rose and went into her bedchamber. She shed her heavy gown and undergarments and bathed in the cool water at the washstand. Though she wanted to stretch out on the bed and rest for a while, she dutifully dressed in a dark green gown to carry out her errands.

"I shall return soon," Rachel said, and placed a kiss on Andrew's curly hair. She adjusted her bonnet at the mirror in the sitting room and was about to depart when Hannah spoke.

"Don't be too hard on Mr. Montgomery," she urged. "Surely Mr. Fontaine did and said equally ridiculous things."

Rachel's stomach rolled over and she feared her dead, departed husband would haunt her for the rest of her natural life. Nevertheless, she could no longer find it in her heart to be angry with Gray. "I shall be back in time for supper," she said, and left the suite.

The afternoon sun was dipping toward the horizon as Rachel emerged from the hotel. She was getting a later start than she had planned but had no intentions of canceling her errands simply because of the hour. Besides, she could not tolerate the confines of her hotel suite right now. She needed to get out, to get some air, and focus her mind on something other than Mr. Gray Montgomery. As always, the man dominated her thoughts, and she wondered if she would see him again after the incident of this afternoon. She had no hold on him and had sought none, though he seemed anxious to seek out her company. Perhaps her harsh words this afternoon would send him back to Claudia for good. And on that depressing note, Rachel headed for the business district.

By the time she reached her destination she had convinced herself that brooding over her lot in life was pointless and that her efforts would be better spent preparing for the house she would soon be moving into. Ridding herself of a portion of her wealth seemed very much in order as she browsed through a general merchandise shop that was one of her favorites. The merchant was very attentive and aided her in that vein as she selected a delicately flowered china pattern, crystal, linens, and a host of

213

other items she had not intended to buy. But it made her feel good so she did it anyway, despite her conscience's warning her of the evils of reckless spending. She made arrangements for the goods to be delivered to her new home and informed the merchant that she would notify him when she was ready for delivery. She took one item with her, a small china figurine that he carefully wrapped. As she left the store, her eyes were on the horizon trying to estimate how much time remained before darkness would fall, and she nearly collided with a gentleman on the walkway. It was Gray.

He tipped his hat. "Good afternoon, madam," he said cautiously. She had been so angry with him that he wasn't sure how she would react at seeing him again so soon.

Rachel was so ashamed of the way she had carried on that she could hardly face him. But she pulled herself together, determined to put the unpleasant incident behind them. "How good to see you again, Gray," she greeted cheerfully.

He was taken aback by her sudden friendliness, but was not going to squander the opportunity to make amends. "Shopping?" he inquired, and glanced at the package she carried.

If Hannah could find humor in their quarrel, certainly Rachel could, too, and it seemed to Rachel to be an excellent way to mend fences.

"I have purchased some much-needed new garments," she told him. "It seems my matronly figure has given rise to a most unflattering rumor."

Gray dipped his gaze sheepishly. "Rachel, I ..." He tried to compose a fitting apology, but no words seemed adequate compensation for the things he had said, so he decided to tell her just that. He looked up, and her lovely face displayed a teasing smile that dispelled his worry. The tension between them broke and laughter took its place.

"I was on my way to see Adam Greely," Gray said.

She was flattered that he would confess his lie to set the record straight. "To tell him the truth?"

"No," he said, as if that was the most unreasonable suggestion he had ever heard.

"No?"

"I was going to tell him what a dim-witted oaf he is," he explained.

"Perhaps it would be better if you let the whole thing drop," Rachel suggested.

Gray nodded. Now that he was back in Rachel's good graces it did seem to be the sensible thing to do.

Noting that twilight had settled upon the city, Gray took the small package from Rachel and said, "Let me walk you to your carriage."

"I am without a carriage."

He looked annoyed. "No carriage? You are out alone at this late hour with no carriage? Rachel, it is not safe for a lady to be unescorted. Need I remind you of the incident of a few nights ago?"

Rachel clearly remembered how frightened she had been when she had unwittingly ventured into a disreputable section of the city, and how relieved she had been when her chance encounter with Gray had saved her from a potentially dangerous situation. But she was not going to stand still and be scolded like a child. Instead she smiled. "As I recall, a very gallant gentleman invited me to supper and I experienced a most enjoyable evening. So you can easily see that I have no fear of being on foot."

She always managed to get the best of him. How was a man supposed to stay angry when being favored with deep brown orbs that threatened to steal his soul? He could do nothing but offer his arm to her. "Then please allow me to escort you to the safety of your hotel."

Rachel slid her arm through his and they leisurely strolled through the streets. A comfortable rapport enveloped them as night closed in, and their amiable conversation made the journey pass all too quickly. Alone on the empty walkway, they stopped in the shadows of the buildings across from Rachel's hotel.

She didn't want to leave him. She didn't want to go inside. The lights from the hotel's windows showed favorably upon his handsome face and reminded her of the first time she had laid eyes on him. She had wanted to stay with him then, as now.

He tucked her package securely beneath his arm and took her hands. Instead of the familiar warmth that usually presented itself at such moments, there was a strange gnawing in his stomach. It was foreign to him, and annoying because he didn't understand it. But there was much that he did not understand about himself as of late. Nor this Mrs. Rachel Fontaine. She had awakened something within him, or altered something, or corrected something, or ... Well, whatever it was felt comforting and exciting at the same time, like two extremes pulling him in opposite directions.

Rachel's ivory skin seemed to glow in the dim light, and her brown eyes sparkled as she looked up at him. To kiss a woman in a public place was unthinkable. No gentleman would ever consider such an unspeakable act, regardless of how beautiful the woman, how inviting the lips, Gray reminded himself. A gentleman could not give in to desire on a main thoroughfare even if it was dark and no one else was about. And being tempted by a ruby mouth

216

that made his knees go weak, or creamy skin that begged to be touched, or—

His lips covered hers and a moan deep in his throat voiced the fulfillment he craved. Her sweet taste delighted him, satisfied him, yet made him want more. He pulled her closer, and the feel of her soft flesh against him sent his pulse to racing. His tongue slid past her parted teeth and eagerly reacquainted itself intimately.

Her feelings for him were most unladylike, to say nothing of her thoughts. His lips on hers, his arms around her, always struck a chord within her heart that threw caution and good sense to the wind. She had no thoughts of stopping him, because reliving the memory of the night in his bed had been all that got her through some desperately lonely evenings. She could not bring herself to call for an end to his embrace, his kiss.

Gray found a tiny shred of self-control and pulled his lips from her. His breathing was ragged as he released her. The innocence of her smile shook him, for the sight opened a door in his memory, opened it only a crack, and but for a split second. Yet a teasing recollection escaped and ricocheted through his brain. It vanished as quickly as it appeared without finding its target.

"Is something wrong?" Rachel asked. A frown was not what she expected to see on his face at this moment.

He shook his head to clear his thoughts. A rakish smile tugged at the corners of his mouth. "Everything is quite right. However, the timing is all wrong."

Rachel blushed, and accepted his arm to cross the street. They said a brief, considerably more respectable good night at the entry of her hotel, and Rachel took her package and went to her suite alone.

"I saved your dinner for you, but it's probably cold by

now," Hannah said when Rachel entered the sitting room. She had Andrew on her lap and he was chewing on the book she had been reading to him.

"I am not very hungry," Rachel said. She walked past her son, which was most unusual because she always gave the child a hug and kiss upon her arrival home, and went to the window that overlooked the street. She pulled back the drape and caught a fleeting glimpse of Gray as he disappeared down the street.

"Did you make your purchases?" Hannah asked.

"Hmm?"

"Your purchases," Hannah repeated. Rachel had become quite distracted lately and she had thought it was due to the burden of buying a business and acquiring a home. Now Hannah began to suspect that there was more to it than that.

"Oh, yes," Rachel replied, and turned away from the window. She handed Hannah the package and took her son into her arms. "How was Andrew today?"

Hannah was in the middle of the detailed recounting of the baby's day that Rachel always insisted upon when a knock sounded at the door. She left mother and son to answer it and returned a moment later bearing an arrangement of fresh colorful flowers wrapped in delicate paper.

"These are for you," she announced.

Rachel was shocked. "Me? Who could they be from?"

Hannah held up a small card. "My intuition tells me you and I both know who sent these."

"Don't you dare suggest Adam Greely," Rachel threatened. Holding Andrew in one arm, she opened the card and written in bold script was simply "Gray." Her smile told Hannah all she needed to know.

"I suppose this puts an end to the quarrel once and for all," Hannah said wisely.

Rachel traded Andrew to Hannah for the flowers and plucked a deep red rose from the arrangements. The flowers and the sentiment were equally beautiful. She walked to the window and saw Gray standing in the streetlight in front of the tobacco shop. Rachel sniffed the flowers' delicate fragrance and waved to him. He tipped his hat. The distance between them seemed to shorten and Rachel's heart swelled with the love she felt for him.

He wished he could have written something clever on the card, but words, at least the right words, had failed him lately. So Gray had signed only his name to the card he had purchased with the flowers and slipped the street vendor extra coins to deliver them. His words were wrong, he did strange things, he couldn't sleep well, and worst of all, he could not understand why these things were happening to him. He wasn't the type of man to be out of control, and he had surprised himself at some of the things he had done and said lately. Even his powers of reasoning had taken a strange turn. Bits and pieces of memories flashed in his mind. But were they memories, or just his imagination? He didn't know, because whatever they were they passed too swiftly and were too hazy to be analyzed. No matter, he decided. He dismissed his concern and watched Rachel at the window as she waved again, then let the curtain fall shut. The problems that plagued him of late seemed unimportant as he turned and walked down the street, whistling contentedly to himself.

Chapter 10

Bernard Wade sat in silence behind his massive desk at the bank, his hands folded patiently in his lap, waiting. He stole a quick glance across the room at his nephew, who paced the floor with hands clasped behind his back. Their eyes met for an instant acknowledging the tedium of the situation. Neither man spoke. Gray continued his carefully measured steps around the room. Bernard turned his attention once again to the blond woman seated across from him.

She had waited over a week for the papers to be prepared, and now Rachel intended to study them carefully and know exactly what they contained before signing her name to them. Bernard had already explained them thoroughly and answered all her questions—and she had had many—but she still wanted to read the documents herself. After all, it was not everyday one purchased both a business and a home.

Gray broke from his pacing and came to stand by her

chair. Bending down, he said softly, "Rachel, my dear, we are not trying to entrap you in any way."

Rachel looked up at him, unaware of the many minutes that had passed or the impatience the men shared. Her dark eyes sparkled as they reflected the lights in the office. Gray's heart fluttered; the sight of her always affected him that way now.

"I learned long ago that some people think widows are easy targets for deceit," Rachel said evenly, then added, "I am glad that is not the case here." She turned back to the stacks of paper and resumed her reading.

Gray straightened up, shrugged his shoulders helplessly, and began pacing once more. Bernard sat back in his chair. When Rachel announced her approval of the contracts both men watched with relief as she signed her name. Gray took the quill and hurriedly scrawled his name beside hers. Now it was official. The mercantile was hers.

"Since it has been rather a long, tedious morning might I suggest we have a bite to eat?" Gray suggested. "Uncle, won't you join us?"

Bernard was busy shuffling the papers into their proper order. "No, no, I have another appointment waiting."

Gray turned to Rachel. "Shall we?"

"Yes," she said, returning his smile. "But first I must stop at the mercantile."

Gray nodded in agreement and they departed, leaving Bernard to attend to his next customer and a full day of appointments all far behind schedule.

Rachel entered her new business filled with a sense of pride and purpose. Her enthusiasm was not diminished by the lack of patrons or the half-empty shelves.

"I will have the carpenters in first to make the necessary changes," she said excitedly," then I will meet with the captain of the next ship that docks and make arrangements to purchase his cargo, if it meets my requirements."

Gray followed behind as Rachel moved up and down the aisles enjoying her excitement. "Just a moment," he interrupted. "I don't want you meeting with any ship's captain alone."

She stopped and turned to him. "It is business."

"To you, yes. But I do not think all men of the sea share your high standards of integrity," Gray pointed out as delicately as possible.

Rachel's cheeks reddened. "Oh, I hadn't thought of that," she murmured.

Gray chuckled and took her hand. "Never fear, my sweet, I would consider it an honor to arrange and escort you to such a meeting."

The shuffling of feet drew their attention to the back of the store where a balding man appeared in the doorway of the small office. "Help you folks?" he called as he rubbed his eyes.

"Good day, Mr. Rhodes," Gray called.

The man settled his spectacles into place. "Oh, it's you. Didn't recognize you, Mr. Montgomery. I was just, ah, going over the books."

From the looks of his rumpled shirt Rachel thought it more likely he was having a nap.

"Mr. Rhodes, I would like to present the new owner of this establishment, Mrs. Rachel Fontaine," Gray announced.

"New owner, huh?" Mr. Rhodes said, and turned his attention to Rachel.

"Mr. Rhodes has been the manager here for about ten years," Gray said.

"A woman. Hmm," Mr. Rhodes said thoughtfully. He

shrugged his slim shoulders. "Well, good luck to you, madam. Hope you can make a better go of it here than the last six owners have."

"Six?" Rachel turned to Gray. "How long did you own it?"

"About eight months or so. Actually, I won it in a card game," he admitted.

"When you were so reluctant to sell I assumed you held a great attachment to the place," Rachel said.

Gray did not want to reveal that his real reason for refusing to sell was simply to use it as an excuse to see her. "But I did," he assured her.

"Couldn't tell it by me," Mr. Rhodes grumbled. "Hardly saw you in here more than a dozen times."

Rachel eyed Gray suspiciously before turning her attention to Mr. Rhodes. "I have many changes in mind, beginning with extensive remodeling."

Mr. Rhodes shrugged. "Whatever you say, Mrs. Fontaine. Don't make no never mind to me."

"Please, Rachel, let us go eat," Gray pleaded. "I fear I may perish from hunger and that would certainly spoil your grand opening."

"Very well," she agreed reluctantly. "Mr. Rhodes, I will be back tomorrow."

"As you wish," the man said as he stifled a yawn and headed back to the office.

Moving day, at last. Rachel and Hannah rose early and anxiously packed their belongings. Their caravan of luggage across the hotel's lobby was even lengthier than when they arrived. This time Andrew walked, his hand held tight in Rachel's as she steadied his often faltering steps.

"My lands, Rachel, I just can't believe this fine house will be our home," Hannah exclaimed as their carriage came to a halt. "This surely is a long way from St. Joseph."

Rachel laughed. "Indeed it is."

The ladies and Andrew climbed down and Rachel immediately took charge as Hannah carried Andrew inside. She stood by the carriage which bore their belongings and instructed the men she had hired on where each piece should be delivered. Then she moved inside and began coordinating the activities there. She took off her bonnet and shawl and surveyed the work that lay ahead. There was much to be done, but with the help of the five house servants it could be accomplished swiftly.

The two housemaids, Selma and Pearl, were directed to begin cleaning the downstairs. The cook, Cloe, was sent to begin preparation of the noon meal. Agnes, who served as the washerwoman and seamstress, was sent to unpack the chests that had been delivered upstairs, while the butler, Philo, hovered about Rachel, opening doors and assisting her in every way imaginable.

"Rachel, I just don't know what to think about all of this," Hannah whispered as they stood in the parlor amid the swirl of activity.

"Don't think about it, just enjoy it," Rachel said with an impish grin.

"But—but all these servants," Hannah exclaimed. "What am I to do?"

Rachel smiled at her friend. "You have only to look after Andrew and have them do everything else."

Hannah nodded thoughtfully then took Andrew by the hand and they set off to explore their new home.

Throughout the morning deliveries were made to the

house, adding to the hustle and bustle. New linens and fine china were brought in and carefully uncrated. The house had come with a good bit of furniture, but Rachel had bought a great deal more. New chairs were placed in the parlor along with a new mantel clock. A large, gracefully carved desk was moved into the study. A more fashionable set of drapes had been made for the parlor and she had put Agnes to work hanging them. Box after box arrived as a steady stream of deliveries were made throughout the morning. Rachel was constantly on the go directing the servants and delivery men and instructing them on how things should be handled. Of course the placement of the furniture was not to her liking so Rachel sent for her new coachman, Jim, who assisted Philo in rearranging. The men had tirelessly moved the heavy sofa for a third time when Rachel was interrupted by a voice behind her.

"Gray!" she exclaimed when she turned and saw him standing in the doorway. She quickly scanned the surrounding area and said a silent prayer that Andrew would be upstairs.

"Did I startle you?" he asked as he strode into the room.

"Yes—no—yes, well, yes, somewhat," she said, then collected herself. "It's just that I had not expected to see you."

"I thought I would come by and offer my help." Gray looked around at everyone busy at work. "But it appears that you have everything under control."

"Miz Rachel, this sofa be powerful heavy," Philo called in a strained voice.

She turned and saw the men still holding the sofa awaiting her next instruction. "Put it over there near the window," she said quickly. "Do you like it there?" she asked Gray.

He watched as the sofa was put in place. "It looks fine," he offered.

"No, you are right, it looks awful," Rachel said. "Have them move it back, would you? And if you will excuse me, I will be right back."

She rushed from the room before Gray could answer. Quickly she went from room to room looking for Hannah and Andrew. When she didn't find them, she hiked her dress up past her knees and took the steps two at a time. To her relief she found them in Andrew's room. "Hannah, I think you should take Andrew to the park," she said breathlessly.

"But why? He is very content playing here."

"Well, there is just too much activity and I am afraid he will get too keyed up to sleep," Rachel told her as she watched Andrew offer an untimely yawn.

Hannah smiled. "This is the calmest child I have ever known."

"Please, Hannah, take him out," she said, trying to keep the sound of desperation from her words.

"All right, whatever you say." She gathered Andrew's things and the trio left the nursery together. At the top of the stairs Rachel stopped.

"Wait here just a moment, then come down. I want to be sure the workmen are out of the way," Rachel said.

"But, Rachel—" Hannah protested.

She didn't stop to listen as her feet flew down the stairs and into the parlor. There, Gray stood fumbling with his hat while Jim and Philo waited obediently by the sofa.

"The sofa looks beautiful there. You were so right, Gray," Rachel said breathlessly as she swept into the room.

"That is where it was before," Gray said.

Rachel took his arm and pulled him across the room. "Gray, I simply must show you the desk I purchased."

"Rachel, dear, are you all right?" Gray asked as he allowed himself to be carried along.

Rachel glanced nervously at the staircase as they crossed the hall and saw Hannah and Andrew beginning their descent. Quickly she pushed Gray into the study ahead of her, then followed him and closed the door behind her.

"Rachel, what is wrong with you?" Gray asked as he regained his balance.

She leaned back against the door trying to still her pounding heart. "Why, nothing," she said innocently. She listened carefully until she heard Hannah's footsteps go past the study and the front door close. "I just wanted you to see the paintings."

"I thought you wanted to show me the desk." He didn't understand her sudden nervousness.

"Well, yes, I did," she said as she gathered her composure and walked over to join him in the center of the room where she had flung him. "But I thought you might enjoy seeing the paintings as well."

Gray looked about the room, its walls devoid of any ornamentation. "What paintings?"

"Oh, well, they are over here in these boxes. I still have so many things to unpack." Rachel led the way to several packing crates and boxes which lined the wall. Suddenly she saw that in one of the open boxes, among some of her personal effects, was Gray's pocket watch that she had taken from him in St. Joseph. She froze in her tracks as panic threatened to overtake her. Then she whirled to face Gray and he had to stop suddenly to keep from walking into her. "But first, I really need your help with the sofa."

She smiled sweetly. "I just can't seem to decide where it looks best," she added helplessly.

Gray studied her for a moment. A woman who had run a successful business, traveled halfway across the country with a baby, purchased a house and another business was more than capable of deciding on the placement of a sofa. He did not understand why she was acting this way. It was totally unlike her. But, well, maybe the strain of business and moving was too much for her, he decided, and he was glad that she needed him for something, though it was a menial task.

"Very well, let's see to that sofa," Gray said with a grin. Women! Who could figure what went on in their pretty heads?

Rachel heaved a silent sigh of relief. She could thank Claudia and her bonnet for the use of that ploy, though it troubled her to act as whiny and helpless as Claudia had when she had stolen Gray away to assist in her selection at the millinery shop. But it had worked and that was all that mattered. Taking Gray's arm, she led him out of the study and closed the door firmly behind them.

It was well after sundown and Andrew was sleeping and Hannah was hard at work on her sampler in her room. Rachel sat miserably alone at her new desk in the study. In her hand she held the pocket watch that had been Gray's. She turned it over and over, her slender fingers roaming the engraved message of love as she recalled the intimate details of the night she had mistakenly taken it from his room. She had known then that Gray was a very special man. Now, all these months later, those feelings had not changed.

Rachel refilled her glass from the now half-empty whiskey bottle beside her and took a sip. She shuddered. It burned her stomach and tasted awful, and she wasn't sure why she was even drinking it except that her father used to consume the stuff in times of trouble, and right now she just didn't know where else to turn.

Her thoughts went again to Gray. She had tried, Lordy, how she had tried to forget him. And she might have been able to if she hadn't come to Charleston and found him here. She had been cool to him, even openly rude on occasion, and still he had pursued her. Now she dared to hope that he cared for her in the same way. Rachel emptied her glass, and her head whirled for a moment, then focused on the problem she was wrestling with tonight—Andrew.

She had spent a good portion of the afternoon looking over her shoulder, listening for footsteps, fearful that Hannah would return with Andrew before Gray left. She had maneuvered him all over the house, finding excuses to slip away and look down the street until he must have thought her quite daffy. She couldn't go on like this forever, she thought miserably. Sooner or later Gray would see the baby. Then what would she do?

Rachel returned the pocket watch to the safety of the desk's locked drawer and poured herself another drink. She wanted desperately to tell him the truth, and the burden of her lies weighed heavily on her. The man deserved to know he had a son. Maybe he would be glad to learn the truth.

She gulped down the evil liquid. How could she tell him after all this time had passed? What proof did she have? Perhaps he would think she had concocted the whole story to trap him into marriage. Marriage! He wasn't interested in marriage. Wasn't it he who had broken off his engagement to Claudia, the Perfect Wife of Charleston? If he had not wanted to be married to her, why should Rachel think he would want to be saddled with her and a baby.

She sighed heavily. Everything had gone wrong, all wrong. She had started out with the best of intentions and now look at how awful everything had turned out.

A knock on the study door interrupted her as she reached for the bottle again. Philo stepped inside and announced that Mr. Montgomery was waiting in the parlor.

"Mr. Montgomery!" Rachel sprang to her feet, and the room tilted. She grabbed the edge of the desk for support.

"Do you wants me to tell him you be too indisposed to receive company?" Philo asked.

"No, no," she decided. "Tell him I will be there momentarily." Philo left the room. She didn't know why he had come by at this late hour, or why she had agreed to see him except that she took such pleasure in his nearness.

Rachel walked on unsteady legs to check her appearance in the mirror. Good grief, she looked a fright! She did the best she could to straighten her hair and pinched some color into her cheeks. Well, that was somewhat better, she thought. Suddenly, she hiccuped. She covered her mouth guiltily. She couldn't let Gray see her with liquor on her breath! She made her way back to the desk and searched through the drawers until she found the box of bonbons that the young desk clerk at the hotel had given her when she had checked out. She stuffed three of them into her mouth. They tasted dreadful after the whiskey she had consumed, but she managed to chew and swallow them, hoping they would disguise the unpleasant scent. Her stomach turned in protest. Drawing together her composure, Rachel left the swaying study and crossed the equally tilted hallway.

"Good evening," she said as she stopped in the door of the parlor and clung to the jamb to stabilize herself.

Gray rose from the sofa and his eyes raked over her. She looked ruffled, much more so than when he had left her this evening, but still beautiful. "I hope I have not come at an inopportune moment. I was passing by and saw your lights and hoped I might assist you further with your unpacking."

"How very kind of you," she said, and walked cautiously into the spinning room. She grabbed the back of a chair to steady herself.

He eyed her with concern. "Are you feeling well?"

"Oh, yes," she assured him, and blinked her eyes to get him into focus.

"Is everything all right?"

"Yes," she insisted. *No, no. Everything is all wrong.*

Gray walked closer. "Are you certain?"

She nodded, and another hiccup slipped out. Her eyes met his, and her heart rose in her throat. Tears threatened as her composure crumbled. "Do you want to know the truth?" she asked meekly.

He had never seen her upset like this; he went to her side instantly. He took her hand. "Of course I do."

"Everything is awful! Just terrible!" she blurted out, and tears began to roll down her cheeks.

Her liquor-tainted breath assaulted his nose and his eyes sprang open in astonishment. Good Lord, she was drunk!

"I have made a horrible mess of my life!" she wailed.

Gray wiped her tears with his handkerchief. "You have a wonderful life," he insisted, unable to fathom her concerns or her unexpected consumption of spirits. "You have a beautiful home, and a new business," he pointed out.

Rachel's tears subsided. Yes, that was true. That part of her life had gone well.

Gray relaxed a bit, glad that she had calmed down. "And you have your son," he added, knowing that every woman took great pleasure in her child.

Her piercing cry shook the room, and tears flowed anew down her cheeks. She dropped her head onto his shoulder. "You don't know what a fiendish person I am! I have done such terrible, awful, unforgivable things!" she cried. What kind of monster would hide a child from his own father!

Gray put his arms around her and patted her back consolingly. "You are a very warm, kind, caring woman," he assured her.

She looked up at him with red-rimmed eyes, "I didn't mean to do such bad things. I tried to do the right thing. But the right thing turned out to be the wrong thing, and everyone will end up hating me."

So that was her problem. Now Gray understood. She had taken on a man's role in life, purchasing a home, running her own business, handling her own financial affairs, and it did bother her no matter how she would deny it. It was an uncommon practice and surely there would be those who would look down on her for what she had done. A woman always had her reputation to be concerned with.

"No, now don't fret so," Gray said softly, helping her to the sofa.

"I can't help it. I have hurt so many people."

He sat down next to her and pulled her head onto his shoulder. "Rachel, you have hurt no one. You are only doing what is necessary, what you have to do."

She sniffed and digested his words, forcing her clouded

brain to think. "Yes, that is true," she agreed. She looked up at him. "But, Andrew, what will he think?"

Gray wiped away her tears. "Andrew will grow to be a fine man, having been raised by a fine mother."

"And you? Surely you have more reason than anyone to hate me."

Gray chuckled and hugged her affectionately. Where did she get such strange notions? "I could never hate you. Like Andrew and all the people who care for you, I know you are doing only what is necessary."

"You really don't hate me?" she asked. This was wonderful! Too wonderful to believe! He held no ill feelings toward her for keeping his son from him. Something else he had said surfaced in her muddled thoughts, and she lifted her eyes to meet his. "You care for me, Gray?" she asked softly.

He smiled with amusement. "Yes, Rachel, I care for you." The strain of the whole, difficult day had clearly been too much for her, and he wasn't one to take unfair advantage of a woman who was emotionally distraught, but her lips were so appealing, so inviting, that he couldn't resist. He lowered his mouth to capture hers, but her eyes fluttered shut and she fell limply against him, sound asleep.

Gray sighed resolutely and laid her on the sofa, fervently hoping this was not a new trend in his way with women. He found Philo and one of the maids, who roused Rachel and got her to her feet.

"Gray, how nice of you to drop by," she said suddenly as he helped escort her to the staircase. "Do sit down and we will chat."

Gray did his best to hide his amusement. "I can't stay. Perhaps another time." He released her into the care of the servants, who guided her wobbly form up the stairs.

233

"Another time, then," she tossed back over her shoulder.

He watched her climb the staircase knowing that tomorrow morning she would suffer from a headache of the worst sort. He turned to leave, recalling the last time he had been so pained. It was in St. Joseph the night the mysterious virgin had come to his room and made such wondrous love—

Gray stopped in his tracks and turned quickly to see Rachel, flanked by the servants, disappear from sight. His brows drew together as a scrap of a memory sped into his consciousness, then as quickly sped out again. He shook his head irritably and stalked out of the house.

"Mr. Hardy, please, must your men hammer so loudly?" Each nail the carpenters drove into the walls of her store felt like it was being pounded directly into her head.

The foreman looked at her with uncertainty. "Well, Mrs. Fontaine, we could get softer hammers but the job would take a lot longer."

Rachel pinched the bridge of her nose. "Just continue on," she directed, and waved him back to his duties.

"Not feeling well today, madam?"

She turned and saw Gray striding into the store. He looked crisp and fresh, immaculately attired in complementary shades of blue, and she felt like she had been pushed through a keyhole. Saints in heaven, why did he have to come by today!

"I am quite well, thank you," she said primly.

He stood next to her. "You look a bit pale this morning," he noted as an amused grin played about his lips.

She was not about to tell him that she had partaken of

234

whiskey last evening, though it had been only a sip or two, hadn't it? What would he think! "I am fine," she insisted, and winced when the rapping hammers began again. "Let's go to my office where we can speak more easily," she suggested quickly.

"That is not necessary, madam, this spot is fine," he assured her, thoroughly enjoying her predicament.

"I insist!" She boldly took his hand and led the way to the small office in the back of the store.

Gray tossed his hat aside and sat down on the corner of the desk. "Are you certain you are feeling well?"

Rachel was busy checking her appearance in the small mirror above the washstand and missed the playful glint in Gray's eyes. Quickly she pinched her cheeks to bring some color into them, then turned to face him. "I assure you, Mr. Montgomery, that I am perfectly well," she said proudly.

"Excellent. Then you can join me for a hearty lunch," he assumed.

Rachel's stomach rolled. "No . . . no, thank you," she said, feeling suddenly ill.

He couldn't resist teasing her just once more. "After working so hard yesterday, you need a good meal. How about a thick, rare steak?"

"Oh, no," she cried in anguish and turned away from him, clinging to the washstand for support. His suggestion was so nauseating she feared she might retch. Rachel closed her eyes, willing her churning stomach to be still.

His gaze swept the fine figure her back offered him, her slim shoulders and narrow waist as she clutched the washstand, and he took pity on her. Wiping the grin from his face, he crossed the small room and stood beside her.

"Let me help you," he said, as he poured water from the pitcher into the washbowl.

She opened her eyes and looked up at him. "That is not necessary," she told him, trying to hold on to the last shred of her dignity.

Gray ignored her and wrang the cloth in the cool water. He sat her down in the desk chair and placed the damp cloth over her forehead. She had no strength to protest and, following his instructions, sat quietly with her eyes shut while he held the cloth in place and supported her head with a hand at her nape. He was thoroughly enjoying himself as he leisurely perused her sensuous lips, the graceful column of her throat, her bosoms that more than adequately filled out the heather gown, her small feet and slender ankles that were stretched out in front of her, and the full skirt of the gown that left his imagination to speculate on what it kept hidden from his view. She was beautiful, like a rare wildflower, independent and strong, that could not easily be picked. And it was just those qualities that drew him to her with a desire to shelter and protect those delicate petals and bask in their radiance.

He realized then that her eyes were open and she had been watching him as if she could read his thoughts. Gray nearly blushed.

He cleared his throat. "Feeling better?" he asked, and returned the cloth to the washstand.

"Yes, much," she answered. While her eyes had been closed, a vision from the night before had crept into her thoughts. She rose. "Did you come by my house last evening?"

His white teeth flashed as he smiled. "Yes, I did."

Her brows drew together as she tried to straighten out her thoughts. It must have been a dream, she decided. A

236

dream in which she confessed to Gray that Andrew was his son and he forgave her instantly. It had to have been a dream. Nothing else made sense.

"I am sorry I was not able to visit with you," she said. "I was very tired."

He chuckled. "Tired? Yes, madam, you were indeed tired."

She smiled. "Come along. Let me show you the remodeling I am planning."

Gray took his hat and gladly followed along behind her.

Within a week, the shop had begun to take shape. The carpenters, under Rachel's close supervision, had cut two large windows beside the front door, added more shelves, and rearranged the counters. A fresh coat of paint brightened the dull interior. There was a new sign added out front tastefully proclaiming the shop Fontaine's Mercantile.

Mr. Rhodes, however, did not share in Rachel's enthusiasm, and on many occasions asked why the changes were necessary at all. She explained that the larger display windows would lure patrons inside, and the wider aisles would improve traffic flow and accommodate the ladies' full skirts. He never seemed to grasp her reasoning, so she stopped explaining and eventually he kept his whining to himself. But nothing Mr. Rhodes—or anyone, for that matter—did or said dampened Rachel's spirits. The shop was coming together nicely and soon all would be ready for the new merchandise.

Rachel was engrossed in mathematical calculations when she heard footsteps enter her small office. The steps were heavier and more purposeful than those of Mr. Rhodes.

She looked up from her ledgers to see Gray smiling down at her.

"What a nice surprise," she greeted. She had not seen him in several days and realized now how much she missed him.

"You are quite a sight, my dear, working so feverishly," he told her, then added softly, "quite a lovely sight."

She was anxious to share her accomplishments with him, but was not unaffected by his kind words.

He seemed to notice little but her.

Rachel rose. "How do you like it?"

"It's beautiful. You should wear blue more often," he said as his gaze freely roamed the gown she wore.

She giggled easily. "Not the gown," she corrected gently, "the mercantile."

"Oh, yes, the mercantile," Gray said, and quickly glanced about the room.

"Not here—out in the shop. The carpenters will be fitting the glass today, then all the remodeling will be completed. Didn't you notice the changes?"

In truth, he had hardly noticed anything in his rush to see Rachel again. To his surprise, she had been much in his thoughts, and he woke this morning knowing he must see her today. "Well, yes, yes, I did," he assured her. "It seems things are quite different. I hope your investment pays off."

"It will," she said confidently.

"Actually, I have come to call for another reason," Gray told her. When she looked at him with those beautiful dark eyes, he wanted so desperately to take her into his arms. Instead, he fumbled with his hat to occupy his hands.

"And what is that reason?" she asked as Gray seemed to have gotten lost amid his own thoughts.

"To extend to you an invitation," he said, finding his tongue again. "I am having a barbeque and ball at Richfield in celebration of Independence Day."

"At Richfield?" Her heart raced at the thought of seeing her home again.

"That is where I have been for the past week," he explained. "I told you I would be living there full time so I have been hard at work seeing that things are repaired and running smoothly. And what better way to show off such a beautiful home than to have a barbeque?"

"Oh, Gray, it sounds wonderful," she said dreamily.

"The ball will run quite late so I suggest you plan to remain at Richfield overnight." Lustful thoughts ran quickly through his mind and he passed a finger across his lips to hide the smile that threatened. "Many other guests will be there as well," he added quickly.

"I am sure it's quite proper," she agreed.

"Then you will come? It wouldn't be a problem for you to leave your son?" he asked with concern.

"No, Hannah takes very good care of him."

"But he is sick so much," Gray said.

Another of her lies come back to haunt her. "This is a very special occasion. I am certain Hannah can handle him this once."

Gray smiled brightly. "Good. Then it is settled. And now for my final reason for visiting. I received word last evening that a sea captain friend of mine from England docked in the harbor. As a personal favor he has agreed to meet with no other merchants until you have looked at his cargo."

Her eyes flew wide-open with excitement. "Oh, Gray! What a dear you are!" Instinctively she took his hand and squeezed it affectionately. Then as quickly she dropped it.

"We must hurry!" Swiftly she donned her bonnet and threw her shawl about her shoulders.

Gray chuckled at her childlike enthusiasm. "There is no need to rush. The captain gave me his word he would wait."

Rachel took his hand and pulled him along behind her. "One must act swiftly when opportunity presents itself," she said wisely as they passed through the mercantile. "Mr. Rhodes, I will be back soon," she called to the shop's less than enthusiastic manager as he idly dusted the shelves. "Clear out all the stock. We have new merchandise on the way!" Mr. Rhodes nodded but did not pick up his slow pace.

Gray walked swiftly to keep pace with her and assisted her into his small, open carriage. She sat thoroughly entertained as he told her of the far-off ports the ship had visited and of the unique cargo it brought back to Charleston.

The purchase of the ship's cargo was accomplished quickly. Rachel had difficulty controlling her enthusiasm for the lovely and unusual items the captain showed her, but managed to appear calm and collected and bought the lot for a price she thought fair. The captain haggled a bit, but in the end it was Rachel who won out. Gray sat quietly in the background watching as she conducted the transaction as well as any other merchant he had seen.

Before returning to the carriage, Gray and Rachel strolled down the dock and he pointed out a clipper ship anchored in the harbor. "I am thinking of purchasing that ship," he told her.

Rachel studied the sleek-looking vessel, then turned to him. "Will it be going to California to join the Gold

Rush?" she asked. It seemed every ship on the coast was headed in that direction.

Gray shook his head. "I have no desire to have my ship rot in the bay while the crew digs for gold. Maybe later, when the fields are played out. There will be lots of people left behind who will need supplies."

"Then where will your ship go, if not to California?"

"England," he said, and his eyes took on a faraway look as he studied the vessel. "It is quite different over there. I should enjoy seeing London once more."

A sudden fear spread through Rachel. "You are not sailing with it, are you?"

Gray smiled gently. "Would it bother you if I did?"

Rachel's cheeks pinkened. "No! Well, yes—no." Her eyes met his. "Yes," she admitted softly. There was no way she could pretend she didn't care for him.

Gray took her hand and brushed a soft kiss across it. "Fear not, madam, I have no intentions of sailing away," he assured her. "Anyway, I am not certain I will even purchase the ship. A friend of mine who is an expert on such things will be in town in a few days. We are considering going into a partnership."

Rachel withdrew her hand from his. "I should get an even better deal on the ship's cargo since I will be acquainted with the owner," she speculated.

Gray smiled rakishly. "I am certain we could work out terms to benefit all parties concerned."

Rachel blushed, not from embarrassment, but rather from the pleasurably wicked thought that Gray's words brought to her.

A catlike purring intruded upon them and Rachel turned to see Claudia approaching on the arm of an older gentleman.

"Why, Gray, darling, how nice to see you," Claudia mewed and touched him familiarly on the arm.

Gray tipped his hat, then extended his hand to the gentleman. "William, good to see you again." He turned to Rachel. "I would like you to meet William Danforth, Claudia's father. This is Rachel Fontaine."

"Good day," Rachel greeted pleasantly.

William's heavy mustache bobbed up and down when he spoke. "So glad to meet you," he said as he rested his thumbs in the pockets of his waistcoat.

Gray concluded the introductions by adding, "You have met Claudia already."

Rachel recalled all too well how the haughty Miss Danforth had been all but openly hostile on their first meeting. "Have we met?" Rachel asked. "I don't recall."

Gray and Claudia's father began to discuss business, and Rachel joined their conversation, easily conversing about the cargos and prices here and abroad. It was clearly over Claudia's head and Rachel couldn't miss the venomous look she got from Claudia.

When their discussion wound down and they had said their good-byes, Claudia suddenly took Gray's arm and rose on her toes to place a kiss on his cheek. In doing so, she pressed her large, rounded breasts full against him in plain sight of her father and Rachel.

"Bye, darling. I'll see you again soon," she purred.

William was obviously embarrassed by his daughter's aggressive behavior. "Come along, Claudia," he said curtly, then took her arm and led her away. She paused long enough to cast a sultry smile at Gray, then went obediently with her father.

Anger and jealously raged through Rachel, and she had to struggle to contain her emotions. Despite the break-off of their engagement, it was apparent that Gray and Claudia were close and still saw each other frequently. And the fact that William Danforth held no ill feelings toward Gray added proof to that notion. How could Gray be interested in such a woman, Rachel thought. What did he see in her? She mentally pictured Claudia's round, curvaceous body and compared it to her own slimmer silhouette. Was *that* it? Was he interested in Claudia for her—?

"I must apologize for Claudia's forwardness. I hope you weren't offended," Gray said sincerely. He searched her face for her response.

"It is certainly none of my concern whom you choose to share an affectionate moment with in public," she said tightly. He falls all over himself for Claudia, and he couldn't even remember the night he spent with her!

"That was hardly an affectionate moment."

"Call it what you will. I have no intention of standing here in the sun discussing the subject any further," she informed him. Rachel's hooped skirt swirled around her as she turned on her heels and left.

"Damn!" Gray swore softly. Claudia had caused him trouble before and he had been willing to put up with it. but now Rachel was angry because of her little scene, and he could not—would not—allow that.

Rachel walked swiftly and determinedly as she picked her way through the crates, boxes, and coils of rope that covered the docks. Foul-smelling sailors and sweaty slaves were busy moving the cargo in all directions and merchants milled about. She had no idea where she was, and it was only a matter of moments before she was lost in the confusion with no idea of which direction she should take.

Suddenly, someone grabbed her arm. Rachel gasped and turned to see Gray beside her.

"This is not a proper place for you to be," he told her sternly. "Come with me. I must talk to you."

Rachel jerked her arm free of his grasp, her anger now threatening to run completely out of control. "It is not your decision to dictate where I will or will not go!"

"You are being foolish," he said as his own anger began to build.

"Save your concern for someone who wants it. No doubt Claudia would lap it up eagerly, but I suggest you continue to do so in private so as not to make a spectacle of yourself in public!"

"Rachel, this is not the place for such a discussion." Gray spoke with slow measured words.

"I have no desire to discuss anything with you," she said through pursed lips.

"Well, I want to discuss it with you!" Gray shouted as he suddenly lost all control.

His voice booming with anger took some of the resistance from Rachel. He seized her hand firmly and led her through the maze of men and cargo to the safety of his carriage. Before she could protest, Gray put his hands around her trim waist and lifted her easily on to the seat. Rachel struggled to subdue her volumes of petticoats as Gray bounded across her to take up the reins and urge horse and carriage away from the docks. When she had at last restored her modesty, Rachel folded her arms and lifted her nose in determined silence. After a few moments it became evident that Gray was not taking proper notice of her anger and she turned her head only slightly to catch a glimpse of him. He stared straight ahead as he guided the horse through the streets, seemingly totally unaware of her indignance. This angered her more and she turned away with renewed determination. How dare he be so calm when she was so upset!

The scenery that passed soon became unfamiliar to Rachel, and as he was about to break her vow of silence and ask where she was being taken, Gray halted the carriage in the shade of a giant oak. Rachel sat in stony silence still refusing to look in Gray's direction, determined to wait him out. The more her mind dwelled on it, the madder she got. Their cross words had been his fault, and it was he who had practically dragged her from the docks and deposited her unceremoniously in his carriage. If they were to speak again it would have to be *his* doing, because certainly *she* was not to blame. Only if he apologized and begged—yes, begged—for her forgiveness would she consider speaking to him again. But then only on rare occasions.

"Rachel."

The soft, mellow tones of his voice melted Rachel's heart, and her anger along with it. She tried to steel her feelings and find the anger that had possessed her, but could not. From the corner of her eye she saw Gray peering around the edge of her bonnet. His slate-blue eyes captured hers and she couldn't resist his boyish look.

"I must talk to you," he requested gently.

Rachel was ready to forgive him and forget the entire incident, but managed to sit quietly, her silence urging him to speak as she turned to face him.

Gray removed his hat and ran his fingers through the inky curls. It was important that he explained this properly, so he considered his words carefully. "I know this may be difficult for you to believe, after what you just witnessed, but I care nothing for Claudia."

Rachel's heart leaped with excitement. Could it be true?

He really didn't love Claudia? But his words did not agree with what she had just seen with her own eyes.

Gray saw the doubt on her face and continued on. "You know that I was engaged to Claudia at one time. It was a long engagement. I kept finding reasons to postpone the wedding, and they were all legitimate. Claudia was very understanding." Gray sounded troubled as he spoke. He sighed heavily. "I suppose I thought it was high time I got married. Aunt Charlotte was always after me to find a suitable wife; all my friends were already married. And Claudia was . . . suitable. She came from a good family, displayed proper breeding, and I was, well, attracted to her," he explained, then added softly, "But I did not love her, and I could not go through with the wedding."

"But you knew you didn't love her when you proposed. What made you decide to call it off?"

Gray shook his head. How could he explain it to Rachel when he didn't understand it himself? He had been willing to enter into marriage knowing full well he did not love Claudia. Then after returning from his last trip West he simply couldn't go through with it. He had realized then that he wanted more from life. More than a wife who was merely suitable. He wanted a loving wife to warm his bed at night. A caring and giving woman beneath him, not a block of stone who simply performed her duties.

Gray's eyes caressed the delicate lines of Rachel's face as he tried to come up with an answer to her question. A strange sense of familiarity came to him as an elusive memory touched his mind for an instant. He tried to catch it, but like so many times before, it was gone too quickly. Perhaps just wishful thinking, he mused. Gray shrugged his shoulders. "I just couldn't go through with it."

"If all of that is true, why are you still seeing her?"

Rachel knew her questioning was bold, but she had to find out while he was of a mind to confess.

"I see her only occasionally," Gray pointed out quickly. "I suppose I felt bad for leading her on then not marrying her."

"Don't you think you are hurting her worse by continuing to see her?" she asked gently.

"I suppose you are right," he admitted. "But I hoped she would find someone else soon."

"If she has truly lost her heart to you, no one will ever take your place." Rachel spoke from experience.

Gray laughed aloud. "In order to lose one's heart, one must first possess a heart. I'm not entirely certain that can be said of Claudia Danforth."

"Oh, Gray! What a terrible thing to say," she scolded.

"It is true. You see, my dear, Claudia loved my wealth and possessions more than she could ever love me. She would never marry for love—unlike you. I'll bet you were desperately in love with Mr. Fontaine."

"Who? Oh, yes, yes, my husband. Yes, we were very much in love. We shared a warm and truly loving marriage. It was a beautiful relationship," she said with as much sincerity as she could muster. She didn't want Gray to think she was as shallow as Claudia.

Yet Gray grunted distastefully and seemed displeased with her reply. He pulled his hat on determinedly and gathered up the reins. "I had better get you back to town before I compromise your reputation," he said sourly.

She covered his hands with hers, stilling the reins. "Why did you bring me out here to tell me this?"

The line of his jaw tensed. How could he tell her now that the real reason was that he cared for her and didn't want her to think of Claudia as a rival? Rachel had just

247

spoken of the great love she had felt for her husband. A man she was no doubt constantly reminded of each time she looked at her son. A man with whom she had surely shared many beautiful moments of wedded bliss. How could he hope to find a place in her heart when her husband so obviously still held his place there?

"As I said, madam, I should get you back to town at once," he said tersely. "I have no desire to make a spectacle of myself twice in the same day." He urged the horse to a brisk canter as they drove away, leaving Rachel in a stunned and confused silence.

Determined never to see Rachel again, Gray's mood worsened with each day that passed. Alone in the solitude of Richfield his mind wouldn't let him rest as his thoughts constantly turned to Rachel at all hours of the day and night. The more he tried not to think about her the more she haunted him. She was in his dreams, so he walked the floors till the early hours of the morning. He imagined her at his side as he moved through the house. The music of her easy laughter came to his ears in the still, quiet house. She was all around him, in his mind and in his heart.

He tried to rid himself of her by throwing himself into his work. There was still much to be done at Richfield, and the barbecue was less than two weeks away. Endless hours were spent overseeing the repairs and remodeling. He pushed himself and the servants to the point of exhaustion. Yet nothing seemed to flow smoothly. There were many problems that continually plagued him. Gray couldn't seem to get control of the situation. He knew that for months he had been wandering through life with little direction or concern for his future. Things had improved for a short time, but now it was even worse than before.

Gray paced restlessly about the library as the early-morning sun peeked over the horizon. He rubbed his hand over the two-day growth of whiskers that covered his face. An achy numbness weighted down his limbs. Gray stopped before the mirror. He hardly recognized the unkempt hair, the dark-circled eyes, and haggard face that looked back at him. He shook his head wearily and turned away. Moving to the window, he looked toward the fertile fields that surrounded the manor house. But he did not see the beauty of it all. He saw Rachel.

He laughed aloud and sank down in the leather wing-backed chair. Well, he had tried to set her out of his mind. He had done everything humanly possible. He had worked diligently for a week. And still he had failed. Now he knew for certain that he could not forget Rachel and cast her from his thoughts. It was impossible to do so. He loved her.

Feeling a sudden burst of energy, Gray took pen and paper from the desk and quickly wrote out a brief message. He summoned the butler, who approached cautiously, unsure of what mood his master would be in today, and then sent the servant away with the letter. Relief flooded Gray as he fell back into the chair once more. He knew he could not fight his feelings for Rachel, so now he would do something about winning her heart. If she still loved her deceased husband, as he feared, then he would dislodge those feelings. He would show her that she could love again. She could love *him*.

Gray closed his eyes and rested his head against the chair as his tired, achy muscles relaxed. As usual, the vis-

249

age of the dark-eyed widow filled his thoughts and he drifted into a welcome slumber.

Though her life had begun to fall into a routine, Rachel felt as jumpy as a cat. She was always on edge, her nerves stretched taut. She continually snapped at Mr. Rhodes until the man showed physical signs of being afraid of her. It took all the patience she could muster to deal with the droves of patrons who flocked to the mercantile daily. She even secretly cursed the success of her business. By the time she arrived home each day, she could do nothing but find fault with the way the house was kept and the food prepared. The servants made themselves scarce. Little Andrew sensed her mood at once and clung to Hannah, refusing to go to his mother. So Rachel abandoned the lot of them and locked herself in the study each evening attempting to do her books. But her mind failed her and she could not concentrate. She sat for hours staring at nothing. Finally she would go up to her bed and spend a fitful night tossing and turning.

A rap at her door woke Rachel from a light sleep. She dragged herself from the bed ready to snap off the head of whomever had awakened her at this early hour.

"Rachel, are you up?"

She heard Hannah's soft voice calling to her and some of the anger left her. She opened the door. Hannah looked bright and fresh, as always.

"This just came for you. The messenger is waiting for a reply," she said, and handed her a letter.

Rachel rubbed the sleep from her eyes and pushed the mass of wild curls over her shoulder. "Who is it from?" she asked as she studied the envelope that bore her name.

"I don't know, but the messenger rode up to the house like he was going to a fire. He said he had to wait for your answer then get back home right away," Hannah said excitedly. "Open it."

Rachel tore the envelope open with considerably less curiosity than Hannah displayed. It was probably a note from Mr. Rhodes resigning his job as store manager, or something equally troublesome. It seemed life held nothing but problems for her lately.

She scanned the letter quickly. Her heart stopped beating. When she had read it the second time her pulse began to race. "Oh, Hannah," she said breathlessly.

"What is it? Who is it from?" Hannah asked, feeling the exuberance that showed in Rachel's eyes.

"Gray," she said softly. Her eyes opened wide. "It's from Gray! He wants to come to call this afternoon!" Tears of joy brimmed in her eyes. Suddenly she looked alarmed. "My goodness! What will I wear?" she cried. Rachel raced across the room and flung open her lengthy armoire. She ran through the racks of beautiful gowns.

"Wait, Rachel!" Hannah called.

"No, I've got to find something special to wear," she insisted.

Hannah joined her. "Don't you think you should first let the gentleman know he will be received?"

Rachel gasped. How could she have overlooked that! She dashed to her writing desk and penned a gracious note to Gray. Hannah took it from her. "I will be right back," she promised and hurried away.

Rachel returned to the armoire and rifled through her gowns. She had to find the perfect dress. And she must wash her hair and allow herself time for a long, hot bath. Her mind whirled with anticipation. She closed her eyes and said a silent prayer of thanks. He was coming to see her. She didn't know what she had done to make him so angry, but it seemed he was over it now. And he was coming to see her!

The morning blended into the afternoon as Rachel prepared herself with the assistance of Hannah and Selma, her maid. Her hair was fashioned in loose curls, accented with ribbons. The gown she selected was the color of buttercups with a flounced skirt and full sleeves that gave it a soft and very feminine look.

Butterflies in the pit of her stomach went into full flight when Philo came to her room and announced that Mr. Montgomery had arrived. Rachel collected herself; she didn't want to appear as jittery as she felt. Before going downstairs she stopped by Andrew's room. He was sleeping soundly. Rachel was thankful that Gray had requested to visit during Andrew's normal nap time.

Rachel entered the parlor where Gray waited. He stood gazing out the window, his face looking tense in profile. Perhaps he wasn't here for a social call, she suddenly thought. She clasped her hands together so he would not notice her trembling. "Good afternoon," she greeted.

Her voice startled him, jarring him from his thoughts. When he turned to her, his handsome face and well-fitting clothes took her breath away.

"Good af—" He cleared his throat nervously and tried again. "Good afternoon." She was so beautiful he couldn't concentrate on what he wanted to say.

An awkward silence fell between them. Finally Rachel walked closer to him and spoke. "Would you care to sit down?" she asked, and seated herself.

Gray twisted the brim of the hat he held. "Oh, yes. That

would be fine," he said, and sat down on the end of the sofa, opposite from Rachel.

"Tea?" she inquired.

The last thing he wanted to do was try and balance a tiny tea cup on his shaky knee. "No, thank you," he told her as he continued to manhandle his hat unmercifully.

They were silent again for several moments.

"How are things going at Richfield?" Rachel asked.

"Fine," he said quickly. "Everything is running very smoothly and should be completed well ahead of schedule."

Silence again.

"How is business?" he asked her, grateful that his mind had finally dredged up some intelligent remark.

"Wonderful," she said brightly. "I do so enjoy assisting the patrons with their purchases. And Mr. Rhodes is such a dear."

Gray nodded a response and quiet closed in around them once again.

Rachel took pity on the beating Gray's hat was undergoing as his strong fingers continually squeezed it. Reaching across the sofa, she took it from him and attempted to restore its shape. "I don't think this hat can take much more of your abuse," she commented.

He pulled at his cravat. It seemed to be cutting off his air supply. The room was closing in around him, stifling him. "Why don't we go for a walk," he suggested anxiously, and stood up quickly.

"Very well," she agreed. It would be a good idea to get out of the house in case Andrew should wake early from his nap. She left word with the butler that she was going out and stopped at the hall mirror to don a wide-brimmed straw hat. Gray watched in silence as she tied the yellow bow beneath her chin, then offered his arm as they left the house.

The day was warm, though the sun had already reached its peak in the blue, cloudless sky. A breeze stirred the air bringing the sound of birds singing and children playing to Gray and Rachel as they strolled along the quiet street. They chatted about the weather; Rachel inquired about the Wades. Their conversation flowed somewhat better than at the house.

Soon they reached the park and sought out the shade of the trees. There were few other people there, mostly women pushing baby buggies and small children toddling along.

Rachel drew in a deep breath. "It's so lovely here. The flowers smell so fresh. Hannah sometimes brings Andrew here to play."

"I've been thinking lately of how difficult life has been for you," Gray said as he stood by her.

"Difficult?"

"Yes. Having a son to raise alone without a man to provide for you must have been quite a chore." This was the subject he wanted to discuss and was glad Rachel had been the one to bring up her son's name.

She shrugged her shoulders. "I had help from friends. I managed."

"Were you married long?"

Rachel's stomach turned over. Oh, no, not questions about her husband. She thought all of that was behind her now. She glided away from him gracefully as she frantically searched her brain. Had she told anyone in Charleston how long she had supposedly been married? "Who is to say what a long time is, or what a short time is," she said wistfully.

"You must have been quite young when you married," Gray commented as he moved to catch up with her.

Rachel fumbled with the ribbon of her hat as she untied it, stalling for time. "Younger than some, older than some," she said with a sweet smile.

"You were lucky to know your own heart at such an early age," Gray said.

Rachel removed her hat. "That is one of the wonderful things about youth, I suppose," she mused. Why did he keep asking these questions! She was running out of evasive answers!

"Tell me about Mr. Fontaine," Gray said. He was getting nowhere with this line of questioning, so he might as well come right to the point.

Rachel froze in her tracks. How could she tell him about a man who didn't exist? He never even had a first name!

Gray readily saw she was reluctant to speak. "Is it difficult for you to talk about?" he asked, his voice heavy with concern.

"Well, yes, you could say that," Rachel conceded as she moved away from him again.

Gray determinedly kept pace with her. He could see that she needed some encouragement to discuss her deceased husband. Though it was surely a painful subject for her, Gray had to learn her true feelings. "Was he a good man?"

"I suppose you could say that," Rachel said as she slipped behind a large oak.

He followed. "You said you loved him a great deal. Did he love you as well?"

Rachel prayed he would cease his questioning. Why was he putting her through this? What possible interest could he have in the deceased Mr. Fontaine? She slid away from the tree. "People usually marry for love," she tossed back at him as she walked.

"Good God, woman!" Gray swore an exasperated oath, halting Rachel's flight. He pulled off his hat and flung it to the ground angrily.

She stood rooted to the spot, stunned by his sudden outburst.

"I have spent a hellish week trying to come to terms with your feelings for your husband! I realize this is a difficult subject for you to speak of. But could you please extend me the small courtesy of standing still while we talk!"

His words hit Rachel like a physical blow. He thought she still loved Mr. Fontaine! She gasped and covered her lips with shaking fingers.

Gray was in front of her in an instant, his face ashen. "I realized this past week how much I care for you. So please, I must know. Can you ever forget the love you had for your husband? Can you love again?"

Rachel's heart nearly burst. All this time he had been concerned about her feelings, worried that her husband was her only true love. Surely Gray was the most sensitive and caring man she had ever known.

She took his hands in hers and squeezed them warmly. "Gray, you are such a dear," she said softly. At least now she could speak the truth. "Mr. Fontaine is but a vague image. Sometimes I can't picture his face. That part of my life was so long ago. It's all over now."

Gray's face brightened a bit. "You no longer feel the love you once had for him?"

"In truth, Gray, I'm not certain what I felt for him," she said honestly.

"You were very young," he agreed. "But what of Andrew? Are you not reminded of Mr. Fontaine each time you look at your son?"

Lies on top of lies on top of lies. Where would it stop? "Andrew was born after . . . Mr. Fontaine . . . died. He is my son. I never think of the two of them as one," Rachel said earnestly.

Gray smiled brightly revealing the relief he felt at hearing her words. "And can you love again?" he asked softly.

"Oh, yes!"

They came together in a warm embrace. Gray's strong arms held her tight against him. He wished he could hold her there forever. Unmindful of passersby, Gray's lips sought out the warmth of hers as their mouths blended together eagerly. Rachel's body tingled as he held her. She knew she wanted to be in his arms always.

Chapter 11

Rachel settled herself comfortably in her carriage as the coachman expertly guided the horses through Charleston's cobblestone streets toward the home of Charlotte and Bernard Wade. While she was hardly a social gadfly, Rachel enjoyed dining with friends, especially the Wades, but she had to admit to herself that most of her excitement over this evening's invitation was because Gray would be there.

Lanterns lit against the darkness shone in the windows of the homes the carriage passed. Rachel sat contentedly watching the scenery. It felt good here; it felt like home. After a difficult period of adjustment, life had settled into a comfortable routine for Rachel. She spent her days at the mercantile, sometimes waiting on customers, or in her office taking care of the books. To her delight, Gray would drop by and take her to lunch. She never knew when to expect him; he would just suddenly appear.

The exhilaration she felt at her business was followed each day by the quiet contentment of returning home at night. The house ran smoothly now and there were few problems. She spent her evenings with Andrew, usually in the garden. It was a safe and happy place for the boy. Surrounded by the tall redbrick wall, Andrew was free to toddle about anywhere his shaky steps would take him. The tall trees shaded the garden from the hot evening sun, making it cool and refreshing with the scent of the many flowers and blossoming shrubs. Rachel would often sit in the latticework gazebo and simply observe Andrew as he explored the garden with unquenchable curiosity. He was such a dear child and Rachel loved him so.

The carriage stopped in front of the Wades' house and the coachman assisted Rachel to the ground. This was to be a small gathering for supper tonight, Gray had explained, to welcome an old family friend who was in town on business. The front door was opened by Gray and he eyed appreciatively the peach gown she wore, especially the bodice which dipped lower than the more modest gowns she normally wore at the mercantile.

Gray smiled rakishly as he leisurely appraised her. "My dear Rachel, your beauty overwhelms me. I shall not be able to pay the least bit of attention to the other guests."

She smiled demurely. She, too, would have difficulty noticing the other guests. Gray was immaculately dressed in shades of brown that complemented his features handsomely and Rachel was unable to tear her eyes from him. "Are the others guests here?" she asked as Gray took her ecru shawl.

"The Lancasters have not arrived yet, but our guest of honor is here and I am very anxious for you to meet him," he said as he escorted her to the drawing room.

Bernard and his guest sat with brandy in hand as Gray and Rachel entered the room. "How good to see you again," Bernard said when he saw Rachel. "Charlotte will be down momentarily."

The other man, whose back had been to her, rose when his host did.

"Rachel, I would like to present my future partner, the man who knows all one can know about sailing vessels of all types." Gray began the introductions as the man turned to face them. He and Rachel recognized each other in the same stunned instant.

"Captain Daniels!" she exclaimed.

"Rachel?" The captain looked harder at her. "Rachel! It is you!"

A wide smile spread across her face as she accepted his outstretched hands. Ezra Daniels was equally glad to see her.

"I take it you two know each other," Gray said, somewhat mystified by this unexpected turn of events.

Captain Daniels squeezed Rachel's hands with fatherly affection. "Just look at you! You have grown even more beautiful," he declared as he appraised her warmly. "Why, the last time I saw you, you were—"

"As big as a barn." Rachel finished the sentence for him, recalling their last meeting in St. Joseph when she was still carrying Andrew.

"Well, what was it? A flaxen-haired beauty like her mother?" the captain wanted to know.

Rachel shook her head. "First of all, it was not a 'she' and, what's more, to look at *him* you would never know the child was mine," she said, smiling.

Gray didn't like being on the outside of anything that concerned Rachel. "All right now, I must insist you two tell me how you know each other," he said good-naturedly and slid his arm around Rachel's small waist.

Bernard joined them. "I've never met a woman so full of surprises," he muttered.

Captain Daniels picked up his drink. "I met Rachel shortly after her husband died. She was one of the shrewdest merchants I have ever known," he said, giving Rachel a wink.

"So you knew each other in St. Louis," Gray surmised.

"Actually it was—" Daniels began.

"Quite a long time ago," Rachel cut in quickly. Upon their meeting in Charleston, Gray had had the mistaken notion that she was from St. Louis and she had let him believe that so he would not associate her with St. Joseph in any way. She certainly could not tell him now that she had misled him purposely. Rachel cast a pleading glance at the captain, begging for his silence. He complied with her unspoken request, though he didn't understand it.

"Gray has told me of his interest in purchasing a ship. I take it you are his partner in that venture," Rachel said, anxious to change the subject.

"Yes, I will be here for a few days to discuss the possibility," Captain Daniels said.

"What a shame you will not be here for the barbecue at Richfield this Saturday," Rachel said, managing to sound disappointed. In truth, she wanted him to leave town right now. He knew too much of her past. More than she wanted anyone—especially Gray—to learn. Rachel had constructed a tower of lies that the captain threatened to bring tumbling down around her.

"I have business up and down the coast. I suspect I will be in and out of Charleston over the next few weeks. Hopefully I can be here for the barbecue. I am most anxious to see this plantation of Gray's," Captain Daniels said.

"I have tried several times to get Rachel to come up and see it, but I can't tear her away from that mercantile of hers," Gray said. He smiled down at her, his blue eyes warm with affection.

Rachel smiled and scolded him gently. "My heavens, Gray, I have no desire to find myself the talk of every old gossip hound in Charleston."

"Fear not, my dear, I would make an honest woman of you," he promised.

A faint blush crossed her cheeks and she stole a glance at him, unable to hide the pleasure his words brought to her.

The exchange did not go unnoticed by Daniels. Their feelings for each other were obvious, which pleased him greatly, though finding them together was an unexpected shock.

The evening passed pleasantly for all but Rachel. She was on pins and needles the whole time, fearful that Captain Daniels would mention something of her past that would conflict with what she had told Gray. She tried to read the captain's expressions for some clue to his thoughts, but was unable to grasp anything definite. He watched her every movement, especially when Gray was near, taking in everything around him. She could only guess what he was thinking.

Rachel went home early with a pounding headache. A sense of doom had fallen over her as the past she thought she had put behind her had somehow found her. And once again her future was threatened. But it was too late to turn back now. She had no choice but to go on.

The morning trade at the mercantile was always brisk and today was no exception. Rachel plastered a smile on her face and assisted her patrons with their selections, sometimes having to make the decisions for them. Many of the ladies who frequented her shop had difficulty in choosing exactly what they wanted. While it irritated Rachel that they should be so indecisive over a purchase as insignificant as buttons, she would stand by them indulgently comparing sizes and colors, pointing out the benefits of each. When logic failed to sway them, Rachel would pick the one she liked best and convince them that this was the perfect choice. The women almost always took her advice.

She found it difficult to listen to the prattling of her customers this morning as her thoughts continued to stray to Charlotte Wade's supper and her unexpected meeting with Captain Daniels. After her initial happiness over seeing her old friend had worn off, Rachel realized the danger Ezra Daniels could put her in. She had spent a sleepless night worrying over the consequences of his visit. He knew more of her past than anyone in Charleston, and if he chose to speak of it she would be cast in a very bad light. Though he knew nothing specific, it was enough to reveal that Rachel had lied about her past and that would no doubt lead to more questions and more answers she did not want to have to give.

When the crowd thinned out, Rachel escaped to the solitude of her office leaving Mr. Rhodes to handle the customers. The man seemed to take everything in stride. He moved at the same pace regardless of whether there were two or twenty patrons in the shop.

Rachel sat down at her desk and tried to focus her thoughts on some of the correspondence which required her attention. The soft shuffling of tiny feet interrupted her work. She turned in her chair and saw Andrew standing in the doorway with Hannah securely holding his small hand. All the fear and anxiety left Rachel when Andrew saw her and squealed in delight. She swept him into her arms and kissed his cheek. "What a surprise!" she said. She glanced quickly through the curtain that separated her office from the mercantile and saw no one there she recognized.

"You kept promising Andrew he could come see your shop, so I decided it was time he learned where his mother worked," Hannah told her firmly.

The poor child never went anywhere except to the park with Hannah for fear this tiny duplicate of Gray Montgomery would be recognized by one of the Wades or even Gray himself. She supposed that going out just this once would pose no problem. Besides, seeing the boy had lifted her spirits greatly. "It's all right," Rachel said, then added, "but just this once."

"You can't keep him shut up in the house forever," Hannah pointed out.

"It's a beautiful home with lots of toys and a big yard to play in. Much better for him than being surrounded by a bunch of strangers. Anyway, he is too fair-skinned to be out in the sun." Rachel defended her position with all the conviction she could muster.

It was a discussion the two women had had many times, always with the same outcome. Hannah, as usual, let it drop. "I want to look around the shop a bit," she said. Her eyes brightened. "Is that Mr. Rhodes?"

"Yes. Please introduce yourself. I'll keep Andrew here with me," Rachel said.

"Oh, Rachel, I saw the most adorable bonnet in the millinery shop awhile ago," Hannah began.

Rachel waved her away. "Take your time. I don't get to be with Andrew nearly enough."

When Hannah left, Rachel resumed her seat at her desk, this time with Andrew on her lap. The child cooed and jabbered happily as his small fingers grasped awkwardly at everything on the desktop. Rachel let him have his way as she contentedly looked on. Andrew was such a joy to be with and she loved every moment with him.

Heavy male footsteps strode into the office. Rachel's heart skipped a beat, and for an instant she was afraid to turn and see who stood behind her. The steps were too purposeful for Mr. Rhodes and she knew only one other man who would enter her office unannounced.

"Good morning, Rachel."

It was Ezra Daniels. Relief flooded her, and she turned to face him. "Captain, what a pleasant surprise."

"I hope you don't mind my barging in. Your man out front said it would be all right," he explained. "I just had to come down and see your business. As I expected, things seem to be running very smoothly—and profitably, I'll wager."

Rachel smiled. "I've been very pleased with the shop's success," she said modestly.

He saw Andrew on her lap. "What have we here?" he asked. "I hoped I would get to see your son before I left."

A chill went up Rachel's spine as Captain Daniels closed the distance between them quickly, his attention centered on Andrew. What could she do? Claim the child was not hers? Hardly. Would he suspect who Andrew's father was? Why should he?

Rachel forced herself to calm down. She turned the child on her lap to face the captain. "This is Andrew," she said softly.

Captain Daniels knelt before them. "What a fine-looking child he is," he said as he appraised the boy's dark curls and blue eyes. "You are right, Rachel, he must look exactly like his father because he doesn't look a thing like you!" he joked. An almost forgotten feeling overtook him and he froze for an instant. He recalled the last time he had seen Rachel in St. Joseph and the unfounded idea that had occurred to him then. He knew now with absolute certainty that that notion had been correct.

Daniels studied the baby's face for a long moment, then lifted his eyes to meet Rachel's. She knew he knew the truth. A sudden wave of calm washed over her. There was no use in trying to deny it. A long silence passed between them. Andrew squirmed impatiently on Rachel's lap until she allowed him to slide down the satin skirt of the teal gown she wore and toddle about the room. Her eyes were locked with those of Captain Daniels.

"I suppose that now you will tell Gray," she said softly.

"You mean he doesn't know?" he asked in shock.

"Of course not," she said simply. "No one knows."

Captain Daniels rose. "How could he not know? All one need do is look at the child—"

"Gray has never seen him."

"Why not?" he wanted to know. He did not understand what was going on here.

Rachel shrugged her shoulders and stared at her hands folded in her lap. How could she explain it all to Captain Daniels?

"Why haven't you told him?" he repeated. "He has a right to know."

Rachel looked up at him, his great height causing him to tower over her. "He has no rights. The child is mine."

266

"Then why did you come here to Charleston to find Gray?" he wanted to know.

Anger rose swiftly in Rachel. "I did not come to Charleston to find Gray," she ground out. "I had no idea he lived here. I was shocked when I saw him."

"I find that hard to believe," the captain said skeptically.

Rachel came to her feet. "Good heavens, I didn't even know his name! You are the only person on this earth who would know that Gray was not registered at Cora's Inn that night! I had no way of tracing him!"

The realization of her words hit him hard. She was telling the truth. "How, Rachel? How did it happen?" he asked softly. His mind was confused as he recalled the events of that night. "I feel as though I am to blame. I should have stayed with Gray that evening. I knew he was drunk, but I never thought he would hurt anyone, or force you to—"

"It was not like that," Rachel said gently. "I knew what I was doing." She held her head up proudly, refusing to feel any shame. She had come to terms with her actions long, long ago, and those feelings had not changed. "I won't explain to you the reasons for my actions. I am not sorry for what I have done." She turned her gaze to Andrew. "Look at the beautiful child I have now," she said with a small smile.

"Then what will you do? It is very obvious that Gray cares for you. What will he say when he finds out the truth? You will have to tell him one day."

"I tried to discourage Gray's feelings, but I found that to be impossible. You see, Captain, I do love him."

He sighed. "I believe Gray should be told the truth," he said with great conviction.

"And will you go to him now and tell him? He will only feel obligated to me and the child and that is not the kind of relationship I want from him. Then when the whole city learns the truth, that I gave myself to a stranger whose name I did not even know, will that bring any honor to the name of Gray Montgomery?" Rachel captured Andrew and lifted him into her arms. "For myself, I care not. I made my decision long ago and will live by it. But what of this child? Will you tell the truth and brand him a bastard for the rest of his life?"

Captain Daniels ran his fingers down the back of his head. There were no easy alternatives. Either way someone would be hurt. Gray and Rachel were both his friends. How could he choose? Making one happy might very well destroy the other. He looked at Andrew as the boy tugged at the bow at Rachel's throat. There really was no choice to make after all. "Very well, Rachel," he relented. "Your secret is safe with me. But you will have to tell him someday."

"I will. When the time is right I will tell Gray the truth," she promised.

Captain Daniels turned to leave. Rachel touched his arm halting his steps. "Thank you," she said softly.

"I only hope you will still feel that way when this charade blows up in your face. And it will, Rachel, one day it will," he predicted, then turned and left her office.

Rachel gave Andrew a squeeze and kissed his cheek. "I will keep you safe from it," she whispered. "Your future won't be jeopardized. I promise."

When Hannah returned a short while later, Rachel made her promise to take Andrew home right away and keep him there. Reluctantly Hannah agreed.

The walls of the mercantile seemed to close in around

Rachel until she could not bear to be inside any longer. Though it was the hottest part of the afternoon when most sensible people tried to remain indoors, Rachel left the shop to run some errands. She needed some fresh air to clear her head. Captain Daniels's words still hung heavy in her office. But as she walked through the streets, she realized that his words could not be left behind so easily. They continued to haunt her as she went about her business.

In an effort to bolster her sagging mood, Rachel decided to stop by the dressmaker's shop and check on the progress of the three gowns she had ordered. She was promised they would be ready in plenty of time for Saturday's barbecue at Richfield, and though there were still several days remaining before the deadline, she felt it would be a good idea to make certain all was proceeding on schedule. Turning her thoughts to a more cheerful subject, Rachel stepped inside Mrs. Wilmont's Dress Shop.

Nearly every square inch of the shop was covered with fabrics and yard goods of every color and texture imaginable. Yet amid the clutter was the meticulous workmanship Mrs. Wilmont was known for. The gowns she created were of superior quality and her reputation carried well beyond the Low Country.

Rachel welcomed the cool of the shop as she caught her breath from the hot walk over. There seemed to be no one else there and she was glad she would not have to wait to see Mrs. Wilmont.

"Rachel?"

A voice from behind caught her attention, and she turned to see Claudia Danforth step from behind a pillar of cloth bolts. She looked cool and refreshed and exquisitely dressed, as always, making Rachel uncomfortably aware of her wilted appearance and flushed cheeks.

"It is 'Rachel,' isn't it?" Claudia asked as she eyed her with thinly veiled contempt.

"Yes," she replied coolly.

Claudia sauntered closer. "Mrs. Wilmont makes the most beautiful dresses. I had no idea she did your gowns," she said with a weak smile.

Rachel's back stiffened. "I would imagine there is a great deal you don't know."

A scowl crossed Claudia's face, but her sharp retort was cut off by Mrs. Wilmont as she entered from the back of her shop. "Oh, Mrs. Fontaine, how nice to see you," the white-haired woman greeted.

"I wanted to check on the progress you are making," Rachel said cordially, refusing to let her irritation with Claudia show.

"Fine! Fine!" she assured her. "I will get the gown that is completed for you to see. Don't worry, all will be finished in time for the barbecue," Mrs. Wilmont assured her, then disappeared into the back of her shop again.

Claudia spun to face Rachel. "Barbecue?" It was a demand more than a question.

Quite obviously Claudia knew nothing of this Saturday's planned festivities. "Why, yes, a barbecue at Richfield," she said casually as she inspected a nearby bolt of blue satin.

"Rich—" Claudia quickly concealed her outrage. "Why, yes, of course. I am certain my invitation is home waiting for me. You see, I have so many social obligations I can't possibly remember them all. My head will only hold just so much."

"Yes, Claudia, I can see why that would be true,"

270

Rachel said dryly. She hoped that Gray had not actually asked Claudia to the barbecue. She had been looking forward to it and didn't want Claudia's presence there to spoil the occasion.

Claudia's eyes smoldered with anger, but she held her tongue. "I suggest you save some of that wit for the barbecue. You will certainly be out of your element," Claudia advised as she swept past Rachel. Pausing at the door, she tossed back over her shoulder, "But I can assure you from personal experience that it will take more than wit to keep a man like Gray entertained." She made a dramatic exit, slamming the door behind her.

The meaning of her words hit Rachel hard. Certainly she had known that a virile man such as Gray would have bedded many women, but it hurt to have his intimacies thrown in her face.

Rachel hardly noticed when Mrs. Wilmont proudly displayed her workmanship. She gave her approval and promised she would return at a later date for the final fitting. She left the shop feeling even more depressed than when she had entered.

There was no sense in moping around, Rachel decided as she walked. She refused to give that ill-bred, bad-tempered Claudia the satisfaction of upsetting her day. She forced her mind on to more pleasant thoughts and went about her errands. Soon she became aware of a carriage that had slowed to match her pace as she walked. Its occupant signaled the driver to stop as the carriage door opened and Gray swung to the ground beside her. He looked handsome and dashing, sporting the new white hat Rachel had purchased and sent to him at Richfield. Though it was bold and assuming to do so, she felt she was to blame for the abuse suffered by the former hat.

"Madam," Gray began somewhat irritably, "do you not realize that proper ladies do not walk the streets, particularly in the heat of the afternoon? If you keep this up you are going to have the face of a field hand." He touched her cheek gently, admiring the beauty of her milky complexion.

Rachel languished in the feel of his fingers against her skin.

He pulled his hand away, trying once more to look stern. "Where are your carriage and coachman? Surely such necessities are well within your means, judging from the success of your business endeavor."

"I confess, sir, that I am without carriage or coachman today."

"Then I shall place myself at your disposal," Gray announced. He took her firmly in hand and assisted her into the cool interior of his carriage. Settling in the seat beside her, he signaled the driver and the carriage lurched forward.

"But, sir, I have not yet told you my destination," Rachel pointed out.

"Next, I shall deliver a lecture on the possible evils of accepting rides from men who pass and see you on foot," Gray told her. He smiled rakishly and said softly, "Though I am not certain my intentions are any more honorable than theirs would be."

Rachel blushed and smiled demurely. His presence and words never failed to rekindle the love she held for him.

He grew serious again and took her hand in his. He captured her eyes. "It is not safe to be alone. You are a very beautiful woman, Rachel, and the men of Charleston can take only so much temptation."

"Very well," she agreed.

"Promise?"

"Promise."

Gray lifted her hand to his lips and kissed it lovingly. The feel of her soft skin sent a shudder through him. He wasn't sure how much temptation he could take, either.

"Am I to assume by your presence here that all is in order at Richfield for the barbecue?" she asked when he had at last, though reluctantly, released her hand.

"I am here to handle a few last-minute details," Gray said, turning his thoughts to more respectable avenues. "Also, I was to meet with a man on some business matters but I was informed at the hotel that he was delayed and will not arrive in town for several more days."

"Your holdings must be quite diverse," Rachel said. It seemed he was always meeting with someone to discuss a business matter.

Gray nodded. "My father left me a good deal. I have added more to that. It never seemed all that important before. It was a game of sorts, like winning the mercantile in a card game. But over these past weeks I have begun to take it more seriously." Gray spoke with thoughtfulness. "I don't understand why, but now it matters to me a great deal."

Rachel could not imagine not taking one's livelihood seriously. But perhaps she would have felt as Gray did if she had not had Andrew to provide for.

"I was surprised to learn that you and Ezra Daniels were acquainted," Gray said. He watched for her reaction.

The sudden change of subject caught Rachel off guard. She tried to sound casual as she spoke. "I was surprised to see him again."

"He spoke very highly of you."

Fear coursed through Rachel. Had Captain Daniels said

273

something of her past after she had left the Wades' last evening? "That was very kind of him," Rachel murmured. She fidgeted uncomfortably in her seat.

"It made me aware of how little I know of you," Gray said. He could see that she didn't want to discuss it, but this time, trapped in the confines of his carriage, she could not escape his questions.

"I believe you know as much of my past as I know of yours," she commented.

Gray nodded. "This is true. Yet I desire to know all about you, especially since you occupy so much of my thoughts."

Even his kind words did not ease the twisting in her stomach. "What—what did Captain Daniels tell you?" She could not meet his eye, but felt his gaze steadfastly upon her.

Gray was silent for a long, agonizing moment. "Very little, actually," he admitted. "It seems no one knows much about you."

Rachel gritted her teeth and turned to look at him. "Then what is it you wish to know?" she challenged.

Gray's face softened. "Only what you wish to tell me."

Some of the tension left Rachel. Of course he should be interested in her past, it was a perfectly normal desire. She must tell him something—anything—to satisfy his curiosity. "I have no family. My parents are both dead. I lived in Louisiana before going to Missouri." It was a very general but truthful accounting of her past.

"And did you meet Mr. Fontaine in Louisiana?"

"Who?"

"Your husband."

There he was again! That man had caused her more

274

problems than any real husband ever could. Rachel nodded. "Yes."

Gray took her hand. "My dear, you have had such tragedy in your life. Small wonder you do not like to speak of it."

She cast her eyes downward and said a silent prayer that this would be the end of their conversation. The continual string of lies she had to tell preyed on her mind. For the others, she cared not, but it bothered her greatly that she could not tell Gray the truth. How could she do that now? How could she admit that she had deceived him from the start? What would he think of her then?

"I won't ask you to speak of it again," Gray promised.

Rachel winced. He was being so nice about it! That only made her feel worse. It seemed she could not come out ahead no matter what. But did she deserve to?

Even before the manor house came into view Rachel saw the puffs of smoke that hung over the tall trees, and smelled the aroma of roasting pork and beef. She knew the barbecue would be held in the grove of oaks behind the main house; that was where her parents had entertained their guests when the Samuelses had owned Richfield. It was a pleasant, shady place a short distance from the house, bordering the rose garden that had been Althea's pride and joy.

The wide, circular driveway was filled with saddle horses and carriages. Guests alighted and were quickly caught up in the festive atmosphere as they called greetings to their friends and neighbors. Servants were busy leading the animals to the barnyard to be unsaddled and unharnessed for the day. Laughing children ran and played about the green lawn. Swarms of ladies and gentlemen in their finest attire milled about the yard and wide portico waiting to greet the master of Richfield, Gray Montgomery, before entering the house and continuing on to the glade.

Rachel's heart pounded with excitement as her carriage halted and she got her first look of her childhood home. The red brick structure with its high, gabled roof looked as stately and dignified as she remembered. The lawn was carefully tended and dotted with the colors of blossoming camellias, magnolias, azaleas, and dogwood. Her coachman helped her to the ground, then pulled the carriage away. Selma, her maid who had accompanied her, would first see to her trunks before joining the other servants at their own barbecue in the slaves' quarters.

Rachel's gaze fell to rest on Gray. Dressed in gray trousers and coat and white linen shirt he looked the part of the successful planter, radiating the hospitality and charm expected of his position in the community. He was surrounded by his guests and he greeted each one warmly. There was a good deal of hand-shaking and back-slapping among the men, while the ladies were favored with a smile and gracious words. Charlotte Wade stood at his side gleefully carrying out her role as hostess.

The sight of the man never failed to stir her emotions, and today was no exception. Mixed with the joy of being at Richfield again was the thrill of spending the day with Gray. It made Rachel feel almost light-headed. She entered the press of people and greeted those she knew as she made her way toward the circle that surrounded Gray. Everyone was in the party spirit, laughing and joking and enjoying the friendship of the gathering.

Finally, she caught Gray's eye and she saw him speak to Charlotte then excuse himself from the guests and make his way through the crowd toward her. He was stopped frequently by those who were anxious to share some bit of news or compliment him on the home he had opened to them.

Gray took both her hands in his. "You are the picture of loveliness," he declared as his eyes hungrily devoured the pale-green gown she wore.

"Oh, Gray, you are so sweet. But how can you say that when there are so many pretty young girls about?"

"Are there other girls about? I had not noticed," he told her. Rachel basked in the warmth of his smile. "Come inside. I want you to see my home."

"But, Gray—your guests," she protested as he escorted her through the crowd.

"Aunt Charlotte will see to them," he said, dismissing her concern. He had little desire to fulfill his duty as host, preferring instead to devote all his attention to this one special guest.

The wide hall which ran from front to back of the house was filled with the laughter and joy of the many people congregated there. Young girls in gay crinoline dresses climbed the graceful staircase giggling and whispering and sharing secrets. Servants moved about bearing trays of cold drinks.

"Welcome to Richfield," Gray said proudly. He guided her from room to room showing off his many fine possessions with modest pride. He was anxious to share his accomplishment with Rachel. It had not been easy for him to decorate the huge manor house.

It was most difficult for Rachel to keep her mind on what Gray was saying as they toured the house. Each room brought back a flood of childhood memories: her father at his desk in the library, Althea conducting evening prayers in the drawing room, Christmas morning, elegant dinners, the laughter of her birthday parties. Past and present meshed together in a happy kaleidoscope of feelings, wants, and desires. For as much as she recalled her past here, the vision of Gray presented itself easily. It was as if past and future were one and Gray belonged within the walls of Richfield as much as her parents did. Rachel had feared that seeing her home again would make Gray seem like an outsider to her. But that had not happened. He belonged here. She belonged here. And there was still a place for the treasured memories she held close to her heart.

"It's beautiful, Gray. The house and the furnishings are all lovely," Rachel praised as they stepped onto the back portico.

He sighed with relief. "I am very much at ease evaluating horseflesh or reviewing a purchase contract. But the selection of drapes and linens found me somewhat ill at ease," he admitted.

Rachel smiled. She wanted to tell him that a proper feminine hand would solve that problem, but dared not be so bold. She accepted his arm as they strolled across the lawn to the grove that sheltered the guests from the hot midday sun.

At a distance sufficient to keep smoke from disturbing the guests were the long barbecue pits and huge pots of sauce. Their rich aroma filled the slight breeze that stirred and tempted the guests with the promise of a fine meal to come. The pits had been burning since the night before and were now troughs of glowing red embers. The meat hung on spits above them, dripping juices into the hissing coals. Under the thickest shade were picnic tables covered with the finest linen. Chairs, benches, hassocks, and cushions dotted the glade.

The older married women were seated together discussing babies, illnesses, who had married whom and why. Children ran about playing tag. Men clustered together talking of politics, the planting season, and sharing news from the local community. Separate from these three groups were the young men of the Low Country vying for the attention of the ivory-skinned maidens. Taught well by their mothers, the girls batted their lashes and laughed easily, displaying only enough of their beauty and charm to attract a proper marriage proposal. Rachel had missed her chance at the courting game and was now obligated to sit with the old women when Gray reluctantly left her to oversee the meal preparation in the cook house.

Rachel settled in amid the women, most of whom she knew, and joined in their discussion of childbirth. Emily Fisk, the wife of a merchant, was expecting her first child in only a few weeks and the ladies were most anxious to impart a wealth of advice. Recalling the strain of her own pregnancy, Rachel felt much sympathy for Emily, who was obviously feeling quite miserable. Presently, and much to Emily's relief, the conversation turned to other topics when Charlotte Wade joined the group.

"I was afraid we would never be invited to Richfield," Mrs. Padgette said to Charlotte.

"Such a shame Gray and Claudia never married," Mrs. Lancaster commented.

"A home such as this should be filled with the laughter of children," Mrs. Covington, mother of eleven, stated emphatically.

"I am certain the house will not be empty for too long," Charlotte offered.

"Oh?" Mrs. Lancaster asked, her interest suddenly piqued.

"Do you know something we don't?" Mrs. Padgette wanted to know.

Rachel's ears perked up and she hoped her expression had not betrayed her feelings.

"Now, now, let us not set our tongues to wagging," Charlotte cautioned. She greatly disliked discussing the subject of her unmarried nephew. It reminded her that she had been remiss in her duty of finding him a proper wife.

"Well, it is a shame all right," Mrs. Padgette agreed and picked up her sampler. "But it is good to be here again after all these years."

"I wonder whatever became of the family who lived here?" Charlotte mused aloud.

Speculation on the whereabouts of Richfield's previous owner had been the topic of many a conversation some years ago. Each person had his own ideas and embellishments to add to the rumors that had circulated through the community.

"Emily, dear, this all happened before you moved to Charleston. The family that used to live here simply vanished." Mrs. Covington eagerly provided the information.

Emily looked as though she could hardly care less, but forced herself to pay attention.

"Now, what was their name?" Mrs. Covington asked as she pursed her lips trying to recall more of the details.

"It was Samuels. How could you have forgotten that?" Mrs. Padgette said.

Rachel's stomach twisted into a painful knot. The women of Charleston remembered her parents after so many years? She had not thought that would happen. But what would they say of her mother and father? She could not bear to sit here and listen as they told the story of the dishonor her father had brought to the family. She couldn't!

Suddenly Mrs. Padgette's voice cut through her runaway thoughts and calmed her fears. "Why, Althea Samuels was one of the finest, most gracious ladies I have ever known," she declared.

The women all nodded in agreement.

"She was absolutely grief-stricken when Mr. Samuels passed away. Poor thing," Mrs. Lancaster recalled sadly.

"She allowed no visitors after his death. Then suddenly one day word came that she had left Charleston. We never knew where she went or what became of her," Mrs. Covington said.

It was true. Althea was so ashamed and humiliated by Frederick's death that she had allowed no visitors to Richfield. And after her mother's breakdown Rachel had done the same, not wishing to give the gossips of the county anything more to discuss of the Samuelses' family tragedy.

Emily Fisk looked properly saddened by the story, but offered no comment. Her own plight was distressing enough.

"Such a pity. There were so many of us who wanted to help," Mrs. Padgette said.

Rachel's heart threatened to burst as the ladies spoke of her mother with such kindness. She had feared for so long that Althea would be remembered only by the reckless actions of her husband. Evidently the ladies had not known, or had since forgotten, Frederick Samuels's bungling of the family business affairs that plunged Althea into bankruptcy and drove her from her home. Relief flooded Rachel as she realized no unfavorable memories lingered to be told and retold.

Filled with exhilaration, Rachel excused herself from the gathering to wander about the barbecue. So much of her weighty past had been lifted from her shoulders now. Happily, she stopped to chat and laugh with the people she knew, and was introduced to many other guests for the first time.

When the barbecue was served, at least a dozen servants were kept busy carrying trays of the delicious meat to the guests. They all drew together in groups large and small to eat and talk and laugh. Gray appeared as Rachel was about to join Charlotte and Bernard and led her to a grassy knoll above the glade. There a servant spread out a blanket beneath a canopy of mighty oak branches, and she and Gray settled there to eat barbecue.

"My heavens, Gray, you should be attending to your guests," Rachel said as she sat comfortably in the circle of her full skirt.

Gray glanced down the hill at the others. "They are all very content," he reported, then turned to gaze at her. "Besides, I like the view better from here," he said pointedly.

A slight blush colored her cheeks. "We shall be the talk of Charleston by tomorrow if we are not careful," she said and smiled coyly.

Gray moved closer to her on the blanket. "Shall we be careful? Or shall we give them something to talk about?" he suggested in a husky voice. He wanted to take her in his arms and feel the soft, yielding curves of her body against him. He wanted to claim her lips with his. It was so difficult to hold his emotions in check when they clamored so loudly to be set free. But wait he must.

Gray's mellow laugh broke the tension between them. Rachel had not the will or the strength to deny him, and she was relieved that it was he who demonstrated this self-control. "We shall let them talk of someone else," he decided, and moved to a discreet distance from her.

Gray's gaze roamed to the stable in the distance. "You must bring Andrew riding."

Rachel laughed gently. "Gray, he is too young for such things."

"A boy is never too young to sit a horse," Gray insisted.

"But he can barely walk," Rachel pointed out.

"Oh." Gray looked perplexed for an instant as he considered the problem. "No matter. He can ride with me until he gets older. Then he will have a pony of his own to ride."

Rachel did not like the thought of her baby aboard a horse. She opened her mouth to protest, but Gray touched her lips with his finger, silencing her. "I will take special care of Andrew," he promised softly. "No harm will come to him." Her eyes met his and she knew she had nothing to fear.

The tranquility of their private picnic was broken by several men laboriously climbing the knoll.

"Gray! Gray!" Mr. Booth called urgently. The four men closed in around the couple with a purposeful look on each of their faces.

Gray was annoyed by this interruption but managed to remain calm and hospitable. "Gentlemen, what is it?"

"Mr. Wilton here doesn't believe you purchased that fine black stallion from Jonas Peabody. I told him you did, but he doesn't believe anyone could have talked that horse away from old Peabody," Bernard said.

"It's true, Mr. Wilton," Gray confirmed. "The stallion is in my stable."

"You have got to settle this once and for all," Bernard declared. "Let us go take a look at that horse."

"But, gentlemen," Gray protested as he glanced at Rachel sitting quietly beside him. It was with considerable pride that he had gotten such a fine horse and he was anxious to show it off, but not at the expense of leaving Rachel when he finally had her alone for a few minutes.

"Well, we do hate to interrupt. . ." Mr. Booth said apologetically to Rachel.

She smiled graciously. "Go show off your horse. I will join the ladies."

Gray saw to it that she was comfortably settled with his aunt before heading off to the stable. Rachel honestly did not mind him leaving to boast and brag to the others about the prized stallion; it was a typically male thing to do.

By late afternoon the guests with small children had left and the ladies had retired to their rooms upstairs to rest and prepare for the night's ball. The men gathered in the library to enjoy a good cigar, a bit of brandy, and talk of life and problems in the Low Country and beyond.

Unlike the other ladies, Rachel had been given a room of her own. She had tried to nap but found it impossible. Each time her eyes closed her mind exploded with images of Gray and of Richfield. Oh, how she loved them both! But would either ever be hers? She refused to let herself think that anything could come between them. Perhaps it was unrealistic, but just this once she would allow herself the fantasy and pretend that all things were possible.

Selma joined her presently and helped Rachel prepare for the ball. Rachel's hair was fashioned in loose curls atop her head and adorned with blue ribbons that matched the trim of her ivory dress. The gown's off-the-shoulder styling revealed the swelling tops of her breasts contrasted by her trim waist and full skirt of tiered lace.

Rachel's heart raced with excitement as she left her room and joined the other women descending the wide staircase. This was Rachel's first ball, and though it was years late, she intended to enjoy it to the fullest. She had been too young to attend such affairs during her previous life at Richfield, but had watched the activities from her hiding place at the top of the stairs. Sitting by her mother's knee afterward she had listened over and over to Althea's retelling of the evening's gaiety. And so at last Rachel was attending a ball; she thought it ironic that it should be at Richfield after all.

Gentle strains of music met Rachel as she moved amid the crowd and entered the ballroom. The aristocracy of Charleston was gathered there decked out in the most glorious gowns and suits imaginable. Couples moved gracefully around the dance floor while others stood around its perimeter enjoying refreshments. Candles in the two huge chandeliers and wall sconces illuminated the room with a soft light. Almost immediately, she was approached by Charles Forsyth, who asked her to dance. He was a young, rather handsome man whom she had seen often in her mercantile, and while she would have preferred to dance with Gray, she accepted Charles's invitation so as not to hurt his feelings.

As the two whirled around the dance floor, Rachel found herself searching the crowd for Gray, but he was nowhere to be seen. She reasoned that he was busy with his guests, as a proper host should be, and turned her attention to Charles.

A continuing succession of men followed Charles, and Rachel danced with all of them, flattered by each invitation. Some were older gentlemen, like Bernard Wade and Mr. Padgette, while others were considerably younger, not to mention more handsome and appealing. She enjoyed each of them, though none were whom she really wanted to be with, and she was totally unaware of the dilemma Gray faced across the room.

A bevy of Charlotte's friends had seized Gray immediately upon his arrival in the ballroom and were anxiously imparting their wealth of knowledge and opinions on his newly decorated home. The women talked constantly, one taking over the conversation immediately when the other seemed to be wearing down. He was held captive by them, unable to graciously break free from them. And what made it even more difficult to tolerate was that each time he glanced about the room he saw Rachel on the dance floor with a different man. He wanted to be the one holding her in his arms, feeling her smooth, soft skin, looking into those huge brown eyes of hers. It took all the patience he could muster to stand still and give some semblance of attention to the well-intentioned ladies.

But when the music began again and Gray saw Rachel sweep past in the arms of Charles Forsyth for the third time—and he was keeping count—Gray could not restrain himself further. "Please, ladies, you must pardon me," he begged, cutting off Mrs. Booth's oration on curtain fabrics.

Chapter 12

"Excuse me, Forsyth, I am cutting in." His tone was not nearly as gracious as his words.

"Sorry, old boy, this dance is taken," Charles tossed back, emphasizing the word "old."

Rachel looked back and forth between the two men, fearful from the venomous look in Gray's steely eyes that they might come to blows.

Gray glowered at Charles and used his greater height to his advantage. "I am cutting in," he ground out, his eyes shooting daggers of hatred at the younger man.

Charles shrank back. The whiskey he had consumed had not been enough to make him foolhardy. He had heard the stories that circulated through the county of Gray's temper. While normally calm and easygoing, once provoked Gray was a dangerous man.

Gray took Rachel into his arms and they fell in step with the other dancers. She had never seen such anger in him. His eyes were cold and his jaw set determinedly. She did not know what could be the cause of his sudden foul mood. Could her innocent dance with Charles have set him off?

"Gray, I did not mean to displease you," she offered softly. She watched closely for his reaction, but he said nothing. "It was only Charles. I think of him in a brotherly way."

"Brotherly!" Gray echoed angrily. How could this woman, who had once been courted and wed, be so innocent in the ways of men! "The man's actions were akin to those of a rutting stag! He did not have one 'brotherly' intention in him!"

Why was he always getting angry with her over things she did not understand? Rachel did not know what she had done to upset him. "But I was only dancing with him," she said helplessly.

Gray suddenly stopped their dance, mindless of the near pile-up of couples he had caused behind them, and quickly escorted Rachel onto the terrace. Holding her arm firmly he led the way down the stone steps and into the seclusion of the garden.

The night air was cool, sweetened by the many rose-bushes that were heavy with blooms. A full moon hung over the horizon casting a soft light over them. The orchestra's music was faint in the background. Rachel sat down obediently on the white bench and watched with wide eyes as Gray paced restlessly in front of her. He seemed so agitated he could not speak.

"Gray, I do not know what I have done to offend you," she pleaded, breaking their long silence.

He touched his brow. "I know you do not understand. That is the problem."

"I was only dancing . . ."

"With nearly every man in the room!"

"But they are all friends of mine," she explained. "They were only being kind."

"Kind? Kind! Rachel, you are a beautiful woman, and a very desirable woman. Charles was nearly drooling all over himself with lust!"

"Are you accusing me of flaunting myself?" she asked hotly, rising to her feet.

Gray stopped his pacing and turned to her. "No, no, Rachel, I am not accusing you of any such thing. But I wanted to dance with you. And instead I was held captive by those old hens, watching as one man after another held you."

"Gray, those others mean nothing to me. I don't understand why you are so angry with me!"

The muscles in his jaw hardened. "Because no man wants to see the woman he loves in the arms of other men on the night he intends to propose marriage!" he thundered.

She gasped audibly and covered her mouth with a trembling hand. "Marriage?" she whispered.

"Damn!" he swore and turned his back to her. He collected himself quickly and faced her once more. "I rehearsed a most eloquent marriage proposal. For days I have practiced. I wanted to charm you with beautiful words of love so you could not refuse me," he said dejectedly. "And instead I blurt it out in anger." Why did he always lose control where this woman was concerned?

Her heart thumped wildly as she flew to him. "Oh, Gray," she said breathlessly.

He took her hands in his and pulled her close. "I love you so, Rachel," he confessed. He looked deep into those brown eyes that haunted him. "I will take care of you, and love you. You will never want for a thing," he promised. "And your son will be my son. I will love him as well."

Rachel's throat tightened and tears threatened to fill her eyes. She had dared to imagine this moment for so long. When he had left her in St. Joseph she had thought she would never see him again. Yet she knew she loved him even then, and the months that she carried his child within her, Rachel had allowed herself only the small hope that she would someday see him once more. Even when they had met again in Charleston and had felt a mutual attraction, she had never fully expected that he would ask for her hand. And now his marriage proposal had caught her completely off guard. She was so stunned she could not open her mouth to speak.

Gray enfolded her in his powerful arms. "Do not give me your answer now. I know you have much to consider," he said gently.

"But, Gray," she said hoarsely, finding her voice at last.

"Shh," he whispered. A small smile tugged at the corners of his lips. "If you turn me down now I shall surely die a broken man. Give me your answer later. Then I will know you gave my proposal some consideration."

She shook her head weakly. When she was in his arms she lost all strength and reasoning ability. "Gray . . ." she whispered. She wanted to tell him—to tell the world! She would marry him! Her heart fairly burst with excitement.

He pulled her closer, and the warmth of his body against hers drained her thoughts. His lips sought hers and she came to him willingly. Their kiss deepened, becoming more satisfying, more demanding. Gray molded her against him and his masculine scent overwhelmed her. His lips moved masterfully over hers as his strong hands sought out her soft flesh, touching and caressing her, sending ripples of pleasure through every fiber of her being. Her mind reeled and she could focus on only one thought: she loved him and this was where she wanted to spend the rest of her life.

The house had long since quieted for the evening. The guests were in their rooms, the master of Richfield had retired to his chamber, and the servants were settled in for the night. A peaceful slumber had fallen over the estate, welcome after the gaiety of the day's barbecue and ball that had brought life to the plantation for the first time in years. The serenity possessed all but one guest, who tossed and turned restlessly on the goosedown bed trying desperately to come to terms with her own conscience. But it gave her no peace in its relentless haunting, and finally Rachel donned her wrapper and slipped quietly into the hallway. She looked both ways, and seeing that no one else was about, descended the stairs with silent steps.

This should be the happiest evening of her life, Rachel thought woefully as she idly strolled through the exquisitely furnished parlor. The man—the only man—she had ever cared for had asked for her hand in marriage. He had professed his love for her, promised a future rich and full, and vowed to fulfill her every whim. After so many years of having nothing but heartache and loneliness, hard work and troubles, she stood now on the threshold of having all the things that she had only dared to dream of.

Rachel slumped down on the sofa and rubbed her forehead wearily. It was all within her grasp. She had but to open her mouth and utter one word and she would be officially engaged to Gray Montgomery, the most hand-some, most sought-after man in the county. The man who had captured her heart, occupied her thoughts and dreams for months, the man she truly loved. She could go right now, in the dead of night, mindless of the scandal it would cause if she was caught lurking outside his chambers at this hour, and she could wake him and tell him, yes! Yes, she would marry him. Oh, how she wanted to do just that.

But she couldn't. Rachel dragged herself from the sofa and continued her aimless walk about the house. She could not accept his proposal. Not now. Not with her conscience screaming at her. For each time she recalled that moment when Gray had asked her to marry him, each time she remembered the glow in his eyes, the warmth of his smile, she also relived his vow to love her son as if the boy was his own.

Rachel's insides twisted into a cruel knot. Was she to forever suffer for her sins of the past? Was she entitled to no happiness because of her actions? Would she always be haunted by the things she had done? She had never meant to hurt Gray by not telling him of the child she had borne him. But when she had first met him in Charleston, she certainly could not have blurted out the truth, and as time went on, her charade and lies had become more complicated until it had become impossible to tell him. But now, now she had to face up to the truth.

She chewed her bottom lip pensively as she stopped at the door of the library. She recalled how her own father used to closet himself away in this room when he had a great problem to solve. Sometimes he would remain within for hours, but when he emerged he always knew what action to take. She found strength in that memory. Rachel drew in a deep breath and walked determinedly into the room. She settled herself on the soft, cushioned window seat and tucked her feet beneath her. The moon was high in the cloudless sky and cast a pale light on the rose garden as she gazed out the window behind her.

The dilemma she faced was truly a double-edged sword. If she told Gray right away that Andrew was his son, he might become angry with her for not telling him sooner. The act she had put on and the lies she had told certainly did not place her in a favorable light. But, on the other hand, if she didn't tell him until after their marriage he would be even more angry with her. He would think her a very deceptive woman for marrying him before telling him the truth. There was no easy answer to her problem. If she confessed before or after the wedding she risked losing him.

For one fleeting moment she considered never telling him, then dismissed the thought. Gray and Andrew both deserved to know they were father and son.

Rachel sighed wearily. There was only one course of action she could take, and deep inside, she had known it all along. She would tell Gray the truth before the wedding and exchange vows with a clear conscience. And if after hearing her out, Gray didn't want to go ahead with the wedding, well ... well ...

Well, she just couldn't worry about that now. She felt a great weight rise from her shoulders. She would tell Gray everything, and she would never have to tell another lie again. What a marvelous feeling!

Rachel was about to rise from the window seat when she heard footsteps in the hallway. She couldn't imagine who would be about at this late hour, but she was not properly attired to meet anyone and certainly in no position to explain why she was up and about at this time of night. Rachel sat perfectly still in the dimly lit room, silently praying that whoever it was would pass by the library and allow her to scamper up the stairs unnoticed. But to her dismay, the footsteps came nearer and the lanterns in the hallway sent long shadows into the room. It traveled across the floor until a tall figure stood in the doorway. Rachel swallowed hard. Oh, Lordy, it was Gray! What would he think of her parading about in her night rail and wrapper? Skulking about his house at all hours, invading the sanctity of his library. She couldn't let him see her, but there was no time to hide. She froze, not moving a muscle, and prayed fervently that he would not see her sitting like a statue in the shadows.

Gray ran his fingers through his black wavy hair as he made his way to the sideboard. He was tired and wanted to sleep. But each time he closed his eyes, the vision of the flaxen-haired, brown-eyed Rachel Fontaine presented itself and stirred his emotions fitfully as he recalled holding her in his arms as they danced. The feel of her soft skin, her creamy bosoms swelling over the top of her gown, her red, inviting lips all lent themselves to an enjoyable evening on the dance floor but made for a damnable memory once he was alone in his bed. And to make matters worse, she was under his own roof. Only a few steps away. And there was nothing he could do. It was maddening!

Gray poured himself a brandy and raised the glass to his lips. The taste of the amber liquid was not as appealing as it had seemed when he had shrugged into his trousers and white linen shirt and anxiously escaped the torture of his lonely bedchamber. He set the glass aside. Perhaps he would sit here for a while and read, he decided. He would try anything to keep the visage of that blond temptress from wreaking havoc with his imagination, to say nothing of his baser desires.

He moved to the desk and took a match from the drawer. As it sparked to life, he heard a tiny gasp from the direction of the window. Gray held the match higher and strained his eyes in the darkness.

"Is someone there?" he called. There was no response, but he detected a slight movement. "Who is there?"

"No one." Rachel shrank back farther into the shadows. Good grief, had she really said such an idiotic thing!

"Rachel?" he asked. His heart began to beat faster. Yes, he was certain that was her voice. "Rachel, what are you doing up? Come over here and— Ouch! God—" Gray shook his hand to extinguish the match, then sucked on his finger both to ease the pain and to halt the oath that clamored to burst forth. His physical discomfort was already distressing enough without adding a burned finger to his miseries.

"Wait a minute, let me light the lantern," he said irritably as he yanked open the drawer again. What was she doing here, in the dark, all alone? Gray swallowed hard, knowing the effort it would take to conduct himself as a gentleman.

Rachel launched herself off the window seat and flew to the desk. "No, don't light the lantern," she pleaded, and covered his hands with hers.

Gray's eyes were not accustomed to the dark and he had not seen her coming. He jumped when he felt her soft hands fold over his. "Why not?" he croaked.

Good grief, she could not let him see her attired in this fashion! What would he think of her? "Because—because I am not dressed."

Gray thought his legs would give way beneath him. "What?" he moaned with a ragged breath.

"I mean—I mean I am only wearing my—" Heavens above, what was she saying! She tried to collect herself. "What I mean to say is that I was not expecting anyone else to be up at this time of night and I—"

"Stop, please, Rachel," he begged, and wiped his perspiring brow with his sleeve. "I need to sit down for a moment," he said, and collapsed onto the window seat. By now his eyes had adjusted to the darkness and he could see Rachel's hips and bosoms outlined in the wrapper that was tied securely around her small waist. His loins throbbed with renewed desire. Oh, but to hold her shapely form against him without the trappings of a woman's daily attire. To feel her soft curves yielding against him, to— *A gentleman . . . a gentleman . . . a gentleman . . .*

"I'm—I'm going to my room now," Rachel said softly.
"Good—"
"No!"
"But, Gray—"
"You obviously could not sleep and neither could I," he began in a reasoning tone, "so we may as well chat for a while."

He looked exceptionally handsome with the moonlight filtering softly through the window behind him. His white shirt hung open and the hair of his chest looked darker than she remembered. Rachel felt drawn to him and she knew it was not wise to remain here, but she couldn't leave now, any more than she could have left his bedchamber that night in St. Joseph.

"Surely we have something to discuss," Gray said lightly. He did not want her to leave him, even though his good sense told him he could do no more than look. Right now, he would settle for that.

Something to discuss, indeed, Rachel mused. Well, she might as well tell him now and get it over with. There would never be a good time for such a talk and at least now they could have some privacy. She drew together her courage and sat down on the seat near Gray.

"Yes, there is something I must talk to you about," Rachel said.

"I imagine you have a great deal on your mind," Gray speculated. He could see her expression in the moonlight.

"No," she told him. "Only one thing, really." She tried to organize her thoughts, but there was no time. She had to say it now before she lost her courage.

"It's Andrew, isn't it?"

Rachel was shocked. "Yes. How did you know?"

"You have something you want to tell me about the boy," Gray said wisely.

How could he have known? "Yes," she admitted.

"It is about Andrew's father."

"Well, yes, but—"

"Don't bother, Rachel, I know what you are going to say."

She looked at him with wide eyes. "You do?"

"I've known for a long time that we would have this discussion as soon as you were ready. You need not look so upset, my dear, I understand completely."

"You do?" Rachel asked. No, he couldn't know! "Gray—"

"You are worried that Andrew won't know who his real father is. Isn't that so?"

"Yes, but—"

Gray reached out and took her hand. "Don't worry, the

boy will know who his father is. I will love the child as my own and treat him as such, but I will never lie to him and pretend to be something I am not."

Rachel winced inwardly. "Gray, please—"

"Shh," he whispered, and touched his finger to her lips, silencing her. "A man deserves to be known to his son, and I will not rob your late husband of that honor."

Rachel was sick. His words pounded her senses unmercifully. He was right, of course, everything he said was true, only he was saying it about the wrong man! Gray was so unselfish and caring and kind, and it made her feel all the worse for not telling him the truth long ago.

"Gray," she begged, "please let me speak. You don't understand." Rachel drew in a deep breath and was about to speak when the sound of footsteps reached her ears. Fear spread through her. "Someone is coming," she whispered.

Gray shrugged. "So?"

Rachel jumped to her feet. "We cannot be found together in the dark, like ... like ... this! Word of it will be all over Charleston by tomorrow."

Gray stood up. Though he was relatively unconcerned about a blemish to his own reputation, he did have to consider Rachel. "What do you suggest?" he asked in a low voice.

"We have got to hide," she said desperately.

"Madam, I do not intend to hide from my own guest in my own home."

"Shh! Come on." Rachel took his hand and pulled him across the room to a tiny chamber where her father used to store guns and important papers and the whiskey he didn't want her mother to learn of. Rachel pulled the door open, urged Gray inside, and followed him in.

298

"How did you know of this room?" he asked in surprise.

She couldn't tell him the truth. "You pointed it out today when you showed me the house," she whispered.

"I did?"

"Certainly. How else would I have known?"

Gray was too taken by her nearness to clearly recall the events of this morning's house tour, and obediently he stepped backward to allow Rachel room to close the door. She left it open a crack and watched as a lone figure came into the library.

"It's Mrs. Covington, that old busybody," she reported in a whisper, "and she is helping herself to your brandy."

In the tiny room, Rachel's backside was only inches from Gray, and her nearness and feminine fragrance stirred his emotions once again. Her hair hung loose about her shoulders and he wanted so badly to run his hands through it, to feel its softness. The silken fabric of the wrapper clung to her trim waist and hung in gentle folds about her hips, sending his desires racing. He had to focus his attention on something else before his instincts took over completely and made him forget he was supposed to be a gentleman. He leaned forward to peer at Mrs. Covington over Rachel's head. At the same instant Rachel backed up to avoid being seen by the servant. Their bodies came together and the soft, round curves of Rachel's derriere nestled snugly against Gray's midsection while her back fell against the muscular wall of his chest.

Rachel gasped, and instantly Gray wrapped his arms about her and covered her mouth with his hand.

"Shh," he whispered. "Do you want her to find us in here?"

Rachel fell silent, but the warmth that radiated from

299

Gray penetrated her thin clothing and scorched her skin. He uncovered her mouth, but his fingers lingered to caress the silky skin of her cheek and wander downward along her throat. His touch made her knees weak and caused her senses to fly in all directions. Gray rubbed his cheek across the top of her hair and drank deeply of its lovely fragrance. All the memories, each intimate detail of the night she had spent in his bed in St. Joseph came back to her, awakening the passion that had long been slumbering. She ached with desire as his touch stirred her feelings, and she wanted to give in to temptation.

Somehow, Rachel kept her wits about her. She could not fall into his arms and give herself to him here and now, no matter how much she wanted to.

Rachel saw Mrs. Covington leave the library and she pushed the door open and spun away from Gray. But he reacted quickly and caught her wrist before she could escape. His eyes were dark with desire, and she realized what a fool she had been for closing herself up in the tiny chamber with him. Her lack of experience with men was always landing her in the darndest predicaments!

"Rachel, my love," Gray said, his voice thick with passion. "I am crazed with desire for you."

She backed away, but he held her wrist firmly. What could she do or say to discourage his advances? How could she tell him no when her own heart was screaming yes? Suddenly her retreat was halted by the window seat, leaving her no other escape route.

Gray slid his arms around her and pulled her close, crushing her breasts against his muscular chest. His hands roamed freely over her back and rose to caress the nape of her neck. All rational thought left him as the burning in his loins took control. His mouth covered hers hungrily, and was met with but a moment's resistance before her lips parted and allowed him to sample the sweetness that lay within.

Her palms touched his bare chest and her fingers dug into its thick dark hair. She pressed closer against him as her desire won out over the threads of logic that she had clung to.

His powerful hands deftly untied her wrapper and acquainted themselves with her trim waist, then climbed to cup each breast. Gray moaned her name and muzzled his face against her neck as his stroking thumbs brought the tiny buds to life. Then his arms moved to hold her tight against him and he gently laid her down on the window seat and stretched out his long form above her.

Gray kissed her greedily as his hand slid over her breast and traveled down the curve of her hip. Slowly, he pulled her night rail upward until it was gathered about her waist, and his hand caressed the silky skin of her outer thigh. He positioned one knee between hers.

Rachel trembled at the fell of his gentle hand. It had been so long since he had first touched her, leaving her with the memories of his mysterious male body. How many times had she wondered if the things he had done would ever again seem so wondrous. Now the memories became exquisite reality as her arms encircled his neck, stroking his hair. His kisses became more demanding, and she returned them with equal ardor. She had no strength, no will to resist his advances.

His anxious fingers kneaded her flesh as they roamed her silky thigh and slid beneath her to caress her round derriere. Her leg moved against his in response, sending waves of warmth radiating to his thigh through the fabric of his trousers. The curve of her hip fit snugly against his palm. She was just the right size, the perfect proportion, and fit against him naturally, like she belonged here beneath him. His hand slid across her ribs and closed over her breast, finding it full and ripe with anticipation. She was warm and giving under his caress, and when his fingers stroked her budding breast, Rachel reacted with unexpected passion.

Unexpected? The thought flew through Gray's mind like a runaway train. No, not unexpected. Not at all. Somehow he had known what her response would be. There was a distinct feeling of familiarity that came over him, stilling his hand, tempering his passion. It wasn't simply that the feel of her body was similar to his experiences with other women. Quite the contrary! It was more, much more than that. A small window to his memory opened a crack allowing a tiny beam of light to enter his consciousness. What was it? What was he trying to remember? Gray suddenly broke off their kiss and searched her face in the semidarkness.

His probing tongue, his stroking fingers, the warmth of his chest tantalizing hers had nearly blinded Rachel with passion. She moaned softly in protest when his lips left hers. She had dreamed of this moment for so long, ached for this moment, wanted this moment so badly that she could not allow it to end. She whispered his name pleadingly and her arms tightened around his neck pulling his mouth back to hers. This time her lips covered his hungrily and her fingers curled through his hair, flexing convulsively. Her leg slid around him urging him downward.

An explosion went off in Gray's head driving away every thought and signaling a tidal wave of desire that washed through him from head to toe. The urgency of his arousal became his only thought as his loins throbbed anxiously, clamoring to escape the confines of the fabric that strained to confine him. Her needs were as volatile as his. He could feel it, he sensed it, he knew it. Yes, he knew it. She wanted him as badly as he wanted her, and there was only one way to satisfy their need. Gray's hand swept over her breast one final time before hurriedly moving to unfasten his trousers. He silently cursed his awkward fingers as Rachel tightened her grip on him, refusing to let him move even inches away. Her hips arched upward, and Gray was afraid he would lose all control.

Suddenly the room was flooded with light, and Rachel opened her eyes quickly. Gray was slower to respond, but finally he, too, turned and saw Bernard Wade standing at the desk.

Rachel gasped and yanked her night rail downward. In doing so, her knee came up and struck Gray solidly in the loins. He cried out in pain and swore an oath that burned even Bernard's ears. He rolled sideways to shelter Rachel from his uncle's view, but lost his grip on the narrow window seat and fell headlong onto the floor, striking his chin on the seat's framework as he went down.

With cheeks aflame, Rachel jerked her wrapper closed and leaped to her feet, narrowly avoiding Gray, who was writhing with pain on the floor. She flew past the slack-jawed Bernard, who appeared nearly as embarrassed as she, raced up to her room, and closed the door firmly behind her.

It was a good hour later when Rachel heard a timid knock at her door. She peered out from under the covers that were drawn up to her chin and decided that she would have to face the world sooner or later. She might as well begin now, even though it would be difficult with the humiliation she had suffered so fresh in her mind. She pulled on her wrapper and tied it securely in place, then eased the door open a crack. Gray was waiting there, now wearing an emerald dressing gown over his trousers.

"May I come in?" he asked in a low voice.

Rachel instinctively grasped the top of her wrapper and held it closed. "I don't think that would be a good idea."

"I assure you, madam, in my present condition I am quite harmless," he told her.

"I am so sorry, Gray. I didn't mean to kick you in the ... the ..." Her cheeks pinkened.

"Please, don't speak of it," he requested, looking all the more pained. "Could I please come in? My guests all seem to have a penchant for roaming about at late hours and I would rather not be seen lurking in the hallways."

Rachel opened her door and Gray walked inside with slow, stiff steps.

"I have come to offer my apologies for my conduct earlier this evening," Gray said when Rachel had closed the door. "My behavior was not that of a gentleman."

She managed a small smile. "Nor was mine very ladylike."

He brushed an easy kiss across her forehead. "Good night, my sweet." He opened the door and stepped into the hall.

"Good night. Sleep well," she whispered as she closed the door behind him.

Sleep? Well, what else could he do, he thought as he made his way to his lonely chamber with painful steps.

* * *

The dawn at Richfield brought to Rachel the same emotions as during her youth here, when happiness and security were all her heart had known. It had been such a long time since she had felt this way. As a young girl living within the strong walls of Richfield, it had been her parents who had caused those feelings; now it was Gray, the man she loved and would wed, who brought such serenity to her.

Rachel walked to the window of her bedchamber and looked out over the grounds. Wisps of white smoke still rose from the barbecue pits, but all else had been cleared away, returning Richfield to its stately former self. The rose garden was directly below her window, and a smile crossed her face as she recalled last evening when Gray's marriage proposal had sent her senses reeling. And suddenly she wanted to see him. She could not bear another moment without him.

But Rachel's enthusiasm was brought up short as the vision of her son flashed through her mind. Andrew. Andrew and Gray. The truth. She still had that to face up to. For all the wondrous feelings of serenity, the joy of Gray's proposal rang hollow in light of the lies she needed to untangle. Suddenly her only thought was to find Gray—at once—and confess the whole story. She wanted to tell him, needed to tell him, had to tell him!

Selma was painfully slow in preparing the bath and helping her dress. Rachel nagged, pleaded, and complained until the maid at long last had made her presentable and sent her on her way. She wanted to see Gray. He was here, only a short distance away, and she wanted to be with him at once!

With cheeks flushed as pink as the gown she wore, Rachel paused at the head of the staircase and, looking down, saw no one. All was quiet except for muffled voices in the back of the house. Raising her skirt to a most unladylike height, Rachel's slippered feet flew down the stairs as if they were wings. She followed the voices to the library and peered past the half-opened door to see Gray seated at his desk speaking with a man whose back was toward her. She didn't recognize him or his voice when he spoke.

Rachel's heart fluttered predictably. Gray was as devastatingly handsome this morning as he had been last night when they had danced until the wee hours of the morning. She yearned to be held by those powerful but gentle arms again. She cursed her luck that the object of her heart's desire should be involved in a business discussion when she was so anxious to have him all to herself. Resolutely, she turned to slip quietly away so as not to disturb Gray and his guest.

"Rachel."

The sound of her name spoken with so smooth and mellow a voice sent a chill up her spine and halted her. Gray crossed the room and held out his hand to her. "Please don't go," he said softly.

His strong, warm fingers folded over hers and their eyes met. For a moment the world stopped turning and the two of them were alone in the universe. Their expressions told more than words, as the love they shared flowed between them easily, gently, and completely.

Finally Gray found his voice. "I would like you to meet this gentleman," he said as he escorted her into the library. "I have expected him in Charleston for over a week now to discuss business and finally he arrived this morning."

The well-dressed man shifted his bulky frame as they

approached. "I am very sorry to disturb you at so early an hour," he offered as he rose awkwardly to his feet.

"No need to apologize," Gray assured him cordially. "Rachel, I would like to present . . ."

Rachel's heart froze in midbeat and her stomach rolled into a painful knot as the visitor turned to face her. She felt the color drain from her. Her mind screamed out in revulsion as her most dreaded nightmare presented itself before her in the person of Fergus Cavanaugh.

She heard herself respond to his greeting and shook inwardly as he placed a wet kiss on her hand. Oh please, God, she prayed silently, don't let him recognize me! Don't let him remember me! Please, God, no! Her breathing stopped. She was afraid to speak, afraid to move, fearful that some mannerism or gesture would jog Fergus's memory and he would blurt out the truth about her past. Light beads of perspiration dampened her temples. Every muscle in her body was drawn tight.

The spark of recognition suddenly gleamed in Fergus's small eyes. He knew who she was! And he saw by the fear in Rachel's eyes that she was aware of his keen memory.

"Always a pleasure to come to the Low Country and meet the lovely young maidens, Miss Fontaine," Fergus said smoothly as his eyes raked over her.

Rachel's heart pounded in her ears. Was he going to betray her? He was toying with her—and enjoying it!

"It's 'Mrs.,' " Gray said. "Rachel is a widow and has a small son."

Fergus looked perplexed, then his heavy lips twisted into a smug smile. Rachel could not bear the man's gaze upon her another second. She must leave! She must get away at once.

"If you gentlemen will excuse me, I will leave you to

your business," she said, and managed to maintain her composure as she swept gracefully from the room. She wanted to turn to Gray, to run into his arms and have him banish Fergus Cavanaugh from her life forever. But how could she go to him? She didn't even have the courage to look him in the eye.

Once out of the library, Rachel nearly collapsed. Her limbs, heavy with fear and anxiety, reluctantly propelled her to the foot of the staircase. She leaned heavily on the banister for support.

Her mind was lost in a muddle of fear and worry. Would Gray learn the truth? Would Fergus gleefully tell all he knew of her past? Why shouldn't he? What did he have to gain by keeping her secret? She would be the laughing stock of Charleston when those rich old aristocratic hens learned the truth of her parents and their disgrace, of her life of poverty in Louisiana, and of how she had left Fergus at the altar and run away with his money. And they would laugh at Gray, too, for his involvement with her. It would all come out now. No doubt everyone would now discover her lies about her trumped-up husband and little Andrew's future would be ruined. Oh why, why did she tell those lies, Rachel berated herself. Why didn't she tell Gray the truth right from the start? Oh, if she could only go back and have another chance. Now her son, her precious little babe, would suffer unmercifully when it became known that he was a bastard.

Fergus's hearty laugh from the library suddenly spurred Rachel into action. She could not remain at Richfield another moment. She could not face Gray when he emerged from the library, not knowing if Fergus had told him the true story about her. Finding her strength, Rachel charged up the staircase. She stopped the first servant she saw.

"You go find Selma and send her up to my room this very instant. Then get out to the stable and have my driver bring my carriage around in five minutes. Do you understand me?" Rachel spoke quietly but with an urgency that left the young girl wide-eyed. "Do you understand me?" she repeated giving the girl a small shake. She nodded and raced away.

Expensive gowns, delicate undergarments, shoes, silk stockings were crammed into Rachel's trunk, heedless of their condition. The maid rushed into her room and was shocked to see Rachel frantically packing, but said nothing. She closed the trunk and left the room behind Rachel.

At the top of the stairs Rachel looked down and made sure no one was in the entry hall before hurrying out of the house and into her awaiting carriage. The driver whistled to the team and they pulled away. Rachel watched out the window as the grand manor house faded from sight. She was sickened to realize that she was leaving the security and love of Richfield for a second time in her life. She had been lucky to get that second chance; it was not likely she would get a third.

Later that evening, Rachel watched from the window of her bedchamber as Gray's carriage stopped in front of her house. Her heart ached as he swung down and strode determinedly up the walk. Oh, how she wanted to rush down to meet him and fall into his arms. But she couldn't, she reminded herself. That would never happen now. Her lies had finally caught up with her.

Upon arriving home, Rachel had given specific instructions to the servants that no one—absolutely no one— would be received until she told them differently. She had made certain everyone in the house understood her wishes before closing herself up in her room for the remainder of the day. Only Hannah had dared to disturb her. Rachel had explained that she didn't feel well, and had managed to sound convincing enough that her friend left her alone with little argument.

A few minutes later, Gray walked back down the walkway. Rachel was grateful that her servants had done their jobs so well. Before entering his carriage, Gray turned and looked up at the house, his gaze searching the windows. Rachel jumped back quickly so as not to be seen. A moment later she heard the steady clip-clop of horses' hooves on the cobblestones.

Rachel wandered aimlessly about her chamber, agonizing over why Gray had come. Was he there to confirm the story Fergus Cavanaugh no doubt had told him? Did he want to hear it from her, giving her the benefit of the doubt? Or was he there to inform her that he no longer wanted to marry her?

Sleepless hours dragged by seemingly without end as Rachel's mind replayed the events of her last few years. She had not meant to harm anyone. She had only sought a better life for herself and, then, for her son. But somehow the world she had created was now falling down around her, threatening to hurt everyone she loved. Her plan for a wonderful life had turned into a catastrophe.

Rachel wandered through the sleeping house, lost in her thoughts, every fiber of her body stretched nearly to its limit with worry and anxiety. Sometime after midnight she found herself seated at her desk, clutching the pocket watch she had taken from Gray so long ago. Her tense muscles relaxed a bit as she recalled the night Gray had made sweet, gentle love to her. It had been beautiful. And despite everything that had happened, she was not sorry for it. No, she did not regret it. It had given her her son and had brought her close, oh, so close, to the life she yearned for.

She didn't budge from the house the following day. Though she had slept little her body was charged with nervous energy and she put it to use running after Andrew. She devoted her entire day to her son, sending Hannah to town for the day and leaving instructions with the servants that no guests would be received.

Her concern over Fergus Cavanaugh was like a giant weight on her shoulders that she could not shake off no matter how she tried to concentrate on other things. Over and over images of Fergus's lustful face formed in her mind. She could feel his foul breath on her skin and his hands tearing at her bodice the night she had fled Louisiana. She was sickened by the thought of him. And this lecherous beast held her future in his hand. She hated that thought; she hated Fergus Cavanaugh.

At midafternoon Gray came by to see her again, but, as before, was not allowed into the house. Rachel was in the parlor and overheard him arguing with the butler, then grumbling angrily when he was still turned away. Rachel could not face him. She knew he would tell her he was ending their engagement, thanks to Fergus's wagging tongue. And why shouldn't Fergus tell all he knew about her after what she had done to him? Rachel cringed when she thought of it. Ah! How Claudia would revel in the retelling of such news. And how hurt and humiliated Gray would be.

In early evening, another visitor came to the house. She was somewhat surprised to see Mr. Rhodes on her doorstep and allowed him to enter.

"Is something wrong?" she asked when they were seated in the parlor.

"No, no," he assured her as he fidgeted with his spectacles.

"Was everything all right at the mercantile?" She trusted Mr. Rhodes to manage things for a short period of time.

"Fine, just fine," he replied. He was perched nervously on the edge of his chair.

Rachel drew in a deep breath and steeled herself for the reply to her next question. "Did anyone come to see me today?"

Mr. Rhodes pursed his lips. "Only Mr. Montgomery. Seemed quite agitated that you were not there."

She was much relieved that Fergus had not been to the mercantile. "Then, Mr. Rhodes, may I ask the purpose of your visit here this evening?" She tried to sound gracious, but in fact she had little patience with the man.

His cheeks pinkened. "I have come to call on Hannah," he divulged.

"Hannah?" she blurted out, unable to contain her surprise.

"I—I saw her in town this morning. She said it would be all right," he hastened to reply.

"Why, certainly, of course," Rachel said after getting a grip on herself. "I will let her know you have arrived." She rose and left the room. Hannah and Mr. Rhodes? Well, why not, she thought. They certainly seemed suited to each other.

Hannah fluttered with excitement when Rachel found her in Andrew's room and told her Mr. Rhodes was waiting in the parlor. "I didn't realize you and he were seeing each other," she said with a smile as she took Andrew into her arms.

"Well, actually we have visited a few times when I was

312

in the mercantile,'' Hannah told her. She smoothed her dress and checked her hair in the small mirror that hung over Andrew's bureau. ''We are just friends.''

Rachel sat down on the rocker Hannah had just vacated and settled Andrew on her lap. ''By the look on his face, I would say Mr. Rhodes has more on his mind than friendship.''

Hannah giggled and covered her mouth in schoolgirl fashion. ''You were married once, Rachel, and you know how men get notions in their heads.''

The gaiety of the moment soured for Rachel. Her string of untruths never stopped haunting her. She picked up Andrew's book and opened it. ''Go on now. I will put Andrew to bed,'' Rachel instructed. She felt a pang of envy as Hannah hurried from the room.

Rachel decided to console herself by spending the evening with her son. But the sway of the rocker and Rachel's soft voice as she read put the boy to sleep after only a few short minutes. Rachel tucked him in bed and spent another restless night plagued by apprehensive thoughts of Fergus Cavanaugh and wrestling with the problem of what to do about Gray.

''Good morning, Mr. Rhodes.'' Rachel spoke an indifferent greeting as she rushed through the mercantile to the seclusion of her small office. Her hands trembled as she pulled the dividing curtain closed, then fumbled with her bonnet for several moments before she successfully untied its ribbons. Her stomach was in knots. She paced back and forth as much as space allowed, trying to calm her jangled nerves.

The day had started well enough. Though she had slept

little and felt wretched, Rachel could not stay away from her business any longer. Drawing together all her courage, she decided to walk to work since the morning was so lovely, hoping the clement weather would soothe her worried mind. But then, only a few blocks from her shop, she had seen him. Fergus must have seen her first because when she noticed him across the street he was already looking at her. He wore a sinister grin as his eyes followed her. He made no effort to cross the street and speak to her. He only watched from a distance, and she could feel his eyes boring into her back as she quickened her pace. The incident left her unnerved and even more distressed than before.

Getting her mind on business matters, she decided, was the best thing she could do to keep from dwelling on her problems. Rachel poured herself a small glass of water and sat down at her desk. Her books had been neglected for several days now and were sorely in need of her attention. She sipped the water and forced her concentration on the ledgers before her.

"Rachel."

Startled, a small cry escaped from her lips and she suddenly sat upright. Her hand upset the water glass as she involuntarily swept the pen across the page of figures leaving a thick black line through the carefully printed numbers. Whirling in her chair to see who had interrupted her, Rachel then sent a stack of papers flying into the air.

"Gray!" she gasped. She didn't know whether to be pleased or upset that it was he who had slipped so quietly into her office.

"I didn't mean to frighten you," he said as he knelt beside her chair to retrieve the papers.

"You—you didn't frighten me," she said quickly.

314

"Then why are your hands trembling?" Gray wanted to know. He stood and dropped the papers on her desk.

He towered over her, his eyes cold and ominous under the brim of his hat. At first he had been worried, concerned that something was wrong with her. He had tried in vain to see her for two days but was continually denied entrance to her home. She had not been at her store. Now he was more than slightly peeved, thinking she was deliberately avoiding him. He asks her to marry him, then she flees his house without warning and cannot be seen for days! He thought some type of explanation was in order.

Rachel clasped her hands together to still their trembling, and turned her eyes from his. She couldn't look at him. She just couldn't! It was obvious he was angry with her; she had never seen such coolness in his expression before. He knew. Fergus had told him. What else could it be?

"You—you just startled me," she said. All right, let him shout out that he knew the truth about her. She had it coming. She deserved his wrath. She steeled herself for what he was about to say.

There was a long moment of silence. Gray could see only her profile as she kept her eyes glued to the ledgers in front of her. The soft morning light from the window behind her bathed her and made her skin appear creamy and delicate. Suddenly he longed to run his hands through that thick mass of hair pinned so carefully in place. He wanted to wind the errant strand at her nape around his fingers and plunge into that blond, inviting mane. His eyes roamed her neck and followed the line of her back down until it disappeared into the volumes of skirts and petticoats that surrounded her. How he ached to know completely what waited under all that clothing. His mind's eye saw curving hips, a soft shapely bottom, warm thighs—

Gray mentally shook himself trying to regain control as turned his attention elsewhere to subdue the sudden warmth that spread through him. Why did she always have this tumultuous effect on him? He took off his hat and wiped his perspiring brow with his coat sleeve.

Every muscle in her body was drawn tight, waiting for him to strike out at her in anger for keeping the truth from him. Why did he not say something? Why was he making her endure his silence? Was he trying to torture her? Did he hate her that much?

She was so beautiful. How could he be upset with her when he was beset with such loving and caring thoughts? Well, surely she must have her reasons for avoiding him and leaving Richfield so abruptly. She would tell him when she was ready.

"You were the most beautiful woman at Richfield."

His rich voice rocked her feelings, and she had to struggle to sit still. She wanted to throw herself into his arms. But he would not want her now. Not anymore. Why didn't he just say it? Why was he toying with her this way?

Rachel finally righted the overturned water glass and rose from her chair. She still could not meet his eye. "Thank you. It was a lovely party," she said. *Now he is talking about the evening at Richfield. He is going to bring it up slowly and cause as much pain as he can.*

Gray stepped back as Rachel eased past him to get a towel from the washstand. The rustle of her petticoats mesmerized him and he devoured her every movement. He had had no woman—wanted no woman—since he had met Rachel and his body was aching for relief. But not from just any woman. No, it was Rachel he craved. It made no sense, he didn't understand it, but his heart made it perfectly clear to him that only Rachel and the aura of mystery that surrounded her could cure what ailed him.

"I wish you had not left so soon," Gray said. He had wanted to see her in the early morning, enjoy a quiet breakfast with her. He had planned to take her for a carriage ride and show her Richfield, maybe have a picnic in the glade by the lake. He wanted to have her alone and not share her with anyone. In the seclusion of the glade, he could take her in his arms and kiss those lovely, giving lips of hers.

Her nerves were stretched tight as a banjo string. Why was he being so cruel? "I'm sorry I left so abruptly, but it was an emergency of sorts," she said in a small voice. *Just get this over with!*

Rachel stretched across her desk to mop up the spilled water. The hoops of her skirt flared out behind her as she bent over and exposed a generous portion of her ankles and calves. Her arms were outstretched, causing her breasts to be outlined in the window beside her.

Gray swallowed hard as the yearning within him suddenly took charge and sent his manhood throbbing uncontrollably. It was too much. Seeing her like this was too much for him to bear.

"Let me do this," he snapped and stepped nearer, reaching for the towel. *Just, please, don't touch me.*

"No, I've got it." She wanted to stay busy so she wouldn't have to look into those eyes of his again.

"I said I'll do it," he repeated irritably. *For God's sake, woman, stand up! How much do you think a man can take?*

"I am finished anyway." Rachel turned toward him as he reached for the towel, and her breasts were suddenly crushed against his chest. Wedged into the small space between Gray and the desk, she had no place to retreat.

Gray froze. Waves of pleasure rippled through him and sent his senses reeling. His eyes homed in on the milky white swells of her breasts that threatened to spill over the top of her gown. She was so desirable! With supreme effort he dragged his eyes upward. Rachel was gazing at the floor, seemingly unaffected by their unexpected touch. He stepped backward, and she moved away. Didn't she feel the same sensations as he?

"An emergency?" he asked.

She stood at the washstand with her back to him an unnecessarily long time wringing the towel over the bowl. Her cheeks were red, she could feel it, and she didn't want him to see how vulnerable she was to his touch.

"A servant came to Richfield with a message from Hannah." Her voice shook. "Andrew was sick and I—I wanted to go to him at once." *Another lie.* God, how she hated herself. "I did not wish to disturb you while you were in a business meeting with Mr. Cavanaugh."

Why wouldn't she turn around? Was she embarrassed by their intimate touch? Maybe she simply felt nothing. "How is he?" Gray asked.

"Who?"

"Andrew."

"Fine."

"He was so ill you had to leave Richfield, and now he is fine?"

Rachel turned to face him, wringing the towel unmercifully. "I stayed with him and took care of him."

"I came to see you."

"Yes, I am sorry I couldn't visit with you, but Andrew needed all my attention. You know how babies are." She

318

could have bitten her tongue off for saying that. Of course he doesn't know how babies are! *And now he will never know.*

"I am glad he is better." He studied her intently, trying to capture her eyes, but she avoided his gaze.

She could not stand it any longer. This game of cat-and-mouse had to end or she would burst. She drew in a deep breath. "How did your meeting go with Mr. Cavanaugh?" The words came out in a rush.

Gray shrugged. "Fine, I suppose. We may be able to do business together. He owns property bordering mine in Georgia and he wants me to purchase it." She would rather discuss a business meeting than her son? That hurt.

"Did he stay long?" She tried to sound casual, but knew she didn't.

"No."

"No?"

"No."

The tiniest glimmer of hope flickered inside Rachel. Maybe, just maybe Fergus had not told him. She had given Gray every opportunity to bring up the subject, but he had said nothing. Feeling bolder, she asked, "What else did you two discuss?"

Why was she being so cold and impersonal? Was she trying to discourage him, preparing him for the rejection of his marriage proposal? He scowled. "Business, Rachel, nothing but business." He clamped his hat on and strode angrily toward the door. "I have another meeting. Good day."

She sighed heavily with relief and held on to the oak washstand for support. He didn't know! Fergus had not told him. A euphoric laugh bubbled from deep inside her and echoed in the quiet room. It was too good to be true.

All her worry had been for nothing. Fergus had not mentioned a word of her past to Gray. Why he hadn't, she could not guess. All that mattered was that—

Her elation was quickly drained and replaced by a different fear. Why had Fergus not told him? He had recognized her instantly at Richfield. What possible reason did he have for sparing her the humiliation of it all? What possible reason, indeed . . .

Cold beads of perspiration dampened her temples. He wanted something. As sure as the sun rose everyday, he wanted something from her in exchange for his silence. Money? No, he had plenty. Power? She could hardly supply that. Rachel had no notion of what his scheme could be, but it scared her and twisted her insides cruelly. Like an ominous cloud on the horizon coming toward her, there was no way to run from it and no place to hide. Fergus would find a way to hurt her. Of that, she was certain.

Chapter 13

He stalked her for two days. Everywhere she went, he was there. Across the street, on the corner, outside the building Fergus suddenly appeared, then as quickly disappeared. He never spoke, never acknowledged her. He only watched her every movement. His evil expression made her feel like a hunted animal. Rachel's already frayed nerves unraveled a little more each time she saw him. She dropped things, couldn't concentrate, could not even carry on a conversation.

A week with little sleep had taken its toll on her. Her hair had lost its luster, dark circles bordered lifeless eyes. She looked sickly. That was one reason she was glad she had seen Gray only once. They had run into each other on the street. Both had been surprised.

"I thought you would be at Richfield," Rachel had commented, stealing a quick glance at him. He looked heart-stoppingly handsome as always.

"I had a few things to take care of this morning," he said casually. He wanted to tell her that he had come to town again just to see her and had gotten all the way to the door of her mercantile before his pride had prevented him from going inside.

Rachel looked around nervously, expecting Fergus to be lurking in the shadows. *Tell him, you fool! Tell him the truth before Fergus does and put an end to this nightmare!* "How is Charlotte? I have not seen her in a few days." *Coward.*

"She has been a bit under the weather." Gray wanted to touch her so badly that he crammed his hands into his trouser pockets to control himself. She looked nervous and peaked. Was she ill? Or was this the way a woman looked when she had to decline a marriage proposal?

"I shall have to stop by and see her." Maybe he would understand. Maybe he could help her. Maybe if he heard the truth from her own lips he wouldn't care about her past and would still want her? Ha! What man would?

"She would like that." Gray wanted to turn away and remove temptation from his sight. He knew he looked like a lovesick puppy. Why did he keep talking to her when she was obviously preoccupied with other thoughts? Did he have no pride left? "May I offer you a ride to your destination?" *No, no pride at all.*

Fergus appeared across the street, standing in the doorway of the tobacco shop, his eyes raking her. Rachel felt her back and neck instantly tighten. She had to get away. She could not stand those eyes upon her another second!

"No—no, my carriage is just down the street." She swept past him without another word.

Gray watched as she hurried to her carriage and climbed inside. What had he done to offend her?

* * *

On the third day it seemed her tormenter had forgotten her. Rachel had grown accustomed to Fergus's relentless pursuit, and now it felt strange that he was no longer shadowing her. Maybe he had concluded his business and left town, or perhaps he had lost interest in following her. Whatever the reason, Rachel felt more at ease than she had in days, but, of course, her troubles were not over since she had not given Gray an answer to his marriage proposal. Oh, sweet Gray, Rachel thought as she sat in her carriage and watched the familiar scenery pass by en route to her home. She rubbed her temples wearily. Honestly, she didn't know where to begin to right the situation.

The front door of her home opened before she reached the portico and Philo greeted her as usual. A quiet evening at home was what Rachel had planned for all day. She would try to put thoughts of Fergus out of her head and give some long overdue attention to Andrew. The thought of her son lifted her spirits.

"Where is Andrew?" she asked Philo as she deposited her bonnet on the table by the front door. The boy usually ran into the room as soon as she arrived home.

"They not back yet," the butler reported.

"Not back? Back from where?" An unfounded fear took root in the pit of her stomach.

"Miz Hannah took him to the park," he explained dutifully. "She said they be home long before you gots here, ma'am."

"The park! I told her not to take Andrew out of this house!" Fear and anger raced through her. She paced frantically about the foyer. What if Fergus's twisted mind had caused him to take Andrew and—

She whirled to face Philo. "Go get Jim and have him

bring my carriage around. You go to the sheriff—'' No, she couldn't involve the law. "Never mind that. You run to the park—and I mean run—and look for them until I can get there. And tell Selma not to let anyone in this house while I am gone."

Philo nodded dumbly, not understanding why his mistress was so concerned. He only knew that he must do as she said. He turned to race from the room when the door opened.

Andrew, in short pants and crisp white shirt, toddled into the house. Hannah was on his heels ready to intercede should his still wobbly legs fail him. The boy saw Rachel and his blue eyes grew big as saucers. He squealed excitedly and trotted toward her, his black curls bouncing.

Rachel dropped to the floor and gathered him in her arms. Tears of relief threatened to fill her eyes.

"Rachel, you are home early," Hannah said brightly as she removed her bonnet.

"No, I am not," she replied tightly, raising her eyes to look at the woman.

Hannah touched Andrew's head lovingly. "No? Oh, well, I guess we just lost track of the time. Andrew was having such fun."

Rachel placed a kiss on her son's cheek and rose. "Philo, take Andrew up to his room."

Care of the boy was not Philo's duty, since he was the butler, a considerably higher position in the household. But he did not want to risk incurring Rachel's wrath so he dutifully took the boy's hand and led the way upstairs.

Rachel's heart was still racing wildly and her breathing was rapid, but she tried to calm herself. "Hannah, I told you not to take Andrew to the park."

"It was too lovely a day to keep him inside," Hannah

said. She always spoke softly and evenly; Rachel had never seen her upset.

She pinched the bridge of her nose in an attempt to ward off the headache that threatened. "We have a lawn for him to play in." She had to struggle to speak calmly.

"But, Rachel, the workmen were there all day."

"What workmen?"

"Pruning the tree next door. Remember Mr. Langdord came over a few days ago and explained that the workmen would be cutting the branches that hung on our side of the fence? It was not safe for Andrew to play there today," Hannah reminded her.

The fight drained from Rachel. She had forgotten all about her conversation with her neighbor. "It completely slipped my mind," she apologized.

Hannah slid her arm around Rachel's shoulder and they walked into the parlor. "You have had so much on your mind lately, it's no wonder you forgot," she said sympathetically. "But don't you worry about Andrew. I love him like he is my own. I would never let anything happen to him."

Rachel sank down on the sofa. Of course Hannah would take proper care of the boy. She was letting her imagination run away with her, thinking horrible thoughts without good cause.

"Andrew is such a sweet child, and so handsome. All the other ladies in the park commented on him today," Hannah said as she paused to straighten the arrangement of fresh flowers on the hutch.

Rachel smiled. "Tell me more." Andrew was her favorite subject.

Hannah eagerly launched into a detailed account of the day's activities. "I think some of those women were actually jealous of how handsome Andrew is. Especially that Mrs. Hartford. Her little girl is the homeliest child I have ever seen, God forgive me for saying so. Since Andrew had not been to the park for so long, the ladies were all commenting on how much he had grown and how well he is walking now. Young Master Andrew was certainly the talk of the town today." Rachel made no attempt to resist the proud smile that spread across her face. "Why, even a gentlemen asked about him," Hannah added.

"Oh?" It was unusual for a man to be in the park, which was usually inhabited by children, mammies, and mothers.

"He was so interested in Andrew," Hannah said as she worked with the flowers. "He asked his name, and how old he was, and when his birthday was. Seems he already knew I was not Andrew's mother like a lot of people think. He was a very pleasant man. We sat and chatted for almost an hour. He asked where we were from and how long we had been in Charleston—all sorts of things."

Rachel drew in a sharp breath. "Who was this man, Hannah? Did he give you his name?"

"Well, of course. He was quite a gentleman, as I said. Now let me think a minute." Hannah tapped her cheek with her finger. "Oh, yes, his name was Mr. Cavanaugh."

Rachel bolted upright off the couch so quickly her head spun. That evil Fergus Cavanaugh! How she hated him. And to think she had let herself believe he was going to leave her alone while all along he had been with her son. She would not underestimate him again. He wanted something from her, and whatever it was he was going to a great deal of trouble to ensure he would get it. Rachel's head pounded. What did he want from her?

"Rachel? Rachel!"from Hannah, and then Philo's "Supper is ready," pulled Rachel from her thoughts.

"You go ahead. I will eat later." She waved Hannah away, and sank down onto the sofa again.

The worry and anxiety and fear she had lived with for the last week left her feeling drained. She had little fear left in her. Now all she cared about was learning what Fergus wanted from her in exchange for his silence. Whatever it was, she would give it to him. By God, she would find a way to give him what he wanted and get him out of her life forever. Fergus had come too close to home now. She would not tolerate him around Andrew. At all costs, she would protect her son.

Mr. Rhodes came to call on Hannah again that evening. She had been all aflutter with excitement. The two of them were seeing each other several evenings a week now and attended services together on Sunday. They seemed well suited to each other and Rachel was pleased. Hannah had been so distraught when Seth died that Rachel was afraid she would never be herself again. She hoped things worked out for her with Mr. Rhodes.

Andrew was tired and fussy after his big day at the park, so Rachel bathed him and put him to bed early. He didn't protest when Rachel snuggled him in his small bed without first reading him a story. His eyes closed as soon as his head touched the down pillow and he fell asleep at once. Rachel knelt beside the bed watching him lovingly. She wound a lock of his dark hair around her finger. It felt like Gray's hair. And this is what he must have looked like as a baby.

Gray. Oh, God, how her heart ached for him. No matter what happened, Rachel would always have this small part of him, Andrew, his son. She would love the boy and protect him, regardless of what it cost her.

Rachel tried to work at her desk but found it impossible to concentrate. She was about to go up to bed when Philo came into the study and announced a visitor. Her spirits soared. Gray had come.

"Tell Mr. Montgomery I will be right there," she said enthusiastically.

"It's not Mr. Montgomery," Philo corrected. "A Mr. Fergus Cavanaugh is here."

Her heart skipped a beat. "Tell him I shall be there in a moment," she instructed, and Philo left her alone. At last, she thought, at last he had come to her. Finally she would know what he was up to. Rachel rose and drew in a deep breath. The sooner she got this over with, the better.

When she entered the parlor, Fergus's bulk lounged casually on the sofa. The sight of him repulsed her, but she pulled herself together quickly, wanting to appear clam and composed.

His beady eyes roamed her from head to toe when she stopped a few feet in front of him. She felt sickened by his perusal. "My dear little Rachel," he taunted, "what a beautiful woman you have become."

"What do you want, Fergus?" she asked coldly. She wanted him out of her house and was in no mood for idle conversation.

He ignored her question and swept his gaze around the room. "And you have done very well for yourself. This is a lovely home you have here. Not to mention the successful business you have. It is amazing what a resourceful girl can do with a little money in her pocket." His eyes drilled into her. "Even stolen money."

His words struck hard, but she held her composure. "That money was my cousin's. It should have gone to me when she died."

Fergus chuckled. "It was my money and you stole it from my cashbox, then slipped away like a thief in the night." He crossed his thick legs. "But that seems to be only one of your many sins."

"I don't know what you are speaking of," Rachel told him.

He disregarded her remark. "Not only are you a thief, but a liar as well, passing yourself off as a fine, upstanding woman from St. Louis, when you are nothing but trash from the wilderness of St. Joseph." He studied his carefully manicured nails. "You see, sweet Rachel, I know all about your past, and how you have kept it all hidden from the good folks of Charleston. They would be so shocked to learn the truth about you."

She looked at him coldly, mentally forbidding herself to show how frightened she really was. "Being from St. Joseph rather than St. Louis would hardly scandalize the aristocracy of Charleston," she shot back.

"But bearing a child out of wedlock would," he said cruelly.

The words cut through Rachel's composure and sliced into her heart. How could he have known? Who told him? She was too shocked to speak.

"You have successfully hidden the truth of your sordid past long enough. I think it is time Charleston learned what you really are," he said slowly.

"I have many friends here—influential friends. No one

would believe your lies." She wanted to sound in control, convincing, but her trembling voice betrayed her.

Fergus slowly lifted his stout frame from the sofa and paced leisurely about the room. Her threats didn't worry him in the least—actually, he found them very amusing. "Perhaps your influential friends won't believe it, but they certainly will have quite a time telling the story of Mrs. Rachel Samuels Fontaine. The daughter of a foolhardy businessman who lost all his money and died in the bed of a whore. That in itself would be quite a juicy bit of gossip. Then, add to it an idiot mother who passed away simply because she could no longer face life. The daughter who shuns a respectable marriage proposal, becomes a common thief, and runs away to live like an animal in a wilderness town, then prostitutes herself and bears a bastard son. Oh, yes, my dear, the fine ladies of Charleston will thoroughly enjoy your misfortunes."

"Liar! You are lying! You're twisting the facts to fit your own sick purposes," she cried. Her small hands curled into fists of anger and frustration.

Fergus laughed. "You are actually going to deny it?" he asked unbelievably.

"You have no proof of your accusations. How do you know I was never married? You have no right to say those things about my son," Rachel declared. "The people of Charleston will be gossiping about you and your ridiculous unsubstantiated claims."

Fergus looked amused. "I have all the proof I need."

"You have nothing!"

His eyes hardened. "I know the date you left St. Francisville, and your dear friend Hannah was kind enough to provide me with the boy's birthdate when we chatted in the park. I can count the months. There was no time for you to wed."

"You don't know that for certain."

"Then where is he? Where is your husband?" Fergus challenged.

Rachel's breath came in short, shallow puffs. "He's . . . he's dead."

"Well, now, isn't that convenient." Those words sealed his case against her.

Rachel pursed her lips and fought to control her racing heart. Her eyes narrowed. She would give anything now to produce the supposed dear departed Mr. Fontaine and slap that smirk right off Fergus's bloated face. But, of course, there was no deceased husband, no one to come to her defense to prove wrong his accusations. Why try to deny his words? Why prolong this conversation?

She took a deep breath and lifted her chin. "All right, Fergus, what do you want?"

He nodded slowly. "I knew you were a smart one. Smart enough to know when your options have run out." He paused and faced her. "What do I want? Nothing. Instead, I am going to give you something." Rachel couldn't follow his thoughts but remained silent, knowing he would reveal his meaning all too soon. "What I am going to give you is something no other man would. I am going to make an honest woman of you. I am going to marry you."

The tension that held her muscles taut suddenly gave way and Rachel collapsed onto the sofe. "What?" she whispered in disbelief.

"I see you are . . . overwhelmed by my proposal," he said smugly.

Rachel shook her head. Surely she had not heard him

correctly. Surely he was joking. Her mind refused to believe what she had just heard. It was ludicrous.

His eyes captured hers. "You will marry me," he assured her.

"No ... no, I won't," she declared, suddenly realizing that Fergus was serious.

"Then who will marry you? What decent man will have you when the sordid truth of your background becomes common knowledge? Who will stand by you when all of Charleston learns how you deceived everyone?" Fergus's nostrils flared as he spat the words at her.

"I don't have to ever be married," she told him. "My true friends will stand by me."

A cruel smile twisted Fergus's face. "Who will stand by that baby of yours when everyone learns he is a bastard?"

"No!" Tears of rage and frustration slipped from her eyes. No, not Andrew. She couldn't let him hurt her son.

A heavy silence hung over the room. Fergus stood above Rachel, gloating over his triumph. He had waited a long time for this moment and he would enjoy every second of it. It had been sheer luck that he had found Rachel in the city, of all places. He had given up searching for her long ago. Now that he had found her he intended to hurt her, hurt her badly. He would make her pay for running away from him in St. Francisville and making him a laughing stock. He was enjoying this greatly.

"So, my dear Rachel, the choice is yours. I can tell everyone about your past and that little bastard you bore. I would greatly enjoy recounting all the lurid details. Or, you can purchase my silence by consenting to marry me. I certainly would not want anyone to know I had married a woman with such a background, so your secret would be safe with me always." He smiled. "It is up to you."

Fergus picked up his hat and strode from the room feeling altogether pleased with herself.

Tears streamed down her cheeks as violent sobs racked her body. She held a small pillow to her face to muffle the sound. Why did this have to happen? Why had Fergus found her? What had she done to deserve this heartache? Rachel's head spun with unanswered questions. It was all so horrible. Somehow she made it up the stairs and fell into her bed.

The first rays of dawn that streamed through her window found a different Rachel. Gone were the tears, the sobs, the wailing. The "why oh why" questions had vanished as well. There was not a drop of any sort of emotion left in her. She had come to Charleston with a purpose. She had worked hard and planned every step of the way. It had been her utmost priority. It still was.

Andrew. Her precious little baby. She would give him the best life possible. Every opportunity would be his. She would not fail him.

Rachel dressed in a dark-blue gown that matched her somber mood and had her coachman drive her to the hotel where Fergus was staying. She dashed off a message and had the desk clerk deliver it to his room. It was early and she was thankful the lobby was empty as she waited for his reply. When it came, she sedately climbed the stairs and knocked on the door to Fergus's suite. The servant who answered took her to where he sat having breakfast. He seemed to be expecting her.

"Won't you join me, my dear?" he asked.

Rachel stood a few feet from the table. "No," she said in a calm, even voice. "I have come to discuss your proposal." Oh, how she wished the sight of him didn't sicken her so.

Fergus stirred his coffee. "I felt certain you would drop by."

"As I understand it, if I agree to ... marry you there will be no talk of my past or that of my son."

He nodded. "That is correct. You have my word as a gentleman."

She fought away the resentment she felt for the man. "Am I correct in assuming we will return to your home in St. Francisville to live?"

"Oh, yes," he assured her. "I am most anxious to present you to my friends there." The same friends who had laughed at him when his beautiful young bride had run out on him. He would show them. He would have the last laugh.

"I would ask that our intention to marry not be made public, and that we not leave the city for several weeks." Silently Rachel prayed that he would grant her this request. He shook his head, but she spoke before he could reply. "I must be given time to sell my shop and house. If it becomes known that I am leaving immediately, the price will surely be less. I am certain that as a businessman you can understand that." And it would give her some time to explain all this to Gray, somehow.

"That does seem to be a reasonable request," he said thoughtfully. "Very well."

Rachel swallowed the lump in her throat. How could she say this? How? For her son's sake, that's how. "Then, sir, on those terms I shall accept your marriage proposal." The bitter words came quietly through her tight throat.

Fergus's wide lips spread a smile across his face. He wiped his hands on the linen napkin and rose from the table. "You have made me a very happy man," he said, taking her hand and placing a wet kiss on the back of it.

Fergus felt her shudder at his touch. It made no difference to him. He would have her in his marriage bed very soon, and whether she liked it or not, he would have his way with her. "Allow me to escort you to your carriage."

Rachel wanted to flee from him but knew she could not. Somehow she would have to accept his company, his touch, his kiss, his ... Oh, God, how would she ever face a night in his bed! She forced the vile thoughts from her head and replaced them with the image of her son. Andrew. He needed her. She would not fail him.

The servant assisted Fergus with his coat and they left the suite together. His fingers closed around the flesh of her upper arm, burning her with his touch as they descended the stairs and crossed the lobby. A few people were gathered there now. Rachel held her head high and kept her eyes forward; she did not care to see the looks on everyone's faces. She wanted to pull away from Fergus but dared not. She wouldn't provoke him, not while they were still in the city. To do so might anger him enough to break off the engagement and send his tongue wagging out of spite.

At least she had bought herself some time by getting Fergus to agree to a long engagement. She could avoid his marriage bed plus find a way to break the news to Gray. Oh, sweet, handsome Gray. How would she explain this to him? He had poured out his heart to her with words of love for her and her son. Now she must refuse his proposal. Her heart ached at the thought. It was a small consolation, but at least he would not learn that she was marrying Fergus Cavanaugh until they had departed the city. She would see to it that they married secretly just prior to leaving. It would not hurt Gray any less when he did find out, but it would keep her from having to deal with it. *Coward. Lying coward.* Who did she hate more? Fergus or herself?

Rachel lowered her eyes as they left the hotel. She didn't want to see anyone she knew and be forced to introduce Fergus, who was still clinging to her arm. She intended to spend the least amount of time with him as possible—and none of it in public, if she could manage. What a mess her life had turned into!

She was jolted to a sudden stop by Fergus pulling on her arm. She had been deep in thought. Had they reached her carriage so soon? She raised her head and looked straight into the blue eyes of Gray Montgomery. Shame and fear washed over her at once as Gray took in Fergus's hand nestled possessively on her arm. His expression turned quickly from surprise to puzzlement to anger. His brows drew together, and the line of his mouth tightened.

"Mr. Montgomery, how good to see you," Fergus greeted.

"Cavanaugh," he replied tightly.

Rachel cast her eyes downward, avoiding his probing stare.

"This is supposed to remain a secret, but I simply cannot contain the good news," Fergus began.

Rachel's head came up sharply. "Fergus—"

"Mrs. Fontaine has consented to be my wife," he announced.

The words struck Rachel like a pounding fist, striking her from all directions. Her heart rose into her throat and choked off her breathing. Horrified, she turned to Fergus and saw his small calculating eyes intently watching Gray. Dear God, he had blurted out the news with the sole purpose of hurting Gray! It was written all over his face. He had seen her with Gray that morning at Richfield and it must have been very clear how they felt about each other. What a cruel man this Fergus Cavanaugh was!

Gray's expression hardened only slightly, and if the news had come as a shock Fergus couldn't tell. Only Rachel recognized the subtle changes in his features that betrayed the hurt he felt. The coolness of his blue eyes, the twitch in his cheek, the tilt of his head. Each gesture tore through Rachel, ripping her heart to shreds. She wanted to put an end to his pain. She wanted to scream out the truth and melt into his arms. Rachel closed her eyes. There was nothing she could say or do. She had come too far now to go back.

The men talked but for a moment before Gray stalked away. He glanced at her only once, and the hurt and anger in his face burned into her memory. Burdened by the guilt she felt, her limbs moved slowly as Fergus deposited her in her carriage; she hardly noticed when he kissed her cheek, and never gave him a second look as her carriage pulled away.

Rachel wrestled with the problem over and over as she sat in her office in the rear of the mercantile. And as the night before, she came to the same conclusion, hurtful and difficult though it was. She could not remain in Charleston subjecting Gray to a scandal and having the truth of Andrew's parentage—or lack of it—become known. That was unthinkable. She loved them both too much to hurt them. She considered running, as she had done to escape Fergus in St. Francisville. But she couldn't pack a bag and disappear into the night this time. Even if she abandoned her house and business and changed her name, she knew eventually she would be found again. And then what? Run another time, to another town? No, that was no life for her son. There was no alternative, no more choices or options. She hated the feeling of being powerless, but she could do nothing except swallow her pride and agree to the marriage.

Storm clouds were gathering on the horizon and the ocean breeze had picked up considerably as Gray slammed the bank's door behind him, rattling its glass, and stalked down the sidewalk. The scowl he wore was a warning to everyone he encountered to stand back and give him room. His muscles were drawn tight. He was like a coiled spring ready to fly with the least provocation.

The argument he had just had with his uncle had been the last straw. He had come to discuss a business deal and get Bernard's opinion, which he valued highly, but when he had advised against it Gray had flown into a rage. He had shouted at his uncle, using a series of very uncomplimentary adjectives, and stormed out of his office leaving Bernard openmouthed with surprise. It was a repeat of an earlier scene at the tailor's when Gray had inspected a fine new suit of clothing and found two loose threads in the coat's lining. He had exploded with anger, thrown the garment on the floor, and told Mr. Hatcher, who had been his tailor for years and always made the finest quality clothing, that if his shoddy workmanship did not improve he would take his business elsewhere. He had left in a huff not listening to Mr. Hatcher's attempt at apology. It had been that way all day. Service was slow when he sat down for his noon meal and he had banged his fist loudly on the table in protest. That attracted the attention of the other patrons as well as the serving girl, and he became so embarrassed over the scene he had caused that he left without eating a bite of the food he had made such a fuss to get.

Gray weaved his way through the pedestrians, annoyed by their slowness when he was in such a hurry. To go where? He had been so deep in thought that at that second he could not recall his destination. He stopped and looked around.

Damn! Not again!

Across the street was Fontaine's Mercantile. This was the third time today he had found himself outside the shop. He was drawn to it like the proverbial moth to a flame.

He pulled off his hat and wiped his brow. Despite the overcast sky and the cool breeze heavy with moisture, he was perspiring. He eyed the store front, then replaced his hat against the glare of the final rays of the disappearing sun. He chewed his bottom lip pensively.

Something terrible was wrong. She would not have done it without good reason. Maybe she had been coerced or blackmailed. Hell—she hardly knew Cavanaugh! She had acted strangely for days. And she had seemed none too happy when Cavanaugh blurted out the news. Something was wrong. He would go to her and make her tell him the truth.

Gray took a step forward, then as he had done twice today already, stopped in his tracks. Like hell he would! He had told her he loved her and wanted to marry her, and had even promised to love that boy of hers he had never seen and that she kept locked away in her house. And, by God, if any child ever needed a strong father it was that poor little fellow. But had she even given him an answer to his proposal? Hell no! She had left him dangling on a string for days, then out of the blue, she turned up engaged to that dog-faced Fergus Cavanaugh. How much could a man take? If that's what she wanted—fine! But he was not about to go to her shop and make a fool of himself again, no matter how much his gut ached.

Well, there was only one thing to do. It had been a bitch of a day with no sign of improving. Gray turned on his heels and headed for the docks.

Thunder rumbled in from the ocean as Rachel locked the front door of her shop and climbed into her awaiting carriage. She glanced at the darkening sky. It would be raining soon, and she was anxious to get home. Mr. Rhodes had asked to leave the shop early today because he wanted to take Hannah to supper at his mother's, then take in the play at the Dock Street. How could she say no? She envied Hannah and the pleasant relationship she shared with Mr. Rhodes. If things had turned out differently, maybe it would have been she who left early today to attend the theater with Gray. She shook the thought from her head. No point in conjuring up things that were no longer possible.

She ate supper with Andrew and they played together in his room until he rubbed his eyes sleepily with his tiny fists and she knew it was his bedtime. She bathed him and dressed him in a warm cotton gown to ward off the chill of the approaching storm. She rocked him for only a few minutes before he fell asleep on her lap, then snuggled him in his small bed and placed a tender kiss in that mass of dark curls.

She had not meant to eavesdrop when Hannah and Mr. Rhodes came into the house laughing and murmuring softly. Rachel was in the parlor trying to force herself to read and couldn't help hearing the intimacies of two people in love. Her stomach wrenched into a knot and her throat tightened. She wanted to cry, but could not. Oh, Gray, she thought. How would she ever learn to live without him? She loved him with all her heart. Why was life so unfair?

She sat quietly as Mr. Rhodes left and Hannah went upstairs, never noticing her in the parlor. After a long time she pulled herself from her thoughts and went up to her room.

A rowdy crowd filled the tavern near the waterfront where Gray sat looking out over the harbor. The promised storm had driven many indoors and a partylike atmosphere had developed. An out-of-tune piano jangled offensively across the room as accommodating women wound through the crowd. The air was heavy with cigar smoke and the smell of ale. Gray ignored them all, most especially the many women who stopped by his table with offers of a pleasurable evening at a reasonable price. He ached for a woman—and had for weeks—but he wanted no part of these rouged strumpets. Finally, after he had turned down enough of them that the rest got the message, they all left him alone. No, there was only one woman who could quench the fire that burned in his loins. A small delicate one with skin as smooth as silk, the color of magnolia blossoms, and eyes so dark they sparkled, lips that were mellow and—

Christ, stop torturing yourself! Gray swore a silent oath and drained his tankard. It had been a long time since he last drank heavily, and the evil brew burned his stomach. But what the hell, he decided, and signaled the serving girl.

"Gray?"

He looked up to find Ezra Daniels standing over him.

He rose and pumped the captain's extended hand, and they both sat down.

"Good to see you back in Charleston," Gray said. "Where have you been?"

"Up the coast a bit, visiting some friends." Because of his years of extensive travel, the captain had friends up and down the Eastern seaboard and stretching to the Mississippi.

They paused in their conversation as the girl delivered them each a tankard and took away the two empties that sat in front of Gray.

"I thought you had sworn off this stuff," Captain Daniels said with a half smile.

Gray shrugged. "Tonight is an exception," he said, and took a long swallow.

"If my memory serves me correctly, the last time you and I drank together, you were about to be married," the captain noted.

Gray chucked. He hardly thought of Claudia anymore, but he recalled that particular evening very clearly. "That, sir, is an evening I shall long remember," Gray said, then added wryly, "What I can remember of it."

"I recall that you had trouble holding your ale that night," Captain Daniels pointed out good-naturedly.

Gray grinned. "Hell, man, you don't know the half of it. I was so drunk I haven't the foggiest notion of how I got up to my room that night." He took another generous swig.

The older man laughed heartily. "You young fool, it was I who carried you to your bed."

Gray looked across the top of his tankard. "You? How? You left early in the evening."

"I came back and found you in such a drunken state

that the innkeeper was threatening to toss you out in the rain. I practically carried you upstairs." Both men laughed.

"Well, there is another mystery surrounding that fateful night I spent in St. Joseph, Missouri," Gray muttered.

"Another mystery?" Captain Daniels asked as he sipped from the tankard.

Gray shook his head and dismissed the question with a wave of his hand. "It's nothing. Just the ramblings of an ale-sodden brain." He was in no mood to discuss the mysterious virgin who had come to his room that night, who had made such beautiful love with him that it totally changed his life. He was in no mood to discuss women at all.

"So what drives you to drink tonight?" the captain asked. "Certainly not women trouble this time, I am sure. Not with a lovely young creature like Rachel Fontaine involved."

The lighthearted expression disappeared from Gray's face instantly. His hand tightened around the tankard and he gulped down the remainder of its contents. "I have no desire to discuss that 'lovely young creature' now or at any time in the near future," he snarled.

"What's this?" When he had last seen Gray and Rachel together, it was very apparent that they cared deeply for each other. He could not imagine what could have happened between them, and he cared too much about each of them to let the subject drop.

"I do not wish to discuss it," Gray informed him, then signaled for another ale.

"You two love each other—it is as plain as day. What happened?"

Gray grew tense under the captain's questioning. He ran his hand through his thick hair. "She is nothing but a

343

fickle, scatter-brained child who does not have the slightest notion of what she wants. And I am damn glad to have found it out before it was too late," he said tersely.

"Gray, you are not making any sense. That doesn't sound like Rachel at all."

"Well, perhaps you don't know her as well as you think you do," he said arrogantly. He pounded his fist on the crude wooden table. "Where is my ale!" Another loud voice was barely noticed in the swirl of activity.

"I don't understand," Captain Daniels said helplessly.

"Perhaps you can understand this," Gray snapped. "She is engaged to marry someone else."

And when the words were spoken aloud they hit each man with unexpected force. Captain Daniels was perplexed, unable to imagine what could have come between Rachel and Gray. They were so happy together, so obviously in love. One could see instantly they belonged together. What had happened so suddenly that Rachel was already engaged?

The tension that had held Gray together all day suddenly drained from him with the realization of his own words. He slumped forward on his elbows and covered his face with his hands. And still the vision of Rachel crept into his mind the instant his eyes closed. Every fiber of his body ached intensely.

"Why, Gray, why?" he heard the captain ask.

Gray wiped his eyes with the backs of his hands. "I don't know," he said softly, wearily. "I learned of it only this morning. I had asked her to marry me, but ..."

"She refused?" he asked in surprise.

Gray shook his head. "No, she did not give me an answer at all. Instead, she told me she was marrying someone else. A total stranger, really."

Captain Daniels could not sit by and let this happen. He knew how much these two cared for each other. And he felt partially to blame, as well. If he had not kept Rachel's secret, maybe this would not be happening. If he had told Gray the truth about Rachel's baby, as he had wanted to, things might be different. No, no, he could not let this happen.

"Gray, something is wrong. Rachel would not reject your proposal unless some outside force influenced her. Go to her, get this problem worked out," he urged.

Gray's back went rigid. "I will not crawl back to her, begging for her hand," he said proudly.

"Good God, man, forget your stupid pride. You love her. Don't let her get away from you again," he pleaded.

"What do you mean 'again'?"

Captain Daniels was sorely tempted to tell him the whole truth, but he restrained himself. It had to come from Rachel. "Believe me when I say that she has something that belongs to you, something very precious."

"She has my heart," he whispered.

"It is something much, much bigger than that. I cannot tell you, but she can."

Now Gray's interest way piqued. "What the devil are you talking about?"

"Go to her, Gray. She loves you, believe me. She doesn't want to marry this other man, whoever he is. It's you she wants."

"But—"

"Go to her—now!" Captain Daniels softened his voice. "Trust me, my friend. I speak the truth."

Gray nodded slowly. He trusted the captain. He would go to Rachel and learn the truth. Without saying another word he left the bar, much to Captain Daniels's relief.

When Gray had arrived at the tavern that afternoon, he had sent a message to his driver at the livery with instructions on where to meet him. He was relieved to find his carriage now parked outside. The strong, cold wind buffeted him as he climbed inside, but it washed away the effects of the ale he had consumed and cleared his head. He shouted his destination to the driver and the horses pulled out into the deserted street. Suddenly, Gray couldn't wait to get to Rachel's house; and he sat nervously on the edge of the seat. When at last the carriage stopped before her home, the storm broke in earnest and raindrops fell from the turbulent sky.

The patter of rain on the window behind her brought Rachel from the depths of her thoughts. They had been all-consuming, and it took a moment to realize she was seated at the desk in her study. The small lantern, the only light in the room, cast a dim light on the ledgers spread before her, and though she had not been able to sleep and had come downstairs to work after everyone else had retired for the evening, she had hardly looked at the columns of figures. Her attention was focused on the pocket watch she held in her hand. Her fingers moved over it lovingly as she let herself drift back in time to the night Gray had made love to her. She closed her eyes and every small detail came back to her—the feel of his soft hair, the strong, corded muscles of his arms and back, his thighs against hers. It was a beautiful memory, filled with gentle, caring love. Would a night with Fergus be the same?

Rachel shuddered at the thought. It was too horrible to imagine. Tonight she felt very alone and frightened, and she wished there was someone who could comfort her. But, of course, there was no one. So she had done what little she could and had slipped her mother's green brocade wrapper over her night rail before coming down to the study. She ran her hand over the fabric, recalling the times her mother had worn the garment and the feeling of warmth and security it evoked in Rachel. She pressed the pocket watch between her palms and rested her elbows on the desk; her voluminous blond hair, free of pins and braids, fashioned a curtain around her face. She indulged herself once more in the memory of Gray.

The pounding noise that intruded upon her thoughts stopped suddenly only to be followed by raised voices and scuffling feet in the foyer. Then the door of her study was nearly ripped off its hinges, and a wide-shouldered narrow-hipped man stood in the opening, filling it, nearly blocking out the lantern light behind him. He stood there for a moment surveying the room, then strode in. She knew at once that it was Gray. Rachel gasped and came to her feet.

"I is sorry, Miz Rachel. I told him it was too late to come acalling." Philo stood in the doorway in his dressing gown, his lanky limbs shaking.

"It's all right, Philo. Leave us," Rachel said evenly, and the servant dashed away. She closed her hand around the pocket watch she held and slid it behind her back as nonchalantly as possible. Gray was watching her from the shadows on the other side of the room and there was no way she could return it to the desk drawer without him seeing it.

Oh, God, how beautiful she looks, Gray thought as he studied her features bathed in the soft light. How could he face each day without her? He couldn't. He wouldn't. He stepped closer to the desk.

"The truth, Rachel. I want to know the truth." He struggled to control his emotions.

Rachel's breath caught in her lungs. She could not reply.

"I know something is wrong. You are being forced to marry Cavanaugh, aren't you?" Anger welled inside of him as he spoke. He would kill that son of a bitch if he hurt her. Rachel was silent. He softened his tone. "I will help you. Whatever it is, I will help you. I swear it."

Oh, dear God, she didn't deserve such a wonderful man. Rachel's heart ached. After all she had put him through in the past weeks, here he was offering to help her. She wanted to blurt out the whole story, tell him everything. But it made no more sense to do so now than before. It would not stop Fergus from telling of her past, or keep her from marrying him in exchange for his silence. Telling the truth now would only hurt Gray more, and she would not do that to him.

Outside, jagged bolts of lightning ripped through the turbulent storm clouds. Rain pelted the window of the study, and for a long moment it was the only sound in the room as Gray and Rachel faced each other in the dim light.

Finally, Gray spoke. "Tell me you don't love me. You have only to say the words and I will leave you." He sounded dejected, yet hopeful. Stepping closer, he placed his hands on her shoulders. "Look me in the eye, Rachel, and tell me you don't love me," he challenged.

Say it! Say the words and send him away! Don't hurt him anymore! Tears threatened to fill her eyes.

Gray searched her face for a clue to her thoughts. He knew she loved him and that it would be impossible for her to claim otherwise. And he loved her, with all his heart and soul, and he knew he would never let her go, no matter what she said. His fingers moved against the brocade fabric, and he marveled at her delicate frame beneath it. Slowly his hand lifted from her shoulder, and his finger traced the hollow of her graceful throat and along the edge of her jaw. He tilted her face up to his. In the glow of the lantern's light her eyes sparkled with a light of their own and his heart swelled with love for her and sent waves of warmth pulsing through his body. He could not deny his feelings, nor could he stop the tide of passion that coursed through him. It felt so right to be with her, as if she was the treasure at the end of his rainbow. He had found the piece of life that would make him complete.

Gray's arms encircled her and pulled their bodies together. The press of her flesh against him sent loose a torrent of passion. His mouth closed over hers hungrily. He was starved for the taste of her, but his lips moved slowly over hers, savoring their sweetness. His fingers moved over the gentle curve of her cheeks, then delved into her silky hair. The last days without her near had been torturous, and the taste and feel of her now filled his senses and evoked an avalanche of beautiful memories. His head whirled, intoxicated by those thoughts and his imagination. No woman had stirred such passion in him before, and he lusted for her now as he envisioned himself nestled within her creamy thighs as she arched up to receive the fullness of his manhood.

The thought confused him. Was it his imagination? Or had it actually happened? His mind teetered with indecision. In the library at Richfield on the night of the barbecue he had experienced these same troublesome feelings. Was he now remembering that night when, had they not been interrupted, their passion would have driven them to an explosive union? Or was he recalling another time, another place?

Thunder crashed violently in the night sky and spurred Gray's powers of recollection onward. The storm. Yes, that felt right. And a woman in his arms. His hands touching her soft skin. A wrapper—a brocade wrapper—beneath his fingertips. It was a hazy memory shrouded in sensuous, desirous feelings of wanting, needing, caring. Peace and contentment countered by urgency. Then his thoughts skipped to the night in the library at Richfield when he was certain the woman in his arms was Rachel. Both recollections meshed together, became one. And the window to his memory flew open wide.

Suddenly a bolt of lightning lit up the recesses of his mind at the same time that another split the night sky. The revelation jolted him, rocked his brain. He pulled away from her. His eyes searched her face, seeing her in a different way now. Quickly his hands ran over the brocade fabric of her wrapper, the line of her jaw, her silken tresses. His heart pounded wildly. "It was you," he whispered incredibly.

Rachel's breath caught in her throat. *Oh, sweet Jesus, not now!*

"It was you." He spoke with more force and conviction.

Rachel shook her head and stepped back from him. "I—I don't know what you mean." But she knew exactly.

"Yes, you do." His eyes were wide, his breathing rapid. "In St. Joseph ... you were in my room that night. We made love."

She must find a way to convince Gray he was wrong. She could not let him know he was right. She was not ready to expose the horrible truth of her past and hurt him further.

350

"Don't be silly," she said lightly and tried to laugh. "We only just met . . . here in Charleston." She sounded miserably unbelievable.

"You are playing games with me. I want the truth, Rachel." He grabbed her arms and pulled her to him. A small object hit the floor.

Rachel gasped and looked down. At her feet was Gray's pocket watch gleaming in the light.

Chapter 14

"What the hell . . ." Gray ran his fingers over the inscription on the back of the pocket watch that had been
a gift from his mother to his father. He moved it closer to
the light and read the words again. The watch had been
his father's pride and joy, and he had given it to Gray
near the end when the fever that ravaged both him and
his wife raged on and he knew their time left on this
earth could be measured in hours. Gray had treasured
the watch with its inscribed words of love, and had been
heartsick when it had disappeared. Now his eyes riveted
Rachel.

"Where did you get this?"

She dragged her eyes guiltily from the watch. "I found
it," she said quickly. She didn't sound very convincing.

"Where?" None of this made any sense to him. How
could Rachel have gained possession of his pocket watch?
Whatever the reason, it was proof that their paths had
crossed before. Was it in St. Joseph as he thought? Was

she the woman who had shared his bed that stormy night? The woman whose virginity he had taken—

Gray rubbed his eyes wearily. It could not have been Rachel. The woman he had slept with was undeniably a virgin, and Rachel was a widow, or perhaps still married at that time. But when he closed his eyes and remembered that beautiful night, his heart told him that Rachel was that woman, regardless of what his reasoning powers deduced.

"I—I don't remember where I found it," she replied as she drifted away from him toward the sofa.

By now Gray was well acquainted with her tactics and knew by the way she slipped away from him that she had something to hide. And he had had enough of it! He was confused and wanted straight answers from her—now!

"Damn it, Rachel, answer me!" he boomed.

His anger startled her and she stopped still. "I don't know what you are talking about," she said defensively.

"You know exactly what I am talking about."

"I told you I don't recall where I found the watch. It—it was lovely and I decided to keep it. There was no one's name on it. I had no idea it was yours." Please, God, she prayed, let her sound convincing.

"It was a gift from my mother to my father and I lost it during my last trip west." He watched her closely. "I am almost certain it was in St. Joseph."

Rachel steeled her emotions. She could tell from the uncertainty in his voice that he was not totally convinced she was the woman who had been in his St. Joseph room, in his bed. She must deny any involvement with him. Somehow, she must find the strength.

"If I had known you before, why would I have not told you so when I met you here in Charleston," she proposed.

He digested her words and could find no argument. "I think your imagination is playing tricks on you." She saw his indecision and pressed on. "After all, it was a long time ago, and it was at night, and you had been drinking heavily."

Gray snapped to attention. "How did you know I had been drinking?"

Rachel's stomach knotted. She had gone too far, said too much, and given herself away. "I—I didn't ... I just assumed ..."

"Stop lying to me!" He took a step closer. "I don't know why you are denying our involvement, but I want you to cease this instant. Tell me what I know is true!"

"I'll do no such thing!"

"Why are you lying?" he demanded angrily.

"I don't want to discuss this further!"

"Because you know I speak the truth!"

"Stop it!" she wailed. "Leave me alone."

"Why are you doing this, Rachel? Why?"

A small whimpering broke the tension between them, and they turned to see Andrew standing in the doorway. Tears rolled down his cheeks and his small limbs quaked.

"Andrew," Rachel gasped. She rushed across the room and lifted him into her arms. "There, there, my baby, it's all right," she cooed as she gently patted his back. She swayed back and forth, murmuring comforting words and quickly his tears stopped. He laid his head on her shoulder, muzzled against her neck, and closed her eyes.

In her concern for Andrew, she had forgotten all about Gray and she glanced over her shoulder now to find him watching her closely from behind the desk.

"There you are!" Hannah swept into the study, tying her wrapper, her hair loose about her shoulders. She

354

clutched her bosom in relief. "I have looked all over for him."

"You should have been watching him more closely," Rachel said angrily. She needed an outlet for her tension, and Hannah was the easiest target.

"The storm must have wakened him. I didn't hear him get up," Hannah explained.

"He came down that staircase all alone. He could have fallen." Rachel held him protectively.

"I'm sorry, Rachel, I was sleeping. Oh, Mr. Montgomery, I didn't see you there. Good evening."

"Good evening," he said mechanically as he joined the women. But it was not either of them that held his attention; it was the babe. He had expected the child to be small and frail from the sicknesses Rachel often spoke of, and he was surprised to see what a big, strapping boy he was. Even at this young age he was quite a bundle in Rachel's arms. Gray reached out and stroked the boy's dark curls. Rachel turned, startled by his closeness, and their eyes met; she glanced away quickly. And for the second time that evening, a jolt like a bolt of lightning ripped through Gray, this time penetrating to his heart.

"I will take Andrew back to bed," Hannah said, and took the sleeping boy from Rachel's arms.

But Gray quickly intervened and took the child into his own arms. He jockeyed him awkwardly at first, then positioned him with an arm under Andrew's shoulders and the other under his chubby knees. The child slept on, unaware of the transfer. Hannah and Rachel watched in silence as Gray carried him to the desk lantern and turned up the flame. The light roused him, and when Andrew opened his eyes, Gray saw his own deep blue eyes looking back at him. They fluttered shut and an instant later Andrew was asleep again.

Gray lifted his eyes and they locked with Rachel's. Now there could be no denying. Andrew was the mirror image of Gray, and the silence that hung heavy in the room further confirmed the boy's parentage.

Hannah, who had not the slightest idea of what was unfolding, took the baby from Gray's arms, mumbled something about the child needing his rest, and left the room, closing the door behind her. Gray was unaware, his thoughts and attention directed at Rachel.

She had not expected him to react this way. In the thousands of times she had played out this scene in her mind, she had never expected Gray to look so awe-struck, so spellbound by the child. She wanted to shout aloud with happiness, run to his arms, and at last share the joy of her child with him. But she was afraid to speak, afraid to move. She stood across the room from him in silence.

Gray could hardly take it all in. To learn the identity of the woman he had bedded in St. Joseph was a riddle he had feared would never be solved. But to find out that that woman was Rachel was almost too much to comprehend. And the boy—his boy—his son! His heart leaped with excitement.

Why hadn't he known? Why didn't he remember her, recognize her? The woman who had changed his life had been right under his nose and he had not realized it. What a fool he had been!

Gray ran his hand through his thick hair and a lopsided grin crossed his face. "A son," he said, mostly to himself. "I have a son."

She wanted to be in his arms to share this moment with

him. But Rachel froze in place when Gray's brows drew together and his eyes turned stormy.

"Why did you keep him from me?" he asked crossly.

The thrill of Gray's discovery drained from her. There would be no happy reunion tonight. It was time to face the consequences of her past actions, time to atone for her sins. And, Lordy, there were so many of them.

"I—I didn't keep him from you, really," she began.

"Yes you did," he snapped.

He was more angry than she had anticipated. "Well, well, yes I did. But not for the reasons you think."

"Christ Almighty, Rachel, I don't know what to think!"

She rubbed her damp palms down the skirt of her wrapper and took a deep breath trying to maintain her composure. What should she tell him? The truth? The whole truth? Well, why not. There was no use in hiding any of it from him now.

"I was ..." Her voice broke. She cleared her throat and spoke again. "I was the one ... in St. Joseph ... in your ... room ... that night."

His eyes drilled her and his tight jaws ticked.

"When I found out I was ... pregnant ... I knew it was up to me to make a life for the baby, since I knew I would never see you again. When things improved, I sold my business and left St. Joseph."

"You told me you were from St. Louis," Gray suddenly realized.

"Your uncle said I was from St. Louis—"

"You didn't bother correcting him," Gray pointed out angrily.

"Well, well, no, I didn't because I thought it would be better if I returned to Charleston with no links to—"

"Returned to Charleston?"

Rachel wrung her hands nervously. "Yes, you see, I used to live in Charleston."

"You lived here? In Charleston?"

She nodded. "I had no idea you lived here. I only came back to give Andrew a decent upbringing in a civilized city. I wanted to give him a good life. I planned to buy back my old family home and raise him with all the prestige due a plantation owner."

"Plantation? You lived on a plantation?" he asked. Good Lord, what was next!

Rachel's mouth was as dry as the cotton her daddy used to raise. She swallowed hard. "Yes," she said in a small voice. "I lived at Richfield."

"Richfield!"

"That's why I wanted to buy it from you," she said. This was getting out of hand. She must explain in to him— he didn't understand! "I didn't want anyone to learn of my past. I wanted to be judged on my own merits, not on the memories of what my parents had done."

"You told me your parents died when you were a child."

"They did. Actually, my father died first and Mama died later after we had moved."

"Moved? To St. Joseph?"

Rachel shook her head. All these lies were so hard to untangle. How would she ever make him understand? It seemed impossible. "Oh, none of this would be happening if Fergus hadn't found me here."

"Fergus? Found you? You knew him?" He wanted to understand, but each time she spoke it only confused the issues and angered him further.

"Yes, in St. Francisville," she said meekly.

"Has every word you have spoken to me in the past

358

been a lie?'' he demanded, and threw up his arms in frustration. ''Have you ever told me the truth?'' He gripped his narrow hips and paced angrily back and forth behind the desk.

Rachel's throat tightened. All right, she deserved this. She had it coming. ''Yes,'' she murmured. He stopped his pacing; his eyes bored into her. ''I told you the truth when I said I loved you.''

''Well, you have a mighty goddamned strange way of showing it!'' he thundered.

Rachel jumped. She was already on the verge of tears and her body was drawn tight with tension, but she faced him squarely.

''You lied to me, my aunt and uncle, to everyone in Charleston. You pretended to be from a different city. You lied about your own parents. You claimed not to know Cavanaugh when in fact you did.'' He grew more angry with each word he spoke. He felt betrayed and hurt, and now he wanted to hurt her. ''And you didn't even have the decency to tell me I had a son!''

Rachel broke. She couldn't take anymore. ''What did you expect me to do? Walk up to you the first time I saw you here, put Andrew in your arms, and announce to the world that this was your son!'' she shot back angrily. ''I didn't even know you lived in Charleston! I didn't even know your name!''

''A likely story,'' he sneered.

''If you don't believe me, ask Captain Daniels! He knows the whole story.''

''He knew that boy was mine and didn't tell me?'' he exclaimed.

Rachel's breasts heaved. ''He only learned of Andrew's

true identity a few weeks ago. I made him promise not to tell you."

"I suppose everyone in the whole goddamned world knew the truth but me!"

"Don't stand there looking so smug in your self-righteous indignance! You know nothing of what I have been through!" Hot tears streamed down her cheeks. "I bore Andrew alone with only memories of a few hours with you to comfort me through my labor. I cared for him, and provided for him myself. I bought a business and worked day and night so he wouldn't have a scrubwoman for a mother. And all the while, I knew you were living in high style somewhere, probably married with other children who were waited on hand and foot, spoiled with every luxury your wealth could provide. I was determined that Andrew would have just as good a life—and he will!"

Her outburst and tears took some of the anger out of Gray. But he was not willing to give up completely. "What about Mr. Fontaine?" he wanted to know.

"Who?" Rachel pushed the mass of tangled blond curls over her shoulder with a trembling hand.

"Your husband," he reminded tersely. "Did he know about us?"

Something inside Rachel snapped. "There never was a Mr. Fontaine!" she shrieked. "I only made him up to escape Fergus, then used him so no one would know Andrew was illegitimate!" Rachel pulled the wedding ring from her finger and hurled it across the room with all her might. What a relief at long last to be rid of that thing. "There was never a husband! There was only you!" She fell into choking sobs that racked her body. She turned away from Gray and leaned against the arm of the sofa for support.

Gray's head was spinning from this sudden turn of events. He had come here tonight to learn the truth, but never had he imagined all of this. The lies, the secrets, the mysteries—how was he suppose to take it? Simply toss it off and forget it? Forgive her for all the things she had done and all the pain she had caused?

Who had endured the most pain, Gray thought, as he watched her small shoulders quake. His anger melted and his heart was flooded with the love he had always felt for Rachel. Surely she had suffered a hundred times more than he, and it was all because of him and his moment of indiscretion in St. Joseph. Oh, God, what he had put her through.

Gray went to her and gingerly touched her shoulder. Startled, Rachel whirled around to face him. "I thought you had left," she said through her tears.

His fingers gathered her tousled hair and swept it back from her face. His heart jumped to his throat. She looked so small and helpless, and he felt like such a brute.

"I shall never leave you again." He spoke softly but with such conviction that it stopped her tears. He enfolded her in his arms and held her close for a long moment. And when the trembling in her limbs had ceased, he wiped her tears with his linen handkerchief and sat her down beside him on the sofa.

"I want you to start at the very beginning and tell me the whole story," he instructed gently. He slid his arm about her shoulders and pulled her closer. "And I do mean the whole story," he added, covering both her hands warmly with one of his.

Rachel snuggled closer to him, her body molding against his chest, her thigh touching his. It felt so good, so right to be at his side. She didn't deserve this. But he had somehow found it in his heart to give her a second chance; she would not squander it.

"Are you certain you want to know?" she asked tentatively. He gave her a little squeeze for encouragement and her words began to flow as freely as the rain from the heavens.

Her whole sordid past became known to him. She spared none of the ugly details, including the circumstances surround her father's death—something she had been too ashamed to tell another living soul—and her mother's loss of her senses. Gray listened intently and sympathetically, but became visibly upset when she spoke of Fergus Cavanaugh and what he had attempted to do. Though it was humiliating, she told him about her cousin who had sold her to Fergus to repay a debt. When she related the incident at Fergus's mansion the night she was forced to wear that horrid, garish gown and Fergus had attacked her, she could see Gray's struggle to control his anger. Yet he held his silence and let her speak. He snuggled her even closer, knowing how difficult it was for her to recall such an awful experience.

Gray was shocked when she told of her escape from St. Francisville and the clever disguise she had used as she made the long trip alone. What grit she had! He knew she was a strong woman, but he had never expected anything like this. He cringed inwardly when Rachel spoke of her pregnancy. He felt like such a cad for putting her through that alone. She sensed the guilt he felt and purposely left out some of the details of her illnesses during that time. But he took great pleasure in hearing about his son. His eyes lit up and a broad smiled crossed his face as Rachel searched her memory for every small detail of their son's life. He was thrilled by every word, and she was equally thrilled to share her memories with him.

When she concluded her story, Rachel rested her head against his wide shoulder, suddenly tired and drained from the ordeal of reliving her past. Gray squeezed her gently and planted a soft kiss on her forehead.

"All the terrible things you have been through," he murmured. "I have caused you such unhappiness."

She shook her head. "Oh, no," she disagreed. "I was never bitter about having Andrew. He brings such pleasure to my life. Nor was I ever sorry about the night we ..." Her words trailed off, and she felt her cheeks redden; she was glad the room was so dimly lit.

Gray chuckled and tilted her face up to him. Her deep brown eyes twinkled in the light. "Nor was I," he confided. "That night changed my life." She raised her delicate brows. "It's true. I was so taken by the woman with whom I made such beautiful love that I could not face life with any other. I was restless and confused, and roamed the country searching for something I could not understand. I broke off my engagement with Claudia Danforth because I could not marry her when my heart belonged to another. Then, when I met you here in Charleston, I knew there was something very special about you. I was drawn to you. I could not stop myself. I knew we had to be together."

Gray brushed a kiss across her forehead and pulled her even closer in his arms. She snuggled against him, and for a long moment they sat content in their embrace. Presently, Gray rose and laid a fire in the hearth to drive away the chill of the damp night air. He took off his coat and sat down on the hearthrug before the blazing fire.

Rachel moved to sit next to him and took his hand.

"There are so many things I don't know about you," she said.

His gaze caressed her face in the glowing firelight. Her tears were gone now, and he saw in her eyes the same sparkle that had been there the night he had first met her. Those beautiful eyes, he thought, and a shudder went through him. Why hadn't he remembered?

"Will you tell me of yourself?" she asked.

Gray smiled. "I fear, my sweet, that my life is not nearly as adventurous as yours."

She grinned. "A normal life seems very interesting to me."

"Very well."

As the storm still raged outside, Gray and Rachel sat before the hearth and talked. They exchanged stories of their youths, some happy, some troubling. They spoke of their families and of childhood recollections, and of growing to adulthood. Opinions on community and national affairs and politics were shared, as were speculation and idle gossip. Theirs was a comfortable exchange of ideas and information, as two minds and two hearts moved ever closer.

Hours slipped by uncounted, unnoticed, and the storm died away. As the first rays of the morning sun flirted with the horizon, Gray lay stretched out before the last glowing embers of the fire, his head propped up on his hand, watching Rachel intently as she sat beside him.

"Gray, I have told you this story three times, and it always ends the same way," she chided gently. "The babe was born and was a fine healthy boy, as handsome as his father."

He smiled lovingly. "Indulge me."

A wry grin curved her lips upward. "Indulging you is

what started this whole thing to begin with,'' she pointed out, and ran her fingers along his firm jaw.

"You are a very indulgent woman," he commented, and closed his eyes as the feel of her hand against his skin sent a shudder through him.

Her hand slid down his neck and toyed with the silky hair of his chest peeking over the top of his open collar, accessible to her since he had discarded his cravat and waistcoat earlier in the evening. Her hand trembled and she closed her eyes as visions of his full, bare chest flooded her mind, and she relived the moments in St. Joseph when she had first seen his wide shoulders and hard, muscular arms. Her breathing became uneven. Her eyes opened and locked with his, burning with passion.

Gray ran his hand through her thick blond hair and pulled her head down to meet his. His lips touched hers gently, and when they parted before his probing tongue, the smoldering embers of desire ignited and burst into full flame. His arms encircled her and pulled her onto the rug beside him as he rose above her and covered her face with hot, searing kisses. There was no reality, no sense of his surroundings, as Gray was consumed by the lust that possessed him. He opened her wrapper and slid his hand down the curve of her hip, his lips reclaiming hers greedily. Grabbing the garment's hem, he pulled it upward and turned his head to view her slender, bare legs. His loins throbbed at the sight, and he ached to claim her, for he had had no other woman since Rachel had returned to his life in Charleston. He turned to capture her lips once more and saw her eyes wide, a mixture of wonder and fright. His passion ebbed as he suddenly remembered that she was far less experienced than he, and her pleasure became uppermost in his mind.

Slowly, deliberately, his hands moved beneath her night rail to caress her thighs and hips as he covered her lips with gentle, loving kisses. A glow deep inside Rachel came to life, and she looped her arms about his neck, pulling him closer. Passion was born within her as the feel of his hands cupping her breasts rocked her senses. His knowing caresses reached deep inside to draw out her love, her desire, and cast away her fear. Her need grew to match his as she rained feverish kisses over his face and throat. He moved above her, unfastened his trousers, and his manhood touched her intimately, scorching her flesh with its heat.

Gray postioned her small form beneath him. His loins burned, aching for relief, but he held back. He did not want to take her brutishly, and he knew that anything but the most gentle union would hurt her; the birth of their child had probably returned her to near virginity. He moved cautiously, gently making them one.

The world about her whirled crazily, and she held him tightly as his movements mesmerized her. She responded in kind and he became bolder, urging her to unknown heights of pleasure.

The ageless rhythm of love ensnared them and wrapped them in ecstasy. Together they sailed upward, reaching, climbing ever higher, until their love burst forth in waves of rapturous delight. They wafted back to earth, limbs entwined, sated in their embrace.

Gray moved to lie beside her and pulled the afghan from the sofa to cover them. He brushed a kiss against her temple. "I love you," he whispered.

She looked up at him. "I love you, too."

They were silent as they lay contentedly in each other's arms. Finally, Gray spoke. "Are you . . . all right?" he asked with a note of concern in his voice. How he prayed he had been gentle enough.

Her delicate brows drew together. "Well, yes, but ... I just can't seem to stop smiling."

He raised up on his elbow and beheld the glow on her face. "Why, you little vixen," he teased. Rachel giggled wildly as he nibbled at her neck.

Gray ran his hand across her firm, flat belly, then peeked beneath the afghan to marvel at the flawless white skin. "I thought that childbirth left its mark on all woman," he said.

"I suppose I was meant for bearing children," she speculated.

His white teeth flashed as a rakish grin parted his lips. "What you were meant for, my sweet, only results in childbearing."

Rachel smiled and snuggled against him, touching intimately. "It feels so right to be at your side," she said wistfully.

"That is where you belong and where you shall always be," he told her.

She sighed. "Oh, Gray, if only it were true. How I wish that could happen."

He looked down at her. "Of course it will happen," he said quite matter-of-factly.

Rachel's eyes widened with surprise. "No. I must marry Fergus."

He bolted upright. "What the hell are you talking about?"

"I must marry Fergus. Otherwise, he will tell everyone about Andrew being illegimate, and I will not allow my son's future to be ruined," she told him and sat up.

"He is my son, too, and I will not have him raised by

another man. Nor will I allow the woman I love to marry someone else," he said angrily.

"Then how do you propose we keep Fergus from talking?"

"Easy. I shall marry you first. We will go tomorrow— no, today—and be married," he told her.

She shook her head. "No, that will not silence Fergus. That will only make him angry and then he will surely tell everything," she cried.

Gray thought a moment. He didn't like this, he didn't like this one bit. He had finally found the woman he loved and, by God, no one was going to take her away from him. "Then I will simply tell everyone that Andrew is my child," he said. There, what could be easier?

Rachel gasped in horror. "And have everyone know I was compromised?"

Well, of course not. That would never do. He brushed the idea aside. "I will challenge Cavanaugh to a duel," he said. Yes, that would solve the problem.

"Oh, Gray, no. Don't do that," she begged. "The scandal ... people would talk about it for years. Andrew's future would be jeopardized."

Gray grudgingly bowed to her wishes, though he would have taken great pleasure in blowing Fergus straight to hell. "We will leave Charleston right away and start again somewhere else. St. Louis, New Orleans, Boston—any place you would like. Just the three of us," Gray told her. He didn't like running from trouble, but he would do anything to keep Rachel and Andrew away from Cavanaugh.

"I would adore going anywhere with you," she said earnestly. She lifted his strong hand, kissed it gently, then held it against her cheek. "But no one knows better than I that one cannot hide from the past."

He caressed her soft skin. "Then come to Richfield with me where Cavanaugh can't get to you."

"If I am at Richfield, that will only lend credence to Fergus's words."

"I have many friends here, and they will not believe the word of a stranger over that of myself," he said.

"But it won't matter who they believe. People will still talk. There will be gossip and rumors and speculation. It will affect Andrew for the rest of his life," Rachel explained. "And I will not do that to Andrew," she vowed. "I will not ruin his life as my parents ruined mine."

Gray tossed off the afghan angrily and got to his feet. "I am not going to stand by and do nothing," he declared as he fastened his trousers.

She looked up at him with pleading eyes. "But you must. Anything you do will only hurt Andrew."

"No. I will not accept that," he said, angry and frustrated by the seemingly hopeless situation.

"There is no other choice."

"There are always choices." His mind worked, searching for a solution.

Rachel stood up. She could see the tension he felt and wished she could help him come to terms with the problem. "Not this time," she said softly. "That is why I am going to marry Fergus."

His eyes captured hers. "Do you mean you actually intend to marry this man? You can't be serious."

She nodded.

"No! I will not allow it."

"You must."

"I won't!" He stuffed his shirt into his trousers.

"The choice is mine, not yours."

"I certainly have a say in the matter," he told her. "The boy is my child."

Rachel searched his face intently. "And it is precisely for that reason that you must not interfere."

He studied her, considered her words. Should he let go of them both for the sake of Andrew's future? Should he condemn himself to a life of loneliness and Rachel to a loveless marriage? Should he? Could he?

He grasped her shoulders. "I will find a way. I swear to you, somehow I will rid our lives of Cavanaugh, and we will be together. The three of us will be a family," he vowed.

"You must not interfere," she pleaded. "It will only anger him."

"I will find a way," he promised.

"No, Gray," she insisted. She paused, mentally selecting the words for a request she did not want to make. "You must not come around me or Andrew again. Promise me."

"I will do no such thing."

"Please, Gray, do not cause trouble. I am engaged to Fergus. You have to respect that."

"I do not."

"You must."

Gray gathered his clothing and turned to her once more. "I will see you tomorrow," he said softly.

"No, I cannot allow that."

He smothered her protest with a gentle, easy kiss, then pulled on his hat and left the house. She watched the doorway long after he had left. Her heart and body yearned for him, and she felt hopelessly trapped by the hand life had dealt her. She would not allow herself the smallest hope that Gray Montgomery would find a way to silence

370

Fergus. She couldn't put herself through that. She had made her decision and she would stick by it. Life had not allowed her to make choices of the heart, only cold, grim choices brought on by reasoning and logic. And she had made her choice and would abide by it . . . somehow.

Chapter 15

"Get out of here."

"Is that any way to address a customer?"

Rachel rose from the small stool where she sat restocking shelves and frantically bobbed up and down trying to see past the large frame that blocked her view. "You have to leave. I haven't seen Fergus all day and he is liable to show up here any second," she whispered urgently.

"Let him," Gray replied with an indifferent shrug.

She scanned the store quickly and saw Mr. Rhodes assisting several ladies at the display near the front door. "Go," she said, boldly pushing him in that direction. But she was no match for his strength and he easily stood his ground.

"How is my son?"

"Shh!" She looked around nervously to see if they had attracted anyone's attention. "He is fine," she whispered.

"The storm didn't awaken him again last night?" he asked.

"Will you keep your voice down!"

The ladies turned raised eyebrows in their direction and Rachel chewed her bottom lip. "Come back here," she instructed. She took his arm and pulled him toward her office. At least in there they would be out of sight. Gray allowed himself to be taken in tow, but followed at an unhurried pace. Once inside, she glanced about the mercantile again, then pulled the curtain closed.

"You promised you wouldn't come around here," she fretted.

"No, I didn't."

"Well, you should have."

Gray tossed his hat on top of the opened ledger and sat down on the desk's corner. "Why?"

"You know why. And don't bother getting comfortable because you won't be here that long," she said. Gray showed no sign of leaving. "I saw you this morning outside my house and again when I went to the bank and then again when I went to the post office. Gray, you have got to stop this. Fergus will see you and—"

"I don't give a damn about Fergus Cavanaugh. I am going to run that man out of your life once and for all. I am going to marry you and raise my son."

Rachel shook her head and covered her ears. "Don't say that. Don't try to get my hopes up. It will never happen."

Gray got down from his perch on the desk and took her hands firmly in his. "Yes, it will."

Rachel looked up at him with hopeful eyes. Oh, if she could only believe that. But she had been let down so many times in the past that now she could not trust anyone. No, not even Gray.

"Andrew is fine," she said suddenly, glad to be able to

change their topic of conversation. He had already asked after his son and knew that he was fine, but Rachel felt she had to change the topic, and knew Gray wouldn't mind hearing about Andrew a second time.

"Good. I shall be by to see him tonight," he told her.

"No! You can't come over. Please, Gray, Fergus knows there is something between us. If he sees us together—"

"How does he know?" he asked, then smiled rakishly. "I didn't realize you were the type to kiss and tell."

"Oh, Gray, please." Honestly, this man could be so exasperating sometimes! "Why are you making this so difficult for me?"

"Let me show you how difficult I can really be." He pulled her into his strong arms and covered her lips with a hot, demanding kiss. She struggled against him but for an instant before giving in to her own desires. When he held her close and kissed her lips so sensuously she lost all her powers of reason and logic. She was totally his to do with as he chose.

When finally their lips parted, she looked up at him with starry eyes. His kiss drove her crazy with desire. Though her experience with men was limited to only two occasions, she was intrigued and mystified by the sensations her body felt. Their encounter the night before had been on her mind all day.

"You do sorely test my willpower," Gray said huskily as he drank in her beauty and sweet feminine fragrance.

"I think I would have enjoyed sharing your marriage bed." The words slipped out, betraying her thoughts. Her cheeks reddened.

Gray chuckled and hugged her tighter. "You will still enjoy it, madam, and enjoy it often," he assured her. His tone became more serious. "We shall be married. Though you may not trust me enough to believe that now, I assure you it will happen. You shall see." With that, Gray retrieved his hat and left.

Rachel didn't know whether to feel happy or angry, upset or pleased by Gray's actions. He always left her so confused. Why wouldn't he simply do as she asked and leave her alone? Somehow she would have to find the strength to forget him, to ignore him. She had tried that before and failed miserably. Well, this time she would try harder and succeed.

She had just bade good-bye to Mr. Rhodes and turned the key in the lock closing her store for the day when she sensed someone behind her. She spun around and saw Fergus Cavanaugh. Her heart sank.

"Do not look so disappointed, my dear. You were expecting someone else?" he asked as his eyes hungrily devoured every inch of her.

He was immaculately attired, as always, but the sight of him sickened her nonetheless. "No," she replied quickly. "I was expecting no one." She had not seen him all day and had begun to hope he would leave her alone.

"Come, my pet, we will dine together tonight." Though graciously phrased, it was a command more than an invitation. She didn't know how she would stomach a meal in his presence, yet was afraid to refuse him.

He offered his arm. "Shall we?"

She didn't want to touch him. She couldn't—

"Cavanaugh!"

They both turned to see Gray striding toward them. Panic swept through Rachel. Would he say or do something to antagonize Fergus? She held her breath as he joined them.

"Cavanaugh, I have searched the town for you. Did you not get my message at your hotel?" Gray asked cordially.

"Message? No, I have been out all day," Fergus said.

Gray tipped his hat formally to Rachel. "Madam," he greeted, then turned his attention to the other man. "I hoped we could get together this evening to discuss that land purchase."

"You told me you were not interested," Fergus said.

"I have put a bit more thought into it and I would like to discuss it further." Gray had no desire to enter into any sort of dealings with this man. Even before he had known about what he had done to Rachel he wanted no part of him. But it was the only ruse available to him at the moment.

Fergus looked at Rachel, then back to Gray. He desperately needed to sell that property and no one else in Charleston had shown any interest in purchasing it. He could see Rachel anytime. He always believed in business before pleasure.

"Rachel and I were just about to have dinner," Fergus began.

"So sorry, I didn't mean to interrupt," Gray said sounding sincere. "But I will be occupied with other matters all of tomorrow."

Fergus turned to Rachel. "I will see you another time. You do understand."

She heaved a silent sigh of relief. "Certainly. Good evening," she bade the men and hurried into her waiting carriage. She looked back in time to see Gray give her a sly wink before he and Fergus continued on their way.

For the next week, every meeting between Rachel and Fergus was interrupted by Gray's well-orchestrated plan to keep the man away from her. Through his network of friends and associates in the city, Gray was able to discreetly learn of Fergus's plans and managed to maneuver some unsuspecting soul into filling Fergus's idle hours. If he had to stretch the truth about the man's pending business deals to entice his associates into spending an evening with him, Gray was more than willing to sustain the tarnish on his reputation if it would achieve his goal. He managed to get his uncle Bernard to meet with him over lunch and even talked Charlotte into inviting Fergus to her party.

Fergus Cavanaugh was not well received in Charleston. Though he looked and acted a gentleman, no one liked him. The men quickly realized he was not much of a businessman, and all wondered privately how he had amassed his fortune. The ladies avoided him for other, less tangible reasons. It was not just his physical appearance that made him unappealing, but a hint of evil that lay just beneath the surface. So it was no small miracle that Gray had managed to secure so many invitations to so unpopular a guest.

Rachel was at first annoyed by Gray's interference. Everywhere she went he was behind her, or across the street, or waiting when she arrived. Though he never approached her or acknowledged her with more than a polite nod, Rachel was terrified that Fergus would see what was happening and become so angry that he would call off the wedding and blurt out the true story of her past. But during a chance meeting with Fergus on the street one afternoon, Rachel saw Gray disappear into the bank and emerge with Charlotte. The older woman bustled over and planted her stout frame between them and insisted that Rachel join her immediately to look at the latest shipment of fabrics just in from England. When they left, Rachel stole a quick glance at Gray standing almost out of sight in a nearby doorway, and the self-satisfied grin he wore told her what he had been up to and that he was the reason she had seen so little of Fergus. The love she felt for him grew all the more, and she was anguished that only a week remained before she must marry Fergus and leave Gray forever.

As that day drew closer, Rachel's pleasures were limited to the time she spent with her son, and visiting with her friends. Since no one knew of her engagement, she was free to attend social functions without having to pretend enthusiasm over her impending wedding. Fergus had at least kept his word and not told anyone of their plans. She had used the excuse that her property would sell for less if it became known that she was in a hurry to sell, and it seemed Fergus was more interested in profits than in Rachel herself. In truth, she had no intention of selling her house or mercantile. Her holdings would be placed in trust for Andrew and would become his when he grew to manhood. That would bring him back to Charleston one day, and maybe then he and his father would meet again. It was a small gesture on her part for all the pain she was causing by separating the two now. She only prayed that one day they would both understand and forgive her.

The jolt of her carriage jarred Rachel from her morbid thoughts, and she looked out the window surprised to see that she had arrived at the home of Bernard and Charlotte Wade so quickly. She pushed all bad thoughts aside and departed the carriage determined to enjoy this lovely Saturday evening with these dear friends. Fergus was supposed to attend with her, but at the last moment he had canceled, having to meet with some businessmen unexpectedly; Rachel suspected that Gray had had a hand in that turn of events.

She put on a smile as she joined Bernard and Charlotte in the drawing room and settled comfortably on the sofa as they chatted easily. Charlotte, as usual, was never at a loss for a topic of conversation, and Bernard and Rachel, being accustomed to that, were content to let her go on, taking what opportunities there were to interject a comment or two. Presently Charlotte excused herself to check on the meal preparation.

"The other guests have not arrived yet?" Rachel asked.

"No other guests tonight," Bernard said. "Just us."

She was pleased that the Wades cared enough to have her over alone. She would miss them a great deal. "I would like to come by the bank to see you," she began uneasily. She had put off setting up the trust for Andrew, knowing all the while that she would have to face it sooner or later.

Bernard nodded. "Monday morning?" he suggested.

"Friday morning will be better," she said. Fergus had told her they were leaving town the next Saturday so she wanted to conclude this transaction as close to their departure as possible so he would not get wind of it. She knew he would be very displeased, but once it was done there was nothing he would be able to do about it.

A knock at the front door interrupted Rachel's thoughts. "Didn't you say there were no other guests coming?" she asked as Bernard rose.

"This man is no guest," he said jovially as he left the room.

Rachel's stomach rolled. Did he mean Fergus had come after all? She rose from her seat and drew back the heavy window curtains. She squinted her eyes in the darkness but was not able to recognize the carriage that waited at the curb. Suddenly depressed by the prospect of spending the evening with Fergus, Rachel turned away from the window only to have her heart jump into her throat at the sight of Gray striding into the room.

He stopped when his eyes met hers and he greedily drank in the refined elegance of her features. The sight of her, as always, whipped his emotions and desires into a frenzy.

She glanced at the doorway realizing they were alone. "I—I didn't—" Her voice broke. Why did he always have this effect on her! She gathered her shattered composure and started again. "I didn't know you would be here tonight," she said softly. She wanted to look away from him, to break the spell he cast over her, but could not find the inner strength.

He walked toward her slowly. "Would you have come had you known?" His eyes held hers captive.

"You know I wouldn't have," she replied finally finding her voice. His masculinity dominated the room, threatening to overpower her.

"You are so bullheaded, woman," he said gently, and stopped before her. Her sweet fragrance titillated his senses. Strength, he prayed, dear Lord, please give him strength. But his heavenly request was unanswered and he gave into temptation. With a will of its own, his hand touched an errant curl of blond hair at her temple and wound its softness about his finger. He cupped her cheek with his palm, then slid his hand down the graceful column of her throat onto her creamy shoulder. The tiny shread of self-control he clung to was suddenly buried in an avalanche of burning desire as his arms encircled her and his lips took hers with molten-hot kisses.

Rachel's arms curled about his neck as her body instinctively responded to his sensual kisses. Her mouth parted before his aggressive tongue and his warmth filled her with passion, a passion only he could arouse, passion she certainly would never feel with—

Fergus.

Rachel tore her lips from Gray's and tried to pull away from his powerful arms. He held her firmly as his lips moved fluidly over her cheek and nibbled at the flesh of her throat.

"Stop, please, Gray, stop," she pleaded as she pushed against the hard wall of his chest. "This isn't right."

"Like hell it isn't," he said huskily against her ear, his tongue playing sensuously about it.

"Do not make this more difficult than it already is," she begged.

He loosened his grip on her and looked her square in the face, his heavy breath hot against her flesh. They stared eye to eye for a long moment before a wry grin twisted Gray's lips. "I will have you," he promised.

Rachel didn't know whether to be frightened or pleased by his vow. Either way, it was unsettling.

A moment later, when Charlotte and Bernard returned to the parlor they found Rachel seated primly on the sofa and Gray leaning rakishly against the mantel. Had the elder couple not been so involved in their own discussion they would have noticed the tension in the air, Rachel's discomfort under Gray's probing eyes and Gray's struggle to hold his wants and needs in check.

It was the longest evening of her life. Without a doubt, the most tedious, nerve-wracking occasion Rachel had ever experienced. Gray's eyes were on her every second, scrutinizing her every action, perusing every movement she made. The meal dragged by slowly as Gray sat across the table with watchful, playful eyes, knowing full well that she was uncomfortable under his gaze. When the meal was thankfully concluded, Rachel had no idea what she had eaten. She only knew that he was up to something. Something devious. Something she was not going to approve of. She heightened her senses, trying to stay one thought ahead of him, trying to anticipate what he was up to. And she was determined she would cut him off, refusing to let him have his way. But as the next hours passed uneventfully with only pleasant conversation in the parlor between the four of them, Rachel began to wonder if she had been incorrect in her suspicions. Seated across the room from her, he conducted himself in gentlemanly fashion. He was witty and insightful, engaging in light discussion of noncontroversial issues selected with the ladies in mind. A gathering anywhere in Charleston where talk of slavery and politics did not creep into the discussion was a rarity indeed, and it made for a very entertaining evening.

Rachel finally cast aside her worries as being unfounded. She had evidently suspected him unjustly of concocting some plan that would not meet with her approval, and now she realized how silly she had been. Of course it was natural that they would be drawn together in the heated embrace that had overtaken both of them earlier, but she had put a stop to it and he had bowed to her wishes. It seemed that she had more control over the situation than she had imagined.

She was sorry when the evening drew to a close. Charlotte gave her a motherly peck on the cheek and Bernard assisted with her shawl as they said their good nights in the foyer. She cared for the Wades greatly and she would be sad to say good-bye to them forever. She had put off that unpleasant task until later in the week.

Gray joined then, pulling on his hat. "Good night, Aunt Charlotte," he said, kissing her full cheek.

"Must you go so soon?" she whined.

"Yes, I am taking Rachel home," he replied quite matter-of-factly.

"What?" Rachel cried, her eyes wide with surprise.

"Oh, how sweet of you, dear," Charlotte gushed, beaming with pride at her nephew.

"But—but," Rachel stammered.

"Isn't he a dear boy." Charlotte spoke to Bernard, but gave him no opportunity to respond. "These dark streets are no place for a lady alone."

"I have my carriage," Rachel interjected.

"I have already sent it home. We will take mine," Gray informed her. He took her elbow and propelled her out the door as Charlotte and Bernard called a final good night to them.

Rachel's small feet froze to the ground, refusing to enter the carriage door held open by Gray. She was so furious her limbs shook.

"After you, madam," Gray said evenly, and reached for her arm to assist her inside.

Rachel pulled out of his reach. "I am not riding home in this carriage with you," she said through clenched teeth.

"There are matters which we need to discuss," he told her.

The heavy night air closed in around her as she tried to control her anger. He was so smooth, so smug, so calm—and it irritated her to no end! "We have nothing to discuss," she informed him crisply.

"We have our son."

"Shh!"

He pushed his hat back on his head and rested his fist on his hip. "Then perhaps, madam, you would like to go explain to my aunt and uncle the reason for your refusal to accept my hospitality," he suggested, and nodded discreetly toward the house.

Turning her head, Rachel saw Charlotte and Bernard standing in the open doorway, still waving. He had her trapped. There was no way she could refuse to ride home in this carriage now. He always got his way and it was infuriating!

Rachel managed a weak smile and waved again to the Wades. She refused to accept Gray's assistance into the carriage, pointedly ignoring his outstretched hand. He might have trapped her into being alone with him, but she still had a few things to show him!

In her haste to enter the carriage, one of her skirt hoops hung in the doorway leaving her half in and half out of the vehicle. She tugged at it twice, but the hoop refused to budge, adding embarrassment to her anger, and she was maddened all the more when she felt Gray's hand on her waist steadying her as he easily dislodged the hoop. Rachel gathered her skirt around her and moved quickly to escape his touch, settling herself primly on the seat, her back straight, head high, silently vowing never to speak to this man again.

"You know the way," Gray called to the driver before waving to his aunt and uncle and climbing into the darkened carriage. He took the seat across from Rachel, tossed his hat aside, and stretched out his muscular legs in front of him, lazily studying her.

She slid to the very corner of the seat gathering her skirt close around her. He had very inconsiderately taken up most of the room in the narrow carriage and she wanted nothing of hers to even so much as brush against any part of him. After the flurry of skirt and petticoats had settled in the cramped area she had confined herself to, Rachel resumed her most dignified pose, refusing to glance his way. Go ahead, she mentally dared, let him try to speak to her. Would she respond? Ha! She would show him!

The carriage swayed through the quiet neighborhood with only the glow of an occasional streetlight illuminating its interior. Several minutes had passed and he had made no effort to speak to her, not a word, not a sound. She pressed her lips together tightly renewing her resolve. She almost hoped he would say something so she could have the satisfaction of not speaking to him. She would take great pleasure in showing this egotistical, stubborn man that she would not be manipulated or used.

"How is my son?" He seemed never to tire of asking that question.

Gray's voice echoed a loneliness that cut through Rachel's determined outrage and struck her heart.

"I see so little of him," he mused in a mournful tone, almost as though he had not realized he had spoken aloud. "He is well, isn't he?"

Merciful heaven, how could she not answer such a question? He sounded so pitiful, so alone, so left out of what was rightfully a part of his life. She couldn't be so cold and heartless as not to tell him about the child. Could she?

"He is fine, growing bigger and stronger everyday," she said in a small voice. Should she tell him every detail of the boy's life and make it all the more difficult on Gray not to be a part of it? Or should she give him only a few small scraps of information to appease him, like tossing a bone to a dog. Neither seemed fair.

Gray nodded slowly, digesting her words. In the brief light that invaded the carriage, Rachel saw a terrible sadness in his eyes that had not been there before. A long moment of silence passed before Gray spoke again.

"Marry me now."

The words struck her hard. No, no she could not go through this conversation again. "Gray, don't start that. You know I cannot—"

"I have sent wires to people in New Orleans, St. Louis, and Memphis about Cavanaugh," he began urgently.

"Stop it!"

"The man is not what he appears to be." He sat forward, trying to get through to her.

"You are wasting your time. Please, Gray, forget it. I am going to marry Fergus. We will be gone on Saturday. And there is nothing you can do to stop it," she cried.

Gray crossed the carriage and sat beside her. "Listen to me, Rachel, I have learned a few things about the man. You could be in danger."

Why did he do this to her! Why couldn't he just accept her decision! "Do you have any proof?" she challenged.

"Well, no, nothing firm—yet," he admitted.

"And you will find nothing!" Rachel's emotions were ragged and torn. "Fergus Cavanaugh is a fine upstanding citizen. He will make a perfectly acceptable husband." Her emotions were churning, a mixture of anger, sadness, anxiety, and outrage.

"And when he beds you each night will he make you feel like this?" Gray challenged angrily as his mouth closed over hers with punishing kisses. He pressed his full weight against her, forcing her down onto the seat beneath him. His hands sought out the softness of her flesh and his tongue ravaged the sweet recesses of her mouth commanding her desire to come alive. His hands tore through her hair loosening the tresses and plunging wildly through them. With skillful hands, he easily opened the bodice of her low-cut gown and pulled free the string ties of her chemise, laying back the fabric. A fiery passion consumed him as his fingers covered the mounds of her breasts, kneading, caressing, exploring, remembering. The tiny buds rose beneath his fingertips sending him to another plane of arousal and he dipped his head to taste their sweetness. The storm that churned inside him threatened to break into full force as his lips worked their way up the column of her throat and claimed her lips once more.

Suddenly his passion chilled as he realized the object of his intense desire lay motionless beneath him, and as the light from outside briefly illuminated her face, he saw tears standing in her deep brown eyes.

Oh, God, what had come over him? Instantly he hated himself. How could he have done this to her? Had he lost all his senses? He had behaved like an animal. What could he say to her to make her understand, to forgive him?

But it was Rachel who spoke first. "Oh, Gray, I love you so much," she said in a choked sob. She threw her arms about his neck, pulling him closer as she pressed her cheek against hers.

"I love you, too," he answered. He spoke the words with all the love, all the conviction his heart held.

The carriage rocked on as Gray and Rachel lay in their loving embrace, contented with their closeness and unfulfilled desires. Their moments together had been but a few, in Charleston as in St. Joseph, yet they embodied the warmth and serenity of two people deeply in love.

Reluctantly Gray sat up and pulled Rachel up next to him. His eyes fell to rest on her breasts, and he drew in a sharp breath as desire tugged at him once more. But this time he controlled himself as he reached for the strings of her chemise. He drew the laces together ever so slowly and after two attempts managed some semblance of a bow at the top. Fingers so deft moments ago failed him completely as he fumbled with the small buttons of her gown. She pushed his hands aside gently and completed the task herself. Rachel arranged her hair as best she could, using the few pins she could locate, then curled contentedly against Gray's chest. He folded his arms around her comfortably as they rode in blissful solitude.

Presently Rachel spoke. "I have been watching the scenery go past and we are nowhere near my house."

He placed a soft kiss atop her head. "I know. I instructed my driver to roam aimlessly about the city before proceeding to your house," he confessed.

She couldn't help but laugh. "You are such a bad man," she gently scolded.

"Humm. Yes, I know," he agreed, and they snuggled closer together.

Finally the carriage found its way to Rachel's house, and Gray walked her to the door confident that Cavanaugh was still engaged in the affairs he had arranged for this evening. In the shadows of the foyer he kissed her softly and said a quiet good night. Rachel watched as he climbed into the carriage and disappeared into the darkness. And somehow, she didn't feel so alone anymore. A tiny glimmer of hope flickered inside her. Maybe, just maybe there was a way for her to be with Gray always. Perhaps if she trusted in him, believed in him, he could make it happen. Perhaps . . .

* * *

On Monday it was business as usual as Rachel attended to her work at the mercantile. It was an especially busy day as word had circulated that Fontaine's Mercantile had, as usual, received the latest and best merchandise from abroad. Patrons were there ogling the goods as fast as she and Mr. Rhodes could stock the shelves. All this hustle and bustle served as a pleasant diversion for Rachel, since the time spent with Fergus the previous day had left a sour residue.

She and Andrew had attended services at church and had stayed for the social gathering afterward. There was a picnic on the lawn with lots of food and fellowship. Fergus had showed up unexpectedly, but in the crowd of people she felt unthreatened by his presence. He had stayed for only a short while before becoming bored with the whole thing and had left promising to see her again soon. Rachel had scanned the crowd all day hoping Gray would be there. She was not disappointed.

A hand closed over her elbow jerking Rachel's thoughts back to the present, and she turned from the display she was preparing. She steeled her emotions when she saw Fergus, hoping her expression would not reveal that her thoughts had been rather unladylike ones involving Gray, not her husband-to-be. But Fergus scarcely noticed her as he took in the crowded store.

"You are doing a very nice business here, my dear," he said. "Very profitable."

She eased out of his grasp without him becoming aware of it. "A small profit, actually," she replied, not wanting him to know how well the store really did.

Fergus only snorted his disbelief before pulling her into a quieter corner of the room. "Do you have a buyer for the business yet?"

"There have been several interested parties, but nothing definite yet," she lied. She had no intentions of informing him of her real plans.

"And the house?"

"The same."

He eyed her sharply. "My affairs here are going very smoothly and we will be leaving on Saturday as planned. I want your properties disposed of before then."

Rachel wiped her hands on the crisp white apron she wore. "It shall be done," she promised sedately.

Something resembling a smile twisted his lips. "Very well."

"Yoo-hoo! Mr. Cavanaugh!"

The shrill of a female voice rose about the noise of the crowd and the patrons parted to allow Claudia Danforth to pass among them. Dressed in the finest apparel her father could provide, Claudia looked radiant, making Rachel uncomfortably aware of the much plainer dress she wore. She stopped before them.

"Why, Mr. Cavanaugh, I have been looking for you all over this city," she said, directing all her attention toward Fergus and deliberately ignoring Rachel.

Immediately taken in by her charm, Fergus replied, "My dear, what for?"

"To give you this." Claudia withdrew an envelope from her purse and presented it to him. "It's an invitation to my party this Saturday evening."

"How gracious of you," Fergus declared as he accepted the envelope.

Claudia's lashes fluttered. "Simply everyone of importance in the city will be there," she said. Claudia hardly knew Fergus, but she had overheard her daddy and several others mention his name and figured that while he was

was extremely unpleasant to look at he must be of some importance and, therefore, must be at her party. "I expect you know most everyone who is coming. Mr. Wade, Mr. Philpot, Edward Davies," she said, then cast a smug smile at Rachel, as she drawled, "Gray Montgomery. Just everybody will be there, everybody who is somebody, that is."

Rachel didn't miss the barb intended for her.

Fergus was about to refuse the invitation since he had already made plans to leave the city on Saturday, then thought again. He had been looking for an insurance policy of sorts to guarantee that Rachel would hold up her end of their bargain. As the time drew closer to leave, he feared she might actually change her mind and decide to risk him circulating the rumors of her past. Now he could make certain all went according to his plans.

Rachel fumed silently, aching to scratch out Claudia's eyes. She was such a witch! But, thankfully, Fergus was leaving on Saturday and the party was out of the question—not that she had been invited anyway.

"Thank you so much, I would love to attend."

Rachel turned to him in shock.

"But could I ask one small favor from so gracious and lovely a hostess?" Fergus inquired.

Claudia dipped her eyes and feigned embarrassment. "Whatever do you mean, Mr. Cavanaugh?"

"I would like to invite a guest to join me," he said.

Rachel's stomach twisted painfully.

"Who?" Claudia's tone was less charming than before. She planned her guest list carefully, avoiding certain younger, more attractive ladies, whenever she could get away with it. She liked a small amount of competition, but only the kind she could win out over.

Fergus touched Rachel's arm. "I would like Mrs. Fontaine to accompany me."

Claudia could barely contain her pleasure. She had purposely not invited the beautiful, successful widow because she hated the sight of her. But now, now that she would be the guest of the unattractive, mildly important, and even less interesting Fergus Cavanaugh, relegated to stay at his side while she herself danced the night away with all the most eligible bachelors in the city, she couldn't pass it up.

"Why, Mr. Cavanaugh, I think that is a wonderful idea and I insist that you bring her along," Claudia told him, smiling broadly.

"I realize, Miss Danforth, that I am but a visitor to this fair city, but I feel so close to the good people here," Fergus began. "I would like to use the occasion of your party to make an announcement."

Claudia's interest piqued. "Pray tell, what sort of announcement?" she asked eagerly.

Fergus cast a glance at Rachel. She held her breath. "That, my dear, is a secret that shall remain untold until the night of the party."

Claudia squealed with excitement. "This is going to be the very best party ever! And I can't wait to tell all my friends of this delightful turn of events." She disappeared into the crowd.

Rachel's blood ran cold. "Fergus, what are you planning?" She dreaded the answer she was sure was coming.

"I just wanted to take the opportunity to announce to the good folks of Charleston that we will be joined together in wedded bliss for the rest of our days," Fergus told her. His eyes darkened ominously. "Unless, of course, you give me reason to make an announcement of another sort."

Rachel cringed. She had not wanted anyone to know that she had actually agreed to marry this man. That would be nearly as humiliating as everyone learning the truth of her past. She had planned to slip away quietly, telling only her few closest friends what she had done. Well, better to have the wedding announced than her biography and that of her son, she reasoned.

"Fergus, I gave you my word that I would ... go through with this." She couldn't bring herself to say the word "marriage."

"You have left me standing at the altar before, if I may remind you. I have simply arranged for a guarantee that you will keep your word this time," Fergus said. "The topic of my announcement at the party is solely up to you. Everyone of importance will be there. It will be the perfect forum for my address." He chuckled as he left the mercantile.

Rachel's heart sank. She closed her eyes and said a silent prayer that Gray would find a way to free her from this terrible fate. She had come to trust and believe in him, and that was something she had not done since she was a small child. And now hope was all she had to cling to.

Chapter 16

"Rachel, you're not serious!"

She looked across at the horrified expression on her friend's face and wished wholeheartedly that she wasn't. "Yes, Hannah, I am quite serious. I am going to marry Fergus Cavanaugh."

"But why? Why marry anyone? And why Mr. Cavanaugh, of all people?"

Rachel shifted uncomfortably on the sofa she shared with her friend, trying desperately to keep her voice and expression emotionless. She knew telling Hannah would not be easy. Unlike the other friends she would eventually have to confide in, Hannah was under no social obligation to accept the news in a gracious, ladylike manner.

"Well, he is a very successful businessman, a fine gentleman ..." Rachel chose her words carefully but quickly exhausted Fergus's attributes.

"What about Mr. Montgomery? I know you care for him, and it's plain to see he feels the same," Hannah said.

She rose and moved uneasily about the parlor. "Things just didn't ... work out between us ... and when Fergus asked me to ... m-marry him, I agreed."

"But this is so sudden. And you will be leaving Charleston. I thought you liked it here."

Rachel turned to face her friend. She knew she was not being very convincing so she resorted to the one argument that Hannah could not refute. "Andrew needs a father."

That quieted Hannah as she thought it through, and Rachel seized the opportunity to sell her on the idea. She resumed her seat on the sofa. "Fergus has an enormous mansion, with acres and acres of land. He has much more wealth that I could ever provide for Andrew. He would have the best of everything, and a father to see that he is raised properly." Rachel managed to put a bit of enthusiasm in her voice. "What do two women know about raising a boy, anyway?" she joked.

Some of the doubt left Hannah's face. "Well, I suppose you do have a point," she relented. She thought it over. Yes, it did make sense. "But must you leave so soon?"

"Yes. Fergus must get back to St. Francisville. He has neglected his affairs there far too long." Rachel took Hannah's hand. "I know this is difficult for you, but please give it some thought. I would like you to come with us, and so would Andrew."

A small tear beaded in her eye. "I held that baby the day he was born and he has been an important part of my life every since. I don't know what I would do without him. But, well, Mr. Rhodes and I have been seeing a great deal of each other and, well, I do care for him so much, I don't know if I could leave ..." Her words trailed off.

Rachel patted her hand consolingly. "I know it's a difficult decision. Think it through carefully. I will respect your choice, no matter what it is." Hannah smiled and dabbed her eyes with the handkerchief she always carried. "Just remember, please keep this to yourself. I want no one to know of the m-marriage." Hannah nodded in agreement, and Rachel rose and walked toward the door.

"Just one more thing," Hannah called. "Do you love Fergus?"

Rachel stopped. She could feel Hannah's eyes on her back, waiting for her response. She tried to form an answer, but the words refused to come. A knot rose in her throat. She couldn't do it, she couldn't say the words. A flood of tears coursed down her cheeks and Rachel rushed from the room and up the stairs to her bedchamber, leaving Hannah with the answer to her question.

Gray came to call that evening, but on instructions from Rachel, the servants refused to let him enter. With the announcement Fergus had planned for Claudia's party hanging over head, Rachel was not taking any chances. She wanted to get a message to Gray somehow, to explain the situation, but dared not risk it. He would have to accept her terms and abide by them.

He was met with the same response when he came again the following evening. Gray knew Cavanaugh would be tied up for hours in another part of the city so there was no chance he would stop by Rachel's house and discover him there. But since Rachel was not aware of this, she wasn't letting him in, Gray realized. He wanted to see her up close, not from the shadows as he had trailed her about the city for the last two days. He wanted to hold her and touch her, he wanted to hear the melody of her voice. Yet there was nothing he could do, short of breaking down the front door, and he left the house in a dark mood.

Rachel's mood was no better. She ached to have Gray near her. Each time she had the servants send him from her door, a little piece of her died. The days dragged by, and each moment that passed stretched her nerves further, testing the limits of her resolve.

Everything seemed to be pulling against her, even the weather. The string of hot, oppressive, humid days finally broke on Wednesday with an afternoon rain shower that cooled the city. Rachel came home from a busy day at the store feeling hot and sticky and indulged in a refreshing bath in her chamber. She languished in the tub letting the tepid water relieve the tension in her muscles.

If only her thoughts could be as easily lifted, Rachel thought as she dried herself on a thick towel. She slipped into her lightest wrapper and sat down at her bureau. She wanted to be left alone for a while to unwind and had not allowed her maid to attend to her bath. She studied her reflection in the mirror, her thoughts alternating between Gray and Fergus and the realization that she had but three days left. It was a depressing prospect.

She shook off her somber mood. Enough of this, she decided, and dismissed the entire subject from her mind. Instead of moping around, she intended to spend a pleasant evening with her son and enjoy the time she had left before doomsday, as she privately referred to her wedding day. Hannah was going out with Mr. Rhodes and she would have Andrew all to herself. She was determined to make the best use of their time together. She wouldn't venture to think what a typical evening at home might be like as the wife of Fergus Cavanaugh.

She swept her hair into a loose bun atop her head and,

unable to face her heavy petticoats and hoops, donned a gossamer chemise and pantalets and a pale-blue day dress that was the height of fashion among the ladies for at-home wear. It had a full skirt and short sleeves, and a deep V-shaped neckline above its button-front closing. Much more comfortable on a hot evening and more practical for frolicking with Andrew in the garden.

Hannah reported the details of Andrew's day over a light meal, as was their custom, then went upstairs to prepare herself for Mr. Rhodes's arrival. Rachel took her son to the garden to play.

"Rachel, I am leaving now," Hannah called from the back portico a few moments later.

"You look lovely," she said as she walked across the lawn to join her friend; Andrew toddled along behind. It was true, Hannah looked radiant. Rachel could not ever remember her being so happy and alive. It must be love, she decided.

"I probably won't be back until very late," she cautioned.

"Don't give it another thought. I will bathe Andrew and put him to bed. You go enjoy your evening," Rachel instructed.

"Oh, I will." Her smile faded. "Mr. Montgomery was here a few minutes ago. Philo refused to let him in."

"Oh?" Rachel said guiltily. She hated not letting him in—she wanted to see him so badly—but what could she do?

"He became very angry this time. Philo was firm, and finally he left," Hannah reported. She looked at Rachel with concern. "Are you certain you're doing the right thing? He seems awfully persistent, and—"

"Please, Hannah, not now," Rachel requested wearily. "Let me have a quiet evening with Andrew and you enjoy yours. Please."

Hannah relented. "Oh, very well. But I still think—"

Andrew suddenly began to squeal with delight as he trotted on awkward legs toward the rear of the house. He jabbered excitedly as he stopped at the trunk of the huge oak that stood by the brick fence and reached up toward its spreading limbs.

"What has gotten into Andrew?" Rachel asked.

Hannah followed the child's line of vision, then called out a greeting. "Why, hello, Mr. Montgomery. How are you this evening?"

"Gray?" Rachel called in disbelief as she, too, recognized him perched atop the tall brick wall.

"Fine, thank you. And you?" He returned Hannah's pleasantries as if they had just passed on the street.

"Gray, what are you doing?" Rachel demanded.

He grasped an available tree limb and swung to the ground. Andrew rushed to him, and Gray lifted him into his arms as naturally as any father would and carried him across the lawn to the spot where the ladies stood.

"Isn't it a lovely evening?" Hannah said wistfully.

Gray turned his head to look at the sun dipping toward the horizon. "Perfect evening for visiting," he stated, and looked directly at Rachel. "Don't you think?"

Rachel was aghast. "What do you think you are doing?" she demanded. "You have no right climbing over my wall, barging into my garden."

"Yes, I do," he told her, and gave Andrew a squeeze.

Well, she couldn't argue with that. "Give him to me.

He's afraid around strangers," she instructed, and held out her arms to take Andrew.

"Oh, Mr. Montgomery is no stranger," Hannah declared. "He and Andrew always have a lovely time together."

She whipped around to face Hannah. "What do you mean?" she wanted to know.

"Mr. Montgomery comes by every day to play with Andrew, that is, if we don't meet him in the park," Hannah explained. She paused. "Mr. Montgomery told me you had said it was all right. It is all right, isn't it, Rachel?"

Her jaw tightened as she slowly rotated her head and glowered at Gray; he diverted his eyes guiltily. "Yes, it's fine," she said through clenched teeth. "Why don't you leave now, Hannah. Mr. Rhodes is growing weary of waiting in the parlor, no doubt."

"Oh, yes, of course. Good night all," she called and disappeared into the house.

"Gray, you should not have climbed over that wall."

"If you had let me in through the front door, as most civilized people do, then such an unorthodox method of entry would not have been necessary," he defended.

"But if Fergus should come by," she protested.

He did not want to hear that man's name mentioned. "Well, he won't. I happen to know that he is in Beaumont and won't return until midday tomorrow," he informed her. It had taken a lot of doing, but he had managed to pull enough strings to get that bastard out of town for an entire evening.

She realized now why he had taken such drastic actions to gain entry to her house, and her anger left her. "Oh, Gray, I was afraid to let you in. You don't know what Fergus is up to."

Andrew played contentedly with Gray's cravat. "What now?"

"He's forcing me to go to Claudia's party on Saturday where he intends to make a public announcement. He said the topic of his announcement will depend on my actions this week."

"There will be no announcement," Gray said flatly, annoyed by this topic of conversation.

"But if he sees you here," she protested.

Gray touched his finger to her lips, silencing her. "He won't know I am here. My carriage is a good distance away, no one saw me scaling your wall—though no one would have believed if they had seen it. There is no possible way he can find out. So put that . . . man out of your mind and let us enjoy this evening. Please." he requested, and glanced toward Andrew. "Just the three of us."

Rachel could not hold back her smile as she nodded in agreement.

"Wonderful!" Gray exclaimed. He put Andrew down beside him. "Let's go, champ!"

Had the garden not been so secluded, the trio would have looked like a typical family to any passerby. Gray shed his coat and hat as he and Andrew romped about the garden, laughing and playing together. The boy's short legs churned fitfully as Gray chased him around the shrubs, overtaking him at will to swing him high in the air. Andrew cackled gleefully as Gray rode him about on his shoulders. They sat with Rachel in the gazebo, where Gray trotted the boy on his knees horsey-fashion as he recited bits and pieces of the nursery rhymes he could recall. It was difficult to say which of the three enjoyed the outing the most. Or who was most disappointed when

Philo appeared and announced that Master Andrew's bath was ready.

"So soon?" Gray asked Rachel as the boy stood on his lap running his fingers through Gray's wavy hair. "It's still light out."

She smiled indulgently. "Babies need lots of sleep, and we must keep to his schedule."

Gray snorted. "A man needs flexibility in his day. He needs to be in command of his life, master of his destiny."

"There will be plenty of time for that when he is out of diapers," Rachel pointed out as she held her arms out for her son. Gray grudgingly gave the boy up after a final hug and kiss.

"Tell Pearl to put him in the tub. I will be up in a moment," she instructed as Philo took the child and disappeared.

She turned to Gray. "It was a lovely evening, but I have to go now and put Andrew to sleep."

"Let me help," he said eagerly and came to his feet.

"I don't know," she said reluctantly. "It is not a very glamorous chore."

"I have never put him to bed before," Gray said softly, his blue eyes pleading.

Oh! He always knew what to say to break down her defenses! "All right, come on," she said, and he eagerly followed her up to the nursery suite.

Rachel sent Pearl away as she donned a long white apron and moved to the small bathing tub on the dressing table where Andrew sat waist-deep in warm water. He splashed happily as he reached for a wooden boat that bobbed on the surface.

"Wait a moment," Gray said as he stood next to her assessing the scene. "What are we doing here, exactly?"

The care of the baby was such a routine to Rachel that she had never stopped to think it might seem foreign to anyone. "Andrew always has a bath before going to bed," she explained.

"Every night?"

She nodded.

"You do that yourself?" he asked. There was a look of concentration on his face as he took it all in.

"Yes, usually. If I am not here, Hannah sees to it. But I like to do it myself."

Gray studied the boy in the tub, the many towels and articles of clothing spread out on the table. "Do you think ... I ... could do this?" He wasn't asking her permission but for an assessment of his ability to perform the task.

"I don't see why not."

Gray squared his shoulders and pursed his lips determinedly. "Very well, then," he said. He rolled his sleeves past his elbows and obediently donned the apron Rachel fetched for him. He slid into it awkwardly and tied the sash into a knot that Rachel had to untangle and retie. He then settled in to the task at hand, lathering the cloth and running it gingerly over the boy's chest and protruding belly. Andrew, who was an old hand at tub baths, recognized a greenhorn immediately, and with one swipe sent a spray of water directly across Gray's face. Rachel couldn't contain her laughter as she toweled the wetness from his stunned expression.

"All right," Gray said, rising to this new challenge, "we shall see who gets the wettest." He attacked the job with more authority and Andrew gave him no further trouble.

Rachel watched the two of them together, both happy and contented, and it warmed her heart. They belonged together—all of them. It was as obvious as the love she felt for them both.

With the wash and rinse completed, Gray lifted the boy from the water and laid him on his back on an open towel as Rachel directed. Quickly she placed an extra diaper between his legs.

"My modesty would not be shocked by such a sight," Gray commented as he dried his hands. "That is something I encounter on a daily basis," he added, and glanced down at Rachel standing at his elbow.

She cut her eyes to meet his as her cheeks reddened. "He tends to be rather spontaneous, and I didn't want you to be christened," she hastened to explain.

"Oh." He drew in a deep breath. "Then we will handle it your way since you have a vast amount of experience in this area," he conceded teasingly, and laughed heartily as Rachel's cheeks turned crimson once more. Andrew joined in with a giggle of his own. Gray pulled Rachel into his arms and she joined in their laughter.

Next, Gray lent himself to the difficult task of fitting the thick diaper around Andrew's constantly moving legs and finally, after much struggling, succeeded in pinning it securely in place. He captured the boy's flailing arms and guided them through the sleeves of the nightgown and worked diligently to fasten its tiny buttons. He lifted the finished product proudly into his arms.

"I had no idea this mothering business was such hard work," he said as he wiped his brow with the tail of his apron. "You do this every evening? After working all day at your shop?" he asked incredulously.

"I enjoy it," she said honestly.

Gray shook his head unconvinced. "Well, madam, what is next?"

"He usually enjoys a story before he gets into bed," she said.

Gray looked troubled. "But don't you have to . . ." He fumbled for the correct word, and finally gestured toward her breasts. " . . . nurse him . . . or something?" He suddenly felt a pang of envy toward his son. He could think of no finer way to end a day than to sip from two such lovely goblets.

"Andrew drinks from a bottle," she explained, and oddly enough felt no discomfort in discussing the subject. "My milk dried up a few weeks after he was born. The doctor in St. Joseph said it was probably due to my working at the mercantile, facing the prospect of raising a child alone, and the anxiety over the loss of Mr. Fontaine."

"Who?"

"My late husband."

"Oh yes, him."

Rachel smiled. "This way, please." She led the way to the adjoining room that served as Andrew's bedchamber. It was gaily decorated with colorful pictures and bright, breezy drapes, and crammed full of every imaginable toy. The baby's bottle waited on the table beside the comfortable old rocker; it was one of the few pieces Rachel had brought with her from St. Joseph.

Rachel tested the milk's temperature on her wrist and was obliged to dribble a small portion of the liquid on Gray's outstretched arm.

"Seems a bit cool to me," he observed, but accepted the bottle when Rachel assured him it was the way Andrew liked it. He lowered himself into the rocker, momentarily juggling Andrew, the bottle, and storybook before settling comfortably into place. He wasn't certain how to feed a baby, but Andrew settled the matter by taking control of the bottle himself and lying back in the crook of Gray's arm as if he had been there every night of his life. Before he had read two pages the baby was fast asleep. Following Rachel's silent directions, he placed his son in the bed and covered him with a light sheet, then tiptoed to the doorway while Rachel turned down the lantern.

"Good job," she whispered as she removed her apron and joined Gray.

"Do you think so?" he asked.

Rachel slid behind him and untied his apron. "You are a natural," she praised, and raised on her toes to lift the garment over his head.

He took one final loving look at his sleeping son and turned his full attention to Rachel. "You have done an excellent job with him," he whispered warmly. It was just one more reason to love her.

Rachel deposited the aprons on the cloak hook and faced him as they stood in the open doorway. "Everything I have done has been for him."

"You have given him a good home." He glanced into the bedchamber at the end of the short hallway. The lantern was lit displaying the turned-down coverlet and her night rail at the foot of the bed. "That is your room," he said instinctively, "right beside his."

"Of course," she replied. Rachel would not dream of being out of earshot should her son awaken during the night.

The stillness of the house suddenly became very obvious. "It is certainly quiet," Gray observed.

She nodded. "The servants retire early, as do I."

"And, Hannah, I suppose she will be back any moment," he speculated.

"No, actually I don't expect her back for a long, long

time." Rachel realized the folly of her admission when Gray's eyes, suddenly smoldering, swept her from head to toe, making her uncomfortably aware for the first time that evening of her state of dress. Without the petticoats, hoops, corset, and shift that were her normal undergarments, the casual day dress clung to her figure revealing the curve of her hips and swell of her bosoms. She was at once conscious of her own vulnerability.

"Well, it is awfully late," she began, and forced a small laugh as she closed the door to Andrew's room. She moved toward the staircase. "I know you are anxious to be on your way. This evening was hardly pleasurable for you, I'm certain."

Gray took her hand, halting her steps. "To my way of thinking, the greatest pleasure of this evening still lies ahead." The cool blue of his eyes deepened to a lustful glow.

Her mouth went dry. "I'm—I'm awfully tired," she began nervously, "and I really would like to go to bed."

"I see, madam, that our thoughts run along the same lines." A rakish grin parted his lips.

"No, no, I didn't mean that I wanted to go to bed." God, why did she keep repeating that word! "I only meant that—that—" She retreated in the face of his steady advance.

His arms closed around her small waist and drew her tight against him. Since realizing that hers was the lithe form in his bed in St. Joseph and experiencing such beautiful love with her in this same house only days ago, Gray had been consumed with a desire to relive those passionate moments. Yet he had fought hard tonight to conduct himself as a gentleman, even though the simple dress she wore outlined her hips with clarity and brought back a recollection too vivid to ignore.

Rachel leaned backward and braced her elbows against his chest. If his expression didn't tell her where his thoughts lay, certainly the warmth radiating from his loins did. She drew in a quick breath and her eyes widened as the evidence of his arousal made itself known through the thinness of her gown.

She spoke in a raspy whisper. "No, Gray, you—you can't do this."

"Ah, but I can, madam, and with great ease."

"Well, yes, yes I know you *can*, but—"

"You placed your brand on me with one night's loving, Rachel. You ruined all women for me, for none could compare with the fervent spell you cast over me," he said huskily.

Panic crept into her thoughts. "I didn't mean to do that. I only—"

"You were made for love, my sweet." His eyes captured hers. "You came willingly to my bed that night, and I, a stranger. Are your feelings different now that you have a name to put to this face?"

She tried to hold tight to her last shred of reasoning and good judgment. "These times are not the same, and ..."

His fingers slowly kneaded the nape of her neck. "Will you deny us both that to which our love leads?"

Rachel closed her eyes as his touch sent ripples of pleasure through her. She wanted to tell him something ... something important. What was it?

His lips found hers trembling with anticipation and they moved together slowly, easily. The warmth of his body drew her to him instinctively and her arms encircled his neck, holding him tightly. All her resolve and determination to avoid him vanished the same second she felt his strong hands moving over her back. What did it matter now that she was betrothed to another, her wedding only days away? All thoughts of Fergus and the future fled. Now, this moment, was all she cared about. A few moments of happiness, a chance to love and be loved. She loved this man, and her body naturally responded to his now as it had only days ago when he had made love to her with a gentle intensity that burned into her soul.

Effortlessly, Gray lifted her into his arms, carried her into her bedchamber, and pushed the door shut quietly. His lips slanted over hers hungrily as her feet slid to the floor. Yet he moved slowly, remembering she was far less experienced than he, and he wanted the pleasure of this night to last them both a lifetime.

He cupped her cheeks with his palms, and ever so slowly his fingers found their way down her neck to her shoulders. His senses tingled as she stepped closer to him, the fullness of her firm breasts straining against the thin fabric of her gown. He traced the neckline of the garment until his fingers reached its buttons, and painstakingly he opened it and pushed it over her shoulders until it fell in a circle about her feet. She extended her arms to encompass his neck and lifted her lips to receive his as his hands acquainted themselves with her soft, round curves through the gossamer fabric of her chemise and pantalets. She moved against him unaware of how enticing she was as she craved for the feel of him. The fullness of his manhood pressed against her and she stopped, suddenly frightened by this rediscovery. Gray slid his hands downward to the soft yielding flesh of her derriere that made his heart flutter. He pressed her closer, moving against her, signaling that what she had caused in him should not be reason for alarm. She understood and followed his unspoken instructions, moving with and against him.

Her pulse quickened as she stepped back from his arms and pulled the pins from her hair sending it cascading over her shoulders. She kicked off her slippers and crawled to the center of the bed where she drew her legs under her and turned her full attention to Gray. He followed, but she held up her hand to stop him.

"I want to see you," she whispered as the lantern light shone softly on her face.

He smiled, understanding what she wanted. Quickly he stripped off his waistcoat and cravat, unbuttoned his white linen shirt, and pulled it free of his trousers revealing his hard, muscular chest covered with thick, dark hair. He shrugged out of the shirt and tossed it carelessly aside, his wide shoulders and arms rippling. He pulled off his boots and socks in one quick motion, pausing a moment as he watched Rachel in the center of the bed. Her face was a mixture of curiosity and wonder, and was relieved to see that when he stepped out of his trousers and undergarments she was not startled by his bold manliness. He stood still as her eyes traveled up his long, corded legs, past his flat, hard belly, over the thick hair of his chest, and came to rest on his face. Her line of vision dipped to his manhood once more, then returned to meet his eyes.

Gray's smile flashed in the dim light and he came to her quickly and sat down on the edge of the bed. Now it was his time to discover the secrets her body held. He pushed the straps of her chemise off her shoulders and unlaced its front. It fell back revealing the pertness of her pink breasts as a rush of excitement surged through his already pulsing veins. He tossed the chemise aside and gently laid her back on the bed, her blond hair fanning seductively across the white linen pillow. Eagerly his hands slid downward, pausing to caress the ripe mounds of her breasts and moved over the soft, flawless skin of her flat belly. Gray untied the drawstrings that secured her pantalets and slowly eased them down as his eyes devoured her hips and slender legs. He cast the garment away.

Love's passion-fire burned strong inside him, but Gray was too anxious to learn more of her to give in to the temptation that threatened to consume him. His hands moved upward along her legs, his mouth following the same path as he learned of the silky softness there before returning once more to the hard buds that rose from her breasts beneath his stroking thumbs. His manhood throbbed unmercifully and he ached to have her, have her immediately. But Rachel rose on her elbow and pressed him down upon the bed, more anxious than he had been to know this male body completely.

She followed his lead as she kissed her way over his strong legs, and since she had had no guidance but his, sampled his loins as he had done hers. He moaned her name as the excruciating pleasure she brought him threatened to overcome his self-control. She lingered there for a moment before delving her hands into the curly hair of his chest and seeking out the small mounds hidden there. She circled her fingers over them and they came alive beneath her touch before she covered them with her hot, moist kisses. Reaching up to meet his lips, the silkiness of his chest hair against her breasts sent a tingle through her.

Together their passion built, fanned by ardent kisses and entwined limbs until their desire demanded to be fulfilled. Gray positioned her small form beneath him. His

411

loins burned, aching for relief, but he held back. He wanted to prolong their pleasure, savor every moment. He moved slowly, deliberately, until they were one.

Rachel clung to him desperately as his manhood overtook her. His touch made every fiber of her being come alive, drawing it out, caressing it. Her heart pumped wildly as the love she felt for him flowed through it.

His thrusts became bolder. She answered him, and they moved in unison. The rhythm of their lovemaking soared higher, ever higher, until it reached its pinnacle, and together they exploded with waves of ecstasy. Their passion ebbed and they languished in the afterglow of their ardent embraces, both overcome by the other's outpouring of love.

Gray moved to lie beside her and drew her near, resting his hand possessively on the curve of her hip. He muzzled her cheek and kissed it gently. "I love you," he whispered.

She turned her head to look at him. "I love you, too. With all my heart."

They were silent as they lay contentedly in each other's arms. They spoke of love in subdued whispers and of the moment they had just shared, but that was all. There was no talk of their future, no hopes and dreams confided, as lovers are wont to do. Gray and Rachel had only this moment. It was theirs and they took it and cherished it, heedless of the world around them.

Gray sighed. "Woman, the things you do to me. Where did you learn of such matters?" he teased.

"I had an excellent teacher," she replied and her brown eyes came alive with mischief. "Actually, I am still learning, and there is one issue I am not clear on."

Gray drew himself up on his elbow and studied her. "And what might that be?"

She chewed her bottom lip for a moment before lifting

her eyes to meet his. "How long must we wait before we can do this again?"

His breath caught in his throat. Rachel had done and said the most unexpected things since he had known her, but nothing in his wildest dreams—and he had experienced some wild ones—had prepared him for this. A wide smile parted his lips. "Allow me to demonstrate," he said huskily, and rose above her once more.

Her arms went around his neck and drew him closer as their lips came together. Gray savored the taste of her, hungrily accepting her kisses. His heart grew as it filled with the love he felt for her. And he had loved her for so long. His heart had known it even before his head had figured it out, and now he was hungry for her, his appetite insatiable. The intensity of her desire had not entirely surprised him because he could easily recall the passion-filled night in St. Joseph, yet her love was a delicate thing, like a tiny bud opening to the world, needing care and tenderness to reach its full bloom.

Soon their kisses were not enough. Cradled in each other's arms and united as one, the cadence of their love increased, taking them to new heights, until, like a shooting star streaking across the night sky, their love burst into millions of tiny lights and drifted contentedly through the heavens.

Chapter 17

Rachel woke from a light sleep. The place beside her that Gray had warmed was now cold and, oh, so empty. She opened her eyes and he was standing over her buttoning his shirt, watching as she had slept. How she wished she could ask him to stay with her tonight and every night.

He sat down beside her and ran his hand through her silken tresses. "I have to leave," he said regretfully. Those were the most difficult words he had ever spoken.

She nodded. "I know."

He took her soft hand and pressed it to his lips. There was so much he wanted to say, so many things in his heart he wanted to share with her, yet he could not find the words. His love for her robbed his thoughts but toughened his resolve to have her as his wife.

She seemed to read his thoughts. "I know you will do your best to end this madness."

"I won't fail you," he promised.

Gray located his clothes which had been strewn haphazardly about the room and dressed quickly. He had to leave and leave soon, for Rachel looked so alluring upon the bed, with the coverlet molded against her barely concealed breasts, that he was afraid he would never be able to go. He fetched the night rail left out for her by her maid and helped her into it.

"I will walk down with you," she said, starting to rise.

"No," he said. "Stay right here. I want to remember you this way." He kissed her tenderly, picked up his boots, and silently left the room. But his heart remained there with Rachel.

Gray's stockinged feet were quiet on the plank floors as he took one last look at his sleeping son, then descended the stairway. He found his way through the dimly lit house and located his coat and hat by the front door where the servants had left them, pulled on his boots, then departed by the back way. The night air was cool and helped to clear his head. He scaled the brick wall easily—indeed, he could have flown over it tonight—and after making certain no one lurked in the alleyway on the other side, dropped to the ground with catlike grace. There was so much in his head and heart tonight that needed to be sorted out. He was glad he had a friend waiting. With brisk steps he headed for the docks.

"I was about to give you up as lost," Ezra Daniels said as Gray slid into the chair across from him.

"Sorry to be late," he apologized as he placed his hat on the table. "I was unavoidably detained."

"Business or pleasure?" Captain Daniels asked, and he signaled the serving girl for a tankard of ale.

Gray raked his hand through his tousled hair. "Business, business," he muttered, and ducked his head so the smile that crept across his lips would not be so apparent.

The captain snorted. "Do you leave every business meeting with your waistcoat fastened crooked?" he asked irritably.

Gray's head snapped up guiltily, then looked down to see that in his haste dressing in the dark he had indeed buttoned up incorrectly. He felt Captain Daniels's eyes boring into him as he righted the situation.

"I can see it didn't take you long to get over your loss of the woman you love," the captain growled.

"What?" Gray asked, not following the thinking of his friend.

"The woman you loved last week. Rachel. Remember?"

Now Gray suddenly understood the reason for the captain's foul mood. He thought Gray had just come from the bed of another woman. "No, Ezra, it's not what you think."

Captain Daniels snorted in disbelief.

"You don't understand," Gray said. What could he tell the man? That he had just come from Rachel's bed? That was no way for a gentleman to conduct himself. Besides, it was none of his damned business.

"When last we spoke—right here on this very spot—you were anguished by Rachel's engagement to another man, and I told you to go to her and resolve the matter before you each made the biggest mistakes of your lives. And now I learn of . . . this!" he said angrily, and gestured toward the telltale waistcoat. He shook his head in disgust. "Damn it all, it's all my fault. I should have never kept silent about Rachel's child when she told me of it. I knew then I should come to you immediately. The girl deserves some happiness. She deserves ..." Captain Daniels's self-incrimination broke off, and he turned angry eyes to Gray once again. "She deserves better than the likes of you!"

"Ezra, listen to me. It's not what you think. I swear ..." he said, then added somberly, "I swear on ... on the memory of my father."

Captain Daniels eyed him sharply, considering the younger man's words. The evidence against Gray was incriminating as hell, but his pledge of innocence carried great weight. The older Montgomery had been an important character in both their lives, too important for such a vow to be taken—or given—lightly.

"All right," the captain said agreeably, and leaned forward in his chair. "Now suppose you tell me just what the devil is going on."

The serving girl delivered a tankard of ale to Gray which he immediately pushed aside. He wanted a clear head now. He needed to think. Time was running out, and still he had not come up with any solid evidence against that Cavanaugh bastard. He studied the weathered face of the man who sat across from him. He had known Ezra Daniels his entire life and had always trusted his judgment, just as his father had done. Perhaps confiding in this man would help. Perhaps discussing the situation, God-awful as it was, would reveal some gaping hole he had overlooked.

Gray rested his arms on the table and inclined his head toward the captain. "What I am about to tell you must always remain in the strictest confidence," he said in a low voice. "It's about Rachel's past. She thinks the world of you and I know she would be humiliated if she ever

417

learned you knew of these things." Captain Daniels had only to nod and Gray was convinced that his friend would respect his wishes. He proceeded to outline the basic story Rachel had related to him.

When he had concluded, Captain Daniels sat back and took a long drink from his tankard. He was amazed by Rachel's stubbornness and distressed that her life had been so hurtful; he mirrored Gray's feelings. And, like Gray, he was angry, angry as hell, at the son of a bitch who was coercing her into marriage.

"Damn it all, we have to do something," he swore, and rapped the table with his fist.

"I have investigated this man's background, and on the surface he seems like a respectable businessman. But, Ezra, I know, in my gut I know there is something wrong."

"Just who the hell is he, anyway?" the captain wanted to know.

"Some bastard named Fergus Cavanaugh." Gray spat the words, not wanting them on his lips.

Captain Daniels sat up suddenly. "Who?"

"Cavanaugh, Fergus Cavanaugh," he repeated. He grew angrier each time he said the name.

"From Savannah?"

"Well, yes, originally. I discovered that through my investigation and by purchasing a worthless piece of property at an enormous price to keep the cad away from Rachel for a few hours. But more recently he is from St. Francisville, Louisiana."

"Sort of a short, portly fellow with heavy features?"

"I think you are being generous, but, yes, that loosely describes him," Gray conceded. "Just what the hell are you getting at? Do you know this man?"

418

Captain Daniels nodded slowly, his brows drawn together in concentration. "I know the Cavanaughs of Savannah and I know a Fergus Cavanaugh, but it couldn't be . . ."

"What?" Gray's stomach knotted anxiously. "You know something. What is it?"

The captain shook his head trying to clear his thoughts. "It doesn't make sense," he mused.

"What?" Gray thundered. He was ready to reach across the table and shake the man.

He turned his attention to Gray and explained. "I have known the Cavanaugh family for years and years, and although I have not actually visited them for a great long while, I know they are a very wealthy, respected family."

"What are you getting at?" Gray asked anxiously. The captain was holding something back; it was written in the expression on his deeply lined face.

"Fergus Cavanaugh would never want to marry Rachel," he announced decisively.

"But—what—" Gray stammered. "Have you not listened to a word I have been telling you?"

He nodded. "I am telling you that never, ever, in a month of Sundays, would Fergus Cavanaugh have the slightest interest in marrying Rachel. Or any other woman, for that matter."

Gray was nearly at his wit's end. He had come to Captain Daniels to pour out his troubles and miraculously the captain had come up with what must be the valuable information he needed. Only the man would not spit it out!

"Ezra, I beg of you, stop talking in riddles," Gray pleaded as he wearily rubbed his forehead. "Simply tell me what you know. Please."

Captain Daniels spoke slowly, choosing his words carefully. "Fergus Cavanaugh ..." he began.

Gray cringed. He would scream if he heard that name one more time!

" ... being the eldest son, took over the running of the family's financial affairs after the death of his father. The other offspring resented this, naturally, but had no choice but to go along with it since it was their father's wish," Captain Daniels continued.

To no avail Gray made a spinning motion with his hand, attempting to speed him along.

"He did an excellent job of rebuilding the family fortune that had suffered considerably in the years before his father died. But, nonetheless, Fergus was always an embarrassment to his family who they all would have preferred to keep locked away."

Gray chewed his bottom lip. "Why?" he asked patiently, and managed to hold his temper in check.

"That is what I have been trying to tell you, boy. The family wanted to disown Fergus for the same reason Fergus could not possibly want anything to do with Rachel," the captain said. Gray stared at him, his face a mask of exasperated tension. "All right, let me just spell it out for you. Fergus's ... preferences ... ran not toward women, but to ... boys."

Gray was so sickened he thought he might retch. He closed his eyes and willed the churning in his gut to subside. "Let me get this straight," he said, turning his full attention to the captain once more. "If Fergus Cavanaugh is so ... inclined, as you say, he could not possibly be interested in Rachel. Yet this man definitely intends to marry her. So how could he be the Fergus Cavanaugh you are acquainted with?"

"I suppose he could want to marry her for appearances' sake," the captain speculated. "I understand that has been known to happen. But if it isn't that, then I don't know who the man is."

Both men came to their feet simultaneously, nearly upsetting the table.

"I'm sure as hell going to find out," Gray swore.

Together they crammed their hats on and dashed for the door.

Gray could think of nothing but Rachel, now lying alone in bed, and how much he wanted to be there with her. For the first time there was a real possibility that he had uncovered something that would end this nightmare once and for all, and he wanted to share it with her.

Rachel lay awake, her thoughts lost amid visions of Gray, having no idea that he had discovered something of significance. She rose the next morning and went about her duties mechanically. It proved to be a long, difficult day.

Oh, no, not again.

Rachel closed her eyes and prayed that when she opened them again he would be gone. But, alas, he was not.

"My pet, you look disappointed to see me."

She pinched the bridge of her nose attempting to ward off the headache that had suddenly overtaken her. "No, Fergus, I am just quite tired." Her already lengthy day showed no signs of ending.

Fergus smiled. "This will all be over very soon," he said, and inclined his head toward the crowd that circulated through her mercantile. "In a few days you will no longer be burdened with this responsibility. Your only chore in life will be seeing to my needs."

Rachel's stomach turned over at such a dismal prospect. She was tired and on edge, and the last thing she wanted was another confrontation with Fergus today. This was the second time he had been into her store, and while that alone was nervewracking, she was more distressed because she had not seen Gray all day. He had not been waiting outside her house to follow her to work, or trailing her about the city, watching over her as he had done for days. She had grown accustomed to his nearness and watchful eye, and it disturbed her now that he was nowhere to be seen. Nor was Gray any longer manipulating Fergus's actions, shielding her from him, and as a consequence Fergus came by to see her as often as he chose.

"Why have you not begun packing?" Fergus wanted to know.

Her thoughts snapped back to reality. "You were at my house?" she asked, suddenly alarmed.

"Am I to assume this means you are not planning to leave the city with me?" he asked. His beady eyes studied her, calculating her every motion and expression.

"No, that is not what it means," she said quickly. How could she tell him that she had put it off, pinning her hopes on Gray rescuing her from so terrible a fate? "I just didn't want to upset the household yet," she hastened to explain. "There will be plenty of time for that on Saturday."

"Don't forget the ball on Saturday night," he reminded her, grinning smugly.

She bit back the sharp retort on the tip of her tongue. "Everything will be handled," she assured him. "I won't forget about the ball." How could she when that dreaded occasion had been their topic of discussion earlier in the day? She had asked him then if they could please not attend Claudia's party, using the excuse that much preparation was required to meet the deadline he had given her. Fergus's eyes had turned cold as he squeezed the flesh of her arm cruelly, insisting that they would attend the ball and forbidding her to speak of it again. Frightened, she had obeyed, but inwardly she had seethed with anger.

"I intend to keep a close eye on your progress," he told her, then departed.

Instead of being relieved that he was gone, a deep depression bore down on her at the thought of seeing him again. She felt like a condemned woman waiting for the executioner. And her only hope for a reprieve—Gray—was nowhere to be found.

She thought he would come by that evening before she closed the shop, but there was no sign of him. At home she kept one ear out for his knock at her door, and in the garden with Andrew her eyes strayed to the top of the brick wall in hopes that he would miraculously appear. He never did. The minutes dragged by finally turning into hours and still he did not come. She paced the floors late into the night, waiting, but to no avail. Finally, nearly exhausted from tension and anxiety, she gave up her vigil and retired to her bedchamber. But she found no comfort there, for the room was filled with the memory of him and their night of lovemaking. Where could he be? Had something happened to him? Was he ill? Had he discovered something about Fergus's past? Could Fergus have done something to him? She sat up in a chair most of the night, worrying and sleeping little. When the dawn broke, her questions remained unanswered, and an uneasiness had crept into her consciousness. Perhaps he had simply forgotten about her. Maybe he no longer cared. Had he found her "unsatisfactory" the night before? Could he have decided a wife and son were a burden he no longer desired after all? Perhaps he had simply walked away, just as he had done in St. Joseph.

The following day brought no answers to her questions. Gray was still not to be seen while Fergus wore a path to her doorstep. Her nerves were stretched taut and it was all she could do to hold her composure and submit to Fergus's constant attention. When she could no longer bear the strain, she slipped out the rear entrance of her mercantile, undetected by Fergus. She had to find out where Gray was. She had to learn the truth—no matter what. Rachel hurried through the busy streets, pensively chewing her bottom lip, hoping and praying that there was no "what" to discover.

If anyone could answer her questions, relieve her anxiety, it was Bernard Wade. He would know. And she would wheedle it out of him right now before she burst.

Rachel was shown into Bernard's office at the bank and took a seat across the desk from him. She filled the first few moments of their meeting with instructions, explicit instructions, then casually mentioned that she hadn't seen Gray in quite some time. She even managed to sound unconcerned when she asked if this behavior was out of character for him.

"Humph." Bernard snorted and sat back in his chair. His brow wrinkled as he thought. "Well, it doesn't really surprise me," he announced after a moment.

"This is not unusual?" Rachel asked. She looked poised and relaxed, and Bernard had no inkling of the storm that raged within her.

"Oh, heavens, no," he declared. "Why, I have known Gray to take off on a moment's notice, heading for God-knows-where, without a word to anyone of his intentions. He has not done it for a while, but, no, it's not unusual at all. And do not worry about him, dear. He will return, eventually."

"He didn't tell you of any trip he was planning?" she asked, swallowing the lump that rose to her throat.

"As far as I knew he was staying in the city. As a matter of fact, he was supposed to have supper with me this evening. Charlotte made him promise to come over before she left for Atlanta yesterday. With her mother taking sick so suddenly, Charlotte didn't want to be worrying about me during her trip," Bernard explained. He smiled and rose from his seat. "Just don't concern yourself over Gray. He does this quite often. I am just glad Charlotte is not here because this type of behavior gets her all stirred up."

Rachel stood, unsure that her trembling limbs would support her. "You will see to the trust for Andrew, won't you?"

Bernard tapped the papers atop his desk that he and Rachel had already discussed. "I will handle everything just as you wish," he assured her. Although he had no idea why she was doing such a thing, Bernard did not question her motives. He had learned long ago that he would get no answers.

She thanked him and left the bank. She almost wished she had not gone there. At least before she could only speculate on the reason for Gray's sudden, unexplained departure. Now it had been spelled out for her and she had no choice but to face it. Gray was gone. He had run away from her just as he had done to escape Claudia

425

when he no longer wanted her. He had changed his mind. He didn't want her or their son. It was blatantly obvious and Bernard, in his own way, had confirmed it.

Rachel felt sick, hurt, and betrayed. And at that moment, she hated Gray. She wanted to cry but refused to let herself. She wanted to strike someone, but the one who deserved her wrath was nowhere around. She had trusted him, believed in him, put her faith in him. Had she been a fool for doing so? It seemed that way. Yet, deep inside, she clung to the hope, faint though it was, that she was wrong.

It was late, too late for well-bred men to come calling. Their appearance was questionable, for each mile of their hot, hard ride showed in their faces and clothing, but Gray and Captain Daniels were not about to stand on formality at a time when so much was at stake.

Though it had been years since his last visit, Captain Daniels easily located the home of the Cavanaugh family north of Savannah. They tethered their horses in front of the large, white-columned house, and Gray took the steps two at a time and knocked urgently on the gracefully carved doors.

Captain Daniels followed closely on his heels. "Keep a cool head, my friend," he cautioned.

Gray paced anxiously, then knocked again. "I am calm," he said tightly.

They had left Charleston during the night, and there had been no opportunity for Gray to get word to Rachel that he and Captain Daniels were leaving and why. He had fretted about it during the long ride. But what could he have told her? There was no concrete evidence to tell of, only a hunch, a suspicion, unanswered questions. He could only wonder at what must be going through her mind now. She was probably worried and concerned. He hated putting her through that. But what he hated more was that with him out of the city Fergus Cavanaugh would come and go as he pleased. He could see Rachel whenever he chose. The thought sent renewed anger through Gray's already pounding heart. He had to find something here in Savannah that would rid his life of that man. He had to. If he was to return to Charleston with no new information, no new hope . . . well, it scared Gray to think of what measures he might resort to in order to lay claim to his son and the woman he loved.

When the door opened, Captain Daniels laid a restraining hand on Gray's arm to prevent him from barging inside. He told the servant that they had come to call on the Cavanaughs on a very important matter, and they were shown into the drawing room.

The house was large and richly furnished, but there was an air of confusion about the place. Packing boxes and crates were stacked here and there, some of the furniture was covered with white shrouds, and the servants rushed about hurriedly.

Gray and the captain had to wait for several moments before a dark-haired woman with plain but pleasant features swept into the room. Captain Daniels recognized her as the daughter of his friend, the eldest Cavanaugh. Gray, too, noted the family resemblance between the woman and Fergus. She looked frazzled and tired, but she smiled warmly as she greeted her guests.

"I am Mildred Cavanaugh Dickerson," she said. "At present, I am the only Cavanaugh on the premises. I was told you are here on an important matter."

"Please excuse our intrusion," Captain Daniels apologized. "I am Ezra Daniels and this is Gray Montgomery of Charleston. I was acquainted with your father some years ago."

There was no recognition in her face. "My father had many friends and business associates. I am sorry, but I knew very few of them. Please, gentlemen, sit down."

The men took chairs across from the sofa where Mildred seated herself.

"To come right to the point," Gray began, "we are here concerning your brother."

"Oh, dear, I was afraid of that," she fretted.

Gray and the captain exchanged a wary look.

"I cannot say exactly where my brother is at the moment," she explained. "You see, my husband and children and I just arrived from England yesterday, and you can't believe the mess I have come home to. My husband is with the overseer now. The house has been neglected, and my attorney was here this morning with most distressing news of the family business affairs. I am sorry, gentlemen, but I don't know how I can help you."

"We know where your brother is," Captain Daniels said.

Her eyes lit up. "If that is the case, sir, you are the only people who do. Everyone I have spoken with since my return claims not to have seen him in several years."

"Years?" Gray asked. "He has been gone for years and you were unaware of it?"

Mildred sighed. "Let me explain. You see, I traveled with my brothers to England about three years ago to visit our ailing grandfather and oversee our holdings there. My brother left England shortly after our arrival and returned here to look after things. As it worked out,

I met a wonderful man there and we decided to marry. We planned to settle in Savannah, but before we departed I realized that we had a child on the way. And then almost immediately there was a second child. By the time the children and I were able to make the long ocean voyage, a great deal of time had passed."

"Weren't you concerned when you didn't hear from your brother?" Captain Daniels asked.

"But I did receive correspondence from him, though it was infrequent. He assured me that all was well, and to tell you the truth, I was so caught up in my new role as wife and mother that I paid little heed to what was going on here," Mildred explained. "Besides, my brother had no control over the family's business affairs. He could do nothing to endanger our finances, although I am certain he squandered the small monthly allowance my father had set up for him."

Captain Daniels looked confused. "Excuse me, but I was under the assumption that your father had left control of everything to your brother."

Mildred laughed. "My word, no. Father had no faith in his business abilities, and rightly so. Bradford could not correctly add a column of figures, let alone made a sound decision."

"Bradford?" Gray blurted out. "Who is Bradford?"

Mildred looked at him as if he had taken leave of his senses. "Bradford is my brother. Isn't that who you were referring to?"

Gray's hopes fell. "No, Mrs. Dickerson, we were talking about Fergus Cavanaugh."

"Fergus?" she exclaimed.

"Isn't Fergus your brother?" Captain Daniels asked.

She looked stunned. "Yes, he is. I have two brothers, Fergus and Bradford."

Gray slowly got to his feet. "It's your brother Fergus we have come to discuss. He is in Charleston and—"

"Mr. Montgomery, that is not possible," Mildred stated.

The two men eyed her sharply.

"Fergus is in England and shall always remain there."

Gray shook his head. "Madam, Fergus is in Charleston. I have seen him with my own eyes."

Mildred smiled indulgently. "Sir, after we arrived in England, my brother died."

"That Claudia! She is so lovely and gracious. And the perfect hostess, as well. Don't you agree, Rachel ... Rachel?"

"Hum? Oh, yes, Mrs. Smith, what were you saying?"

"I said that Claudia was a gracious and beautiful hostess," Mrs. Smith repeated.

Rachel followed the older woman's line of vision across the room to Claudia. Immaculately attired, she stood between two of the county's most handsome young men, fawning and flirting and teasing them unmercifully.

"Yes." Rachel simply agreed, since she dared not say what was really on her mind.

She was seated with the matrons, spinsters, and widows, well back from the mainstream of Claudia's party, which was in full swing. The gentle strains of the orchestra took graceful partners effortlessly about the dance floor, while others clustered together chatting, laughing. The refreshment tables were heavily laden with the finest of dishes, and servants passed through the guests offering trays of beverages. Young couples, such as Claudia and her many attentive beaux, drifted out through the French doors to the terrace and garden beyond. Businessmen, planters, and leaders of the community gathered together talking of politics and the like. It was a festive, happy occasion. For everyone but Rachel, that is.

Faced with the chore of packing, she had risen early that morning and set the servants to work. She still did not tell them of her plans; she couldn't bring herself to say the words aloud. Her thoughts had been so consumed by Gray that she had gone about the task mechanically, hardly aware of what she was packing and what was being left behind. There was still no sign of him, no word, no message, so her imagination was left alone to speculate on his whereabouts and the reason for his sudden departure. She wanted to believe in him and have faith that somehow he would come through for her, but her optimism was all but gone. Fergus had come by the house twice, once to make certain that she was packing, and again later in the day to check on her progress. His proximity grated her nerves but she managed to conceal her emotions until he was gone. And to top the afternoon off, Hannah had told her that after a great deal of soul-searching she had decided to stay in Charleston. Rachel's heart sank. She would need a friend in Fergus's home, and she had hoped and prayed that Hannah would be there. But she could not blame Hannah for wanting to stay, and managed to conceal her bitter disappointment when Hannah broke the news.

Fergus had arrived early to pick her up for Claudia's party and was annoyed to find she was not ready. He shouted unkind things, accused her of stalling, and refused to listen to a word she said. They rode to the ball in stony silence and, once there, Fergus deposited her in a chair and ignored her. That really suited Rachel fine since she didn't want to be around him anyway.

Time dragged by slowly as Rachel sat with the ladies and tried to keep her mind on their chatter. Her eyes continually scanned the crowd, keeping tabs on Fergus as he huddled with the other gentlemen. It was still early and Rachel felt certain he would not make his planned wedding announcement for some time yet, but she wanted to keep an eye on him just the same. And she wanted him to see her, as well, and know that she was conducting herself according to his instructions.

Rachel's eyes swept the crowd as she wistfully prayed that Gray would suddenly appear. But instead her eyes met Claudia coming her way.

"Why, Rachel, dear, it always amazes me how you can make the most matronly of gowns look appealing," Claudia said, sitting down next to her. Rachel was in no mood to exchange verbal punches with her. When Claudia received no response she went on. "It seems that your Mr. Cavanaugh has all but forgotten about you. But I suppose you are accustomed to being unable to hold a man's attention." Rachel only stared at her coldly. "I hope you don't mind, but I have told a few people about Mr. Cavanaugh's announcement," Claudia said. "Everyone is on pins and needles to find out what it is. There has been speculation of all sorts, and some have predicted that wedding bells are in the air."

Rachel drew in a deep breath. No wonder everyone had been looking at her so strangely tonight. She pursed her lips and managed to hold the sharp remark Claudia deserved. She knew full well that it was Claudia who had started that rumor.

"This is so exciting!" Claudia said. And she so hoped that Rachel would be stuck with that dull, unattractive old toad for the rest of her days. "Rachel, I think the two of you make a perfectly matched couple." She delivered her final insult and flitted away on the arm of the first available young man.

Rachel came to her feet, seething with anger. She had to get away, outside for some fresh air before she exploded. Turning to leave, her eye caught a familiar face in the crowd. It was Gray. Gray! She looked again. On his arm was another woman.

All the tension drained from her and she fell back into her chair. As if in a trance she watched him wind his way through the crowd, speaking to his many friends, smiling and nodding cordially. Rachel could hardly believe her eyes. He was here . . . now . . . across the room . . . with another woman.

Neither did Fergus miss the entrance of the couple. But it wasn't Gray Montgomery who had caught his eye, it was the woman on Gray's arm. Recognition flashed in Fergus's eyes and turned to anger. He silently cursed them both before hastily excusing himself from the gathering of businessmen and forcing his way through the crowd to where Rachel sat.

"It is time for my announcement." Fergus clamped his hand around her arm and jerked her to her feet.

She dragged her eyes from Gray. "But—"

Fergus looked at Gray and then back to Rachel; his face was twisted with fury. "You can thank your precious Mr. Montgomery for having the whole world know the truth about your deceitful past and that little bastard you have got."

Rachel's heart froze in midbeat. "Fergus, what are you saying?"

"If I am going down, you are going with me," he hissed, and pulled her toward the center of the room.

Panic rushed through her like wildfire. "Please, Fergus, I beg of you, don't do this," she pleaded, trying to pry his fingers from her arm.

He tightened his grip painfully. "You could have had it all, you little tramp. Now I will see to it that you end up with nothing."

Rachel looked over her shoulder at Gray making his way toward her. Her eyes met his and sent a silent plea for help. She saw him quicken his pace as Fergus dragged her through the crowd in the opposite direction.

"May I have your attention!" Fergus's voice rang out over the crowd silencing them and the musicians.

Rachel's heart pounded in her ears and she felt the color drain from her face. This was the moment that had hounded her thoughts, had turned and twisted itself in cruel nightmares. The cream of Charleston's aristocracy was assembled before her to hear the lies and deceptions she had perpetrated upon them. And Gray was here, too, to witness her mortification and to share in it.

"I have an announcement to make!" Fergus began.

The guests crowded around them in a half circle, and Claudia appeared from nowhere to stand next to Rachel.

"This is so exciting!" Claudia declared.

Rachel's breath came in shallow puffs, and she feared she might swoon. From somewhere she found the strength to pull herself together, and she held her head up proudly as Fergus began to speak.

"I have some news to share with you," he said.

At that moment, Gray appeared between Fergus and

Rachel. He slapped the man on the back, much harder than was necessary, and smiled at the gathering of guests.

"My good friend Fergus Cavanaugh is anxious to tell you all of some wonderful news," he called out. He casually locked his fingers around Fergus's wrist with near bone-crushing strength until he released Rachel's arm.

Claudia's face went white. "Gray, I—I didn't know you were here."

"Please, Gray, leave," Rachel whispered. "I don't want you to be hurt by this."

Fergus began to move away, but Gray drapped his arm over the man's sloping shoulders to prevent his flight.

"But instead, I will have the honor and privilege of announcing to you," Gray continued, slipping his arm around Rachel's waist, "that Mrs. Rachel Fontaine has made me the happiest man alive by accepting my proposal of marriage."

"What?" Claudia gasped.

Rachel's head spun crazily and she couldn't comprehend his words. She looked up at him helplessly.

"Smile, my sweet," he whispered. "Show our wonderful friends how happy we are."

Blindly, Rachel obeyed as she clung to his arm for support while the guests closed around them offering congratulations. She was vaguely aware of an unexpected face in the crowd when Captain Daniels appeared beside Fergus for an instant before they both melted into the throng of people.

"Let's get some air," Gray said when the well-wishes had ended.

Rachel was still too stunned, too confused to do anything but go along with him as he took her through the French doors onto the terrace. To her surprise, Captain

Daniels, Fergus, and the woman Gray had escorted into the party were standing together in the corner.

"Gray, what is the meaning of this?" Rachel asked as they joined the group.

Gray's features grew hard as his hate-filled eyes bored into Fergus.

"What is this all about?" she implored. "Captain Daniels?" The two men riveted Cavanaugh with anger. In desperation, she turned to him. "Fergus, what is happening?"

Gray slid his hand around Rachel's small waist and pulled her to his side. "This, my dear, is not Fergus Cavanaugh," he told her.

"What?" she gasped.

"This is my brother, though I am ashamed to admit it. Bradford Cavanaugh," the woman said.

Rachel's head spun. "But—but I don't understand."

The woman turned to Rachel and touched her arm. "My dear, I am so very sorry. I cannot tell you how sick I was to learn of this," she apologized.

"I don't understand," she replied helplessly.

Finally Gray spoke. "Rachel, may I introduce Mildred Cavanaugh Dickerson, sister of Fergus and Bradford Cavanaugh."

"Please," Mildred said, "allow me to explain." She related the story of her journey with her brothers to England, and Fergus's death shortly after their arrival in that country.

"And you had no idea what your brother was doing while you were still in England?" Rachel asked.

"Not until I returned and learned that no one here knew that Fergus had died," Mildred explained. "Who would imagine that a man would masquerade as his own deceased brother?"

Cavanaugh broke his silence with a hearty laugh. "Fergus and I always looked a great deal alike. It was a simple matter to assume his identity, draw out all his cash resources, and start again in St. Francisville. No one knew Fergus there. It was easy, so easy."

Rachel, just beginning to comprehend it all, turned to Gray. "How did you learn of this?"

He gestured toward Captain Daniels. "Actually, we can thank Ezra for it. It was he who knew that this man was not Fergus."

"Gray and I left for Savannah immediately," Captain Daniels told her. "We met Mrs. Dickerson there and pieced it all together."

Rachel looked up at Gray with wide eyes. "You mean he is not ..." Gray shook his head. "And I don't have to ..." A wide smile spread across his face as the full realization dawned on Rachel. "And now we can ..." She threw her arms about his neck as relief flooded her. She felt the weight of the world lifting from her shoulders, and she laughed gaily as tears of joy slid down her cheeks. Gray held her securely in his arms, laughing with her, more pleased than she that this nightmare had finally ended. He released her and dried her eyes with his handkerchief.

Standing at Gray's side, Rachel turned to Bradford. For the first time, she no longer feared him. "What will happen to him?"

"Mr. Montgomery and Captain Daniels have graciously consented to drop the entire matter on the condition that we leave for Savannah this evening and never return to Charleston again," Mildred said. Her eyes bored into Bradford. "Under the circumstances, I feel they are being more than generous."

"What? Let him go?" Rachel was outraged. "He should be whipped . . . imprisoned—for life."

"Rachel, dear, please," Gray said, trying to calm her.

" . . . dragged behind wild horses . . . tarred and feathered . . ."

"Rachel—"

"Shot in the foot . . ."

"Rachel!"

She turned her flashing dark eyes to Gray. "He deserves to suffer," she said angrily.

Gray took both her hands and bent to whisper in her ear. "Think of the gossip, the scandal this would create if we pursued it."

"But—" She was unwilling to give up so easily.

"Think of our future," he urged. "We can put this behind us and get on with our life together."

Rachel shook her head. "He should—"

"Think of Andrew." And as he knew it would, those words silenced her protests.

"Well, all right, I suppose you are right," she said reluctantly.

Mildred turned to Rachel. "Thank you. And don't worry, you will never hear from Bradford again." She lowered her voice. "He doesn't know it yet, but I am sending him to England on the next ship. Frankly, I think he will be glad to go."

"And if I ever see your miserable face again, Cavanaugh, I am going to blow your head off," Gray said coldly.

Bradford looked shaken for the first time. He shrugged past the others and reentered the house, anxious to put some distance between himself and those cold, steely-blue eyes.

Mildred said a quick good-bye and followed after her brother.

Rachel took Captain Daniels's hand. "You have been a true friend to me, and helped me many times. How can I ever repay you?"

"Marry this man and raise that boy up proper," Captain Daniels said. "Then I can die with a clear conscience."

Rachel slid her arm around Gray. "That is one request I will gladly oblige."

Rachel and Gray left the party and climbed into Gray's waiting carriage.

"You know the way," he called to the driver as he closed the door and settled into the seat next to Rachel. The carriage jerked forward and Gray lowered the window shades, leaving them secluded in semidarkness. He put his arm about her shoulders and drew Rachel near.

"I can hardly believe this madness is over," Rachel said. She felt happy and carefree, almost giddy.

"I told you to have a little faith in me and I would find a way to keep us together," Gray said. He didn't let on that he had been worried about exposing Cavanaugh before it was too late. He and Ezra Daniels had ridden hard to Savannah and returned with Mildred Dickerson, hoping and praying that he could reach Claudia's party in time to silence Cavanaugh. He would tell her another time. Right now he was content to bask in the glory of his accomplishment and Rachel's happiness.

"I thought this would be the worst evening of my entire life, but instead it's the most wonderful," Rachel told him.

"And I know how to make it even more wonderful," Gray predicted. He scooped her off the seat and placed her on his lap. Rachel giggled as his arms encircled her and he nibbled at her neck. His lips found hers, and as their kiss deepened he pressed her down onto the seat. Lying beside her, his hand eagerly caressed her soft shoulder. His desire grew as he deftly loosened the buttons of her gown and plucked at the laces of her chemise.

She suddenly pulled her lips from his. "Wait, Gray, don't do this," she said.

Heated with passion, his lips tried to reclaim hers.

"Please, Gray, stop."

"What?" he asked, suddenly aware that something was amiss.

"Please, don't do this," she said softly.

He drew himself up on his elbow. "Don't worry, my love, we are alone. No one will disturb us," he assured her, and slanted his lips over hers once more. The long journey to Savannah and back with the memory of their lovemaking so fresh in his mind had fired his loins with a passion only she could quench.

She tore her lips from his probing kiss and pressed her hand against his chest. "Gray, this is not the time," she pleaded.

"Why not?" he asked hoarsely. This was a hell of a time for her to decide to keep her virtue intact.

"Because we have to talk," she said softly.

"Talk!" he exclaimed. He was burning with desire and she wanted to talk! He tried to compose himself. "Rachel, dear, there are things about men that you must become aware of," he began, trying to choose his words as delicately as possible under the distressing circumstances. "Men have . . . needs that must be fulfilled, and—"

440

"I have to tell you something," she murmured guiltily.

Oh, God, another confession. His passion cooled considerably. What else had she done and never told him about? He braced himself.

"Very well." He righted himself and pulled her up with him, positioning her once more on his lap.

Rachel settled the flurry of petticoats around her. "This isn't very easy to say," she began in a serious tone.

Gray tried to focus his attention on her face, but his eyes strayed to her open bodice and were tantalized by her creamy white breasts that undulated seductively with each sway of the carriage. "Please, Rachel, say it," he begged.

Realizing the cause of his distraction, Rachel picked up the laces to fasten her chemise. "This is important," she scolded.

"No! Don't do that! Please!" His hands closed over hers, halting their work. "I am listening. You have my undivided attention," he assured her, still holding her hands.

She was skeptical, but drew in a deep breath and went on. "After I tell you this, you may not want to marry me. And if you don't, well, I can't blame you. So don't feel quilty about telling me the truth. And, and don't worry that I may be carrying your child once more, since I do take your seed with great ease, because—"

"Rachel," he interrupted gently, and kissed the back of her hand. "What is this terrible thing you have done?"

It was difficult to say, but she had to tell him the truth. She could not begin her life with him unless she told him everything. "Well, when you were in Savannah I didn't know where you were or what you were doing." She low-

441

ered her eyes in shame. "I thought you had left for good because you did not want any part of me or Andrew, that you had deserted us. And I hated you for it." she said in a small voice.

Gray heaved a sigh of relief. "That's it?" he exclaimed.

Rachel's head came up quickly. "What do you mean, 'that's it'?" she demanded. "I just told you that I hated you!"

Gray began to laugh. "I thought you were going to tell me that you really were married to that Fontaine character and have four more children hidden away in that house of yours."

"Oh, Gray! What a terrible thing to say!"

"You must admit that coming from you, this is a very minor admission," he chuckled.

Rachel began to laugh, too. "Yes, I see your point."

Gray pulled her into his embrace and held her close. She looked up at him with loving eyes. "Up until now, I have given you little reason to trust me or have faith in what I say to you. So I cannot blame you for thinking what you did when I suddenly disappeared or for hating me. But, madam, I intend to spend the rest of my years demonstrating that your faith in me will not be misplaced."

Rachel smiled. "Does that mean you still want to marry me?" She knew what his answer would be; she only wanted to hear him say the words.

He growled deep in his throat. "If I don't soon marry you, woman, I will surely go mad."

His lips covered hers with a hot, sensuous kiss as he pressed her upon the seat once more and followed her down. Rachel moaned contentedly as she wound her fingers through his thick hair. His hands began to wander, taking up where they had left off earlier. Desire gripped Gray and Rachel simultaneously. He would never tire of the feel of her or the taste of her. Sampling her sweetness now made him crave for more. But the confines of the narrow carriage and the yards and yards of fabric that surrounded her frustrated him and brought a temporary end to his lusty pursuit. Lord, he couldn't wait to get her home.

"I suppose I shall have to learn to dress in the dark," Rachel said as she sat up and fastened her bodice.

Gray laughed huskily. "As my wife you only need to undress, and I shall be at your constant disposal to offer my services toward that end."

She smiled contentedly. It seemed that they belonged to each other, though they were not yet husband and wife. It was a good feeling, one that marriage vows could not improve upon.

Rachel curled up in Gray's strong arms and rested her head on his shoulder. "I could stay right here in this carriage with you forever," she said wistfully. Then realizing that the journey to her house had taken much longer than usual, she said, "In fact, I think I have been in here forever. Did you instruct your driver to roam about the streets again? Honestly, Gray, what will people think?"

"Fear not, madam, your reputation is quite safe. I instructed my driver to take you home."

Unconvinced, Rachel sat up and pulled back the shade from the window. She saw no streetlights or lanterns in the windows of her neighborhood, only the pitch-dark night. She sat back and turned to Gray. "Where are we?"

He shrugged his wide shoulders innocently. "As I said, madam, I am taking you home." He raised the shade beside him and directed her attention out the window.

Rachel leaned across him and her eyes widened in surprise as the glowing lamplight from the windows of the manor house came into view.

"But, Gray, this is Richfield."

He shook his head. "This is home," he corrected.

"But—"

Gray took her hands and looked deeply into her eyes. "Home," he said softly. "This is home. Our home."

Her heart fluttered as his love flowed through her. But as wonderful as it sounded, she knew of the obstacles.

The carriage jerked to a halt and Gray climbed out.

"But, I can't stay here," she protested. "Andrew is—"

"Where he belongs," Gray said as he lifted her to the ground. "Upstairs in the nursery."

"Here? Andrew is here? she asked in amazement looking up at him. "But how?"

"I stopped at your house when I returned from Savannah this evening, thinking that perhaps you had not gone to Claudia's party after all. Seeing that you were all packed I had Hannah bring Andrew and your things here," he explained.

"Hannah is here, too?" Good Lord, she never knew what to expect next from this man.

"Certainly," he told her. "So you need not worry. Our son is being properly cared for until he adjusts to his new home."

Her eyes searched his face. Oh, how she wanted to stay here, in this house, in his arms. Would the time ever come when she could?

"Gray, my love, I want to be here with you always," she said gently. "But I can't. Not yet."

His brows drew together. "And pray tell, madam, why can't you?"

"I cannot just ... live here with you. It's not proper. People will talk. Think of the gossip," she explained. Why didn't he ever think of these things?

"I fail to see what is so scandalous about—"

"What?" she exclaimed and looked at him in horrified amazement.

A lopsided grin twisted his lips. "I fail to see what is so scandalous about a man and his wife living under the same roof." He looked at her with amusement as the soft light from the manor house illuminated her features.

"Gray, we are not married," she explained wearily.

"But we shall be."

"Yes, dear, but until then we must conduct ourselves accordingly," she told him.

"Like this?" Gray took her into his arms, crushing her against her chest, and covered her protests with a warm, gentle kiss.

"Tomorrow," he said when he released her.

"Tomorrow?" she questioned, her head spinning slightly from the effects of his nearness.

"Tomorrow," he repeated. "The preacher will be here at Richfield at three o'clock tomorrow to marry us. As I was leaving your house this evening I asked Hannah to go immediately and make the arrangements; she was more than happy to comply."

Rachel was shocked. "Tomorrow? Tomorrow! Oh, Gray, I can't possibly marry you tomorrow."

"Why not?" he wanted to know. He had been through

a great deal for her and there was no way he would let her get away from him now.

"A wedding must be planned. There are invitations to be sent, food to plan, music to arrange. I have no gown," she explained. Men just didn't understand these things.

He grasped her arms firmly. "Now listen to me, woman. The preacher will be here at three o'clock tomorrow. I don't give a damn about guests, food, or music. I'm going to marry you if you are dressed in a gown or your shift."

All of Rachel's arguments vanished and she realized he was right. "Whatever you say," she said softly.

Gray had prepared himself for more protests from her and was taken aback when she agreed so quickly. "Well," he said, and tugged at his waistcoat, "then that settles that," he declared, closing the subject.

He looked deep into her dark brown eyes. Despite the hurt and pain of the past, they still held the childlike innocence that had burned into his soul so long ago. He had never known real love before, and now that it was in his grasp he would hold tight to it and never let it slip away.

Rachel giggled as Gray lifted her into his arms and carried her down the brick walkway toward the house. The problems that had threatened only a few hours ago were gone, and for the first time she and Gray had more than the moment to share. Now the future was theirs also.

She looped her arms about his neck. "You are like the knight in shining armor I used to read about. You have rescued me once again. This time from the evil dragon Fergus Cavanaugh."

"Once again?"

"Yes," she said happily, "just like you did in St. Louis."

Gray stopped in his tracks and his brows drew together. "St. Louis?"

She chewed her bottom lip. "Oh, dear, I guess I forgot to tell you about the night in St. Louis." Gray snorted and climbed the steps. "I didn't forget to tell you on purpose. I wasn't trying to hide anything from you," she explained quickly. She didn't want him to be upset with her. "It simply slipped my mind," she added as they crossed the wide portico.

"I have only one thing to say to you, madam," he said sternly as he opened the front door and carried her across the threshold. Rachel braced herself. "Welcome home," he whispered, and he closed the door behind them.